The Long Voyage to Peace

The Long Voyage to Peace

ERNIE MOULTON

ISBN: 978-1-63821-032-0 (Paperback Edition)
ISBN: 978-1-63821-033-7 (Hardcover Edition)
ISBN: 978-1-63821-031-3 (E-book Edition)

Some characters and events in this book are fictitious. Any similarity to real persons, living or dead, is coincidental and not intended by the author.

Book Ordering Information

Phone Number: 315 288-7939 ext. 1000 or 347-901-4920
Email: info@globalsummithouse.com
Global Summit House
www.globalsummithouse.com

Printed in the United States of America

PROLOGUE

George Mictackic, better known as Mista, since most people had trouble pronouncing his last name, stood in the pilothouse of a 82 foot motor sailor. He had a line tied around his waist and the other end secured to the wheel, since the boat was rolling and pitching in the steep swells and high winds on the edge of a hurricane. Mista stood six feet tall and kept himself in top shape, but did not trust his own strength in this storm.

Three of his companions were on deck to man the sails. Mischal Yoeder was an easy six foot nine and weighed close to 300 pounds. The other man, Jeremy Bates, was a lawyer in training. He too was fit, but he knew that his strength was limited, and his wife, Charly, was on deck working alongside him. Charly was a trained sword fighter and was larger and stronger than her husband. She ignored the fact that she was carrying her first baby. She had named him Charles Jeremy, sure in her mind that it was a boy. All three had safety lines tied around their waists and to a secure point on the boat.

Mista shone a hand lantern on the main sail and flashed it three times. That was a prearranged signal to bring the sail down, since he knew that he would not be able to make himself heard over the wind.

Once the sail was down and secured, Mischal untied his safety line and worked his way back to the wheelhouse. "I'll take over for a while. Take a break, Mista."

Mista said, "Would you check on the engines and fuel first?"

"Sure." They could feel the twin Caterpillar 420 hp engines throbbing below decks. Mischal worked his way carefully back to the engine room hatch, waited until the boat was relatively stable, and ducked inside.

Everything looked fine, nothing loose and the pumps were keeping up with water that came in.

"Purrin' like two contented cats," Mischal said on his return.

"How's the fuel?"

"Probably two days, maybe three."

"Good."

"Okay. Let's keep it bare poles for now. If the jib goes, it goes. I'll go check our position and the weather. Call Jeremy and Charly in."

Mista untied himself, and worked his way back to the charthouse, opened the door and stepped inside, slamming the door behind him. Chandri Yoeder was his navigator and had lashed herself to the chart table. She looked up as he came in and said, "Wild ride, isn't it?"

"Yeah. I don't think we are in danger, though. Let me see your plot." They all remembered a similar time 12 years ago when the boat they were sailing to Bermuda hit a sudden storm and went down. Chandri stepped back and let him see her chart. They were in the Gulf of Mexico and she had marked their position and their track on the chart. She had also marked the position and track of the hurricane they were trying to avoid. It had crossed Cuba and then picked up strength again. It was now heading for the Tampa, Florida area. They were west and slightly north of the storm and were heading southwest, and the hurricane winds coming almost dead astern. The winds would get stronger for a while, but then begin to subside as they left the storm behind. This track took them closer to the storm for a little, but kept the wind behind them. They would have had better sailing on the east side. There they could have kept the head of the ship close to the wind and been sailing into the wind and waves. But the storm had changed course suddenly and left them on the west side.

"How accurate is our position?" Mista asked.

Chandri shrugged. "Haven't had access to a satellite in over 24 hours. It's my best guess."

"And the storm's position?"

"Got a weather update this morning. I know where it is."

"Good. I'm going down and get some coffee."

"You can't make coffee in this storm!"

Mista grinned. "A sailor always has coffee at hand."

"Yeah, right. I'll believe that when I see it."

"I'll be right back. I filled the thermos jugs before the storm got bad. Hope it's at least still warm."

He went down the hatch to the main salon, making sure that the hatch was secure behind him. There were a total of eight people on board, including his wife and two daughters. When it became obvious that they would experience severe weather, he had called them all into the salon and laid down the safety rules for them. "Make sure that all the portholes are closed and dogged tight. Make sure that every door and hatch stays closed at all times. If you go through one, close and secure it behind you. We are going to rig safety lines inside the rails for those that have to go topside, but nobody goes up unless they absolutely have to. If it gets too bad, I want everyone to put life jackets on."

"Those smelly things?" asked Janice, his twelve year old.

"If you happen to go overboard, you won't have time to grab one on the way over."

Robin, his eleven year old, said, "It's hot down here with the windows closed. Besides, I want to see the storm."

"Portholes," Mista said. "If you open one you'll be breathing water instead of air. You want a little hot or a boat full of water?"

"All right. But it's stuffy down here."

Mista filled a Styrofoam cup with coffee. It was just a little more than warm, but it was coffee. "The wind is kicking up. I'm getting about 40 knots now. Time to put the life jackets on." He already had his on, since he had been topside. He made sure that Janice and Robin had theirs on and that they were tied securely, and then he went back up.

Charly and Jeremy had just come into the wheelhouse. Mista said, "You two better get below and get warm."

Just then, Robin opened the hatch and climbed up. "I want to stay with you, Daddy." The boat took a sudden lurch and she lost her footing, slid across the deck and out the open door and over the side.

Mista did not hesitate, but jumped over after her. Her life jacket had inflated automatically when she hit the water, and Mista swam to her and held onto her; then turned and looked for the boat. He pulled Robin into a life saving hold and swam for the boat, not believing that he had a chance to get there; but he had to try.

Mischal throttled the engines down as much as he dared. He had to keep enough speed that the boat kept steerageway, or the waves and wind would turn it and swamp it. Jeremy stepped out and called, "Hold me, Charly!" She grabbed his belt in one hand and hung on to a rail in the wheelhouse with the other. Jeremy snatched a life ring off the bulkhead and threw it at Mista. He used mind power to send it directly to Mista, and then sent a mental message, *Grab the life ring and I'll pull you in.*

Mista sent, *Where?*

Coming your way. It bumped Mista on the head.

Got it. You better take the wheel and let Misch pull me in.

Roger. Hang on.

Charly said, "You get back in here. Can't lose you both."

Jeremy handed her the lifeline. "He has the ring, just pull him in."

Charly said, "Take the wheel. Misch, come help me pull them on deck."

Mischal stepped out to the safety line and waited. When Charly had pulled Mista up to the side of the boat, he lay down on deck, held the rail with one hand and reached down. Mischal tried three times to grab Mista's hand when he rose on the swells, but could not get a grip. Chandri heard or sensed the commotion, and stepped into the wheelhouse. She yelled, "Make a bight!"

"What do you mean?" asked Charly.

"Here. Give me some of the free line."

Charly picked up some of the line that she had used to pull Mista in and handed it to Chandri. Chandri quickly doubled the line, making a loop, or as she had called it, a bight, and then passed the line back through the loop. She yelled, "MISCH!" When he looked back, she pushed the line back and forth through the loop, and then handed it out to him.

Mischal showed the line to Mista, and he reached up for it. Mischal dropped it to Mista, and Mista put the loop around Robin. When Mischal pulled up on the line, it tightened around her and he pulled her up. He held a fistful of her shirt and life jacket in one hand and looked back at Charly. "Now what?"

Charly passed the life line that Mista was hanging onto to Chandri and said, "Give her here. I'll hold her. You pull Mista up."

Mischal dropped the line back down to Mista. He put the loop under his arms and tightened it, and Mischal flipped the line around his wrist and heaved. Mista grabbed the rail and pulled himself on board. Mischal called "Get the engines up to speed, Jeremy!"

"Roger."

When Mista came inside, Robin leaped into his arms. "Don't yell at me, Daddy."

Mista said, "I know you like to get wet, Honey, but this is not the time or place."

"I didn't do it on purpose!" She hung on and cried.

"It's all right Little Bird. I was afraid I'd lost you. You're all right now." He looked out at the sails. "Bring her a couple of degrees to starboard. Watch your helm, the wind will try to push her back around."

Jeremy eased the wheel over and the boat changed its motion as the relative direction of the wind and swells changed. "Okay, that's good," Mista said. "With any luck, we'll be out of this in a couple of hours."

Mischal said, "Want me to take the wheel, Jeremy? Good thinking, throwing that life ring. We couldn't have turned back."

"Well, I knew it was right out there and already had a line on it."

Mista took Robin down below to get her some dry clothes. Her stateroom was aft, so they went there first. "Get some dry clothes on, Hon."

"But ..."

"I'll turn my back."

She came to him a few minutes later, dry, and said, "Thanks, Daddy. I thought I was losted."

"Well, you remember, sometimes you need to obey without question. It could save your life. This was one of those times. You stay below, now, okay?"

"Yes, Daddy. Are you mad at me?"

"No, Honey. I can't get mad at you. Maybe I would have been mad if I'd lost you though." He took her hand and said, "Let's go to the salon. I can't carry you; I'm still wet."

CHAPTER 1

This had started when George Mictackic, known as Mista, and his friends, had come to Florida to catch a man suspected of providing underage girls to clients for their sexual pleasure. He had taken in some 11-year-old girls to work as bait. The man they were hunting had taken the bait and kidnapped two of the girls.

They were ready for him, and had rescued the girls, but the man made his escape. However, they now know who he was and where he lived. The next step would be to return to their home in Georgia and make plans to find and capture him.

After rescuing the girls, Mista and his friends spent the rest of the week relaxing and preparing for the trip back to Georgia. Each family had bought a camper or motor home to use when on an extended job away from home. This time they would take all the campers back to Georgia. Njondac and Mischal planned to clean each one inside and out and make any repairs necessary in Toccoa during the spring. Njondac also had a steel gate built across the road into his property and hung a sign on it saying, "Private Road No Trespassing".

Mista looked at it and approved. "You are having the water and electric turned off also, right?"

"Right. I should of done thet gate when we first set this up."

"No. We wanted trespassers then. We didn't really want the last one that came – but it worked out, and gave us a lead to the source."

In the process of the hunt, they had come across several other men with abnormal interest in pre-teen girls. One of them, named Campbell, seemed to be running a network of perverts. He had multiple mailboxes on E-Mail and his activities had led them to David Brumley in Louisville, Kentucky. Now they needed to pair his screen names with actual addresses and people.

"Yah. Cudda been worse."

"Well, I'm going to look at houses."

"Ya'll spend a chunk of money down on tha beach."

"Yeah, I know. But it will give us a base of operations here. Also a place to come in winter or anytime to get away from it all for awhile." The irony of 'getting away from it all for a while' on the Florida beaches at the height of tourist season somehow escaped him.

He walked back to his trailer and asked Sharra if she was ready to go look at houses.

She shrugged. "Any time. You sure you want to spend that much money?"

"No, but I do want to take a look at the houses that are available. Might be a really good investment."

Robin said, "Can I go, too, Daddy?"

"Sure, Honey. Let's go."

Janice hung back. "You want to go, Janice?" Mista asked.

"I guess."

"Well, you don't have to. But I would like your opinion."

She brightened. "Okay, I'll go."

Sheila went with them, also.

The first house was of modern construction and looked bigger than it actually was. With only 1700 square feet, it would be too crowded for the whole group. The second house they looked at was older and built in Key West style. It was on the waterfront and had a dock and a swimming pool.

Robin said, "Get it, Daddy. We could go swimming any time we wanted to."

"Well, it does have some advantages. Being on the water would really be good. Only three bedrooms, though."

"They are big rooms, though," Sharra said. "The three girls could share one room, and Em and Sheila could share one."

"That leaves eight others homeless, assuming that Njondac really wants to stay with his camper. We could partition off this huge room on the ground floor."

Sheila said, "Do we all have to live in the same house? There are some small houses nearby."

"No, we don't all have to live here. But I wouldn't want to force someone to buy a house just because I like the area."

"Why don't you ask them?" Sharra said.

"Okay, good idea. I think I'll make an offer on this house. You like the house, Sharra?"

"I do, but it's terribly expensive."

"True, but it should not lose any value over the years. And who knows? If we live long enough to retire, this would be perfect. I'll make a really low offer. High enough to be a serious offer, but low enough that he will want to make a counter offer. That will give me time to talk to the rest."

As it turned out, Mischal liked the modern house, and Charly and Jeremy wanted a small cottage nearby. The owner surprised Mista by taking his first offer.

Sharra said, "What about the property in Georgia? You can't sell it – you told Njondac that you would not."

"We'll keep it. Our best prospect for work is still the occasional assignments from the Georgia State Police. We could always spend summers in the mountains and winters on the beach when we were not on assignment."

The last night before leaving for Georgia, Thursday night, Robin was cuddled with Mista and Janice sat cross-legged on his knees, reading. She read six pages and stopped. She had gotten more and more competent in her reading. "Is that enough, Daddy?"

"Yes, Honey, if you want to quit. What's bothering you?"

"Nothing."

"Uh-huh. Nothing. Still upset over your kidnapping last week?"

"No. I'm over that."

"You learn anything useful?"

Janice grimaced. "Yeah. Don't accept rides from strangers."

"Even if they say that they are not strangers?"

Robin said, "He said he knew you, Daddy."

"Well, you know, kidnappers have been known to lie."

"I didn't want to go with him," Janice said.

"If you didn't want to go, then why did you?"

"It was my fault," Robin said. "I said it was probably all right, since he knew you."

"How can someone else's action be your fault?"

"Because," Janice said. "She always gets her way, and anyway, I didn't want to be a stick in the mud."

"Hmmm," Mista said, rubbing his chin. "This the nothing that is not bothering you?"

"Well …"

"Robin, please go to your room, or to our room and wait with your mom for a few minutes, okay?"

"Do I have to?"

"You do."

Robin walked slowly to Mista's room. "Close the door, please."

"Now, tell me what's really bothering you, my charging Tanker."

"It's nothing, really. I just… I don't want to get Robin in trouble."

"This is not about Robin. It's about you and me. He scooted her closer to him and put his hands behind her back. Are you jealous of Robin?"

"No, not really. It's just …" She looked away to hide the tears in her eyes.

"Janice, I really want you to tell me what you are thinking. I can't make you talk, but I really want to know. If I know what's wrong, maybe I can fix it. If you don't tell me, then it just gets worse."

She looked back at him. "I don't know, really." Two tears rolled down her cheeks, and she wiped them away furiously.

"Ahhh. That's better. You really don't know? You aren't just saying that so you won't have to talk?"

She shook her head. "I really don't know."

"You want me to ask Mom to read your mind and find o—"

Her eyes widened. "NO!"

"Ahhh. That's one problem. You are afraid that she does anyway?"

"Well, she said that she wouldn't, but …"

"How many times do you think she has read my mind?"

"I don't know. Lots."

"Only once. When we first came here, we found out that a bad man had messed with our minds and hidden our memories from us. Sharra and Jeremy and Molly took turns reading everyone's minds to open up our memories. That's the only time she ever did."

"Why not?"

"She wanted to take me on faith. Love is based on trust. If you can't trust someone, it is very hard to love them. If she had to read my mind to see if I were telling the truth, then she would not be trusting me. I don't think she has ever read your mind. We take you on faith."

"You didn't take Robin on faith."

"That's true. We had to know what was going on with her. Now that we do know, she does not read her mind. But that's not what's really bothering you, is it?"

Janice looked away again, without answering.

"Is it?"

"No."

"You're not telling me anything. Are you afraid to?"

She looked at Mista and looked away. "A little."

"Hmmm. Maybe if I read the bumps on your head. Let's see. This is the knowledge bump. Nice and fat. That's good. This is the courage bump. Wow. That's a really big one. Now here is the love bump. Wait a minute. I can't find it. Oh. You've got a dimple there instead of a bump. Where is your love?"

Janice jerked her head away. "I have love."

"You love me?"

"You know I do."

"Then why are you afraid to talk to me?"

"Because."

"Oh. Because. Let me guess. If you tell me what you really think, I might not love you any more."

She did not look at him, but nodded slightly, holding her breath.

"And Robin already gets all the love, and you get left out."

"How did you know?"

"I really can't read minds, but I can a real good impression of what you are feeling by the way you talk, hold your shoulders, look at things. There's more. Robin is pretty, and you are not, therefore, I must love her more. Right?"

She looked away and did not answer.

Mista shook her. "Right?"

"Yes."

"You think I love people because they are pretty?"

"Doesn't everyone?"

"No. You will be pretty one day. I told you that. Remember when I got the Barbies the first time? I told you that you would look just like her?"

"But I didn't."

"Are you still afraid that I will be disappointed in you and send you away?"

"Yes, sometimes."

"All right. I won't tease you about that any more. I don't want you to be insecure. I will never, never send you away. It doesn't matter if I am right or wrong about your future beauty. And I believe that one day you will be a beautiful girl. I love you just because you are. Something inside you calls out to me, making me glad that I found you. I like your courage, your loyalty, your spunk. I like everything about you. You need have no fears on that score. None."

Janice slid forward and put her arms around his neck. "It just all seems too good to be true. I keep waiting for it to end."

"It won't end unless you decide that you want it to. But Robin gets all the loving, and that leaves you more and more outside, right?"

She hugged him tighter and buried her face in his shoulder. "Yes."

"She gets loving because she wants it. You could have just as much, but it's not your nature. You want a little and then want to go your own way, right?"

"Yes."

"But you could wish I'd give you just as much attention? I do, actually. You are a very smart girl. That's why we are working on your reading. And you are getting very good at that, by the way. We'll work on some other things, too. You have good coordination, that's why you're a good fighter. Maybe Charly will let you fight against my staff one day. Would you like that?"

Her eyes widened with excitement. "Yes."

"Maybe I've teased too much about sending you away. I won't do that any more. And I can't tease you about being skinny, because you are filling out in all the right places. And you skin is smoothing out since you are getting better food. I love you both equally, Tanker, but I deal with you differently, because you are different. Never think that being cuddled means being loved more. Okay."

"Yes. Okay." She leaned up and kissed him. "I do love you, Daddy. I don't ever want to lose you."

"Well, you won't lose me unless you want to."

"I've never had anyone to love. I don't know how to do it. I've probably got it all wrong."

"No, Honey, you are doing just fine. One thing bothers, me, though."

Janice caught her breath. "What?"

"You are afraid that if you don't turn out to be pretty, then I won't love you."

"I know you said, but …"

"Well, let's think about the people in my camp. Charly. Too tall, too strong for me, runs faster than I can, so I must not love her, right?"

"I don't know. I guess you do. Sort of."

"I do love her very much. She was ten when we adopted her. Then there is Chandri. Too short, skimpy yellow hair, I must not love her, right?"

"You probably do."

"Yes. Very much. She was eighteen when we found her. Then there is Molly. You don't really know her, but she's done terrible things to us. Tried to seduce Mischal, tried to have me killed. I must really hate her, right?"

"You probably love her in spite of it."

"You're getting the picture, right? Then Mom. I married her because she's drop-dead gorgeous, and I couldn't stand to live without her."

"But … I don't think she's drop-dead gorgeous. She's not even real pretty."

"Who's not," Sharra asked. She had just come in to see what was happening.

Janice covered her mouth. "Oops."

"Tell her what you think, dear," Mista said.

Janice looked from one to the other and grimaced. "Well. He said you were drop-dead gorgeous and I said I didn't think so."

"That's not exactly what you said, Janice," Mista said.

"All right. I said you weren't all that pretty. But I still love you."

Sharra came over and knelt beside the chair and took Janice's chin in her hands. She kissed her on the forehead. "Honey, in this family you can say whatever you're thinking. We both want you to feel free to express your thoughts on any subject. I know I'm not all that pretty, and since I know you were not being mean, it doesn't bother me at all to hear you say it."

Mista said, "I married your mother because I thought she was a wonderful person, not because she was beautiful. We'll be through here in a few minutes, and then we'll call Robin back in. You can stay if you want. This is not secret from you."

"No, I'll let you two talk."

"I have an idea," Mista said. "Let's go to the computer and get on the Internet. We want to find a picture of the person you think is one of the most beautiful women you've ever seen." Janice sat on his knee while he started the computer. "Now, if we search for …"

"I know how to search."

"Okay. You search." After a few minutes Janice said, "This one. She is beautiful."

"Okay." Mista printed her picture. "Now we'll get someone to make a mask of soft rubber that looks just like that, and then we'll put it on you. That will make you her."

"No it won't. I'll still be me."

"Oh. That didn't work, then. Okay. We'll take you to a beauty salon and have them paint your face up and make you really beautiful. That'll change you."

"No it won't, Daddy. My face isn't me."

"Then what is the real you?"

"It's what is inside … Oh."

"Exactly. I love you, not your face. If you grow up to be six feet tall and stay skinny as a rail, your hair is frizzled, you have a beak nose, and your ears stick out like sails on a boat, I'll still love you."

Janice giggled. "I hope I don't look all that bad."

"I do too, but the point is, it won't matter. Now, Robin is cuddly, and likes to be cuddled. So I give her that. You want attention … you did really well on the computer. Have you used one a lot?"

"No, never did. Robin showed me how."

"Well, you learned fast. How would you like for me to teach you how to really use a computer, not just surf the net?"

Her eyes lit up. "I'd love that."

"Okay. You could turn out to be a computer genius. We'll get started as soon as we get back home. Want to call Robin back in, now?"

"Yes. ROBIN!"

Robin came running in. "Did you tattle on me?"

Janice said, "No."

Mista said, "We weren't talking about you. We were talking about Janice, but it needed to be private. What did you do that needed tattling?"

Robin looked away to hide her tears. She had not found room to get into his lap, yet, so she was still standing. "You'd find out sooner or later. I dropped my Wii in the ocean this afternoon. It doesn't work any more."

Mista shifted Janice and pulled Robin up. "When were you going to tell me?"

"When I got up the courage. But I didn't lie to you when you asked."

"That's true Honey. Well, it's yours. You can drop it in the ocean any time you want to."

8

"I didn't do it on purpose! Can we get it fixed?"

"I don't know if it can be fixed. We'll have to see when we get home."

"It's going to be a long ride without it."

"Well, we certainly won't be able to get it fixed before we leave in the morning. And that reminds me, we do want to leave first thing in the morning. Your room in the camper is completely ready, right?"

"I think so," Janice said.

"Well, let's go take a look."

As soon as they went into the girl's bunkroom, Janice ran to the other side and picked up a lone shoe. "Missed one."

Mista said, "Put it in the box. Straps on the cabinet doors, okay. Let me see how your clothes hang."

Janice unlatched the closet door and showed him. "See?"

"Okay, that's good. All you have to do is make one trip with stuff unsecured, and you'll find your room a total mess when you get there, and some of the stuff will be broken."

CHAPTER 2

They hitched the trailers up and stowed the wires, hoses and leveling jacks while Sheila and Em prepared the breakfast. They were on the road by 8:00.

Janice asked, "Mom, can I ride up front with Dad?"

"Why?"

"I want to navigate for him. I can do it. Can I?"

"What did you do to her last night?" Sharra asked.

"Threatened to beat her with a spiked board if she made a sound on the trip."

"You did not, Dad!"

Mista grinned and shrugged. "I just told her that she was smarter than the average bear."

"I want to ride up front," Robin said.

"Sharra said, "Ride with me, Hon and help take care of Sam, okay?"

"Okay, but I get to ride up there some."

Janice got the map and Mista marked the route that they would take. "Keep track of where we are, and tell me before we have to make a turn. If you tell me after, we might get lost."

"How long before?"

"At least five miles. That gives us five minutes to get ready. Then see if you can spot the actual turn when it comes in sight. Don't worry about it right now. It's kind of complicated getting onto the Interstate."

Since there were six vehicles in the cavalcade, they did not try to stay close, but depended on the radio links in case of trouble. Neither Sheila nor Em had a radio imbedded, so they followed Mista in second place.

Janice told Mista that I-75 was coming up. After they made the turn, Mista asked, "How long will we be on this road?"

"All the way."

"No, I don't think so. Where are we going?"

"To Atlanta. Oh, no. Toccoa. I don't know how long."

"Measure it. Find a scale on the map that says how many miles to the inch, and then measure the distance."

"But it has curves – it isn't a straight line."

"True, so you will be a little off. Look at my odometer and write down the miles. Then see what it says when we get to Atlanta, and you will have a pretty good idea how to adjust for that kind of rough estimate."

After a few minutes, Janice said, "I think it's about 300 miles. I don't know how long that is, though."

"Well, how fast are we going?"

"Sixty-five."

"So how long will that take us then, at sixty-five?"

Janice got her pencil out and studied the problem. Em had taught them how to do long division, but it was still new to her. Mista glanced over and saw her puzzled look. "If we are going 65 miles in one hour, how long does it take us to go 65 miles?"

"One hour. That's easy."

"How do you know?"

"Divide 65 into 65?"

"Right. That a gives you one. How long to go 130 miles?"

"Uhhh. ... Two hours."

"Right. How long to go 300 miles?"

After a minute she said, "Four and a remainder of 40."

"Hmmm. What does that mean in real words?"

Janice frowned. "Four hours and 40 somethings."

"Forty miles, maybe?"

"Yeah. Forty miles left over."

"Okay, so we drive four hours. What do we do with the leftover miles?"

"We drive. But I don't know how long that takes."

"Well, you could put a decimal point after the four and keep on dividing. You will get something like 4.6153. Six tenths of an hour is about 37 minutes. Or you could figure out how many miles we go in a minute, and divide that into the forty remaining miles."

"That's hard. "How did you know that it's 4.6153?"

"Oh, I did in my head. But, you better do it on paper. I might have made a mistake. They didn't take that into consideration when they invented hours and minutes."

"When did they invent hours, Daddy?"

"About 5000 years ago."

"Who lived that long ago?"

"Lots of people. The Egyptians had a 10 hour day plus 2 hours of twilight, and a 12 hour night. The Babylonians had a base-60 number system. The Maya Indians had a base-24 number system. We have lots of twelves in our language, dozens of things. We count to twelve, and then drop to the decimal system, thir-teen. German and Latin does, also. Why don't you look it up on the Internet and see what you can find?"

"How? We are on the road."

"Use my laptop. Pull it out from its rack under the dash. The server is up and running back in the trailer, so you should be able to get on."

Janice forgot about navigating while pursuing her search. She was still working when they pulled into a Love's truck stop for lunch two hours later. She looked up, surprised, when they slowed down. "Oh. I forgot to tell you when to turn."

"We haven't turned, yet. This is lunch and leg stretch. According to your figures, we still have a little over two hours before turning again."

Atlanta was hard for Janice. Mista had already turned onto I-285 to go around the city when she finally figured it out. "Oh! I would have had it in time."

"Not in time. You should have looked ahead. Now, where will we turn again?"

She studied the map for several minutes before she found Toccoa. "It's not on an Interstate highway."

"Right. There are several ways to get there. Pick the best."

"Well," she said after a long study, "it would be easier for the campers to go on I-85 and then turn off just before we get there. We would have less time on these little roads."

Mista laughed. "That's correct. But they aren't really little roads, just small lines. Some of them are little. You figure out how to tell, and we'll talk about it this evening, when I can look at the map with you."

Janice could hardly wait until things settled down enough after supper to come show Mista what she had learned. She brought a handful of maps in and jumped up into his lap. She told him all about federal highways, state highways, county roads and other symbols that she had discovered, including the mileage between points.

"So, if you had known about the mileage points, you wouldn't have had to measure?"

"Right. But, that's okay. I learned about the scales on maps. Now, can I always be your navigator?"

"Well, Sharra usually does that. Are you trying to supplant her?"

"What does supplant mean?"

"Take her place."

"Oh. No, I can't take her place, Daddy! I just want to be navigator."

"Well, ask her. She might be willing to give you the job. But she might not like riding in the back all the time. And Robin might think I've suddenly made you my favorite, like you thought she was. Could you navigate from the back seat?"

"Sure. I don't think I'm being a favorite. I just want to help."

Robin came in about that time. Mista heard her coming down the hall, squishing. He said without looking up, "Go get dry, first."

Robin put her hands on her hips. "How'd you know? You didn't even look up. I have a frog."

"I heard you coming. Go change."

She came back a minute later and said, "Move your maps, so I can get up there."

She climbed up and showed Mista her frog.

"Where did you find him?"

"Down in the creek. Had trouble catching him."

"I imagine. You didn't change completely."

"Yes, I did!"

"Then why do I feel wetness?"

"Oh. I dint change my underwear. I was in a hurry, and I have dry clothes on top. Is it okay? You've talked to Janice all day, and now you're fussing at me."

"It's okay, Sweetheart. I love you even when you're wet." He gave her a squeeze and kissed her forehead.

"Now I'm going to watch TV for awhile and relax after my long drive. You can stay here, or go play. Janice, you did good with your maps. You also need to study some maps of the ocean. They're called charts. I don't know what all is going to happen this summer, but I think we will be buying a boat and spending some time at sea. And Shawnah, I haven't seen you all day."

"He, he. I was riding with Jasmine."

CHAPTER 3

The next morning Mista called his investment broker, Catherine Golightly. She said, "I have your annual report just ready to send. You will have to pay taxes this year."

"I presume that by that you mean that you made me some money. Good. You know, I've been thinking. I hear people talking about putting money in some kind of shelter. Is that a possibility?"

"It's done all the time. Some people buy losing businesses just to show losses. Others move their money to an off-shore account, such as in the Cayman Islands. You might think about real estate investments."

"The first two don't sound legal. I guess nobody likes to pay taxes, but I'd rather pay what I owe than lose it deliberately in a losing business."

"Well, the losing business could be either legal or not, but personally, I don't see losing money with one hand and making it with the other. Off-shore moves are probably illegal. Depends on how you do it."

"What if I incorporate my little group and then put the property I own or acquire under the corporation name."

"So long as the purchases are legitimate for the business, it would probably work. You could claim depreciation and maintenance as expenses. You need to discuss that with a lawyer."

"I'll do that. Don't reinvest any profits, yet. I –"

"It doesn't work that way, Mista. Some of your profits are dividend payments, but much of it is increased value of the stock you own. You will owe taxes on the stocks that were sold at profit. That money has already been re-invested, to keep it at work."

"Oh, I see. I have decided to purchase a house in Florida as a second base of operations. I will incorporate and buy that as a corporation. That means that I have to pay myself a salary, doesn't it? I'm not sure if I should pay cash or mortgage it."

"As I have told you, I can make no firm predictions. However, if we can continue at anything near the present rate of growth, then any money you leave at work will make about twice as much as the mortgage interest. I would leave it invested and make a mortgage. Mortgage interest is also tax deductible."

"Sounds good. I'll need about $100,000 for down payment and expenses."

"Okay. I'll show your investment gains as monthly income on the statement that I am sending out. You can use that to show income when you arrange the mortgage. Or, if you prefer, send me the details, and I'll get our mortgage department to advance your mortgage."

"I like that idea. I'll send you the property details. I have tentatively scheduled closing for May 1, depending on financing, title search, and other issues. There will be two houses. One house is for my sister."

Mista started to disconnect, but remembered that he had one more request. "I have one other thing, Carolyn. I want to buy into a freight company called Darkling Freight, or something like that. I want to buy a substantial number of shares."

"I'll check it out for you and call you. You'll be home for a while?"

Mista laughed. "I might be anywhere, but the number you have is my cell. You can reach me wherever I am."

Mista called his lawyer next and started the process of incorporating. "I'll have the principals' names and the amount of money they will put into the common fund for you sometime this week."

After lunch he asked his friends to meet for a few minutes in the common room. The building that he called home had once been a research facility. He had acquired it when it turned out that the company which had built the facility did not have title to the land on which it stood. Now it was home to Mista's family as well as those of this friends.

The friends had formed into an official group four years ago and worked under contract to the Georgia State Police as undercover investigators. Over the years they had fought battles and worked together, and grown by marriage and the birth of children. The original seven now numbered 24.

Mista looked around at the group as they came in and took seats. He had not intentionally formed a group in the beginning. It had just happened. Seven people came together and pooled their talents. The first had been his wife, Sharra Darkling. They had been assigned to the same project and rubbed each other the wrong way at first. Only over a period of time had they come to love each other. Their first two children had been murdered, and the third, Samantha, now two years old, had cerebral palsy.

Then Mischal Yoeder and Mista had paired up on several projects. Mischal was ex-Marine and Mista ex-Navy, but they had enough in common that they bonded immediately. He, Sharra and Mischal had rescued a girl named Chandri from a Satanic group, and eventually Mischal had married her. They had two children. Mischal was six foot nine, and walked with purpose. People unconsciously moved out of his way. As he came in with Chandri, Mista thought, *Who would ever have thought that that giant would marry a five foot two girl?*

Njondac came next with his wife, neither of them over five feet tall. Njondac's first name was Sean, but he would not answer to it. He had once owned all this mountain valley and had sold the block with the buildings on it to Mista as a base of operations. They chose to sit at the table with Jasmine, their Nurse-practitioner. She was the sixth member of the original group. She was still their local doctor, but also had a license as a Baptist minister.

Charly and Jeremy came next. They had found Charly Talljohn when she was ten years old, newly orphaned. Jasmine had adopted her and everyone in the group had helped to raise her. She had declared her intention to be paladin – a holy warrior – when they first found her, and had kept her vow. She had married Jeremy Bates some years ago and was expecting her first child within a month.

Sheila Demallis came in with Em Evockovic. Mista had found his sister quite by accident three years ago, after she had been missing for 25 years. Em was a nurse who joined the group just a year ago to help care for Samantha and to home school all the children.

Mista stood and said, "I guess you are wondering why I suddenly called a meeting. I have decided to form a corporation. It could include just Sharra and me, and leave each of you independent. Or you could join me. This is not about what we do, it is about money. I intend to put almost all my assets into the corporation. The corporation will be the entity that contracts with Karl, or anyone else, for the projects that we do. The benefits are that all the assets will accrue depreciation and require maintenance. That is deductible for taxes. The houses that I am buying in Florida will be owned by the corporation, and so they become an expense item. If I leave them as personal property, they are just money spent. Good money, good purpose, but just spent. No tax benefit."

"If we do not become a part of your corporation, what happens to us?" Mischal asked.

"Nothing. You each have the gold and diamonds you brought back. It continues to grow. You each receive your share of any contract payments. The difference would be that as it stands, you pay taxes on your investments and your income. You have almost no tax-deductible expenses. If you put your vehicles in the corporation, they can be expensed, and reduce your share of taxes. Any houses that you buy could remain personal property, or corporation property – your choice."

"If we do that, we will no longer own anything," Chandri said. "Not that that is bad in itself."

"No, you would own a proportional share of the corporation. We would issue stock certificates. If you decide that you want to leave, you could sell your share for cash, or cash plus any property that you want to take out."

"I don't understand how we would benefit," Jasmine said.

"Last year we only had one contract, $150,000. Each of us got a share, which was not a lot. But you had income from your invested treasure. If you had $1,000,000 invested, then your income would be about $150,000. Your stock increased in value, but until that is sold, it is not income. That means you would owe about $50,000 in taxes. If that were in the corporation, the corporation would pay that tax, but it would not be that much, because the corporation would have expenses to offset the income."

"How long do we have to decide?" asked Mischal.

"As long as you want," Mista said. "I am going to form the corporation this week. If you want in now, then now. If not, you can always buy a share by putting your assets under the corporation. I don't want anyone to be pressured into this. The corporation will benefit me most, since I can claim these buildings and staff as corporate expenses, and the houses in Florida as expenses. You each will probably benefit, but only you can say for sure. If you don't want in, it changes nothing in our personal relationships."

Silence held for a few minutes. Then Mista said, "That is the official meeting. We can stay and talk about details as long as you want." He sat down.

Njondac walked over to Mista's table. "I thought ya weren't goin' ta sell tha place."

"I'm not. The corporation is still me, for all practical purposes. It's just a way to save tax money."

"But, iffn everybody buys in, then everybody owns it."

"Yes, that's true. But as far as I am concerned, it is virtually community property anyway. I told you all that at the beginning."

"Whut iffn I wants ta put all my money in, and then wants ta buy a new truck or something?"

"Hmmm." Mista rubbed his chin. "I don't know. We could pay everyone a salary, say $50,000 a year, or whatever we want to set. If you had $1,000,000 in it, and that portion earned $150,000, like I said, then the corporation would pay the tax on it. If the corporation paid you $50,000, you would owe tax on that much. The corporation would show a salary expense of $50000, reducing it's tax liability from $150,000 to $100,000, but you would have to pay your own tax. About the same thing either way. Or we could issue everyone say one share for every $100. Then if you wanted to take some out, just cash in enough shares to get the cash you want. The value of the shares would increase as the investments grows. So, if we had done this last year, each share would now be worth about $130."

"I think I like it better tha way it is."

"Fine. No problem. The more I think about it, the more problems come up. I intend to incorporate my holdings. Maybe I should just leave it at that."

Mischal came up and asked, "Could each one of us incorporate our own selves?"

"You could. We would have to talk to an accountant and a lawyer to see how much you would benefit. For me, it's a no-brainer, since I hold title to this building and now two houses in Florida, and I pay staff. Like Em. She travels with us and is really part of the group, but is technically staff. I pay her salary, since her original job was just Samantha. I could take their salaries, the fence maintenance, the house maintenance, and the vehicle depreciation as expenses. Like I said, the corporation idea is about money, not about what we actually do. Remember, I have eight people on staff, now. Not a big problem, but if I could claim their salaries as expense, I can save a lot of tax."

At the end of the afternoon, Mista and Sharra were the sole owners of the corporation. The idea was so new to everyone else that they were afraid that they would lose too much.

Mista and Sharra spent the day in Atlanta on Wednesday, signing papers setting up the corporation. He decided to call it Mista Consulting.

Thursday evening Karl Spicewood and Molly Greene came down. She had not been there when they came home, and Mista did not know where to contact her. Had it been important, they had other means, of course. He could always have asked Karl where she was.

Molly said, "Karl and I want to be married on May Day, up by the waterfall. Is that okay?"

"Mayday is a special day, you know, for the witches around here," Mista said.

She bristled. "You calling me a witch?"

Mista grinned. "Not at all, but remember how we found Chandri?"

"Oh, that's right. But that was Hallowe'en, wasn't it?"

"Yes, but they have eight special days. Beltane, or Mayday, Halloween, Midsummer and Midwinter."

Molly said, "That's four."

"Those are the best known names. Then you have spring and fall equinoxes, February second and August first, awakening of life after winter and harvest."

"Oh. Well, we'll just have to be out of there by nightfall." She grinned. "That shouldn't be a problem."

Jasmine said, "You still want me to do the ceremony?"

"You betcha!"

Mista said, "We'll have to put off our house-signing date. How long do you plan to stay around after the ceremony is over?"

"Are you kidding me? We'll be gone by sunset. Unless you mean future. We'll be back. I don't want to quit working. You understand, this spring we had too much to do for me to be gone."

"Okay. It's going to be a busy summer. I have set up a corporation. Right now, it's just Sharra and me, but anyone could join."

"You merge our investments and then I don't have to pay tax on them?"

"That's about it. Put in as much or as little as you want. Your car could go in, or you might just want to keep that free.."

"Count me in. I like saving money. Just leave me enough to meet expenses."

"Profits on your share of the investment and your shares of reward money would be paid to you as income for you and expense to the corporation "You would have to sign papers authorizing transfer of your funds."

"No problem. You want me to be your secretary/treasurer? I'm good at that."

"Sure, why not."

Karl said, "Now that the routine stuff is over, I have a visitor coming up to see you tomorrow. I think we have a job coming up. Interested?"

"I don't know. Depends on what it is and how it works. I'm still following up on Sheila's captor."

Karl smiled. "I think you will be interested."

CHAPTER 4

Later that evening Janice, Shawnah and Robin were playing online, when suddenly Janice said, "OH! I hate it when that happens."

"What is it, Hon?" asked Mista.

"I was in a chat room for early teens. All of us are 11, 12 or 13. I got three invitations to go to porn sites, and had four notes in my e-mail when I finished. They know we are all less than 13. Why do they do that?"

"You haven't been to any of those sites, have you?"

"NO! I don't even want to. I think it's sick."

"Well, I trust you there. I do have the logs if I need to check."

"I swear to God, Daddy, I haven't been to any of them. Well. I got onto a couple by accident, thinking it was something else, but I didn't stay. One of them wouldn't let me out!"

"How did you get out?"

"Had to reboot the computer."

"Oh. It's happened to me, too. You should learn how they do that, and how to defeat them. There aren't any teen porn sites, are there?"

"Depends. Here, I'll show you one. Not really porn, I guess, but they have girls that are less than 12 and they show everything."

"I'm not sure I want to go there."

"You ought to know that it's here. It might be part of that sex ring we were chasing."

"Not were. Still are."

"Here you are. I was searching for teen or pre-teen model sites, and this is what I got." The home page showed face pictures of six girls, all of whom looked to be about twelve. "Looks innocent, doesn't it? But when you click on a picture…"

"Hmmm," Mista said. "That's an off-shore site. Wonder where it comes from?"

"How do you know it's off shore?"

"You'll find spelling errors on sites from time to time, and grammatical errors. But Americans don't make mistakes like this one with the number not matching the verb, or leaving out some of the verbs. That is the way oriental languages are constructed, and it comes into their English usage. It might not be literally off-shore, might just be someone from another country. We should try to locate the site."

"Well, it gets worse. There are some pictures of them completely naked. You shouldn't see that, Daddy."

"Fine with me. I don't need to see it. But, sites like this disturb me. Adult sites are one thing, but when they put young girls up… I thought that it was illegal. Why don't you make a list of this kind of site, if you find others?"

"Okay. But I wasn't looking for this when I found it. You have to believe me."

"I believe you, Honey. Don't worry about it. I could check, but I'm not going to. It is the same kind of thing like Mom not reading my mind to see if I am telling her the truth. I want to always be able to take you on trust."

"I want you to, also, Daddy. I like it much better that way."

Robin said, "I learned my lesson. You can take me on trust. You can look at my logs, too. You won't find anything."

"Little Bird, if I look at your logs, that won't be trusting you. I like it better when I can trust you. Just always be straight with me, okay?"

"Okay, Daddy."

CHAPTER 5

Their promised visitor arrived just after 10:00 the next morning. Karl met him at the door and ushered him into the common room, where everyone was waiting. Mista stood up when he came in and said, "Well. I never expected to see you here, Mr. Ross."

Karl said, "You two have met before?"

Ross said, "You could say that. I saw him in action in Louisville, Kentucky, and I wanted to come down and talk to him."

Mista said, "I thought that it was settled that we had done nothing wrong, Mr. Ross."

"It was. I was impressed with the speed and dedication with which you handled your investigation. I told you then that I apologized for any ill feeling that I had caused. If you had told me then that you had official ID from Commander Spicewood, here, I would have listened to you much sooner."

"But that would have been improper, since we were not on official business. We have no direct connection with the state police except when we accept a contract. Even then, we are not on payroll."

"As I told you, Paul," Karl said, "there is no paper trail until after the affair has been concluded. They trust me to keep my bargain with them, and I trust them to operate within the rules. That way, there is no official record of them as officers on duty, and they are free to decide how and when they will work. There can be no leak from anywhere in the department, since no one knows that they are on assignment except me. Naturally, I have cleared this process with the powers that be, and have an authorized budget should I need them."

"I applaud your decision not to use your IDs to short-cut the investigation, Mr. Mictackic. It would have been unethical, but some would have done it under the theory that the ends justify the means." He pronounced the name correctly, but a little stiffly, making it sound almost like 'Mistakich' instead of 'Mistaskich'.

"That is never a valid stand, Mr. Ross. We are able to do some things that while ethical within themselves, do not generate admissible evidence for use in court."

"Yes. I have trouble believing that anyone has the ESP powers that you claim to have, but your demonstration was effective."

Karl said, "I can guarantee you that they do have these powers, Paul." He did not mention that he was marrying one of the persons who had ESP.

"I appreciate your support, Karl. Mr. Mictackic –"

"Just call me Mista, Mr. Ross. Everyone else does."

"I have no trouble with your name, Mista, but if you prefer Mista, then fine. Call me Paul, please. I have a proposition for you, Mista. Karl has told me how you work. You really opened a can of worms when you went after Mr. Brumley. He is one of Kentucky's richest men, and he is well connected. No one knows just how rich he is, since he holds his cards close to his vest."

"Rich is not necessarily good, Paul. In fact it is often the opposite of good. It's hard to get rich by legal means. Not impossible, but hard. Unless he had inherited money."

"I don't think he inherited money. He started Darkling Freight about 20 years ago and has done remarkably well. I agree with you, that the easiest way to make money is seldom legal."

Mista felt Sharra start when he said that Brumley started the company. *Started it, did he? I'd say he inherited money, but not from his parents, but from my father.*

Pull your claws, dear. Let's see what his public image is.

"He started a company from scratch?"

"I don't really know if he started it or bought it. Here is an interview that was posted in the "Growing Louisville" magazine. He doesn't say much about it, but says that he took over a struggling company and made it profitable. Keep this copy and read it at your leisure."

"You think this article is not entirely factual?" Mista asked.

"I think that the picture that he paints of himself may not be strictly true."

"You can say that again," Sharra said.

"You know something about this man?" Paul asked.

"He was my stepfather. I guess he still is," Sharra said. "He married my mother after my father died, or was killed, and took over the company."

"That's where the name 'Darkling' came from?"

"Yes. That was my father's name, and my maiden name. I refused to change it to Brumley."

"Then you have a personal interest in this man?"

"I do now. I have had no contact with him for about ten years, until this spring."

"Well, you know that the man who kidnapped your daughters called himself Sam Smith. We do not know who that is. There are a number of people who have that name, since both names are quite common. However, we do not know who took your girls. We do not know if his real name was Sam Smith. We do not know if this man actually is David Brumley."

"What do you want us to do, Paul?" Mista asked.

"Cut to the chase, eh? Prove that this man is the infamous Sam Smith. Prove that he is involved in illegal activities. He owns multiple freight venues. He has a truck line, a charter service, a special delivery freight service, shipping lines and probably other things that we cannot trace to him. For example, you may know that much trade with the Caribbean and with Central America is carried by small motor vessels. Often known as 'banana boats'. He owns a number of them. It is hard for the small operators to make a profit, but often it is a family business, and they survive. However, if his boats also carried a few pounds of cocaine along with the bananas … you see where I'm going."

"Do you know that he does traffic in cocaine?" Mista asked.

"No. We have not been able to prove it, but we do suspect it. Another thing. The kidnapper was apparently running a string of pre-teen and teen girls. We do not know exactly what he did with them, b—"

"I can tell you exactly what he did with them," Sheila said.

"You came to my office with Mista, as I recall," Ross said. "How can you be so sure?"

"Because he kidnapped me in just the way he did those girls when I was eleven. He forced me into prostitution and kept me captive for ten years or more. And I was not the only girl that he had."

"Did he rape you?"

"No, sir. He played the kindly gentleman role. But he kept me in a locked room and sent men in for me to service. I can't tell you exactly how long, because he kept me drugged."

"How do you know that it was Brumley?"

"I don't, really. But the pattern is exactly the same. It has to be him."

"The pattern people use in the commission of crimes helps to identify them, but does not prove that a particular man is guilty. What state was this in? Statutes of limitations differ from state to state."

"It was Florida."

"Oh. Florida has a limitation of five years. However, if you had DNA evidence, there is no limitation. Too bad it was not Kentucky. Kentucky has no limitation."

"It might have been in Kentucky at times. I do not know where I was kept. DNA? Fat chance."

"Well, you would have to bring evidence that he harmed you. If you have evidence that he kidnapped you and transported you across state lines, then federal laws apply."

"I have no way of collecting evidence of a crime committed 25 years ago."

"Maybe, and maybe not. If you can track down criminal activity for him and prove that he does these things, then we can bring him to trial. You might not get to prove that he harmed you yourself, but you can have the satisfaction of seeing him punished for other similar crimes. And you might just come up with evidence against him. You also will have the option of a civil suit."

"So you want us to trace his activities and find out if he is committing criminal acts. And then, of course, prove it."

"Correct. I know that this won't be easy, and might prove impossible. He might not be guilty. I am thinking a six-month investigation. I have no money budgeted to pay you, and am not inclined to offer a contract agreement like Karl has done. However, we do have reward money available. If we paid you $500 per day and assumed an average work force of 5 people for six months, that would be about $450,000. I can arrange a reward of $500,000 for successful capture and sentencing. Nothing if you fail."

Sharra said, "You are offering us $500,000 to prove that my scoundrel of a step-father actually *is* a scoundrel? You're on!"

"I rather hoped that you would see it that way, although I did not know that he was your step-father."

CHAPTER 6

Mista picked up his cell and called Robin. After four rings, he disconnected and called Janice. She answered almost immediately. "What are you girls doing, Sweetheart?"

"Working on the Internet."

"Okay. We have visitors. Please come down to the common room and meet them. Make sure Robin is dressed appropriately."

Janice giggled. "Okay. We'll be right down."

While they were waiting, Mista said, "We have a number of children here in the valley. Some are of school age and a couple are nearly old enough."

"With all the traveling you do, how do you manage school for them?" asked Ross.

"We have a teacher, Em Evockovic. She has a home schooling license and works with all of them. Ah, here are the girls."

"Oh, yes," Paul said. "I remember them."

They came over to Mista's chair and each stood on one side or the other. Robin said, "Am I a propriate."

Shawnah giggled.

Mista laughed. "You are always appropriate, Little Bird. The question is, appropriate for what? Now, I want you two girls to meet Mr. Paul Ross. He is an FBI agent."

Janice said, "Are we in trouble?"

Robin asked, "Did the adoption not work?"

Mista put an arm around each one. "No, you aren't in trouble. He wants us to help find the man who kidnapped you."

"Would you know him for sure if you saw him again," asked Paul.

"You betcha," Janice said.

Shawnah said, "I sure would."

Mista said, "He might have been in disguise when he picked you up, or he might now be in disguise."

"I'd know him anyway," Robin said. "He looked older than Daddy, and Daddy is older that dirt. So maybe he was disguised."

"So how can you be so sure that you would know him?"

Robin said, "Once I meet someone, I will always know him."

"Oh." Ross assumed that this was simple an example of youthful overconfidence. No one told him that she was training her developing ESP talents under Jeremy's tutelage.

Janice asked, "Are we going to Louisville again and catch him?"

Robin said, "I think he went back to Florida."

"Do you know that, Robin, for sure?" Mista asked.

Her eyes rolled up and to the left as she thought about that. "No. Not for sure. I just think that he did."

"Well, that is one reason why we bought a house in Florida. We are going to do a lot of different things. Chandri, I want you to work on the Internet. Look for anything you can find about him, see if you can trace any activity. Janice you can help with that and learn at the same time."

Janice said, "I've already found some things. Mr. Ross, Daddy said he thought it was illegal to show 11-year-old girls naked on the Internet. Is that true?"

Karl said, "Pornography is a slippery subject. It is generally illegal to show the privates or breasts of girls under eighteen, since that is usually done for the purpose of exciting men. Or women."

"Well, they said that they were 11 and 12. Even thirteen."

"Follow up on it, Mista. You might expand your search some and bring down some other felons. But remember, Janice, pornographers sometimes lie."

"Yeah. Kidnappers do, too," she said, looking at Mista.

"They might not be eleven. Or the ones who say that they are eighteen might not be eighteen. She showed me one site. The language looked like translation English."

"You familiar enough with languages that you can be sure of that?" Asked Ross.

"I have some familiarity with a few languages."

Sharra said, "Some familiarity? He can read Greek, Latin, German, French and Spanish and translate as he reads. I'd say he's familiar. He speaks fluent Spanish with a friend we have in Puerto Rico. If we had a friend in Greece, he'd probably speak fluent Greek with him."

"Good thing you don't have a Latin friend," Ross said, thinking that since Latin was a dead language, the friend would be dead.

"That's the same as Spanish," Janice said. "The friend you have in Puerto Rico would be a Latino."

Mista smiled. "That's what we say, isn't it? Spanish is a derivative of Latin, but so is Italian and French. French is much closer to Latin than Spanish, but we don't call the French Latinos. No, he meant a friend who spoke Latin. And since no one speaks Latin any more … People call it a 'dead' language. I guess I'd have to be dead."

Paul said, "It might well be an offshore account. Or it might just be someone with imperfect English."

"Or it might be deliberate. It is almost as if they wrote it in another language, oriental probably, and then used a dictionary to make a word substitution. Brush up on your navigation, Chandri. I think I'm going to buy a boat and spend some time on the Gulf of Mexico."

Mista got up to leave the room. "I'll be back in a few. You staying for lunch, Paul? You're welcome."

"Thank you, I will." He turned to Sheila. "You aren't the cook, are you?"

"Oh no. I can cook, but not for this crowd. We have a cook. However, this would be a good day for a cook-out. What do you say, Mischal? Steaks and tube steaks?"

"Sounds good to me," Mischal said. "I'll get the barbeque pit ready."

Ross said, "I don't know how to ask this, but you don't look old enough to have been eleven 25 years ago."

Sheila laughed, a tinkle. "I really am that old. That boy over there," she pointed to her son Gary, "is my firstborn. He is 25 years old. Like I said earlier, they kept me on drugs and my memory of those years is real hazy. I do not know how old I was when he was born. I also have a nineteen year old daughter away in college." She did not mention her 15-year-old, not even knowing if she was still alive.

Paul just looked at her. Finally, he said, "You are incred-- Please forgive me. I don't know how to say it." He thought she was beautiful, but did not know how to say it without sounding like he was trying to flatter her.

Sheila tossed her hair. "Are you trying to flirt, Mr. Ross?"

He blushed. "I guess I am. I see a lot of the bad side of life, Sheila, and hardly know how to handle myself in social gatherings."

"If you call this a social gathering, then you are doing quite well." Her eyes took on a hooded look, and her voice was low. "*I've* seen the bottom side of the bad side of life, Mr. Ross. You ain't seen nothing yet."

"My dear woman," Ross said, "I can't imagine how bad it must have been for you. I am amazed that Mista managed to even find you after all that time. How did he do that? If you don't mind my asking."

Sheila smiled and touched his arm. "No problem. It was quite by accident – serendipity, you could say. He found my daughter and took her in. She looked pretty much like me, which means she looked exactly like Mista. But he had no children at that time. He began to wonder if she could have been mine, and then if perhaps I was still alive. He traced her beginnings, and that led him into conflict with the organization that held me at that time. He destroyed that organization and thus found Gary and me." She paused for breath and then smiled and said, "The last thing he said to me before I was taken was that if anything happened to me, he would not stop looking for me until Hell froze over. I'm sure glad it never froze."

Mista had left the room to make some calls. Sharra was right on his heels. As soon as she was out of the room, she said, "What were you two looking at last night?"

"I don't know, exactly. Janice told me that she had found sites showing pre-teens partially undressed. She showed me. Come on back, I'll show you."

He logged onto his computer and did a search for pre-teen models. "Well, that's odd," he said. "Last night I got a lot of hits on that search. Actually Janice did the search, and I didn't check to see how many hits there were, but today there are only about 50. And I don't see the sites that she took me to. You know, I also followed another link. There is a lot of controversy about sites that show pre-teen models. Some of the sites are quite evidently legitimate. The poses look normal, and the models are available for work."

"Then what is the controversy?"

"Criticism of sites that show models in skimpy clothing and suggestive poses. That's what I saw last night. I did not see any undressed. Janice told me that she had followed links to sites that did have nude models. I didn't need to see them, so I didn't check them out. The funny thing is, not even the sites that we visited are showing tonight."

He kept looking and found three references that promised nude preteen models, but when he clicked on those sites, he either got nothing at all – a blank page – or a 'page-not-found' error.

"Looks like they were scared off. Well, if I know people, they'll be back soon enough. I'll ask Janice to keep a look-out for them. Now, the reason I came back here was to talk to our financial advisor about buying a boat. It will probably cost over a million to get one large to accommodate the entire group. Of course, they might not all want to come."

"That's a lot of money for a boat. You sure you want to spend that much? It's your money."

"It's *our* money. I won't do it without your approval."

"You know what you want. I'll go along with whatever it is. You've got the head for it."

"Well, she said to mortgage the house and let the investments accrue interest. That the interest would be several times the cost of mortgage interest. I expect she will say the same thing for a larger purchase."

"Whatever you want, dear."

"I just want to explain my thinking to you. If it costs $2,000,000 and I pay for it in five years at 10% interest, the interest cost will be about $500,000. If she continues to get 25% return on investments the interest income will be more than each annual payment. That means, that the boat will not cost anything except lost income. And since it will be under the corporation, the interest cost will be deductible."

Sharra reached up and kissed him. "Mista, you know what you want. Just do it."

Carolyn Golightly said, "I was just about to call you. Your investment in Darkling Freight? Forget it. You can't. There are about a dozen companies with some variation of that name, and they are all privately and completely owned by a man named David Brumley. You cannot buy into them. I even called him and told him that I had a client who was interested – not mentioning your name, of course – and he said flatly that he was not interested."

Mista stroked his chin while he thought. "Well. He knows he is approaching retirement, perhaps, and has more than enough cash on hand. Maybe he simply does not want to share control. Or, perhaps he does not want a meddler to know what he really is doing. I vote for the latter."

Carolyn said, "You sound like you know the man."

"I do. I knew that he was primary owner, but did not know that the companies were not public. That means that we have no real knowledge of how much he owns and what his net worth is. I suppose the IRS would know, but I don't think they will talk to me about him. Oh well. I have another request, Carolyn. That's why I called you."

"What is it?"

"I want to buy a large sailing boat. 100 to 150 feet long. It is likely to cost several million dollars. I suppose your advice would again be to finance it, and leave the capital alone?"

"That is correct. That is a significant chunk of what you have. You sure about this?"

"Quite sure. It is business. If you keep up your performance it will only cost me lost income. That is a cost, but not like paying out what I have. And if you keep it up, I'll have to pay you a significant bonus."

"You already provide me a significant bonus. Every dollar I make for you gives me some money, too, remember."

"I know, but I want to add even a little more incentive. How about this: If you can show another year at 25% gain, I'll increase your percentage by another percentage point?"

"That's a lot of money, Mista."

"Yes, but it will be worth it."

"You've got it. I'll definitely aim for that extra money. Of course, as always, if the bottom falls out …"

"Of course. I understand. I'm going to contact a broker. Could you start the loan process there? I don't have a hard figure, yet, but I expect several million."

"I'll get it. With your reserves, you should not have a problem."

Mista sent e-mail enquiries to two brokers expressing a serious interest in some of the boats that they had listed on the Internet, and then returned to the common room just in time to follow the others out to the barbeque pit.

After the lunch, Ross expressed his appreciation for their hospitality and then said he would have to leave. "Just one more thing. You are undertaking to hunt down a very rich and powerful man. If I took on this job myself, I would probably not survive. I have too little evidence. If he got wind of the investigation, and he most surely would, and placed a word in the right ear, I would be sent to the North Dakota weather station. If you bring me enough credible evidence, then I will move forward and nail him.

"You, on the other hand, have no visibility. Even if he hears that you are asking questions, you have no official standing, and so appear to be no threat to him. However, he might well be suspicious. He might feel that he can retaliate without fear of prosecution, if he keeps his person isolated from his felons. In other words, he is not likely to attack you himself, but he could send someone who could not be traced back to him.

"Therefore, you must be very careful. One, you must not let him or anyone know that you are doing an official investigation. No one must know of my visit to you. Keep any evidence you turn up in a secure place, such as a safety deposit box, or several boxes. I will not tell you how to conduct your investigation, since you seem to be adept at that."

"Thank you for the warning," Mista said. "We have taken on powerful men before, and know the risks. We will be careful. Have a good trip back."

After he had gone, Mista said, "We have all worked together for a long time. I do not need to tell you to be careful. However, we have three new girls. Gather around, girls."

They all came over to him and then he said, "You have been kidnapped once. It seemed easy for him to find out about us and to find you when he wanted you."

"He couldn't have known we were down at the river," Janice said.

"Don't be so sure. He might have sent the three men who attacked you at the riverbank. We'll never know, but it is entirely possible. He might have had a spy in the woods who alerted him when you went off by yourselves. He probably knows where we are now, and will know if you're ever alone. Robin, I called you this morning and you didn't answer."

"I left my phone in my room."

"Keep it on you at all times, even here. And don't forget the button on your watches that will call me. Do not hesitate to use that. Don't wait until you're at the airport."

"But, if it had been a false alarm?" Janice asked.

"No harm done. I would rather have a false alarm than find out too late."

They all nodded.

"Remember. Any man who will shoot at people just because they might be following them has no conscience. He will do whatever he wants to. And if he decides that he should kill you for his own safety, since you could identify him, then he will do that and it won't bother him at all. You understand?"

Again, they nodded.

"Now in your work or play on the Internet, you must not breathe a word about what we are doing. Not one word. Not that we are private investigators, not that we are tracking down a kidnapper, nothing at all. People listen in on other people's conversations. You will be listening in on some of theirs, if we can. You can be sure that they will do the same thing to us.

"Also, you must never, ever go off alone. Even on shopping trips, stay with us. We will take you up and show you the waterfall and pool where we swim. But you must never go up there alone."

"We can all swim, now, Daddy," Robin said.

"That's not the point. If he wants you, he can put spies on the land. They can hide up in trees, or behind bushes and you won't see them. But if you go up there alone, they will know. You might come back feet first."

"Feet first? Why?" asked Shawnah.

"When people carry a dead person, they carry her feet first."

"You're scaring us," Robin said.

"Good. This is scary business. And because you have been kidnapped once, you are in the most danger. I told you three that we do dangerous things. This is one. Shawnah, you still have an out. If you don't want to be a part of this, we can take you home."

"No, I'll stay. I like Jasmine. She would adopt me, but my mother would never agree. Anyway, I don't want to go home."

CHAPTER 7

David Brumley had left his rented house on Fourth Street, intending to return later that evening. He changed jackets in his hotel room and decided to leave the Sam Smith jacket behind. If anyone had made him they probably would find the room and the coat could be a red herring. He made sure that he left nothing else. He did not check out when he went back downstairs; he would call later and cancel the room. He had paid in advance for three days.

His driver was inspecting the limo carefully. "Any more damage James?" Brumley asked.

"No just the tire. Whoever that was, it was a great shot. Or just lucky."

"Only one shot, right? Maybe he was really good."

"Nah. I think he was just lucky. Guess he decided that that was not a good neighborhood for a gun battle. Boys must have disabled their car. They didn't follow."

James held the door and Brumley got in. "Home, James. No. Go to the office first."

Inside the car he addressed his chief of security, Arnat Karackish, "That was pretty rash, shooting a strange car, Arnat."

"Did you notice that he had a gun in his hand while yelling for you to stop? Who knows who he was or what he wanted. But it looked like an imminent attack on you, to me."

"No, I didn't see the gun. I have no idea who he was. Oh, well, that's what I hire you guys for."

His cell phone beeped. He answered, "Yes?" Only a few people knew that number. He never identified himself when answering. If they did not know who he was, then they had no business calling him.

A man said, "Smith, I thought you said that girl was safe! She was a demon! Knocked me down and stomped on me, picked the lock and ran. I followed her, but her daddy was there, and he had called the police. They have me downtown. You have to get me a lawyer."

"You know the risks. I'll call a lawyer, but I'm not responsible for anything that happens to you. The girl was docile enough with me."

He turned to a quiet, slim man sitting in the corner. "Nathan, call the legal office and tell them that it would be worth their while to defend Ebenezer Snood. That he is being held downtown."

"What if they refuse, boss?"

"Don't give them a chance. Tell them what you want and hang up. I'm not responsible for these guys' legal defense."

Brumley sat musing while his secretary called. *Mictackic was there? How? Sure he had missed her by now, but how could he have known that she was in Kentucky? Surely Mictackic had no connections in Kentucky. Even if he did, how would he know that she was here? And where she was? Must be an accident.* Brumley did not believe in coincidences, and this one disturbed him.

At the office, he called his general manager, Tom Bronack. "Tom, I have to go to Florida again for a few days. We have anything that can't wait?"

"No, sir. Have a good trip."

The Darkling Freight Company was not a large company. He had a fleet of 24 trucks that had mostly regular runs with clients. Seven of them could be sent anywhere at any time. He had spun off several other companies, some under the Darkling name and some under his own. Each company had its own management team, and Tom was the general manager. He could have invested more of his profits in rolling equipment, but this was about as much as one man could manage. He already had enough to retire and live wherever and however he wanted. He only still worked because he preferred working to doing nothing.

After he called Tom, he told Nathan to have his jet ready. "Gate time 1900 hours. Clearwater." Nathan could handle the details. He would call the crew, schedule the departure time and give them the destination so that they could file a flight plan.

Then he called his wife. "Have to go back to Florida, dear. Sorry for the short notice, but something came up. Probably be there several days."

"Okay, dear. I'll see you when you get back." He was good to her, and not particularly demanding, but he did expect complete obedience.

He did not stay only a few days, but was gone for two weeks. He was surprised to find that she had company when he did return.

CHAPTER 8

Mista took the girls up to see the waterfall the following Sunday. They had never seen anything like it. Robin wore a tank top and shorts, and Janice her usual jeans. She loved the idea of having dresses, but only wore them for dress up. They headed straight for the water.

Mista said, "Robin, you should take your shoes off if you happen to go wading."

"Do I have to?"

"I would appreciate it."

"Okay." She waded out a little ways, and then decided to see if her shoes would float. Janice watched for a while, and then took her sandals off and went in with Robin.

Janice said, "I wonder how deep this is? We can see bottom for a little, but then it gets too deep."

"Want to find out?"

"Not today. We should have worn our bathing suits. We will next time."

After a while, Robin said, "Let's go see if there is a cave behind the falls. I've seen movies where they hid in caves behind the waterfalls."

Before they got there, Robin stopped and put her shoes back on. The stones hurt her feet, and the shoes were wet by this time anyway. When they got close, Janice stopped outside the spray area. Robin said, "I think I see a cave. Want to go look?"

"We'd get all wet."

"So? I want to see."

"You'll get in trouble."

"No I won't." She ducked under the waterfall, and came back a minute later. "Come and see. There is a cave." She went back behind the veil again.

Janice hesitated. She did not really want to get wet, but a hidden cave behind a waterfall? What a cool idea. She went.

Robin said, "Isn't this cool? I wonder if anybody else knows about it. It could be our secret cave."

"I bet Daddy knows. He knows everything."

"Yeah. He probably does. Let's go ask him."

Mista had just missed the girls, and asked Sharra, "Seen the girls?"

Robin popped out from behind the falls and called, "Daddy! Did you know that there is a cave back here?"

Janice popped out beside her. Mista looked at Sharra and said, "I might have guessed."

"Didn't you know they would go there first thing?"

"I should have known. Come on out, girls and I'll tell you about the cave." He and Sharra had already crossed to the other side of the pool, so the girls splashed across the pool and joined him. Mista sat on the large flat rock in the center of the meadow on the back side of the pool and waited. Sharra took a seat next to him.

Robin said, "Can I sit in your lap? There isn't room on the rock."

"As wet as you are? I don't think so. Sit in the grass."

Mista said, "This place has a lot of history for us. Njondac's people are buried just over the hill in a family graveyard. We have had picnics and parties up here. Even this rock has its history."

"What happened on the rock, Daddy?" asked Janice.

"We caught a witches circle about to make a human sacrifice here. Broke them up, of course. We couldn't allow that to happen."

"No, you didn't! Did you?"

"Sure did. And that cave? I was curious, like you were, so I went and looked. Found a big pile of money there. That's where we got the money to get us started in this business."

"Wow!" Robin said. "How much did you find?"

"I don't remember, exactly. Enough to get us started, but not enough to live on very long, so we still have to work."

"That's why you can buy cars and things, and don't worry about how much we cost you," Janice said, worldly wise at almost twelve.

"Yep," Mista said. Figured that right out, didn't you? Of course, there is a limit, but it's not something that I worry too much about."

Sharra said, "We came up here one day, and Daddy read to me from one of his Greek books."

"He did that to me one night," Janice said. "I couldn't understand a word."

"Neither could I," Sharra said. "But I guess you could call that our first date."

"Wow!" Robin said. "That was a long time ago, wasn't it?"

"Yes. Depending on how you look at it, before you were born, or four years ago. Time is real funny, sometimes."

"That doesn't make sense, Daddy," Janice said.

"I know. I'll explain it some day. I guess we better get back. You girls ready?"

Robin said, "I need to wash off the dirt." She ran out into the pool and swished off any dirt that might have stuck to her.

Mista said, "I thought you were going to leave your shoes on the shore."

"You didn't say that. I didn't wear them in."

"Hmmm. They seem to have gotten pretty wet."

"Yeah. I tested them to see if they would float. They did, for a while, and then began to sink."

"And since they were wet, anyway, you just put them back on?"

"Right."

"Well, unfortunately, you will have to walk home. I don't want my car all wet."

"Daddy!" Robin said. "You can't leave us."

"Sure I can. Just follow us, and you won't get lost." He and Sharra went down to the creek and crossed where it was shallow, and then he started toward the car.

The girls got there first, since all they had to do was wade across the pool. Robin said, "I'll jump on you and get you all wet, and then *you'll* get your car wet, and then I can ride, because the car will already by wet."

"Sharra murmured, "Perfect logic."

Mista grinned. "Hop in the back. Just don't drip on anything. Where are your shoes, Janice?"

"Oh. Up there." She ran and got them.

After supper, Mista asked Sharra when she wanted to go visit her mother. "I didn't know I had planned to do that."

"Well, you know, all this revolves around your stepfather. We ought to at least visit your mother, don't you think?"

Sharra sighed. "Yes. I know I should. Might as well get it over with."

"You might find out what happened to your father."

"You think she would tell me? If she even knows."

Mista shrugged. "Never can tell. Won't hurt to ask. If she doesn't know, or won't talk, then nothing is lost. If she does …"

"Yes. You're right. Can it wait a little? Molly is getting married next Tuesday, and we still have a lot to do."

"Sure. How about the Thursday after? We could drive up; that's about eight hours. Flying takes almost as long, considering the hour or so to the airport, the two hour wait at the airport, arranging the rental car and all. Be a good chance to find how good a road car your Lincoln is."

"Good idea."

The girls came in a little later and climbed into Mista's chair. He said, "I think my chair is breaking."

"Why?" asked Robin.

"Because you two girls are growing so fast that you weigh too much."

"Oh. Buy a bigger chair," Janice said.

Sharra looked at him and said, "Female logic. Always right."

"Yeah, Daddy. Female logic," Janice said. "So there."

Mista groaned and said, "I wonder if I could trade you in for a couple of boys. Boys tend to be rascally, rambunctious, dirty, and self-willed, but at least they don't jump on you and smother you."

"You wouldn't be happy," Robin said.

Mista rolled his eyes. "I think you are probably right, Little Bird. Now, tell me, what do you two want? It's not bedtime and you're not dressed for bed."

"We just want to sit here and watch TV with you," Robin said.

"Yep, that's all," Janice said. "Why do we have to want something?"

"I don't know why, but you usually do. What do you want to watch?"

"Whatever you are watching," Janice said.

"Well, let's see if there is something new and interesting on the History Channel."

"Yuck! More lessons?" Janice asked.

"What would you like, then?"

"How about the Sci-Fi channel?"

"I didn't know you were interested. Most of that is fantasy."

"Yeah, but sometimes they have interesting stories."

CHAPTER 9

What they found was an old movie, and they all lost interest after a few minutes. Mista let it play on, but no one was really watching. Janice scooted up onto the arm of the chair so she could put her arm around his neck, and Robin snuggled into the crook of his right arm. Mista looked at Sharra and asked, "You think I could turn them back in?"

"I don't think I could live with you if you did."

"Yeah," Janice said. "So there. Don't even think about it."

"Well, I'll just have to keep them. Guess I'll have to buy a stronger chair."

They sat and watched the movie for a few minutes more, and then Mista tossed the control to Sharra. "Find something else or just turn it off."

Sharra searched for a few minutes without finding anything of interest, and then turned the set off.

After a few more minutes, Robin said, "Daddy, am I in trouble?"

"Well, now, that is an interesting question. As far as I know, you are not in trouble. What have you done that makes you ask?"

Robin and Janice exchanged glances, and she said, "Nothing."

"Hmmm. You thought maybe that enough time had gone by since last time you were in trouble that it was time for the trouble machine to automatically make you in trouble?"

She giggled. "No. I just wondered."

"Unhum. Just wondered. Well, I believe that you must have done something to make you ask such a question. Care to tell me?"

"No, nothing."

"Okay. I guess you don't want to talk. He pushed the chair back to the halfway position and closed his eyes. After a few minutes, Janice asked him to tell them about the strange time problem. "How could you have met Mom four years ago, but it was before I was born? That doesn't make any sense. You promised to tell us."

"Well, I always keep my promises, but I can't tell you without telling Robin, and she doesn't want to talk to me."

"Yes I do!"

"Oh. Well, you haven't answered my question."

"But I did. I haven't done anything."

Mista laid his head back and closed his eyes again. After a minute or so, he felt Janice reach across him and poke Robin. She did not respond. Robin lay cuddled against his right side and a little later her felt some wetness. He felt Robin make a sudden move, and knew that she must be wiping her eyes.

She lay still for a minute and then asked, "Daddy, why are you mad at me?"

"I'm not mad at you, Honey. I don't know any reason why I should be. Do you?"

"No, but you act mad."

"No, I'm just waiting for you to decide to talk."

"But … I was just wondering if I was in trouble because I went under the waterfall and got us all wet."

"No. I knew that you had gone in – I saw you come out, so I knew that you must have gone in first. Why would you think you were in trouble? I do kind of wish you would grow up some."

"Janice said I'd be in trouble if I went in, but I went anyway. Charly is grown up, and she still likes to get wet."

"Hmmm. So you are going to outdo Charly?"

"Might."

"Little Bird, why were you afraid to tell me?"

"I was afraid you'd get mad at me."

He squeezed her and held her for a little and the kissed her forehead. "I won't get mad at you. I want you not to be afraid to tell me anything that you do, or ask me anything. The only time I'll get mad at you is if you do something really bad, like try out drugs or something. Even then, you better tell me, because I *will* find out, and then I'll be *really* mad. I'd be mad because you did drugs, and then really mad because you didn't tell me. Understand?"

"Yes, Daddy. I love you."

"I love you, too."

"Now will you tell us?" asked Janice.

"This is what you really came in for, isn't it?"

"No," Janice said. "We came in to love you. But you could go ahead and tell us, since we are already here."

Mista looked over at Sharra. She was holding up one little finger and making motions like wrapping something around it. Or someone. Mista smiled.

"I guess I could. It would be four years ago that I met your mother. Met her right here."

"Not exactly," Sharra said.

"Well, no. We actually met when her boss hired me, and that was in Texas. But the job we were working on was here, and that's where we got to know each other. Then Mr. Spicewood, you remember him? He is marrying Molly."

"Yes," Janice said.

"He offered us a job. After we finished that project, we went sailing out on the ocean, and a big storm came up and the boat sank."

"What happened to you?" Robin asked. "How did you get off?"

"We were in the middle of the ocean. We died."

Janice punched him. "No you didn't. You couldn't have died. You're still here."

"You sure about that? How could we survive if the ship sank?"

"I don't know, but if you had died, you wouldn't be here now."

"Well. What do you think about magic?" Mista asked.

"Magic doesn't work. And anyway, it wouldn't bring you back to life."

"What do you know about parallel worlds?"

"What is a parallel world?"

"You might have read a book or seen a movie about them. The idea is that when a major decision happens, the world splits. One world does one thing, and the other goes another way. There could be thousands of worlds because of decisions made. One world might have us like we are in America, and another might have us as still a colony of England. Even further back, one world might have America as a separate continent, and another might have America and Europe as one continent."

"That doesn't seem possible. Where would all those worlds be?"

"In another dimension of space. I'm not sure how it all works out. However, when our boat was going down, a man popped in with a magic device. He took us to an alternate world. The land was different, and there weren't any cars or TV. Everybody rode horses and fought with swords. Magic worked on that world. A lot of people we know here were also there, but a little different. Mr. Spicewood was a duke."

"So how long did you stay there?"

"We stayed there twelve years. But time was different. Only two years passed here. We found Charly when she was ten years old, on that world. Njondac met his wife there. We fought wars there, and got rid of some very bad people. We did a lot of good, and then another man appeared one day with the magical device and said it was time to come home. So we came, and Charly and Jeremy and Molly came with us."

"Were you a magician there?" Robin asked.

"Yes. Magic worked, and I was a magician. I also taught in a school of magic. Jeremy was an ESP instructor there. He had a lot more power there than he does here, and magic does not work here at all."

"Are you glad you came back? Or did you have a choice?" asked Janice. She would not have had Mista for a father if he had not come back. She wondered if he were sorry.

"I liked a lot of things about that world, but I am glad to have come home. There were a lot of parallels, and I might have found another you there. Or I might not have. Not everything was the same. I'm glad I did come home."

CHAPTER 10

The girls were left pretty much on their own the rest of the week. Molly came up and stayed, and everyone was busy getting ready for her wedding. Robin still had her afternoon classes, but Em did not hold any school that week.

They played outside and spent some time on the Internet. Robin asked Janice what she was doing.

"Looking for those sites where they show girls undressed. Also looking for anything about the Darkling Trucking."

Shawnah asked, "Why do you want to find sites like that?"

Robin said, "Why would you want to see girls undressed?"

"I don't. I just want to find the sites and get the addresses."

"Oh." Robin and Shawnah spent most of their time in on-line chats. They had not gotten any sexual perverts in their chats, or at least no one had admitted to it.

Robin found pictures of girls getting wet and muddy. Not girls, but women. Some of them seemed old to Robin, and even ugly. She liked to get wet, but did not think she would want to have movies made of her doing that.

Then one night she found a site showing both men and women naked. Some of the scenes showed simulated or actual sex. She didn't like it at first. She knew what sex was all about, but had never spent any time thinking about it. It did not look like fun, but they seemed to enjoy it.

One night she found a picture that she could not get out of her mind. She didn't like it, but could not forget it. *Yuck. Gross! But they seem to like it. They looked grown up. Maybe old even, like 25 or 30.*

She found a few more like that, and kept coming back to them. Her fascination grew. She was repulsed by it and attracted at the same time, and did not really understand her fascination.

On Saturday evening when she came into the work room she found a printout of the picture she could hot forget on her keyboard. "Janice! Did you do this?" she asked.

"Nope." Janice had seen Mista lay it on her keyboard, but when she started to ask him about it, he merely put his finger to his lips and left the room.

"Gross!" She wadded it up and threw it in the trash can. Then she logged onto her computer. She was surprised to find that her favorites list was gone. She went to Google and tried a search, but most of the things that she was used to seeing were not there any more. "What happened to my computer?" she asked.

Janice said, "I haven't touched it."

"Well, I can't find anything."

Janice just shrugged and kept on working.

"Is your computer working okay?"

"Yes. Mine is fine."

Robin sat and looked at her screen. She responded to a couple of chat friends, but had no interest in talking and signed off after a few minutes. *Now I'm really in trouble. He must have found out what I've been doing. But I don't know how. It's not in the chat logs, and I didn't download any pictures. And how could he know that I had seen that one picture? He said not to go to the porn sites, and that is just what I've been doing. I guess I have to tell him. He already knows, but he said I have to tell him. But that'll just make it worse. Can't get worse. Well, it can, too. Wonder if he'll give me my privileges back if I confess real good. Probably not. Boy, I've really blown it now. Now he doesn't trust me any more, and he won't even let me do anything. Wonder if he'll send me away? He said he wouldn't but … But anyway, looking at those sites is not really bad. Not like smoking or drinking or something. He did say not to do it, but it's not really bad. Maybe a little bad.*

She felt tears run down her cheeks and just let them run. Nothing mattered any more. She pecked at her keyboard a couple of times, but really had no interest. Janice asked her once what was wrong.

"Nothing. I don't feel good."

"That picture bother you?"

"No. Well, yes, but that's not it."

After a while she got up and went to her room. It was still early, but she had nothing interesting to do, so she got ready for bed and lay on top of her bed, trying to figure out what to do. She knew that she had to tell Mista, but dreaded it. He probably wouldn't say or do anything, and that just made it worse. Now he might not even love her any more. She lay there thinking and worrying until she heard Janice go in and give Mista her good night kiss.

She waited a little longer and then went in to see him. She stood by his chair without saying anything for a long time, just picking at the leather on the arm of the chair. Mista looked up once, but he did not say anything, either. She knew she was in deep trouble.

Finally, she said, "Daddy."

"Yes."

"I think I've been bad."

"Either you have or you have not. Surely you know the difference."

"Yes. I know. I have been. Will you forgive me?"

"Well, now you think I should forgive you without knowing what you've done?"

"You know."

"Okay. I forgive you."

"It can't be that easy."

"Hon, I love you and I'll forgive just about anything you do."

"You know what it was."

Mista did not say anything.

She started to climb up, hesitatingly. Mista put his arm around her and lifted her. She huddled against him and started crying. After a while she asked, "Do you hate me now?"

"No, Robin, I don't hate you. I love you very much."

"You trusted me. And I went to all those porn sites. It was really an accident. I dint like them."

"Maybe the first time was an accident. But you kept going back."

"Oh." *How could he know that? No point in denying it, though.* "How could you know that?"

"I told you. I can always know what you are doing on your computer. I don't look over your shoulder, and I trusted you to stay away from the filth. You have no business on those sites."

"I know. I don't know why I kept looking. But it wasn't something really bad."

"Well, that is a matter of opinion. It's not good. It gives you a wrong impression of life and love, and it's something you need to stay away from."

"I will, now. I promise."

"You already promised, and you broke that promise. Now I can't trust you."

Robin broke into sobs. "But you *can* trust me, Daddy. I promise I won't do it any more."

Mista did not say anything, and Robin said, "Are you going to spank me now?" She turned so that her bottom was up, steeling herself for the pain that she knew would be sure to come.

"No, I'm not going to spank you and I'm not going to yell at you. I have already told you that I'm not ever going to send you away. I'm just badly hurt and disappointed in you. I thought you were going to be a fine girl and make me proud of you, but you didn't. I don't know what to do now."

"I promise I'll be good."

"Well, I'm going to leave your computer restricted for a while and let you think about it some more. I need some evidence that you really can be trusted."

"What can I do?"

"Well, now, that's a problem, isn't it? What can you do?"

"I don't know."

After a while, Mista said, "You need to go on to bed. Good night." He kissed her good night and watched as she slowly walked out of the room. She did not sleep for a long time.

CHAPTER 11

Sunday morning church was more or less normal, except that Robin was unusually quiet. She did not have anything to say at dinner, either. After dinner she changed into shorts and sneakers and walked up into the woods. She even waded through the creek, but this time it was no fun at all.

She walked up into the woods and just kept on walking. She did not know what to do. Nothing was fun any more. Maybe she should just walk away. No, that wouldn't do any good. Suddenly a man said, "Well, little girl, what are you doing up here?"

"Oh! Who are you?"

"Just a man up hunting and guess what I found. Come here."

Robin backed away. The man was between her and the house. She kept on backing until she came into the road that went up to the falls. He kept coming after her, so she turned and ran.

"You can't run away. There's nowhere to go." When Robin kept running, he gave chase. She ran faster, but he was gaining. He had almost caught her when she popped into the clearing by the waterfall pool. She did not hesitate, but ran out into the pool until the water was over her head and she had to swim.

The man said, "You can't stay out there, little girl. Come on back in before you drown."

Robin thought, *Daddy said take off my clothes if I ever fell in and had to swim. Can't do that with than man there. Shorts aren't heavy, though. I could take off my shoes.* She took a breath and ducked under, untied her shoes and let them drop. It wasn't much over her head so she knew she'd be able to find them later.

When she came back up, the man said, "See, you can't stay out there."

Robin had a thought. She reached out with her new power and untied his shoes. She tried to tie them together, but that was too much. However, he did not know what she had done, and stepped toward the water. He stepped on one lace, and tripped when he tried to take another step, falling face forward into the water. "I'll get you for that!"

When he stood up, Robin could see that he had a gun in his pocket. *Wonderful.* She reached out with her mind and *moved* each bullet from the gun and dropped them into the water.

Robin moved deeper, and then thought about the cave behind the falls. *He doesn't know about that. I'll duck under again, so he thinks I'm drowning. I've heard that if you go down three times you'll drown.* She ducked under and tried to swim toward the falls. She had done a little underwater swimming at the beach, but was not good at it.

When she came up again, he said, "See, you're going further out. You'll drown." He started into the water to try to get her.

Robin ducked under again, and swam toward the falls again. This time she heard the falls above her, and when she came up, she was in the cave.

She heard the man say, "Now you've gone and done it. Oh well."

Meanwhile, Sharra's alarm had gone off when the man started chasing Robin. She sent her a call, but Robin was too panicked to respond. She thought it was just part of her panic and pushed the thought aside. Sharra called Mista. "Robin's in trouble."

"Where is she?"

"I don't know. I saw her going into the woods earlier."

"Let's go." He ran to the Range Rover and they headed up the road, looking for any sign of her. They got to the falls just as the man was walking out of the water. Sharra sent another call to Robin. *Robin! Where are you?*

Here, Mom. Behind the falls. That man tried to catch me.

Okay. We're here. Stay hidden.

Mista, he tried to catch Robin, but she hid behind the falls.

Mista whipped his staff out and shook it out full length. It was heavy aluminum and telescoped out to three feet in length, or folded together to an eight-inch length. He always carried it in a pouch on his belt.

"What are you doing up here?" he asked.

"Hey, man, just looking for deer sign."

"Sure you were. You were trying to catch my daughter. This is private land, and posted besides. Put your hands behind you. I'm taking you in."

"Sure you are." He pulled his gun. "You just stand out of my way, now, and I'll be gone." He did not realize that the gun was empty.

Mista said, "Turn around. What can I use to tie his hands?"

"I'll bind them," Sharra said.

Mista walked quickly toward the man, raising his staff. The man aimed his gun and fired. He pulled the trigger several times without result. Mista swung his staff and knocked the gun out of his hand. "Now. Hands behind your back. Sharra, hold him if you want, but there's line in the back of the truck. That will be more permanent."

The man tried to pull a hunting knife from his belt, but Mista punched him in the stomach with one end of the staff and then reversed it and clubbed him on the back of the head while he was bent over, gasping for breach. Sharra brought Mista the coil of line, and bound his hands behind his back and then pulled up his legs behind his back and bound his ankles and tied the ankles to the wrists.

"Why did you do that?" asked Sharra.

"We have no way to secure him in the back of the truck. This will be pretty uncomfortable for him, but it will keep him from doing anything till be get him to the house. You want to call the sheriff while I look for Robin?"

"Sure. Have him meet us at the house?"

Mista called, "You can come out, now, Robin."

She came out from behind the falls and ran to Mista. She jumped into his arms, and said, "I was so scared. Oh. Now I've got you all wet. I'm sorry."

"That's okay, Honey. Let's go."

"Wait. I need to get my shoes. They're right out here."

He took a stick and lifted the gun by its trigger guard and dropped it into the back of the Range Rover. Then he dragged the man to the truck and heaved him into the back and closed the back gate. He opened the back door and asked, "Ready to go, Robin?"

She shuddered. "Do I have to ride back there with him?"

Sharra said, "No. I'll ride back here. I can keep an eye on him that way. You ride up front with Daddy."

Mista headed the truck back down the road. He called the sheriff on the way home and told him that he had an intruder who had tried to molest his daughter. "I have him secured in my vehicle at the moment."

"We'll have a deputy there to pick him up in a few minutes. Was anyone harmed? Are you currently in danger?"

"No, we're fine, thank you."

He clicked off and turned to Robin. "What are you doing up here alone, Honey?"

"I didn't come up here. Not on purpose. He was chasing me, and I just ended up here." Her eyes got big. "I'm not lying, Daddy. Please believe me."

Mista looked into her eyes and then nodded. "I believe you, Honey. It's all right."

After a minute, Mista asked, "Where did he find you?"

"I was in the woods. I probably went too far in. I was feeling pretty bad, and not really paying attention."

"Did I ever tell you not to go off alone?"

"Yes, Daddy. I'm sorry. Nothing mattered any more because you were mad at me. I can't stand that. If you stay mad at me, I don't know what I'll do."

"I'm not mad at you, Sweetheart. Just disappointed. Did you try to call us? Or even push the alarm button your watch?" He had bought them GPS locator watches with a silent alarm built in.

"No. I never even thought about it. I would have in time, but everything happened so quick."

"Well, they are for your protection. I'd be lost if anything happened to you."

Robin pulled her phone out of her pocket. "I tried to call you, but I think it's broken."

Mista looked at it and said, "Yep. Not a good idea to go swimming with your phone in your pocket."

Robin felt better about things in general since Mista had come to her rescue and then assured her that he was not mad at her. Still, with no computer privileges, she felt lost. Her dolls were not much fun any more, and the Wii was still broken. She read some, but did not enjoy it. She was miserable.

She came in that night to get her good-night loving and asked if she could have her computer back.

Mista said, "You have your computer. I'm not going to restore your full privileges for a few days. I want you to think about it."

She snuggled closer and leaked a few tears. Mista felt the wetness, but ignored it. He thought that the tears were real, and not just to get his sympathy, but decided that the best course of action was to ignore them.

After a while, she said, "I've learned my lesson, Daddy. Nothing is any fun any more."

"Not even getting all wet?"

"No. Even that."

"Well, you said that last time we had a problem."

"About lying? I did learn. I told you everything."

"Did you think about not telling me?"

Robin sat up and looked into his face. "Yes. I don't know how you know, but I did think about it. I was tempted, but I knew I'd have to tell you. You have no idea how hard that was."

"I think I do. It is important to me that we have a good relationship. You're not perfect, I'm not perfect. But if we do something wrong, then it is important to confess to the other person and ask forgiveness. That's not always easy, but it is very important."

"I did that. But it was so hard."

"I know. But still, important. Have you talked to God about this?"

"No. Why would I?"

"Don't you think he would be interested in what you do?"

"I never thought about God caring about what I do."

"Being a Christian is not about obeying a bunch of rules. It's about having a loving and obedient relationship with God. He does care, or he would not have worked to hard for us. Do you think it didn't hurt God to have his son die for us?"

"I guess it did, but I just never thought about it. God is so far away."

"Actually, no. He's right here with us. If you've done something that you ought not to have done, then you have hurt your relationship with God. You need to confess to him and ask forgiveness."

"How would I do that?"

"That is one of the things that prayer is all about. Just talk to him as if you were talking to me. You probably won't hear an answer, but you will feel a whole lot better."

"Okay. I'll do that tonight. Good night, Daddy." She kissed him and left, already feeling a little better. She did not realize that part of the Internet call to her was to visit the forbidden sites. She knew that she could not, but if allowed back on, she probably would have risked detection and done it anyway. Mista knew that, and the three-day banishment was to allow time to mute her desire. He had not actually set a time, but with the wedding two days away, and the planned trip to Louisville later that week, he knew that it would be a while.

CHAPTER 12

The wedding went down without a hitch. Karl was supported by two of his officers. The wedding was a private affair, but 24 officers and men from various divisions of the Georgia State Police were there anyway. The marriage was not secret, they just did not have it in a public place, and had made no public announcement.

Mista gave the bride away. Molly did not ask him, she simply said, "You *are* giving me away, aren't you?"

Mista said, "I don't own you, how can I give you away?"

"You did own me once, but you wouldn't dump Sharra, so you couldn't keep me."

"Well, since you ran off after your year, you're on your own. You wanted emancipation – you have to give yourself away." Molly had served as a servant in Mista's household some years before in lieu of a sentence of death for treason. Mista had thought that he could change her attitude toward moral behavior in a year, but she had merely bided her time and then gone back to her old lifestyle as soon as she was free.

"Hey. When I came to my senses and realized that what you had tried to teach me was right after all, I came back, didn't I?"

"True, but did you give yourself to me?"

Molly raised one eyebrow and tilted her head back. "I probably would have, if you had been interested. But you weren't, so now you have to finalize your loss. If you don't agree quickly, I'll just have to get Sharra to make you do it."

Mista grinned. "You know I love you. I'm glad to see you happy with a man like Karl. I think you'll be good for each other. You know I'll give you away." He gave her a tight hug and let her go.

Njondac had cut lumber and he and Mischal had built an arched bridge across the creek below the pool. They did not expect visitors, but neither of them thought that Molly would want to wade through the creek in her wedding dress.

Sharra helped her decide on a dress. Molly said, "I could buy a wedding dress for the occasion, but it seems like a waste of money. It's just us."

"True. With all the dresses you own, surely you have one that would work?"

"Well. I have a white organdy dress that Karl loves."

"That's easy, then. Wear that."

Tuesday was a clear, sunny day, and Em and Sheila prepared food for the reception after the wedding and took it up to the falls that morning. The only problem was that the ride was bumpy, to say the least, and they worried about the cake surviving. That was the only thing that had been catered. It did survive, however, and the whole affair went well.

Molly and Karl made their escape by subterfuge. Knowing Robin's love of the water, Molly bribed Robin with a new Wii. As soon as they had thrown the bouquet and garter, Robin walked to the edge of the pool and faked a fall into the water. While everyone's attention was on this apparent accident, Karl and Molly made their escape. The family was not surprised, but none of the guests knew Robin and assumed that it was an accident and that she needed to be rescued. Njondac helped. He pulled his truck across the road when Karl left, and then walked into the woods and disappeared. By the time they had found him and moved his truck, it was all over. They had told no one where they would spend their honeymoon.

Wednesday was dedicated to planning the trip to Louisville. Sharra knew that she had to go, but dreaded the trip. She wanted no one to go with her except Mista. Mischal said flatly, "That is foolish. You are walking into the lion's den alone. You think you are a Daniel?"

"I don't consider my mother to be a lion."

"I understand that, but I believe that the man that she is married to is highly dangerous. I don't think you should go alone."

"Well, I will be safe with my own mother, and I don't want an audience. It's hard enough just to go back to see her. You don't have to make it harder."

"Why do you not like your mother?" Charly asked.

"It's a long story, Charly. You remember the first battle we did with the woman I thought was my mother. My memories are now totally confused. I am not sure that what I think I remember about growing up is the implanted memories about the false mother, or real memories about my real mother. I remember her as loving, but totally devoted to her husband. I remember that husband as being a pervert, and apparently this man is a pervert. At least he sells perversion, whether or not he is himself a pervert. One memory says that I ran away when I was sixteen. The other says that I went off to college and never looked back. I am pretty sure that when I went to college it was effectively running away. I did not tell them where I went, and I paid my own way. I do not hate my mother, but I believe that she would support him against me if it came to that."

Charly stood a minute without replying. Then she said, "Aunt Sharra, we are going with you. I believe that if you face this man alone, he will attempt to kill or capture you. And I do not believe he would care particularly which happened. We do not intend to let him do that, Aunt Sharra."

Charly had not called Sharra 'Aunt Sharra' in a long time. It was an indication of her love for her that she wanted her to know that she saw her participation in this mission as loving support, not opposition.

They decided to take two cars. Jasmine rode with Mista and Sharra, while Charly, Jeremy, Mischal, Chandri and Njondac went together. Mischal thought about a car with five people in it, three of them larger than average, and decided to take his Jeep also. Chandri looked at him and said, "I know you like your Jeep, but we've got an eight hour trip. You won't be able to unbend when we get there. Let's take the Mercury."

The girls came in on the tail end of this conversation. Robin said, "I want to go."

"Me, too," Janice said.

Shawnah said, "I'm going if they are."

Sharra and Mista looked at each other. Finally, Sharra said, "Sure. Let's just take the whole army."

Mista said, "It will change the way your mother reacts. For the better, I hope. And if Brumley is there, they will probably recognize him."

57

"If I see him, I will know him," Robin said. "Even if he is wearing a disguise."

"Well, you might as well get baptized into what we do for a living," Sharra said.

Jasmine said, "In that case, I'll ride with Chandri, since they are taking her car."

Chandri said, "Since everyone is going, I'm going to take Biscuit this time. Never know, he might alert us to some danger that everyone else misses. I'll ride in the back with him." Biscuit was a bobcat she had found as a kitten abandoned by his mother. Shawnah was thrilled to get to sit near a real bobcat.

CHAPTER 13

They were all up and loading cars shortly after sunrise. They knew that they would have to spend one night there, possibly two. The girls stood around and watched until Mista asked them if they were packed already.

Janice said, "Packed? What do you mean?"

"You need a change of clothes or two unless you mean to wear that until it falls off."

"Oh. We didn't even think about that."

"We don't have luggage for you, so just use one of the grocery bags. Don't forget your toothbrush and hairbrush. And underwear."

"And makeup. I can think, just didn't think about packing."

"Makeup? You? Already?"

"Of course, Daddy. I'll be twelve in a couple of weeks."

"Oh. And Robin, you need at least three pairs of shoes and several dresses. Maybe some extra shorts and jeans."

"For one night?"

"Well, we will cross several rivers and go by at least one or more lakes."

"So?"

"If we happen to stop near one, you will have to change clothes. We can't have everybody in the car stay wet for the whole trip."

Robin put her hands on her hips and stamped her foot. "Daddy! It's not that bad."

Mista tousled her hair. "It's all right, Honey. Do take some extra, though. You, too, Janice. Think some dress-up. We'll have to eat somewhere, and might go to a really nice restaurant."

When they were ready to leave, Janice asked, "Can I navigate again?"

"Ask your mother. It's her seat."

Sharra shrugged. "Daddy knows the way. But you can sit up there. I guess I'm permanently relegated to the back seat."

"Thanks, Mom." She unfolded the map she was carrying. "See, I marked the roads all the way to Louisville last night."

Mista took it and studied her map. "I'm going to throw you a curve. We aren't going that way."

"Why? That looks like the shortest way." She had used an orange highlighter to mark the Interstate to Atlanta, Chattanooga, Tennessee, Nashville, and then Louisville.

"It might be the shortest way or not. I'm not sure. See where I-75 goes off to the right at Chattanooga? I thought it would be interesting to go up that way. It goes through some mountain country, and then horse country in Kentucky. Let me see your marker." He marked I-75 to Lexington, Kentucky and then I-64 to Louisville.

They stopped for a break just north of Chattanooga, and Robin said, "It's not fair, Daddy. I want to ride up front some."

Mista said, "We'll be on I-75 for a long time. Let her ride up front for awhile, Janice. Are you going to give your mother a turn, too? I think she might still like me."

When they had been on the road a while, Janice said, "Would you tell us about your mother, Mom? I didn't know you had one. I mean, I know you were born, but you never mentioned her, and …"

Sharra patted her knee. "Yes, dear, I had a mother. It's a long story. I was kind of skinny and all arms and legs, kind of like you were when we first saw you."

"I wasn't skinny!"

"Well, you were pretty thin," Mista said. "I'm not sure just how thin you have to be to be called skinny. But you were close."

"Well…"

"It's all right, dear. Some people are, and some are not. I was. Then when I was about eleven, I started filling out, like you. I never filled out all that much, as you can see, but life changed for me. I barely remember my own father. He owned a trucking company and drove trucks like all his men. He didn't come back from one trip. I never knew why. No one would talk about it."

"How old were you," Robin asked. She had to sit sideways in her seat to listen and almost regretted asking to be up front. She started to take her seat-belt off to get more comfortable, but Mista put a finger on her hand.

"I was five or six. Six, I think. I remember him, but not much. He always used to give me a bear hug when he came home and brought me presents. She married again, seems like right away. The man she married hardly spoke to me. He didn't say hello or good-bye or anything. I might as well have been a piece of furniture that came with the marriage. That all began to change when I was eleven. He began to notice me. I'd see him staring at me. Made me feel dirty."

"Yeah, I know," Janice said. "Like those men that came to see us in that house. Creepy."

"Yes, good word for it. He started coming into my room without knocking or anything. Just open the door and walk in. Caught me changing clothes once, and just stood there while I threw on a shirt. I started locking my door when I was changing. I told my mother and she just shrugged. Said something like, that he was harmless, he wouldn't hurt me. Then when I was thirteen, he told tried to catch me in a corner in my room. I didn't really believe it at first. But he was serious about it. Tried to catch me in a corner several times. Used to stand in the hall or doorway so that I would be forced to brush against him if I went by."

"Did you tell your mother?"

"Yes, but she said it must be my imagination."

"What if Daddy tries something like that?" Robin asked.

"Your daddy wouldn't. He is not that kind of man." She looked at Mista with a raised eyebrow. "If he ever does, though, you tell me. I'll clean out his brain."

Mista laughed. "She would, too. Trust me, if I were interested in deviant behavior, I have had many opportunities to try something. You're safe with me."

Robin said, "Like when you told me to take my shirt off –" Sharra stiffened. "and then wouldn't let me even start. Told me that if I felt like I should not do something then I ought not to do it, even if somebody said to?"

"Yes, Hon. I would not have let you do that. I just wanted to make a point with you. If I ever ask you to do something that you feel bad about, then don't do it. But. Be sure that we can talk. That's one reason that I insist that you tell me when you have done something. I want you to know that you can tell me anything. You can, and should, tell me if you feel bad about doing something that I ask you to do."

Sharra sent to him, *What's going on here?*

It was a lesson in obedience when the girls first came. I told them that they should do what I ask, even if they don't really want to. But that if they REALLY didn't want to, or felt bad about it, then they should not do it, and that they should tell me why. So to drive home the point, I told Robin to take her top off. First she said no, and then started to go ahead and do it. I stopped her, and told her that I really didn't want her to, but wanted to show that it was alright to say no to me if she thought something was wrong.

Okay. I just wondered. It didn't seem like you.

This only took a few seconds, but nevertheless, it was a pause in the conversation. Robin looked from one to the other, and then said, "Did you two just mind-talk to each other?"

"Yes. Why do you ask?"

"I thought you were."

"Did you hear something?"

"No, but I felt something in my mind. Not words, just something."

"Good. Your talent is still growing. I thought it was strange that Daddy would ask you to take off your shirt."

"Well, it was just a lesson. He didn't really want me to."

"I understand. I wish my step-father had had some lessons like that. Whenever I complained to mother, she always said it was just my imagination. But she also said, that since he was now my father, that I should do whatever he asked me to. That he had the right."

"Did you?" asked Janice.

"Certainly not! We had some arguments about that before I finally left home. She believed that she was duty bound to do whatever her husband told her to, and never argue with him. And that as a child, I was even more duty bound. I grew up unwilling to take orders from anyone."

"You don't do whatever Daddy says?" asked Robin.

"Mista and I had lots of discussions about that before we got married. It gets real complicated. Marriage is giving and sharing. I will generally do whatever he askes me to do, not because I have to obey orders, but because I love him and want to please him. And he never gives me orders."

"Never?" asked Janice.

"Never. Well, almost never. When he did it was because something was going on, and he didn't have time to ask. He has probably told you that there will be times when you must just do what he says and don't ask why."

"Yeah. Said it might save our lives," Robin said.

"That is very true. But does he normally give orders to you and expect you to just do them?"

"He hasn't ever done that," Janice said. "Except when we were on the Internet he said to never take dirty pictures of ourselves. I guess that was an order. Like we needed to be told that!"

"You did need to be told. Not that you wanted to, but you needed to know that it was not something that I wanted you to do. Just in case you had a conflict, and the man asked for pictures, and you might think I wanted you to do whatever he said."

"We understand."

"He tried to rape me when I was fifteen, and several times after that he tried to corner me. I took to staying in my room all the time with the door locked. I put a chair under the doorknob at night. Several times I woke up hearing the door rattling. I thought about running away, but didn't know where to go. So when I went off to college, I told them that I was going to University of Kentucky, but when I left I went the other direction. I made good enough grades that I got a scholarship at Kentucky Wesleyan, so I went there. I worked and saved my money, and then went to Purdue and got an MBA. Took all the money I had saved, plus student loans. But when I got out, I landed a really good job right away, and paid off my loans. Anyway. I never called, or wrote or visited after I left for college. I was afraid to."

Robin said, "You aren't afraid any more?"

Sharra smiled. "I am very much afraid. But it is something I have to do."

"Oh, yeah, that's courage," Janice said. "Daddy talked about that one night. Courage is doing something even when you are afraid."

Sharra smiled. "Your daddy is a very wise man. You should always listen to him."

"Not always wise," Robin said.

"What do you mean," Sharra asked.

Robin scooted over against her door and said, "He won't give me my computer back."

Sharra asked, "Why did he take it?"

Robin looked back at Janice. "Because I was going to porn sites, and he had told us not to."

"Well, I'm sure he will give it back when he thinks the time is right."

She leaned up so she could talk straight to him. "It's been almost a week. Isn't that long enough, Daddy? I'll do anything you say. I just want it back."

Mista reached out and pulled her head over next to him. "Be careful what you promise, Sweetheart. I might ask you to clean out the barn."

"What does that mean?"

"Well, you know, horses and cows mess wherever they are. We have to come behind them and clean it up."

"We don't have a barn or horses. Can we get some horses?"

"If you'll clean out the barn."

"I'll do it."

"We'll talk about it after our trip is over. And we'll talk about your computer after the trip, too. You think you have really learned, or do you just want it?"

"I really have learned my lesson."

CHAPTER 14

They came into the Louisville area about 3:30, just as the exit traffic was starting to build. Mista asked Sharra, "Do you know where the office and or truck terminal is?"

"Not exactly. I remember that it's somewhere on Strawberry Lane, or at least that name sticks in my mind. Daddy used to take me there, I believe, on weekends. My stepfather took me sometimes on Saturdays until I started growing up. He didn't much like me, but I wanted to go so bad that he took me. I guess I don't really remember my father taking me, but the guys at the dock kept telling me that he did."

"Okay. Where's Strawberry Lane?"

"I have no idea. In Louisville."

"Hmmm. Janice, look it up on your phone. You have a map ap."

It was almost five when they pulled up in front of the terminal. The office girl was just getting ready to leave, and was talking to the general manager in the main office when Mista and Sharra walked in.

Tom Bronack, the general manager, recognized Sharra immediately. "Sharra? Sharra Darkling? Good Lord girl, I thought you must be dead or something." He opened his arms in an invitation to hug.

Sharra instantly responded, and hugged him back. "It's good to see you, Tom. Been a long time."

"Sure has, girl. I've missed having you around. You quit coming when you were about eleven, but I've often wished I could see you again. Whatever happened?"

"Long story, Tom. Lots of things happened, mostly all bad. I was suddenly not getting along with my step-father, and … well …"

Tom's eyes clouded. He cut his eyes toward the office girl and said, "Well, things happen, you know. What can I do for you?"

"I want to try to mend fences. First step is to go see my mother. We used to live in St. Matthews, but I suspect that she's moved. That's why we came here first."

"Yeah, they've moved. Sally, call Mrs. Brumley and see if she is available."

Mista sent, *Pick the number and address out of her mind.*

That's an invasion.

I believe from Tom's comment that she is an enemy. She's not likely to give it to you, and I bet Tom doesn't know.

Oh. You're probably right.

The telephone number and address were associated with the person, and were on the surface of her mind as she called. She said, "Mrs. Brumley, this is Sally Fielding. There is a lady in the office that says she wants to come see you. Will you be available?"

"Just a moment. Your name, ma'am?"

Sharra said, "Sharra Mictackic," not wanting to say Darkling, even though she had kept her maiden name when she married.

"Mrs. Brumley, it's something like Sherall Misterskitch."

"Yes, ma'am. Sorry to bother you."

"She's expecting company tonight, and will be busy tomorrow. Would you like to try to schedule a day next week?"

"No, that will be all right. Thank you for checking," Mista said. "Glad to meet you Mr. ..."

"Bronack."

"Mr. Bronack. Sharra has fond memories of you. We'll be in touch." He gave him a business card, and was pleased to see the glint of amusement in Tom's eyes when he read the name. He apparently knew some Serbic names.

Mista ushered Sharra out before she could speak.

On the way back to the car, she hissed, "I wanted to visit with Tom."

"Not with that girl present. She's an agent if I ever saw one. We have to be real careful, dear."

"Yes, you're right. I knew this would not be easy."

"You get the address? Let's head out."

When they got in the car she gave Mista the address and number, and he wrote it on the back of a card. "La Grange. Do you know where that is? Obviously not in Louisville any more."

"No. I didn't go out much when I was in high school, and when I left, I left."

"Okay. Miss navigator, find La Grange for us."

Janice unfolded the map of Kentucky all the way and started at the top, looking for La Grange. Mista said, "Here is a lesson in problem solving, Tanker. First a story. How would you eat an elephant?"

"Eat an elephant? I could never eat a whole elephant."

"Sure you could. You eat it one bite at a time. Might take you a month or so, but you could do it."

"Oh. Well, you didn't say that. So what does that have to do with this?"

"Where is La Grange? Since the man works here, and it did not appear to be a long distance call, let's assume that it is somewhere near Louisville. So start looking near Louisville. If you don't find it, expand your search."

"Oh. Okay." It only took a minute. "Here it is. On Interstate 71. About 30 miles."

"Okay. How do we get to I-71 from here? I am going to head back out to the loop around the city."

Mista had come to the outside beltway and turned north on it by the time Janice had figured it out. "You go to I-265, go north about 25 miles to I-71. Then north another 10 miles or so. There is an exit right there."

"Okay. Sharra why don't you call information and get the number for the local police there, and then call them and see if there are motels available. We will probably see some, but I'd like to know. Or there might be a Bed-and-Breakfast. That'd be even better. Oh, you might ask them where Old Sligo Road is. That's a weird name. Might be a farm road."

"Gotcha."

A few minutes later, Sharra said, "There is a Bed-and-Breakfast on US 42. They said go north on Ky 53 to US 42 and turn right. Just a few miles from there. Said we can't miss it. Old Sligo Road turns off of KY 53 about a mile from town."

"Good. Same direction. You get a phone number for that B-and-B?"

"Yes."

"Call them and reserve a few rooms. You get all that, Miss Navigator?"

"No. Wait a minute." She spread the map and found La Grange again. "Okay here is 53. It's in a circle, but doesn't say KY on it. Is that the right one?"

"Yep. The circle means it's a state highway, and this is mostly Kentucky."

"It's all Kentucky, Daddy. I don't see Old Sligo Road, though."

"Well, let's head that way and see what we see."

They found the road about a mile north of town, as advertised. It had a county road sign, but also had a street post with the name on it. Mista followed it, watching the numbers rise. The land was hilly and covered with trees at first. After a couple of miles the trees all disappeared, and the land opened into rolling pastures with black horse fences along both sides of the road. They came to a house that should have been the right number, but did not see a number on it. It was a large brick house that appeared to be three stories, with an attached four-car garage. It sat on a corner lot in the middle of about five acres of mowed grass, well back from the road.

Mista slowed down and looked, but could not find a number. He drove on. The next house had a higher number. "That must have been it. Let's go back."

"He can't live in that house!"

"Why not? If my estimate of his net worth is anywhere near right, it fits him."

"I can't see my mother living there."

"Well, let's go knock on the door and see."

He called Mischal and told him he thought that that was the house and that he was going back.

Right. I'll pull off on this farm road here and wait. You want to leave the girls with me?

No. I'll let them wait in the car until we see what the climate is.

Next, he called Charly and told her. *Okay. I'll pull off on this farm road and wait.*

Be careful. Misch is also going to do that.

Oh. Well, I'll go back up the road to the next farm road above the house.

Mista pulled into the driveway and stopped. There was no sidewalk in front of the house, so he and Sharra walked through the grass to the front door. He leaned back into the car when he left and said, "Keep the doors locked. If someone comes up, lie down in the seats so you won't be seen. We do not know what to expect here, so be ready for the worst. If nothing happens, then fine. If something does happen, we'll be ready. Don't forget your emergency button on the watches if somebody does bother you. If we are okay in our visit, I'll come back out and get you."

Janice climbed into the back seat and the two girls started a two-person game on the Wii. They were so absorbed in the game that they almost did not hear the car drive up behind them. They ducked down, hoping that the dark windows kept anyone from seeing them.

CHAPTER 15

As they walked around the house, Mista said, "Looks like they don't welcome casual visitors."

"No. I guess most people have an appointment or an invitation. They probably meet them at the back door. But, since they aren't expecting us …"

Mista rang the doorbell and waited a long time before a man came to the door. "Yes?" he asked. "May I help you?"

"We are looking for Elizabeth Brumley," Mista said.

"Is she expecting you, sir?"

"No, I don't think so," Sharra said. "Please tell her that her daughter is here."

"Just a moment, please." He closed the door and they waited.

He came back a minute later, opened the door, and said, "Come in, please. Mrs. Brumley will see you."

She was cool but cordial. "Well. Did you decide to come home. You haven't taken care of yourself. You look more like 40 than 28."

"Well, Mother, you look well. Yes, I have put this off long enough."

"Who is the man with you? Are you married, now?"

"Yes, this is my husband, George Mictackic."

"Oh. That's what that girl was trying to say. That is an unusual name. What do you want, Sharon?"

"I don't want anything. Well, I do want –"

"I knew you must want something. I guess you found out how well my husband is doing."

"You don't understand. What I want is to try to restore relations between us."

"Well, I never understood why you ran off. Said you were going to college, but you never got there."

"I know. I went somewhere else. I did not want your husband to know where I was."

"He would have paid for any college you wanted to go to."

"I paid my own way. You never did believe me, did you?"

"Believe your wild accusations? I never saw any evidence for your charges. You always were wild. Probably not even married, now. You could leave this man and come back home."

Mista took her hand and sent, *Easy!*

Sharra squeezed his hand and said, "I am married, Mother. Church wedding and all. We have children that are making us proud. Would you like to meet them?"

She sniffed. "I suppose that I should. When would you like to bring them?"

"They are out in the car," Mista said. "I'll go get them." He walked out as Brumley came in through the garage.

Mista went to the corner of the house and waved to the girls. They opened both doors and popped out and ran to him. "You just missed it," Janice said breathlessly. "A big old limousine just came in and parked in the garage. I don't think they saw us."

"Well, it doesn't matter. Come on inside."

He sent to Mischal, *Taking the girls in. Charly, take notice.*

Careful. Brumley just came in. Same limousine that we almost chased.

Mista stopped at the front door. "If you recognize this man, do not say anything. Nothing at all. Hold your faces as still as an Indian. Do not under any circumstances reveal that you know him. If it is the same man, and I believe that it is, he will surely recognize you. Even if he says something to you, like 'remember me?' pretend that you do not know him."

"That would be lying, Daddy."

"Yes. I suppose it is. Would you rather be dead?"

"Then it's all right to lie if you think your life is in danger?" Janice said.

"It's not that simple. We'll talk about it tonight, if we're still alive."

Janice looked at him for a minute, and then said, "You're scared, aren't you?"

"You got that right. You girls be on your best behavior. Sharra can contact you if she needs to, but her mind is focused on seeing her mother."

"Okay. We'll be good," Janice said,

"Me, too," Robin said.

Mista opened the door and took the hands of both girls and walked in. Janice turned to close the door, but the butler was already there, closing the door.

When they entered the parlor, Brumley was attempting to hug Sharra. She stood stiffly, hands at her sides and let him. He stepped back and said, "You don't seem glad to see me."

"We did not part on good terms."

Mista felt the girls' hands tighten on his when they walked in. He squeezed their hands. "Mr. and Mrs. Brumley, I would like to introduce our daughters. This is Janice, on my right and Robin on my left. Girls, this is your grandmother and grandfather."

Mrs. Brumley started forward to embrace them and then stopped. "My goodness, Sharon. You must have had them before you left for college. Or your husband was previously married. In that case, they aren't really mine."

"Relax, Mother. We adopted them."

"Oh. Is that working out for you?"

"More than you would ever believe. They are lovely girls."

Brumley strode forward and opened his arms to embrace them. "My pleasure. Glad to meet you."

Janice kept her cool and dropped Mista's hand and held out her hand to shake hands. "How do you do, Mr. Brumley?"

Robin copied her and held out her hand. "How do you do, Mr. Brumley?"

He recovered and took Janice's hand and then Robin's. "Very well, thank you. And how are you?"

The girls did not answer, but turned and looked at each other. Robin thought, *I think he recognized us.*

Janice felt the force of the thought, but did not know what she was feeling. She did not 'hear' the thought, but she knew that something had happened. She stepped back behind Mista and took Robin's hand.

Mrs. Brumley said, "What do you need from me, dear?"

Janice remembered her radio and keyed it. *Daddy I think he recognized us. Or course he did. Be very still.*

"Nothing at all, Mother. I was just trying to reconcile."

"Well, you need to reconcile with your father, first."

"He is not my father, and until he changes his ways, I have nothing to say to him."

Elizabeth Brumley's hand went to her mouth. "Well!"

"I have done you no harm, Sharon."

"Not because you didn't try. I presume that you are still at it."

"I'm afraid that I don't know what you are talking about."

Mista sent, *Cool it. We better go and come back later.*

She gripped his hand. *All right.*

Mista said, "I guess we should be going. Nice to meet you, Mr. and Mrs. Brumley." He turned and walked out, leading Sharra. The girls followed.

Janice opened the front door at the car, but Sharra said, "Get in the back, Honey."

She took one look at Sharra and climbed into the back.

Mista backed out and headed back to La Grange. He said, "You should read his mind and find out what's going on in there."

Sharra shuddered. "It's a sink hole."

"Just surface thoughts."

"Okay."

Mista turned on KY 53 and headed north. He turned onto US 42 and found the B-and-B almost immediately. A tall gray-haired man met them at the door. "Welcome. You are our only guests tonight, so the place is all yours. I'd invite you to supper, but we don't have enough prepared for ten extra people."

Mista said, "Suppose one of us goes to town and brings back KFC?. You would be welcome to join us if we may use your dining room."

"That would be fine," the host said.

Mista called Mischal, *Would you like to go back and get us some chicken? I invited our hosts, too.*

Sure. Be back in half an hour. He turned around in the driveway and headed back. Mista walked into the old house with Sharra and said, "We would like to use your common room for a private meeting while we are waiting."

"No problem. We live in the back. Just knock on the kitchen door if you need anything. Would you like coffee?"

"Coffee would be most welcome."

Charly came running in a little later, and Jeremy and Njondac followed more slowly. Charly hugged Sharra and said, "What happened, Aunt Sharra. You look like you've seen a ghost."

"I'm afraid I didn't handle that well. Sit down, everyone and I'll tell you what I just learned."

Mista said, "Did you girls recognize him? I felt your hands tighten."

"Yes," they said together.

Sharra said, "He knew you, of course, but he does not know that you recognized him. He thinks that you are my children, twins, born the year I finished high school. He thinks that is why I left home, thinks that I ran off with my boyfriend. Which is funny, since I didn't have one of them."

Janice said, "That would make us eleven?"

"Yes. I graduated in 1997. My mother believes him. How could she?"

"Well, think about this, dear. Suppose my mother had come to us and told you that the girls were really mine by a secret marriage. And that their mother had gotten into drugs and run off with another man, leaving her with the infant girls. And now she was bringing them to you, since you were now my wife. Would you believe her?"

"No. I know where we got them."

"No, I mean if you didn't know. If you had never seen them before."

"Oh. No, I know you better than that."

"Exactly. She thinks she knows her husband. What has he told her about you?"

"That I was a tramp and came on to him all the time."

Janice snickered. "*I* don't even believe that."

"Well, she does. I guess there is no point in going back there. What's next?"

"You girls understand that you are now in great danger?" Mista asked.

"Yes," Janice said.

Robin said, "But we didn't say anything."

"No, and that's a good thing. That's why I warned you. He thinks that you don't know who he is, but he will still be scheming to get you, especially since your mother insulted him in front of her mother. Not that he didn't have it coming, dear. I intend to do more than insult him when I meet him later."

Mischal came in with the chicken. "Delivery Man! One drum each."

"What?" asked Sharra. "Only one piece each? What did you do, insult Colonel Sanders?"

Mischal laughed. "No. There's plenty. Two barrels. One regular and one crispy."

Mista said, "Sharra, fill Misch and Chandri in while I call our hosts. And Jasmine."

When they had finished, Mista said, "Five rooms, right? All upstairs? The girls would prefer single beds, if you have them, but double beds are all right."

"Four rooms upstairs and one down. One room has a double and a single. All doors are lockable, and we have a safe for any valuables you want to lock up. Breakfast in the morning from 0630 till 1100."

After they left, Mista said, "We need to try to find out what happened to your father. You think you could entice Tom Bronack to meet you somewhere away from their shop?"

"I think so. I'll call him in the morning."

"Better let somebody else call, in case that girl recognizes your voice."

"I'll call," Jasmine said. "I'll even drop into patois for you, Mista."

"Let me," Shawnah said. "Let me. I can do it real good."

"Okay, honey," Jasmine said, "let's see how good you are."

"She's good," Sharra said. "We thought it was real when we interviewed her."

CHAPTER 16

The next morning they took a leisurely breakfast, and then Shawnah called Darkling Freight. "I got to talk at Mr. Bronack."

"He's busy right now. Can he call you back?"

"Naw. I got t' talk at him rat now."

"I'm sorry, miss, but he's busy now. Give my your name and number and I'll call you back."

"Naw. I'll wait."

"You can't do that. You'll tie up my lines."

"Don' yo be tellin' me whut I can an caint do. I got t' talk at him rat now."

Finally the girl said, "Oh all right. I'll go and get him."

Shawnah grinned. Tom came on the line. "May I help you ma'am?"

"This private?"

"Just a minute." He pushed the privacy button. The receptionist fumed. "It's private. Now to whom am I speaking, please?"

Shawnah handed the phone to Sharra. "That was my niece, Tom. I've got to see you today, if you possibly can. Away from the shop. Meet me for lunch at Koch's, downtown?"

"Sure, honey. I'll be there. Noon?"

"Noon. Thanks Tom. I owe you. I'll put Shawnah back on to make your receptionist happy. Take it off private."

Tom clicked off the privacy button and said, "Are you happy now, ma'am?"

"Yo jes be sure yo do what yo said, yo hear?"

"I will. Oops. Clicked on the privacy button. Have a good day, ma'am."

Sharra did not want anyone there for her meeting except Mista. "But, it's unfair to ask you to forego a great meal. You can come, just don't be at my table."

Tom showed up right on time. "Hi, Miss Sharra."

"Thanks for coming Tom. Have any trouble getting away?"

"No. In fact, I took the afternoon off." He grinned. "I'm entitled."

"I'm treating, Tom, so order whatever you want."

"You don't have to do that, Miss Sharra."

"Yes, I do."

They ate in silence except for small talk. Sharra ordered coffee but no dessert after the meal. When it came, she called Mista over. "I can't drink this stuff."

Tom was surprised. "Why didn't you join us for the meal?"

"I asked him not to. I don't really know why."

Tom shrugged. "Whatever. Now what can I do for you? You sounded really urgent on the phone. And why that subterfuge with the little black girl?"

"Oh that. So your receptionist wouldn't know who was calling you. Tom I need to ask a really big favor. I want to know what happened to my father."

"Oh. I'm not surprised. You didn't need all this charade to find that out, though. I would have told you."

"Thanks, I thought you would. But there is something evil about my stepfather, and I didn't want you to get in trouble with him."

Tom shook his head. "You're right about that. I sure miss your father, even after all these years. He was a good man. This man – he's something else. I do all the day to day operations. I know that he has far more money than we make. I don't know what else he does, but it can't be right."

"I know some of it. I suspect other things. He captures little girls and charges people to have sex with them. Holds them captive until they aren't any more use to him and then gets rid of them."

Tom closed his eyes and groaned. "I can't believe that. That's pedophile. Are you sure?"

"My sister was the first that I knew about," Mista said. "He took her when she was eleven, and I just happened to find her years later. She is only one of many."

"That's hard to believe. But I guess I'm not all that surprised. He won't hire women. That girl must be a mistress. He has a new one every month or so. You were right to avoid her if you wanted to keep this secret. Well, let me tell you about your father."

"He was coming home from a long drive. He stopped in Madison, Indiana. That's only an hour or so away, but it was raining and he had been on the road too long already. Over his limit. So he spent the night there, and called me the next morning. He left about seven. He sounded rested, and said he felt fine, that it was a good thing that he stopped over. On the approach to the bridge at Madison, he suddenly swerved and ran off the road. You might know, the bank is not steep there, and he ran straight into the river. The Ohio makes a turn there, and runs deep. Took a few hours to hook and pull the rig up. He had no marks on him, except for his seat belt."

"Oh," Sharra said. "An accident? Somebody run him off?"

Tom was silent a long time, turning his coffee cup around and around. "No. I don't think so. I don't think it was an accident. That's the way they wrote it up. Said he drove too long the day before and must have been over tired. Went to sleep at the wheel. No, Miss Sharra. He called me just before he left. He was not sleepy. The truck window was open."

"I have to go up there, Tom. Would you come with me?"

"I'd love to. Let me call my wife."

"Don't tell her where or why."

"She won't talk."

"I believe you, but I know who we are dealing with."

"Okay." He punched her number. "Honey, I've got an emergency job I've got to finish today. I'll be late tonight, okay?"

"Love you too."

The three cars stopped at the top of the hill going down into Milton, Kentucky, across the river from Madison. Tom looked back. "You have a tail, Miss Sharra."

"I know. I should have told you, Tom. They are friends and they came with me because they know about David Brumley, too."

"Oh. Good friends? They came all the way from wherever you came from?"

"Atlanta. Very good friends."

"Oh. You can see the approach to the bridge very well from here."

"Yes. If they wanted to kill him, it would be easy from this hill."

"Yes, but going the wrong way."

"It could happen on the way up, too," Mista said.

"Yes, but it would have wrecked the truck totally. I think someone was in the truck with him and did something to make the truck swerve before they got to the bridge, and then he swam out the window."

"He would have had to have air tanks."

"So? I think that is what happened. If he had gone off on the way up this hill, they could not have claimed sleepiness. You don't sleep on this hill."

Sharra said, "All right." *Jeremy! Can you come up here?*
Be right there.

Sharra got in back and took Robin in her lap. Jeremy opened the door and stepped in. "What's up?"

"This is the site where my father was killed. Can you sense anything? It was 21 years ago."

Jeremy closed his eyes and let his mind go out. Five minutes went by, and then another five. He opened his eyes. "Truck?"

Tom said, "Yes. How did you know?"

"The windows were open?"

"One was – yes both were open."

"He threw something out and tried to swim out. Something held him. Some one."

He closed his eyes again. A little later, he said, "Sorry, Sharra, that's all I can get. Whatever he threw out might still be there."

"Let's go to Madison and get a diver," Mista said.

"I better go back to my car," Jeremy said. "Too crowded in here."

They pulled up on the edge of the road across the river. Mischal said, "I can dive. Need to find a dive shop."

"Good," Jeremy said. "I can guide you and tell you what to get."

"Just tell me now."

"I don't know exactly. When I see it, I'll know. Or if I am in your mind, when you see it."

Two hours later, Mischal was in the water. He started upstream, since the current was swift here. He swam up river just fast enough to slow his motion to a drift. Suddenly, Jeremy sent, *That box. Get that box.*

Mischal kicked hard, grasped the box and rose to the surface. Then he swam to the shore. He took off his flippers and handed the box to Sharra. "Here you go. Must have been important."

Sharra took it and examined it. It was a steel waterproof box. "I wonder if the seal held?"

"Only one way to find out," Tom said.

Mischal dried the box thoroughly and then looked for a way to open it. "Ah. Combination lock. Must be an internal latch. Have any idea what the combination was?"

"Try my birthday."

"Yes, he always made a deal about your birthday," Tom said.

Mischal punched in the numbers, but nothing happened. "Might have been it, but whatever opened it doesn't work any more. We'll have to cut it."

"Let me look at it," Jeremy said. He put his fingers on the ring of numbers and let his mind search. The combination looked free. He *pushed* a little here, a little there, and then *pushed* down on the latch. It moved down and the lid released. "The springs were rusty. When new, it would have popped open. It's all yours."

She lifted out two notebooks and three sheets of loose paper. The top sheet said, "Saw Arnat Karackish in the truck stop tonight. Wonder why he is here. He is not a driver. Close too Brumley. Could be trouble."

Janice said, "That's the man that was in the car when they picked us up in Florida. He's the one that stuck us with the sleepy drug."

"If I ever see him again, I'll know him," Robin said.

"Have you ever made mental contact with anyone," Jeremy asked.

"No. Almost, but not quite."

"We'll have to work on that."

The notebooks were logs of events and incidents that Harry Darkling had observed and written down. He had observed actions by some of his drivers and then watched them closely. He had recorded payments made to three of them by Brumley. The last note was the conclusion. "It has to be drugs. I don't know how he gets them into the country, but he's putting them on my trucks and paying off the drivers. I believe I have heard a girl's voice in a couple of rigs, but can't be sure of that."

One of the loose papers was blank. The other said only, TO: FBI AGENT IN CHARGE.

Sharra held the paper in her hands and stared at it. "He was going to turn that in when he got back. Never made it."

"Well," Mista said, "We can turn it in for him."

"I knew that he must have been killed. This doesn't bring him back, but at least now I know. Thank you, Tom."

"Don't thank me, Miss Sharra. This explains a lot of things. Brumley had been hanging around your mother every time your dad was away."

"She wouldn't have had an affair. Totally against her nature."

"I think you're right. She's sweet, but old fashioned strict. But he was hanging around like a wasp around a honey jar. He married her just a few weeks later. Consoled her in her grief, offered to run the company like your dad had, knowing that she had no clue. That means that all his extra money must be in drugs."

"And prostitution."

"If you're right about that. He does mention hearing a girl cry in the rigs. Could be."

"Well, let's get you home, Tom," Sharra said. "I want you to know that we are on his trail. He will be dead when we are finished with him."

"How can you do that, Miss Sharra? I understand that you are upset, but ..."

"Tom, this group of people that you see has the will and the skills. Your boss is a dead man. I'm trusting you to be on my side in this. If you aren't – you'll go with him."

He paled at the implied threat. "Trust me, Miss Sharra. I'll be glad to see him go. And all his thugs. But what will become of the company?"

"You can have it."

"No, no. I can manage it, but I'm not an owner. It'll probably go to you."

"I'll be surprised if it does. But if it does, I want you to continue to run it. Turn all the profit into profit sharing with the men and women who are the company."

"Only men. He never hired a woman. Except the bimbo in the office."

"Well, hire women if you want them. Run it the best way you can. I mean it. I don't need the money and I want the men to have it. If you want, you can form a holding company and have the employees buy the company. That will guarantee that they get the profits."

"If it comes, I'll ask them. Might be great for us."

Mista said, "Will you drive, Sharra? I want to call Ross while we are driving back. I wonder if that guy has fingerprints on file anywhere."

CHAPTER 17

They dropped Tom off where he had left his car in a mall parking lot and then went to supper at the Kingfish restaurant. Back at the B-and-B, Mista relaxed in the only comfortable chair in the common room. Most of the chairs were either antiques or were straight chairs. Sharra had gone on to bed. She was not sleepy, but did not feel like talking. Jasmine and Chandri went to her room to give her company, even if she didn't want to talk.

Robin came in and said, "Daddy, there isn't room for us in this chair."

"I know. You'll just have to sit on the floor."

"There's a little couch over there, about half as big as the other couch. It looks comfortable."

"You want me to move so you can have my chair?"

"No, we want you to move so we can sit on you," Janice said.

"Okay." Mista moved and they piled on him on the love seat. Robin said, "Daddy, you still haven't told me when I can have my computer."

"I know. We need to talk about that."

"We could talk now. Then when we get home I could get right on it."

"You could anyway."

"Yes, but it's no fun without privileges. I don't care if they hear."

"Not right now, Honey. There's too much else going on."

Janice said, "When is it all right to lie, Daddy?"

"Why don't you ask Mischal that question. He should be able to give you a good answer."

"Okay. Mischal, when is it okay to lie?"

"Well that's easy. Never."

"But, what if it will save your life? Like this afternoon, if Mr. Brumley had asked if we recognized him, could we say 'no', so he wouldn't know?"

"No. That would be a lie."

"But then he might kill us."

"So? You would die honorably."

"But, I don't want to die."

"Better think through that one. Everyone dies."

"I mean right now. It would be better to lie than to die."

"No. You are going to die. Whenever God decides to take you, then you will die. On the other hand, you cannot be killed until he is ready to take you. You cannot add one minute to your life by anything that you can do."

"Daddy said not to tell him."

"Talk to your daddy about that. You asked my opinion. His might be different."

"The trouble with lying is that once you do, then no one will believe you. Ask Robin about that."

"What does he mean, Robin?"

"You know. I got in worse trouble for lying than if I'd just told the truth."

"Well, I don't particularly care if Mr. Brumley believes me or not."

Mista said, "You have to decide for yourself what you will do in any given circumstances. Now, be careful with that statement. There is a thing called 'situation ethics' that many people adopt. Some people think it is a modern idea, but in fact it goes back to the ancient Greeks. In simple terms it means anything can be right – what is right is what brings the greatest good to the greatest number of people. There are times when you have to weigh relative good or bad actions, but that philosophy fails."

Mista rubbed his chin and thought for a few minutes. "Let me give you an example. Suppose that our friend Karl had done something that made him a hero. Stopped a riot or something and saved a lot of lives. And then he got elected mayor of Atlanta, and since he is a very smart and good man, he became a very popular mayor, getting reelected say three times over. And then suppose somebody broke into his house one night and killed him and raped his wife, Molly. What would people want to happen next?"

Janice said, "Why, to catch whoever did it."

"Exactly. Everybody would want him captured and punished, from the Governor on down. But he didn't leave any clues, and nobody could find him. The search goes on for weeks, and people want this man *caught*. Now, suppose one day a man walks into the police station and confesses. Everybody is happy. The governor, the police chief, Molly and their children – they would have some by this time, of course – we would be happy, since they are good friends. He goes to trial and gets the death sentence.

"Turns out that you find out that the man actually is a little crazy, and he wants to be punished for something, whether he did it or not. And you find out that he was not even in the state when it happened. You know that for a fact. What would you do, Janice? Come forward and tell that this is an innocent man? Or just let him die. Remember, he wants to die, so everybody would be happy, including the man to be put to death and the man who got away with it."

Janice said, "Me?"

"Yes. What should you do? You are the only one that knows, except the man himself, and he doesn't want you to tell."

"I would have to tell."

"Why?"

"Because."

"Because why, Janice. The 'because' thing doesn't work here."

"Because he is innocent. It isn't right to put an innocent man to death."

"But if you do, you will ruin everyone's happiness, including the actual murderer, who is about to get away."

"It doesn't matter. It's the only right thing to do."

"So, you see, 'the greatest good for the greatest number of people' doesn't always work. Some things are just *right*, and some are just *wrong*. Unfortunately, there are a lot of things that you have a hard time deciding about. Sometimes you just have to choose between the lesser of two evils."

Janice said, "Thanks, Daddy. I can't sleep now, thinking about this."

CHAPTER 18

Janice did sleep, though. She shared a room with Robin and Mista and Sharra, and they talked a while before going to sleep. "What would you do, Robin?"

"If I knew who the murderer was, I'd burn him up."

"Yeah, but I don't know what I'd do. I'd have to tell, but then we would have to find the real murderer."

The B-and-B had a no-pets rule, so Chandri had to put Biscuit out at night. The owner said, "I'm sorry, but we must insist on that rule. Other guests want a clean room, and some might be allergic to cats. I wish it weren't so, because we have coyotes out here in the country."

"That's okay. He can take care of himself. Coyotes don't climb trees well, if I remember correctly."

"By the way, we set the security system at night. You can move freely around the house, but if you need to go outside for something, we will need to disable it."

She rubbed his head and scruffed his back. "Guard, Biscuit. I'll save some good breakfast for you in the morning." *Chances are, he'll bring me some breakfast. A rabbit or something. He doesn't understand why I'm not overjoyed at his generosity.* Biscuit purred and rubbed the point of his jaw on her leg, and then ran and jumped on a tree, climbing out of sight in a few seconds.

When they went to bed, Mischal noticed that Chandri had her pistol strapped to her leg under her skirt. "Why did you bring your piece in? Expecting trouble?" Even after being out of the Marines for years, Mischal still called his weapon a 'piece'.

"Not really, but then, you never know. You have yours, don't you?"

Mischal grinned. "You betcha. You can bet Mista has his staff, and Njondac has his axes, too."

Jasmine shared a room and bed with Shawnah. Before she went to bed, she found Mista and said, "I have a funny feeling about tonight."

"What do you mean?"

"I would not be surprised if someone tried to stop us from taking that evidence to the FBI. You know who I mean. I'm going to set a ward around the house. If you hear a panther scream, you'll know someone is out there."

"Biscuit?"

"It will sound a lot like Biscuit, but louder. He is not as big as a panther, but has the same kind of scream."

"Okay. Good idea. I hope it doesn't happen, but it's best to be ready."

Sometime after midnight Chandri woke up with the sound of a scream echoing in her mind. She was a trained ranger, and instantly alert, listening for any unusual noise. Then she heard another scream. *Panther!* It sounded like a woman in anguish, but she knew her animal sounds. It was not Biscuit. Perhaps he had screamed first and that was what woke her. She called softly, "Misch!"

"What?" He too was a warrior. She knew better than to touch him, and he came awake instantly at her call.

"Somebody out there. Biscuit screamed and then a panther."

"I bet that was Jasmine's ward against intruders. I'll go call Mista."

Chandri opened the window, forgetting about the alarm. Nothing happened, so she assumed that the upstairs windows were not alarmed. The window opened onto a flat roof over the back part of the house, the part where the owners lived. She climbed out onto the roof. The night was dark, with no moon and overcast skies. The light which spilled out behind the house from a security light on the front side was enough for her to be able to see. She reached back inside and got her pistol and then crawled out onto the roof. Two shots rang out, and she dropped flat on the roof.

She heard Mischal in the room behind her. "Stay there, but throw me a pillow."

She pushed the pillow up in the air, and four more shots rang out, two of them hitting the pillow. Mischal called, "You better get back in here."

"No, I'm going to see who it is. She crawled to the back of the house and then pushed the pillow up again. Another shot rang out, and feathers puffed from the pillow. *Biscuit! Scream!*

Instantly, he screamed. She did not know if the attacker or attackers knew what a bobcat sounded like, but if they did not know, then they would think it was her and that they had hit her. She crawled on toward the back of the house, where the shots had come from. Just before she got there, the alarm went off, a wailing siren followed by voice, "You have violated a protected space. Leave immediately. Police have been called." It repeated the message again a minute later. She assumed that she had tripped it after all, and that it was a delayed response.

She looked out onto the field behind the house. Her eyes were nearly as good as a cat's eyes. Suddenly she saw movement. A figure rose from the ground holding a piston in his hand. She raised hers, clicked on the laser beam and double tapped. The figure flew backwards and then fell to the ground. Another man rose and aimed toward her. She tapped twice again and he fell. Then a bullet came from the side and hit her in the buttocks. She ignored the pain and turned to see who it was.

She spotted a man up in the tree next to the house and tried to draw a bead on him, but he was behind the trunk of the tree. He reached around and fired in her direction, and she fired back, but could not hit him. She called, *Biscuit! Get him!* Biscuit leaped halfway up the tree trunk and climbed on up. The man heard him coming and looked down just as Biscuit leaped onto him, bearing him to the ground 15 feet below. Chandri said, *Get his gun hand. Firestick.* Biscuit clamped onto his gun hand wrist and bit clear through it. The man screamed and dropped his gun, but Biscuit held on. *Hold him!*

Meanwhile, Mischal crawled through the window and crawled toward the front side of the house. He stopped while still in the shadow cast by the side of the house and looked. He spotted a man running toward the back of the house, and followed him with his gun. His Kimber Desert Warrior spoke once and the man fell. He did not see anyone else, but stayed prone behind the wall, watching.

A man broke the glass in the front door and forced it open, setting off the alarm. Since Njondac was sleeping in the front room, he was up as soon as the alarm went off. He grabbed his axes and stepped into the main room to see a man pouring gasoline on the floor, and then backing toward the door, leaving a trail behind him.

"No ya don't." He threw one ax, hitting the man in the near shoulder. He threw his hands up in reflex, throwing the gasoline can and splashing gasoline all over himself. Terrified, he turned and ran. The second ax hit him in the back just as he cleared the edge of the front porch, and he went sprawling. Suddenly, he burst into flames, and his gasoline soaked clothing flashed into a fireball.

Then Njondac saw another man jump from the car parked in the driveway and run toward the house, carrying another can of gasoline. Njondac had no weapons, having thrown both axes, but he stood ready to take the man apart with his bare hands. Before he was half way there, he, too flashed into fire. Then the car itself flashed into fire, and a man opened the driver's door and crawled out, his clothing burning.

Robin was standing in front of the bedroom window in Charly's room. Something had jarred her awake, and she thought she had been dreaming about a man trying to set the house on fire. She ran to her bedroom window, where she could just see a car in the driveway. A limousine. She ran into Charly's room in the front of the house and looked out. When she saw the man running out with a gasoline can in his hand, she didn't think, but set him on fire. Then she saw the other man leave the car and head for the house. She set him on fire, and then set the car on fire for good measure.

Sharra came up behind her and put her arm around her. "Good work, hon."

"Want me to burn him, too?" she asked, pointing to the man running from the car.

"No. Let's hold him and question him."

Jeremy and Charly were both awake and watching Robin at work. Jeremy formed a band of energy around the man's ankles, and he went sprawling, still burning. A police car roared into the driveway, lights flashing, with another right behind him.

The security company had called when the alarm went off, and the house owner had said that there were people shooting at the house, that they better send more than one officer.

The first officer jumped out of his cruiser with fire extinguisher in hand. While he was extinguishing the burning man, the second officer called the fire department and EMS. They would let firemen deal with the burning car and the two small fires near the car, not knowing that the two small fires had once been men.

When the fire was out and the man sat up, Robin said, "That is the man who was in the car with Mr. Brumley when he captured us."

"You sure?" asked Sharra.

"Yes. I can tell."

"Well, I guess we can get fingerprints on him. If he has any left."

Mischal saw a man jump up in the field behind the house and run when the police cars arrived. He raised his Kimber to shoot, but then lowered it. He did not want to shoot with police coming in, and besides, the man could carry a message to his boss, whoever that was.

The house owner came out when the police arrived and greeted them. The first officer said, "I am Joe Donnelly. What's going on?"

The owner obviously knew the officers, and said, "Good morning, Joe. You guys got here quick. I don't know what's going on. Some men were shooting at the house, and then somebody else tried to burn it down. I think that is them, out in front. Looks like the fire got them before they had the house ready to fire."

Chandri came out the front door, leaning on Jasmine. Jasmine had healed the wound, but it still hurt. Chandri said, "I'll have to borrow a pillow to ride home on."

"Be glad it didn't hit a bone," Jasmine said. "Could have crippled you."

Chandri called Biscuit, *Bring me your man.* The cat did not speak English, but Chandri was able to communicate with it. She could not explain it, but she was able to send images and the cat responded. He came around the corner, dragging the man behind him.

Officer Donnelly said, "What it this?"

Chandri said, "He was shooting at me. My cat is very protective. You'll find his gun somewhere around there."

"Your cat? That's a bobcat, ma'am."

"I know. I raised him from a baby." *Let him go, Biscuit.* Biscuit dropped the man's hand and walked over to Chandri as if nothing had happened.

The officer approached Chandri to get her ID, and Biscuit growled. Chandri stroked his head and said, "It's okay, Biscuit."

Donnelly said, "Jim, go around back and see if you can find a gun while I get her name."

The other officer took his flashlight and headed around the house. Donnelly's eyes widened when Chandri showed her badge and ID card. Chandri said, "We were just up here to visit relatives. I have no idea what these men wanted."

Officer Donnelly took all their names. He knew something was going down when they all had the same address, and all were police officers, but he did not want to say anything in the presence of the two assailants who were still alive.

The other officer came back a few minutes later, carrying a gun in a plastic bag, and said, "There are three more out back, all dead. What did you people do, have a little war out here?"

"It looks that way," Mista said. "We were all asleep when it started, so you will have to ask them what they were doing here."

Donnelly said, "Three?" He looked around. "Who shot them?"

"I shot two," Chandri said. "They were shooting at me."

"How do I know that they were shooting first?"

"I put two bullets in each of their hearts. How many times do you think they shot after that?"

"How do you know that you hit his heart?"

"I don't miss."

They put the men in the EMS wagons and took them to the hospital, Jim Calvin escorting the ambulance. Donnelly said, "Where can I reach you?"

Mista gave him a card. "You can call this number, also, to find out where we might be at any given time." He wrote the number and FBI, Paul Ross, on the back of his card.

Officer Donnelly called for assistance. He took statements from each of the people there, and then removed the bodies. He recorded the license number of the burned car in his notebook and had it dragged to a salvage yard. He whistled when he checked the registration. He had waited to check it, knowing that the car was not going anywhere. Now he wished he had checked earlier. It belonged to David Brumley.

After everyone had left, Mista said, "Well, let's see if we can get some sleep in what's left of the night. Better set your ward again, Jasmine, just in case they try again."

"Yeah, really."

He told their host, "I see that you have some broken windows. Probably other damage. It is obviously our fault. Surely they would not have attacked had we not been here. I'll walk around with you in the morning and give you a check to cover the damage."

"Insurance should pay, sir."

"You can file with them, too. But I will cover your costs anyway. You need to make some repairs right away."

CHAPTER 19

The sheriff came by while they were walking around the property. He asked Mista and others some pointed questions and examined the sites where the bodies had been found. "Well, it looks like the men carrying gasoline were a bit careless. I can't imagine why they would be carrying cans of gasoline around at 2:00 in the morning. Shooting at strangers, though."

"They shot first," Mista said.

"It seems so. Hard to shoot after a bullet pierces your heart. Mr. Mictackic, were you planning on staying here for a while?"

"No, sir. We were scheduled to leave this morning."

"I'm going to ask you not to leave the area until after the weekend, to give us a chance to check everything out. I need to verify your status and get a history on each of you, since you are strangers in the area. I understand that the car found here belonged to Mr. Brumley, a respected businessman in the community. We want to know why it was here, also."

Mista gave him Paul Ross' name and number. "He can probably give you some information on our status."

The sheriff punched the number into his cell, and he looked up with a raised eyebrow when the person answering identified themselves as FBI. Ross said, "Let me call you back, Sheriff." He did not ask for a number, and immediately disconnected.

The sheriff looked quizzically at his phone. "He said he would call me back, but did not ask my number."

"Maybe he wants to place the call through your office?" Mista said. "You could also call Commander Karl Spicewood, Georgia State Police. Oh. You might not be able to find him."

The sheriff's eyes narrowed. "Why do you think it would be hard to find him if he is State Police?"

"He's on his honeymoon."

"Oh."

"Here is his personal cell number, if they won't give it to you at his office."

The receptionist said, "Commander Spicewood is on vacation, sir."

"Could you get a message to him?"

"Well, of course, but … well, it's his honeymoon, sir."

"It's important. Please ask him to call Sheriff Nottingham at this number."

"I'll send him a message, sir."

The sheriff tried Karl's cell, but got voice mail.

Mista said, "Sharra why don't you ask him to call?"

"Sure. What is your number, sir?"

Sharra sent, *Molly?*

Ummm. Sharra? Call later, okay?

Can't. Have to do this now.

This better be important!

It is. Call this number. It is Sheriff Nottingham.

"Karl, darling, you have to call in."

"Now?"

"Yes. It's Sharra. She says it is important."

"Okay. Good timing."

Sharra said, "I think I interrupted something."

Mista raised an eyebrow. "Oh?"

"Well, they *are* on their honeymoon."

"What do you mean, you interrupted something."

"It's a family joke, sheriff. You wouldn't understand."

The sheriff's phone beeped. "Sheriff Nottingham."

"This is Commander Karl Spicewood. I have been asked to call."

"Yes. I am talking to a George Mictackic here. He says you can tell me something about him."

"Let me speak to Mista, please."

"Mista?"

"Mr. Mictackic."

"Oh. Just a moment."

"What's up, Mista? Is this for real? Like I need to ask you that."

"Yep. We had an interesting night last night."

"Are you clear? Say, 'Sorry about you car,' if you are not under duress."

"Sorry about your car."

"Okay. Put the sheriff on."

"Sheriff Nottingham."

"Mista and his family have done excellent work for me, sheriff. You can trust whatever he tells you."

"Okay. This is a homicide. It looks justified, but I have to investigate."

"If Mista is involved I'm sure that it's justified. Do whatever you have to do."

"Thank you, sir."

He closed his phone and it beeped again immediately.

"Sheriff Nottingham."

"Paul Ross, FBI. You had some questions?"

"Yes. I'm talking to a George Mictackic here. He says that you can verify his status."

"You understand, I had to verify to whom I was speaking. When you called me, you were just a voice. Let me speak to Mista, please."

The sheriff handed the phone to Mista. "Everyone wants to talk to you."

"When you do the kind of work I do, they want to be sure that they do not give information to the wrong people. Mista here."

"What have you got, Mista?"

"I was going to bring you the information that I found yesterday. Apparently someone did not want that to happen. The sheriff is investigating."

"You clear?"

"Yes. He has to know something. But this is a local county. Not much, understand?"

"Gotcha. Let me talk to him."

"Sheriff Nottingham."

"What can I do for you, sheriff?"

"Do you know this Mictackic?"

"Yes. I know him. He's clean."

"Is he FBI?"

"No, not at all. Did he say he was?"

"No, but he gave me your number to call."

"Well, something must have happened."

"Yes. We have a homicide here. I'm going to ask him to say around for a few days."

"That's your prerogative. I do not interfere in local affairs."

"He says he works for the Georgia State Police."

"He has done some work for them. I do not know if he is currently on their payroll."

"He says that he is not."

"You would have to ask them about that."

"Can you tell me what he is involved in up here?"

"No, sir. He does not work for me, so I do not know what he might be involved in, if anything."

"Well, thank you for your information."

He closed the phone and turned to Mista. "I'm going to ask you to stay in the area for a few days."

"Fine. We do not have to be anywhere in particular. You mind if we do some sightseeing? Like Mammoth Caves?"

"So long as you are back tonight."

"You have my cell number. You can call now, if you want to verify it."

Sheriff Nottingham punched the number. Mista answered, "Mista." And closed the phone. "Satisfied?"

"Yes. This might be a very high profile case."

"Only if you make it so."

"Not me. You know whose car that was out here?"

"No. No idea."

"It was registered to David Brumley."

"So? I am not a local resident. Is he someone important?"

"One of the richest men around here."

"If you say so."

"Well, I guess you wouldn't know."

TV reporters were the next to come. They interviewed the owner and the guests and took pictures of the picturesque old inn and left. The man the cat had dragged around was identified as Samuel Johnston. The man who had leaped from the car was identified as Arnat Karackish. Neither had a criminal record. Arnat Karackish was kept under guard in the burn ward of a local hospital, since he had third degree burns. Johnston was released on bail and sought treatment for major bites and scratches. They never found the supposed panther that had attacked him.

Arnat Karackish told police that they must have been bandits. They had stopped the car as he was returning from an out-of-town trip for his employer, claiming that their truck had broken down. "I never saw them before. Looked like Mexicans to me. Can't trust those people." In fact, none of them were Mexicans, but the police were not able to identify them. When his burns healed, he was released on his own recognizance, pending investigation.

Mista did visit Mammoth Caves that Saturday, but stopped to deliver a box to Paul Ross. He called him while driving into Louisville and asked Paul to meet him at Paul's office.

Ross was already there when Mista arrived. He said, "I'm here. On a Saturday. What's the rush? The stuff you found yesterday has been there for 20 years."

"More like 30," Mista said. "Either someone knew that we had found it, or someone just doesn't want us to survive. The B-and-B that we stayed in last night was assaulted by at least four gunmen and two men with gasoline trying to fire the house. The police have two men in custody. One is Brumley's right-hand man. He is the one who shot up Mischal's rental car when we were here before. He was inside Brumley's limousine when it suddenly burst into flame. The driver got away to report back to Brumley."

"You let him get away? I assume that you could have stopped him."

"We could have. Sharra made mental contact with him. We will have a tap on information, now." Mista held up his hands. "I know, that is not legally admissible information. But it could be enough to lead us to what we need."

"I don't suppose you had anything to do with firing his car?" Ross asked.

"We were all inside the house, fending off the gunmen. Maybe they got careless with their gasoline. I don't know what will happen next, but I think the fun has only just begun. What we have here is not proof of anything, but indication of what went down. Her father already suspected Brumley and his crew, and had made a series of notes. He was bringing them to the FBI the day he was killed."

"I thought that was an accident."

"It was logged as an accident. It was rigged to make it look like an accident. However, we know that it was not. It will be pretty hard to prove it, though. What we know is not considered evidence. But, we know."

"More of your mental powers?"

"You got it. Not to fear, that will never be made public. No one would believe us, except a few. And they would be likely to want to use us for their own gain. It will be kept a close secret."

He handed Ross a list of screen names. "Paul, I need names put to these internet screen names. I don't have the power to do that. I intend to interview the people involved and see what we can learn."

"You cannot use this to coerce them."

"Don't intend to. Just need to know who they are and where they live."

"I'll get it for you. Just be careful."

When they left his office, Sharra said, "This is Saturday. Are you sure that you want to go to the caves today? There'll be a million tourists down there."

"So? What better place to hide. You have anything better to do?"

They returned to Georgia the following Tuesday. The rest of their stay was pleasant and uneventful. Only Robin was unhappy about the extended stay. "I'll never get my computer back."

Tuesday night she climbed up into Mista's lap with a sigh. "Are you ever going to give me my computer back?"

"Is it that important to you?"

"No, not any more. I mean, I like having it, but there are other things to do."

"That's what I was waiting for. Why did you go to all those sites if it wasn't important?"

"It was then. But I don't know why they fascinated me so. It doesn't seem all that bad."

"Would you put pictures like that of yourself up on the 'net?"

"NO! I don't know why *they* would. But, like Janice and I take baths and showers at the same time. We don't mind seeing each other."

"Would you want me in there with you?"

"No! You wouldn't, would you?"

"No, of course not. You know, we do not know if those girls put their own pictures up on the 'net. We don't even know if they know that they are there."

"They could go look."

"Not necessarily. Not everyone has the same privileges that you girls do. You have them because I trust you. If I can't trust you, then I can't restore yours."

"You can trust me. I'll never go back to them."

"All right. I'll do it tonight. Now, I don't want you to be afraid to use it. You might come across a site from time to time, and I expect that you will. Just don't be going back to them time and again."

"Okay. I promise."

Janice came in a little later. "Daddy, remember that man that said he was from Louisville? A long time ago?"

"Yes."

"He IMed me just now. Said he heard we were up in Louisville and wondered why we didn't contact him."

"How would he know?"

"I don't know. I wondered about that."

"Hmmm." Mista rubbed his chin. "Must be part of the network. Means, someone in the network knew that you were up there. Well, just be careful. We are tracking them down."

"I'll tell him that we weren't there very long, and didn't have a computer with us."

"Let me know what he says to that."

Janice came back a few minutes later and said, "I don't want to talk to him any more. He got nasty. Said next time we ought to take a computer and stay longer. He wanted to see me, and even asked for a better picture."

CHAPTER 20

The driver made his escape without detection, as far as he knew. He ran down the road for a quarter of a mile and then hid in a small stand of trees beside the road until all the emergency vehicles had left. Then he walked back to the Brumley house, about three miles. The eastern sky was beginning to lighten before he arrived.

David Brumley was waiting in his home office. He had dozed in his recliner, but had not really slept well, and was grumpy. "Took you long enough, James. You get lost somewhere?"

"No, sir. Had to walk home. They was waiting for us."

"So what happened? You get careless and set off an alarm?"

"No, sir. Like I said, they was waiting for us. They shot Murphy, Jonas and Kline out in the field before they even got to the house. Maddox and Linders must of got careless. They set themselves on fire carrying their gasoline cans before they even got to the house. And then the car blew up. Don't know what caused that. Actually, I think Linders got inside, but he must of set off an alarm. You could hear it half a mile. Police were there a few minutes later."

"How did the car blowup? I don't see how that could happen."

"I don't know, boss. Maybe they threw a firebomb into it. Windows were open. I jumped out when it burst into flames and ran, and Arnat, he got out the other side, but he was burning. He tried to run, but tripped up. Probably just as well. He was burned so bad they took him to the hospital."

"What about McIntyre? He was supposed to be coordinating this."

"I don't know what happened. I looked back and saw what looked like a big old bobcat dragging him around the side of the house. They had police cars, ambulances and fire trucks there, so there was plenty of light. Cat dragged him up and then ran off. If I didn't know better, I'd of thought it was a pet, but nobody can tame a bobcat."

"You sure it was a bobcat?"

"Well, I was pretty far off, and it was as big as a big dog, but didn't look like no dog."

"So, where is McIntyre now? Why didn't he come with you?"

"Don't know. They took him off in an ambulance."

Brumley dropped his head into his hands and groaned. "Half my people dead, leaders in the hospital. What next? No car. Police will have to wonder how my car got there. And I have an important meeting this morning. Funny how you can be on top of the world one day and then one person comes along and it all turns to dust."

"We can use your wife's car to get to town, Mr. Brumley."

Brumley was silent for a minute. Then he raised his head and said, "Right. Get some sleep. We need to leave at 8:30. I'll get a new car later today. I expect we'll get a visit from the sheriff today, also."

CHAPTER 21

The following Monday they all drove to Florida to close on their houses. They had bought from several realtors, and were able to set up closings on all of the houses on the same day. Mista took both the Range Rover and Sharra's Lincoln, since he planned to stay a while. He needed the space to carry the computers he would need to set up operations there.

His house was the only one that was already empty, and he took possession immediately. Mischal and Jeremy drove their motor homes and parked them on Njondac's land. None of them wanted Mista and Sharra down there alone. Chandri even made a point of bringing Biscuit, especially since he had sounded the alarm in Kentucky and helped capture one of the men.

Mista looked around his empty new house and said, "I guess we better get some furniture. What should we buy first?"

Both girls said, "Buy a bigger chair. You have to have one, and you said the old one was getting too small."

"Well, I can't buy me a chair and make the rest of you sit on the floor."

"We would share it with you," Janice said.

"And Sharra, too? That will take a really big chair."

"I'm not that big," Sharra said.

"No, but with three other people already in the chair ..."

"You could get two chairs," Robin said."

"Hmmm. That would work. Have to make two trips, but we can do that. We need to buy a couple of air mattresses, too. We can sleep on them tonight, and then stow them for company."

"Hummph." Njondac said. "I gots a perfectly good truck. I'll haul 'em."

While Mista was shopping for furniture, Sharra picked out sets of cookware, dinnerware and flatware. She also bought a basket full of general kitchen utensils. She would need appliances, but they could wait.

Mista and Sharra looked around the nearly empty rooms after everything was brought in and Njondac and Mischal had left. Mista said, "Well, two chairs do not a home make."

Sharra smiled. "No. We need everything, don't we? Sofa and chairs for the living room, dining furniture, beds. I need more stuff for the kitchen, too. Toaster and Microwave, for starters. Want to go back?"

"We could go and get some small things. Get your appliances, get some deck chairs and maybe pick out some bedroom furniture for later delivery. But, we have the trailer with us. We can sleep there tonight."

"Okay," Sharra said. "But we also need basic things, like soap and towels. Brooms, vacuums, and general household things. We could get a start tonight."

When they had nearly everything that they wanted to buy that night, Mista said, "You know, we could initiate the house by cooking a meal there. Anyone like chili?"

"Yes, yes," the girls said.

"Okay. Let's get what we need and I'll make us a big pot of chili," Mista said.

Sharra said, "I don't think I've ever seen you cook."

"I did once."

"Oh. I must have missed that."

"It can't be hard. They print directions on things."

Sharra knew better, but chose to remain silent. "Well, let's see what you can do."

Mista took his time. First he picked up a carton of Bloemers chili base and read the directions. Next he bought two pounds of pre-packaged chili ground round beef, a package of chili seasoning, a can of special chili tomato sauce, with seasoning. "We have to have beans," Sharra said.

"Oh, okay." He read the directions on the chili seasoning package. "Two cans of beans. Hmmm. Let's get four, for good measure." He bought two cans of kidney beans in mild chili sauce and two in hot sauce."

When they got home, he read the directions again. "Brown meat in skillet and add chili base."

Robin said, "Want me to cook it, Daddy? I cooked all the time for my mother and me."

"No, this is my treat, honey."

He opened the packages of meat and dropped them in the largest skillet Sharra had bought. The pre-packaged hamburger was in small blocks. He browned one side and flipped them over to brown the other side, and then added the container of chili base. It two was a block. Next he sprinkled the package of chili seasoning over the three blobs of brown meat and added the can of tomatoes, then all four cans of beans. "Simmer on low heat for 20 minutes."

"Okay. You girls open the dishes and wash them. We'll be ready in twenty minutes." He covered the chili and let it simmer.

After twenty minutes, he took the lid off the skillet. "Well, smells all right, but looks funny," he said.

Sharra came into the kitchen for the first time and said, "What's wrong?"

"I don't know. The blocks of meat didn't melt down or anything. Looks kind of like a cake with beans for icing."

Sharra put her hands on her hips. "You have to break up the meat! You are supposed to squeeze it in your fingers and break it all up."

"But it's too hot to put my fingers in it."

"Silly. Break it up before you brown it."

"Oh. Well, too late for that."

"Here. Take the plastic spoon and break it all up, stir it good and let it simmer some more."

Ten minutes later, he served up six bowls of chili with a flourish. "Enjoy!"

Sharra took one bite and said, "Mista, this is awful strong."

"I just followed directions."

"Let me see what all you put in it."

He showed her everything. "You used chili base, chili seasoning, and chili seasoned beans and chili seasoned tomatoes? How much water did you add?"

"No water. Didn't call for water."

"Phew. No wonder Charly says you aren't allowed to cook. It does call for water."

"Oh. Must have missed that."

"You can plan battles, heal broken hearts, counsel married couples and teach wisdom, but you can't cook. You don't need chili base *and* chili seasoning. *And* seasoned beans. One or the other. Put it all back in the pot and we'll add about a quart of water and try again."

Thinned down, the chili was not half bad. Sharra said, "I appreciate the effort, but I think somebody else better be cooking for us. How about it, girls?"

Robin and Janice looked at each other. They had each managed almost a whole bowl of chili. Janice said, "Well, it was filling."

Em said, "If you had asked, I would have been glad to cook it."

Mista said, "Well, maybe I could do better on steaks or chops."

"No way," Sharra said. "You just stay out of the way."

Sharra poured the remainder of the chili into a bowl and the girls cleaned up the dishes and loaded the dishwasher. Mista walked out onto the deck to watch the sunset. He found Sharra already there, sitting in one of the deck chairs. He walked up behind her and put his hands on her shoulders. "You haven't said much the last few days, dear. Are you all right?"

"Yes. I'll be all right."

"Don't you like the house?"

"I love it. But I'm not sure we should spend all that much money. And you still want to buy a boat."

"What else would you rather do with it?"

"Live on it. We don't have a steady job, you know."

"Honey, we could pay for the houses outright and pay for the boat outright and the interest on the remainder would still be over $100,000 a year. That's enough to live on. Money is of no value if you don't put it to use."

"Just as long as we don't go broke."

After the sun had set they went back over to where they had parked the trailer on Njondac's land. Everyone else was seated around a roaring campfire. Charly said, "We wondered where you all were. There's still some chicken left."

"No, thanks," Mista said. "We decided to initiate the house by cooking supper there."

Sharra showed the bowl of chili and Charly lifted the lid and smelled. "Smells good."

Sharra said, "Mista cooked. Want some?"

Charly closed the lid. "No thanks. I ate some of his cooking once."

Robin pulled on Sharra's hand and whispered, "I'd like some chicken, Mommy. I'm still hungry."

"You'll hurt your daddy's feelings," she whispered back.

"Oh. Well, I'm not that hungry."

"Get you some chicken, honey. If he says anything, I'll hit him on the head with his chili pot."

They talked for a while and then went down to the trailer. Em came in a few minutes later, carrying Sam. "She's ready for bed. What about living arrangements after you move into the house?"

"We didn't buy you a house, did we?" Mista asked. "You have been living with Sheila, and that's all right if you want to. Or you could live with us. We'll set up a room for you."

"Well, we've all been living kind of together, you know," Em said. "Either in a camp or in the big house. Now we are splitting up. I'll still be available for the teaching tasks and caring for little Sam. I just wondered what the best place would be."

"We always lived in separate houses until we came back to Georgia," Mista said. "We traveled together and campaigned together, but it's good to have some space. We have lived as a group ever since you joined us, haven't we? Whatever you want to do. It might be easier for you to work with Sam if you live with us. We can make you a separate room, or make an apartment downstairs for you. You could still share the house with Sheila if you'd rather. I also thought I'd ask Jasmine if she wanted to share Sheila's house. I looked for a house big enough for all of us, but couldn't find one."

"I think I'll stay with Sheila for a while. But, I like the idea of having a separate apartment in your house so I can be near Sam. It would make it more convenient to set up teaching rooms there, also."

Em left and Sharra started to put Sam to bed. Mista said, "Girls, I would like for you to help take care of Sam. You can start by helping to get her to bed tonight."

Robin said, "What's wrong with her? I mean she doesn't talk or walk or anything. I know you said it was CP, but will she get better?"

"She will grow and get better, but it takes a long time. Her brain was damaged when she was born, and she doesn't have enough muscle control to walk or talk. She is smart, though."

"She seems slow," Janice said.

Sharra sent, *Tell her, baby.*

Sam sent, *I not slow. I fast.*

Janice jumped. "How did she do that? You did that, Mom."

"No, she has mind-speech. But at a little less than two, she doesn't have too many words yet. She understands pretty much whatever you say to her though. And she knows a lot of sign language. You could learn that and talk with her. Sam, can you say 'Janice'?"

"Djannnch."

"Good try. How about 'Robin'?"

"Wobb."

"You have been too busy with everything else to pay much attention to her."

"We have not," Robin said. "We play with her some and hold her and change her. I just wondered if she would ever talk."

When Sharra came back, she said, "The girls are staying with her till she goes to sleep. I'm going on to bed. I'm tired tonight."

Mista pulled her down into his lap. "You sure you're all right?"

"I'm just angry. You know what he's done? Killed my father. Stole my mother and alienated her. Took over my father's business and made it into a racket. Kidnapped my girls and tried to kill all of us. I hate him."

"Now, …"

"I know. I have to get rid of the hate and I will. But I might just kill him with my own two hands first."

"You can't do that."

"Oh, yes I can."

He put his arms tight around her and rocked gently. "No, you really can't. I don't mean that you don't have the mental or physical ability. But it won't do for you to kill him. It would leave a wound in you that might never heal."

"You think I don't already have a wound that won't heal?"

"No, I don't. It's a serious wound, no doubt. But it will heal. But if you kill your father. …"

"Not my father. Don't ever say that."

"He stood in for your father, like it or not, for ten of your formative years."

The girls came in, ready for bed and stopped when they saw Sharra in Mista's arms.

Sharra said, "I'll get up and you can have him."

Mista said, "No. It's your turn. Go away, girls."

They went back into their room and pulled the door almost shut.

Sharra resisted at first, but finally settled down. After a while she began to cry softly. "I don't know how you do this to me."

"You need the release. I'm here for you. I do love my girls, but you know that I love you more."

After a few minutes, Sharra dried her eyes and said, "I can't let him get away with it."

"He won't, trust me. It just can't be you that has to kill him. It might not be any of us. It won't be me, either, unless he attacks me directly, or one of you four."

"I'm not afraid to kill him. You know what I always say – I have no compunction about killing an evil man. It severely limits the amount of evil he can do in his lifetime."

"I know. But this would hurt you more than it hurts him. You think your mother is alienated now? Wait till you kill her husband."

"She can't love him!"

"Oh, but she does. She might or might not know what he really is, but believe this: she loves him."

"She loved my father, too. But she married that man within days."

"You assume that she loved your father. Maybe she didn't? Maybe she was part of a plot to get rid of him and marry this man?"

"I don't believe that! That would be totally out of character for her. Even if she didn't love him, she would have been obedient and dutiful. She would never have been a party to killing him."

"Maybe not, but she could look the other way. Don't count her out. I don't accuse her, either. But don't be blind to facts."

"You're right. I need to keep my eyes open. Can I go to bed now? The girls are standing behind the door, dying to get in here."

CHAPTER 22

They spent the rest of the week furnishing the houses and setting up housekeeping. Paul Ross came down on Friday and Mista invited him to stay for the weekend.

"I have several things for you. First, your friend, Mr. Brumley has apparently escaped any connection with the caper at the B-and-B where you stayed in Louisville. He says that his car was hijacked. The only person that they could prove was in the employ of Brumley was his head of security, Arnat Karackish. The other man that they caught – or you caught—claims not to know Brumley, and visa versa. He must have connections, however. Someone made his bail."

"Why am I not surprised," Mista said. "So that's the end of that?"

"Looks like it. You probably know that Karackish was burned severely. He has been released, and Brumley and he and some other unnamed persons have departed for Brumley's vacation home in Grand Cayman. He will be out of the picture for a while."

"I doubt that," Mista said. "Out of the country, but not out of the picture. When it gets hot there, he'll probably be back."

"That may well be," Ross said. "I have some information for you. Here is a list of screen names, matching telephone numbers and account names that own the screen names. I say it that way, because the person setting up the Internet account might not be the person actually using the screen name."

"Yes, I know," Mista said. "I have several people using screen names on one or another of my accounts. Since I have my own Internet server, they are really tied to user accounts in my own network."

"That is probably true of some of these screen names. It might not be a personal Internet server, but one where they work. Whatever. It is leads for you. If it is a corporate server, then the telephone number is probably the company number. They probably don't know what their employee is doing on company time."

"Probably true. Well, thank you. We'll start tracking down some perps."

"Just be careful. That list must remain in your possession. No copies. If you get your information the wrong way, you will not be able to use it as evidence."

"Don't worry. I am not as much interested in preserving evidence to match court rules as in stopping the practice. If the perp is bad enough, we will be sure to send him to see a judge. With intact evidence. I am also interested in putting Mr. Brumley out of business, and out of this life. That is not a threat against his life. But, if I gather as much information as I hope to, then some prosecutor is going to have a field day. He might sit on death row for 20 years, but I believe that he is going down."

"Again, be careful. I believe that you have tagged the right man, and that he is a dangerous man. The incident in Louisville proved that."

"Now you believe me when I say that he is responsible?"

"I do. Just don't make any unprovable assumptions. By the way, nice house. I didn't know you had a house down here."

"It is the town where I was born. A couple of streets over is where Brumley went cruising and picked up my sister. He appears to be still operating in this area, and I will focus my investigation here."

They started calling numbers on Monday afternoon, using Mista's cell phone, since his number would not show up on Caller ID. The first three numbers were corporate numbers.

In each case, Mista asked to speak to the network administrator. "Good afternoon. If your company does not have Internet usage controls in place, it probably should," Mista opened with without preamble.

Typically, the first question the administrator would ask was, "Who did you say was calling?"

"I didn't say. However, you might want to check on the kind of email is going out under the screen name of ___." He named the screen name in use at that number and disconnected before the network administrator could ask anything else. The hint should be enough to cause the network administrator to look at mail going out, whether or not they had a policy about personal use. The screen name used might or might not be the name on that person's network account. There was a good chance that the person might be on the network staff.

The next three names were in different states, one in Washington, one in California, and one in Illinois. He gave these to Janice and asked her to email them expressing an interest in talking to them. "Just say that you got their names from a friend and wanted to know more about them. Let things develop as they will from that. If they do not answer, then just drop it."

The next name had a Florida area code, somewhere in the middle of the state. Mista said, "We need to go shopping. I want to buy a pay as you go cell phone and use that number for callbacks. That way it cannot be traced to a name."

"It won't be an 800 number," Sharra said.

"Hmmm. There is that. Well, let's try it and see what we get. We can get an 800 number later if this doesn't work. Tell them that a donor bought the 800 number for us. We need to pose as a charity."

"We can't do this on the phone, you know."

"Yes, I know. The phone call is to find out where they are. I guess I could ask the FBI to get the city that the number is in. If we had every phone book, they have their exchanges listed."

"Maybe the telephone company would give us the city that matches that exchange?" Sharra said.

"Maybe. Or maybe we could get it on line. There is a number of telephone listing services. I bet at least one of them can give us a reverse listing."

"You could try."

"I'll put the three girls on that. Something useful for them to do. You know, I've heard or read that city police departments have reverse listings. They are looking for addresses. Which is what we are looking for, actually."

"They wouldn't give you that."

"No, probably not. But I bet there is a national database of phone numbers, or maybe one for each state or area code. Ross should be able to get that for us."

"Let's ask. I don't think this call back scheme is going to work," Sharra said. "I certainly would not give my address to an unknown caller, no matter what he said he was."

"Yeah, probably right."

Mista sat musing, staring sightlessly at his list of numbers and names. He turned to the second page and then back to the first page. After several minutes had passed, he suddenly said, "Listen, what do we really know about these people?"

"Not much," Sharra responded.

"No, not much. They are on Campbell's buddy lists. Seven of them. We don't really know why he had seven separate lists."

"He had seven screen names."

"Well, yes, and each name had it's own list. But why so many? We know that he had more than one personality, but I don't think that there were seven. I guess there could have been, but I don't think so."

"Maybe it was simply to separate the people he talked to. We know that our four girls were each on a separate list."

"Yes," Mista said, stroking his chin. "So when he talked to one, the others did not even know that he was on line. But how did he know that they were all in the same place?"

"How do you know that he did?" Sharra asked.

"Hmmm. Well, I don't know that. Maybe he was simply being careful and didn't put a new name on a list until he had talked long enough to the newest names on that list that he felt safe with them. Then, if he wanted to talk sex to one of them, he didn't add any more names as long as that name was active."

"Yeah, could be. He never talked sex with Robin or Shawnah, for whatever reason. Maybe he just worked one or two at a time."

"Yes. Probably. Then when Candy sent him a picture of Robin, he saw a connection and immediately switched over to the screen name that had talked to Robin and IMed her. And showed up here minutes later, wanting to see both girls."

"Go on."

"Well, if he took Robin's screen name from this list, for example," he turned to the fourth page, "and called her and asked her about their Internet chats, she would be all innocent. And we know that their chats were innocent, until the very last one. Same with Shawnah, and not much with Janice. Like he was just starting to develop her."

"So, any name that is on a unique list could be an everyday routine chat. Could be work acquaintances, friends that he met on line or otherwise, or could be a sex chat."

"Right. We cannot assume that all his calls were sex chats. And I did that when I called the first three companies. Good thing I did not identify myself. They might check out the logs and find nothing at all objectionable."

"Or they might find something really bad. On the other hand, the names that appear on all of the lists are probably his contact points for the sex rings."

"Yes, he was one confused individual. Looked like he was part of a ring that tried to kill the Internet sex talk with minors. And we know that he was part of the Sam Smith ring that promoted Internet sex talk and action."

"With underage girls."

"Right. And that is almost certainly David Brumley. Someone contacted Janice a long time ago and said he was from Louisville. He contacted her again a few nights ago and said that he had heard that she was in Louisville recently and had wanted her to contact him there."

"David? I refuse to call him father. How else would he know that she was in Louisville?"

"Could be. Or part of his network. I wondered about that, too. However, I just thought about something. She changed her screen name after the first contact. David would know her current screen name and the fact that she was in Louisville. But how would he know that she was the same person that he contacted under a different name several months ago?"

"Good question."

"Well, he can afford to hire good detectives. I wonder just how much he does know. You know? I ran across a service on the Internet that can give you a history of any name in the country. Every address, every marriage or divorce, and I don't know what all else. Several levels of service. The free service was spotty. But there were several levels of paid service that promised everything. I bet if I signed on and ran these names, I would get an address and telephone number. It gave every person that had that name, and for common names there might be hundreds of people with the same name. But we should be able to pull out names that paired with the same telephone number that we already have. We'll have to try that."

"They wouldn't have screen names, would they?"

"No. It looks like a database pulled from public records. But we already have the screen name that goes with the personal name. We just need to know where they currently live."

Mista read through the names that were common to more than one of the lists. He said, "There are two that have local numbers. Let's go visit them."

"Shouldn't we call first?" asked Sharra.

"Probably. But let's assume that he or she works during the day. We should go to the immediate area this evening and call when just minutes away. Let's say that we are trying to save children from Internet pedophiles, and see what happens."

"Well, that is what we are doing."

"That's true. That is exactly what we are doing. Some of these names might be people who want to help, also. I don't think I will call ahead. We'll just knock on the door and see what happens. Worse case, you see them and then you can make mental contact and see what he really thinks. If he is truly on our side, we leave him alone."

"I don't like reading people like that."

"I know, but if he is the enemy, we move one step forward. If he is a friend, no harm is done, and you can back out."

"Well, let's try."

They walked up to the front door together just before sundown. They wanted the man inside to be able to see them, and see that they were not armed. The man of the house opened the door and said, "Yes? What can I do for you?"

Mista said, "I am George Mictackic and this is my wife Sharon. We are working on systems to protect children using the Internet from pedophiles. We would like to talk to you about it if you can spare a few minutes."

"My name is James Armstrong. What are you selling?"

Mista smiled. "We are not selling anything at all. We could use your help if you are interested. I will not ask for money. If you do work with us and come to have confidence in the operation, they you might wish to support it. I will never ask you to give money."

Armstrong gave Mista a wry smile. "You are simply offering some services at a reasonable cost?"

"Not at all, Mr. Armstrong. There are many levels of help, but if you are not interested, then we will not bother you any further. Again, I am not asking for money, nor will I ever ask for money."

Sharra sent, *He's on our side but he doesn't believe your pitch. He thinks it is just a ruse to get inside and then beg for money. He's seen several encyclopedia salesmen.*

Gotcha.

"Mr. Armstrong, this is not about money. No doubt you have been approached by door-to-door salesmen who say they are not selling anything, but once inside you can't get rid of them. That is not us, but I don't know how to convince you of that. This is about protecting our children. Perhaps you do not have children, or do not understand the seriousness of the threat against them. We won't take up any more of your time. Here is my card, should you want to talk to me in the future. Good night, sir."

Mista took Sharra's hand and they walked back to the car. He had two major reasons for taking the Range Rover. One, it was a tough and flexible vehicle in case they ran into trouble. Secondly, he hoped to allay the natural suspicion people would have that he was asking for money, if they saw that he was driving a $100,000 truck.

As they drove back to the house, Sharra told him, "He is part of the network of users that search for children and make their acquaintance and try to offer them some protection. After he has chatted with a girl or boy for a while and is satisfied that he or she really is a child, he gives them his telephone number and address and tells them that if they ever get in trouble they can run to his house or call, and that they will be safe there. I didn't go deep, but that seems to be a genuine concern for him. He really is working to help. He thought at first that it was just a money-making scheme. Then he thought that it might be some one following up on a child's report of that number and address. He thought that we might be the enemy."

"Well, our primary purpose is to flush out the enemy. If he is not one of the enemy, then our visit accomplished its goal. We'll try another one tomorrow evening."

CHAPTER 23

Meanwhile, Em had set up a classroom in the large basement room of the house, and the girls' lessons were on schedule. After lunch they rode their bicycles for a while and then went down to the boat dock. Robin headed for the water, but as she walked past the land end of the dock, she heard a noise under it and a loud 'hssss'.

She stopped, frozen in place. When she heard another 'hssss', she called "Janice, come here. Something's under the dock."

Janice and Shawnah came back and looked under the dock with Robin. It was dark and they could not see anything moving under the dock. Robin got down on her stomach on the sand and started to crawl under the dock to look. She did not mind that the sand was wet.

Janice said, "Be careful. It might be a snake."

Robin stopped. "You think?"

"I don't know. Could be."

"Hand me a stick."

Janice found a stick and handed it to Robin, who pushed it into the grass between the dock and the sand. Something moved and hissed, and Robin jerked back. Whatever it was, it was not a snake, she was sure. She waited a minute and then crawled under the dock. A small kitten jumped and hissed and then backed as far under the dock as it could.

Robin crawled under the dock further and finally got close enough to reach out and grab the kitten. It hissed and scratched and tried to bite her, but it was so small that was not able to seriously hurt her. She backed out, crooning and stroking the kitten. "I'm not going to hurt you, baby. I'll get you some food and be good to you. I won't hurt you." She stood up, cradling the kitten in both hands. "Look!" Robin said. "It's a calico. He's pretty. Let's go get him something to eat." The kitten backed as far into the crook of Robin's arm as it could, trying to hide.

No one was in the kitchen, and Janice poured a little milk into a bowl and heated it for a few seconds in the microwave to take the chill off. The kitten almost forgot it's fear and lapped up the milk. "Cool! He's starving. See if there is something to eat in there."

Shawnah found the bologna and took a piece out of the package. "No cat food, but maybe he'll like this."

"Sure. Warm it up a little," Robin said.

The kitten ate a few bites and then looked like it wanted to run and hide. Robin grabbed it up. After a few seconds it relaxed and began to purr. Janice said, "Well, it's not wild, anyway. Wonder where it came from?"

"I don't know. I'm going to keep him. I'll call him 'Patches'."

"How do you know it's a him?" asked Janice.

"I don't know. It just seems like a boy."

"Well, look and see."

"How do you tell?" Robin asked.

"Silly," Shawnah said. "Don't you know the difference in a boy and a girl already?"

Robin blushed. "Oh. Yes. Are cat's the same?"

"Sure they are," Janice said. "Look and see."

Robin turned the kitten over and pulled its fur back. It squirmed and tried to turn over or escape, but she persisted. "I don't see a thing down there, so it must be a girl," Robin said.

"Thing?" asked Shawnah. "Don't you know the right name?"

"Of course I do. I just don't like to use it. Mom and Dad never use that word."

"Well," Janice said, "I don't have to talk like them. I'll say whatever I want."

"I will, too," Robin said. "But I don't like that word." Pictures she had seen flashed through her mind.

Robin cuddled the kitten in her hands and lifted it up to her face. She said, "You like me, don't you, Patches?" She kissed the tip of its nose. "I'm going to keep it."

"You better ask," Janice said.

"I'll keep it down here. They won't know. I can sneak food out for her."

"Just ask," Janice said.

"They might say no. If they don't know, then they can't say no."

"You'll get in trouble," Janice said. "You better ask."

Robin found a box and put it in a corner of the boathouse and put the kitten in the box. She promptly curled up and went to sleep. Then Robin put the milk in the box and broke up the rest of the bologna slice and dropped it in the box. She stayed with the kitten all afternoon, talking to her and playing with her when she was awake.

Every meal after that, she would keep back some of her meat and sneak it into a napkin when no one was looking, and then take it down to her kitten. Mista thought he saw her wrap some meat up in the napkin twice, but his mind was on other things and he did not worry about it. Monday night he was sure, but that was the night they went to call on the first of the contacts, so he said nothing to her.

The next morning they had bacon and eggs for breakfast. Mista carefully watched Robin out of the corner of his eye without seeming to notice her. She ate only a little of her bacon and then folded the rest into her napkin. When she left the table later, Mista waited until she had gone outside and then looked to see where she was going. "Hah! The boathouse."

Robin glanced around before opening the door and going into the boathouse. As soon as she was inside, Mista walked quietly down and followed her in. He leaned against the doorjamb watching her feed and pet her kitten.

"I'll see you later, Patches. Okay?" She stood up and turned to leave. She squealed and then clapped her hand to her mouth when she saw Mista standing there.

"What have we here?" he asked.

"I ... I found her under the dock. She likes me. Can I keep her?"

"Looks like you have already decided to keep her."

"Well, I did, but can I?"

"What will you do when we travel?"

"She could go with us. She could learn to ride."

"Hmmm. Seems to me that we had an agreement. Something about talking to me? Asking permission? Telling us what is happening?"

"I know. But... She was lonely and scared. And she likes me."

"That is not the point."

"But ... "

"Sweetheart, what will you do with her when we have to travel?"

"She could learn to ride in the car or the camper."

"She could, but you would be adding another layer of trouble."

"I guess I can't keep her," Robin stared at the ground and kicked at imaginary rocks on the floor. She tried to hide her tears, not wanting him to think she was playing on sympathy.

Mista said, "It's you I'm most worried about. You are supposed to talk to me, to ask when you want something, or want to do something. Am I so hard to talk to?"

"No. It's just …"

"We have a problem. We can talk about it tonight. During the day, I want you to think why you are afraid to ask me for what you want."

"I'm not afraid …"

"Whatever. I guess in the meantime we can confine you to your room for a week and let you think about it."

"NO! Please!"

"That's the most gentle thing I can think of …"

"It's not me. Patches will starve with no one to take care of her. If you lock me up, you have to find a home for her."

Mista looked down at her. She had grown several inches during the year. He placed his hands on her shoulders and she looked up at him, eyes wide and troubled. Mista said, "You are more concerned about the cat than about yourself?"

"Yes. I know I messed up. You can do whatever you think is fair. I don't know why I keep messing up. But you can't just leave Patches out here to starve. I've been saving some of the best part of my meals to give to her."

"I know."

"You knew? You already knew? You dint say anything."

"I've been too busy. Look, we have some bologna in the fridge. Give her some of that at noon – I think she'll like that, and it would be better than scraps from your plate."

"She loves --" she clapped her hand over her mouth.

Mista smiled. "You have already sneaked some? We'll talk tonight. You have school now."

Robin reached into the box and petted her kitten's head. "Goodbye, Patches."

Mista watched Robin walk up to the house, head down and feet dragging. He sighed. *Every time I think I understand what makes her tick, something else goes wrong. She desperately wanted this kitten, but walked away from it with no argument. Maybe it's her life up till now. Never having anything she could call her own and being able to count on keeping it. She can have the kitten, but I want to try to use this as a springboard into her mind and heart.*

Mista went up to the house and found Sharra. He told her about the incident with the kitten, and she said, "Do you mind if she has a kitten? So long as she takes care of it."

"Don't mind at all. What I mind is her trying to hide it from us."

"Well, obviously, she was afraid that we would not let her keep it."

"Yes. But that is the problem. I don't want her to be afraid to talk to us."

"You have to give her time. She's probably been beat down all her life. That's why she clings to you so. Don't be mean to her. You told her she could keep it, right?"

"No. I said we'd talk about it tonight."

"Don't be mean to her."

"I guess she does see it that way. But I want her to talk to me. Okay. Let's go get whatever she needs to keep and raise that cat. You know we'll probably have to buy two more."

"Not three cats! They'll just have to share."

They went shopping at the nearest pet center. Mista went down the rows dedicated to cats. "Toys?"

"Toy. Here. Get a bag of little white mouses. Mice."

"Okay. Kitty litter, scoop, deodorant and litter pan. Here is an automatic electric litter pan."

"No. Let her learn to keep it clean, and then we can look at electric later."

"Works for me. Food. Dry kitten chow, and meat. These little plastic cups are a good size and easy to open and close. Anything else?"

"Fleas."

"She probably already has fleas."

"No, something to kill fleas."

"Hard to do with a kitten. I think washing her in a dip. Can't use drops, can we?"

"Not until she gets older. The pet store variety is probably weak, anyway. Let me see." She read through the directions and precautions. "No. She has to be 12 weeks old. We'll get some from a vet later."

"Okay," Mista said, "I think that's everything. Oh, let's get her a sparkly collar. With fake jewels on it. Maybe that'll make Robin feel better."

Sharra said, "Let's not visit any of the contacts tonight. We need to settle this with Robin early."

At supper, Robin only picked at her food. Sharra said, "Eat your supper, dear."

Robin looked up at her and then glanced at Mista, wondering if they had talked about her. She assumed that the kitten was gone, or about to be gone, and was not saving food for her. She just didn't want to eat. "I'm not hungry, Mommy."

"You thinking to fill up on ice cream later?"

"No. I don't even want ice cream."

Sharra looked at Mista and raised an eyebrow. *You have a fence or two to mend.*

Yeah. Got my work cut out for me. Well, I put the little collar in my pocket so I can bribe her.

After supper, Mista watched the evening news and then picked up a book to read. Janice logged onto her computer, but Robin went to her room and closed the door. After a few minutes, Mista called her. "Robin! Come here, please."

She walked slowly out and stood by his chair. He patted her bottom, legs and felt her feet. "Not wet."

"Not funny, Daddy."

"Come up here." He picked her up and set her in his lap, facing him. "We need to have a very serious talk."

"I know. I'm in deep trouble."

"No. You're in a little bit of trouble, but not deep. We can resolve it with just a little bit of talking. First question. Why are you afraid of me?"

"I ... I'm not afraid of you."

"You act like it."

"How?"

"You won't talk to me. You won't tell me what you want. You sneak to get the things you want or want to do."

"I ..."

"Go ahead. Why?"

"I'm afraid you'll say no. And then I won't have anything."

"Hmmm. Let me get this straight. I always say no to anything you ask for, just automatically."

"No. You don't. But I'm afraid you will."

"I see. What have I said no to, so far. You haven't been here all that long, so I haven't had a chance to say no too many times."

"Nothing, yet. But …

"Hmmm. Nothing yet, but since I am basically a mean guy, I'm just liable to say no, just for meanness."

"No! You aren't mean."

"Then what?"

"I don't know. I'm just afraid."

"All right. I'm trying to understand you here. Don't think I'm mad at you, or yelling at you. Have you ever had anything that you really liked, that was just yours? A favorite doll, stuffed animal, favorite dress or anything?"

"No. Never."

"Not ever? Maybe had one you loved but lost it or had it taken away?"

"Yes. I never had anything very long. My mother would search my room when she was mad at me and throw things away."

"Did that make you angry?"

"Yes. But it didn't do any good."

"Well, I'm not your mother. Have I given you every thing you asked for?"

"Yes, so far. Except Patches."

"And have I taken anything away from you?"

"No. You took Internet privileges for a while, but you gave them back."

"Yes. That was a lesson. I will not promise to give you everything you ask for. That would be foolish, and not good for you at all. Now, here's the problem. Parents are supposed to give good things to their children. They are supposed to *want* to give them things. At the same time, a good parent knows that it's not good to give them everything. When they do that, then things have no value. Do you understand what I'm getting at?"

"Not really."

"I *want* to give you things. I *want* to say yes to your requests. I *want* to be good to you. You don't have to hide things from me and sneak to do the things you want to do. I want you to be happy."

"But you might say no to something that I really want."

"I might. But I want you to ask. I want you to not be afraid to ask for anything that you want. You know, you've heard people pray in church. A lot of them say, 'if it be your will'. Why is that?"

"I don't know."

"They are thinking that it is not a good thing to ask for something just because we want it. I don't believe that. I will ask God for anything that I want. I am not frivolous, and I don't demand that he give it to me. But I'm not afraid to ask. I want you to be the same way with me. Anything you want. I am not promising to give it to you, but if I don't say yes, I'll give you a good reason. Okay?"

"I guess."

"Okay. Let's test it. What would you really want, right now?"

"I want Patches. But you said …"

"Yes? What did I say?"

"You didn't really say anything. Said we'd talk about it."

"Well, we are talking about it." He reached into his pocket and pulled the collar out. "You think you could find something to do with this?"

She put her hand to her mouth, and then said, "Is it … is it for Patches?"

"No. It's for you. For you to do whatever you want to do with it."

"I'd want to use it on Patches."

"Well, then, use it on Patches."

"Really, Daddy? You're not kidding?"

"Really. I have no problem with your having a kitten. Just your not being willing to tell me."

"Oh! I love you, Daddy!" She threw her arms around his neck and kissed him four or five times. "I love you."

"I love you to, Sweetheart."

"Can I go give it to her, now?"

"No. We have a few more things to discuss. First, I want you to promise to ask me for what you want, and not sneak around. Can you do that?"

"It's hard, Daddy. I never dared ask my mother. She would say no, just to spite me."

"I promise not to do that. I want you to ask. Secondly, you cannot own a cat. The cat owns the humans. She will choose her master. You can't claim that she is yours alone. I'd have to buy two more, and we can't have three cats. So she is family. But you have to take care of her. Feed her, bathe her, clean up after her."

"I will, I will! Can I go now?"

"Yes –"

She was halfway to the door when he got the next word out. "But there is one more thing."

"What?" she said, skidding to a stop.

"There is a bag of stuff in the backseat of the Range Rover for you."

Robin ran out. She ran back in a minute later. "There is a litter pan there. Can I keep her inside?"

"Yes, but you have to clean up after her. You have to scoop her pan every single day. You might be able to bribe Janice to help you, but you cannot demand it. If she travels with us, she has to be clean."

"Okay."

Robin came back a few minutes later holding Patches in both hands. She rubbed her head against her cheek and listened to her purr. "You want to hold her while I fix her litter pan? Where should I put it?" She handed Patches to Mista. He cupped her in one hand, and she curled up and closed her eyes and began to purr again.

"Probably in your bathroom. But that means that you have to leave the door open."

"Even when we have to use the bathroom?"

Mista smiled. "No, of course not. But listen for her when you are in there. She will probably want to go in with you. Cats can't stand closed doors. They don't really want in, they just want to go through the door."

CHAPTER 24

They took the next local name on their list after supper the next night. A young man came to the door and listened to their introduction. "Come in, I'd like to hear more. I have two young girls and they'll be using the Internet in a few years. I've heard all sorts of things about the Internet, and would like to hear what you are doing."

Sharra sent, *He's genuine. Member of a group that monitors the Internet for sites that promote kiddie porn.*

He took them into a small living room and introduced them to his wife. "I'm Steve Bagel, and this is my wife, Ann. Would you like some coffee?"

Mista said, "Sure. Just black, please."

Sharra said, "Thanks, but I don't do coffee."

Steve said, "I am a member of a group trying to keep the Internet safe for our kids. And adults. We regularly monitor any sites that show pictures of teens and pre-teens., especially sites that claim to have teen and pre-teen models for hire. There are many legitimate sites, but there are some that are not. As long as their promotions seem proper and the pictures that they show are decent, we are content. Every once in a while, we find a site showing girls and boys nude or partially nude. We go after them and shut them down."

"It must take some effort to actually find them. Physically, that is."

"Yes. Some have open addresses. The legit sites almost always do. The porn sites hide. We have uncovered quite a few, though, and shut them down."

His wife returned with two cups of coffee. Steven said, "My wife and I always work together. I want to avoid any suspicion that I am looking for porn for personal reasons."

They talked for nearly an hour about their work and their successes and frustrations. Mista finally said, "We have to be going. Here's my card. Call or email if you need some help."

Steven also handed Mista a card. "That is my phone and E-mail. I'm careful who gets that card. But if I can help you with something, don't hesitate to call."

The next night they called on the last local name. He was polite but cool when he opened the door. "May I see some kind of ID?"

Mista showed him his driver's license, and he wrote down the name and number. "There is so much craziness, I don't trust unannounced callers. Come in, please."

He led them to a large formal living room and offered them seats. He did not suggest refreshment. "What can you tell me about your activities?"

Sharra sent, *Be careful. This one is an enemy.*

Mista said, "We have known some girls who were tracked down by men that they met on the Internet and raped. There is no other word for it. We are working with other people to offer some kind of protection for girls like them before others get hurt."

"I see. Seems to me that parents should be responsible for their own children."

"I would agree, but sometimes things happen that parents cannot control."

"Perhaps, but I do not see how you could interfere. If that is what you have in mind, I don't believe that I'd be interested."

"Sorry to take your time," Mista said, rising. "Have a good night."

They left and returned home. In the car, Sharra said, "That was a trip."

"What? His coldness?"

"No, his mind. Pure evil. He is still wondering who we are and what we really want. He identifies girls who are the right age and seem interested, and makes their acquaintance. Then he gets their real names, telephone numbers and addresses and posts that to the account that we know is Brumley, along with their screen names."

"Well, at least we know one source of names. Otherwise, I'm not sure that this exercise is doing us any good. We already know what Brumley is doing, and we were pretty sure that men like this one were collecting names for him. We haven't learned anything, and even what we know we can't use."

"You could close down one conduit, couldn't you?"

"I can do that." She closed her eyes and reached out with her mind. After a few minutes, she said, "Done. Now every time he sees or talks to a girl under 12, he will think that they are an adult police officer, and that they are suspicious of him. The illusion will fade in time, like a post-hypnotic suggestion, but he should have an interesting few months ahead of him."

Mista was quiet for a few minutes, and then said, "You're right. We're spinning our wheels here. We need to actually catch them doing something that we can put them away for. If we could divert his mail to us…"

"I could leave him a suggestion that he blind copy us on every message to Brumley."

"Okay. That's something. I'll set up a mailbox just for that. If we can find the others, we can do the same thing there. Except I doubt that you'll get much from him for a while."

"No. He won't be sending names until that suggestion wears off. Might generate some interesting excuses as to why, though." She grinned.

Mista said, "We need to catch them or at least him doing something illegal. Passing names to another account is not in itself illegal. We know the purpose behind it, and that purpose is illegal, but we can't prove that."

"Kidnapping our two girls was illegal."

"True. Who kidnapped them?"

"You know that it was Brumley."

"But we cannot connect him with the kidnapping. We cannot prove that he was Sam Smith."

"No, but we know he is. We could just kill him and be done with it."

"Not in this world. We'd be up for murder one. You could kill him and no one would know how it was done, since no one believes that people really have ESP. But it cannot be you. It would leave a scar."

"That man? After all he's done? I have no compunctions about killing that one."

"Don't kid yourself. Any other man, yes, but he is in the place of father. Stepfather, to be sure, and not a good one, but still he occupies the position. You cannot do it."

"I guess you're right." She leaned back against the corner of the door and her seat and wrapped her arms around herself.

"Jeremy could, but wouldn't. Now, if Molly's daughter were a little older, and he did something to her ... he'd be dead before he knew what was happening."

"Humph. You're probably right about that. But she's only four. We can't wait seven years."

"On the other hand," Mista said, "If he did something to Shawnah, Jasmine might call down fire from heaven."

"Yeah. She would. Or Robin. You saw what she did at that B-and-B. If he touched her she's liable to burn him without even thinking twice about it."

Mista smiled. "Yep. But I don't think he'll bother our girls again. Or if he does, he'll spirit them away someplace where we can't find them. However. He has ships and airplanes, right?"

"Yes," Sharra said. "He has a freight company."

"And makes far too much money for freight alone to account for it."

"Well, his prostitution business accounts for a lot of it."

"True. But I'd lay odds that he ships in drugs on his ships. Do you know what ships he owns?"

"No. There ought to be a registry somewhere, though, showing who owns what ships."

"I'll get Jeremy to search for it. Might not be all that useful, though. Might be owned by a business that is owned by another business that is owned by Brumley. Or some kind of chain of ownership like that. Still, it's worth a try."

"And if we knew what ships he owned, then what?"

"Find out what they're carrying. Chances are, no one on the ships knows of anything that is not legitimate cargo. We keep watching and hope we get lucky."

"And if we find some?"

"I don't know. We'll cross that bridge when we come to it."

Sharra leaned back and closed her eyes. They were almost home when she suddenly said, "I don't know if you are afraid to go after him because of his money or just aren't interested. I would think, with your own sister involved, that you'd be a lot more aggressive. And, you dote on those two girls, and they were taken and you do nothing."

Mista's jaw tightened. *Careful. She just wants action.* "I do intend to see him brought down, but we have to be sure that —"

"We know he is the one!"

"Okay, yes, *we* know that. But we can't prove it yet."

"I don't think I want to wait for you to build your evidence bit by bit. I'll be old and gray before you can prove anything."

Sharra went straight to their room when they got home. She did not go to bed, but curled up in the easy chair there and began making her own plans. After about half an hour, she knew what she wanted to do. Her first thought was to make him hate women. But, she knew that he probably already hated women, saw them as less than human. All right, she though, she would intensify that hatred, make it active and virile. Let it rule his actions. He would shrink even from touching a woman or girl. Next she would twist his mind so that all of his male associates would rouse sexual fantasies in him. She did not simply intend to make him homosexual, but to raise active sexual fantasies triggered by every male that he dealt with, especially his close associates.

She sent her mind out to contact him. She did not know or care where he was – once she had made contact with him visually, she could contact him wherever he was. Her contact did not reveal his location to her, although his thoughts and what he saw might tell her. In this case she had no interest in knowing where he was. First she intensified his hatred of women. She thought, *if he is in bed with mother at this point that could be interesting.* She implanted a suggestion that would make him shrink from any physical contact with a woman or girl. Then she left an illusion that he was attractive to all males, and wanted to pursue active sexual contact with any man that he happened to be dealing with at any time. She knew that her changes would fade in time, but hoped that it would speed up the hunt for him. Even if it did not, she took pleasure in his embarrassment when he reverted to normal and remembered things that he had done.

Satisfied, she dressed for bed and went out to give Mista a good-night kiss with a self-satisfied smirk.

Mista raised an eyebrow, sending a signal to ask what she was thinking. She shrugged and kissed him, saying only "Good night."

Mista thought, *Well, she'll tell me what she is thinking when she is ready.* He checked his e-mail and found a message from the broker he had contacted about buying a sailboat. He had located two that he thought were a perfect match for Mista's specs.

CHAPTER 25

The next day Arnat Karackish was released from the hospital with instructions to take things easy for a while. Brumley had his driver pick him up and bring him to the house. When they arrived, Brumley said, "Arnat, I want to go to the Caribbean for a few weeks and take a break. It'll give you a chance to rest and complete your recovery, too."

"Whatever, boss."

Brumley had already told his wife and his general manager that he would be going. He looked at Arnat like he was a new man. He wondered why he had never noticed before how sexy his man was, and wondered if he felt the same way about him. Strange, he thought, he didn't remember being drawn to men this way before.

He called ahead and left word for his driver in Grand Cayman to meet him when he landed that evening. Karackish detailed two of his men to accompany them. He never traveled without a guard, but now he was doubly cautious. He was afraid that one or more of the group that they had attacked in that bed and breakfast up the road would be waiting for them.

On the way to the airport, Karackish said, "I called Smirnoff and told him to take a couple of girls down for company, since you said we would be there for several weeks."

"Oh, fine. I'm not sure I'm in the mood right now, but that's okay. Can't hurt."

"Well, he said he had a couple of new ones, some he picked up in Florida. You'd be the first to have them."

"Not the two that we tried to get last month, are they?"

"Oh, no. Those girls blew our local operation up in flames. I've got plans for them. Going to the Caymans will be good."

"Well, be careful. I don't know how, but they tracked them last time, and are liable to do it again."

"Yeah," Karackish said. "They must have gotten a message out somehow. I'll be careful."

The next morning, Brumley joined Karackish and Smirnoff for breakfast in a large airy dining room. He looked around at the old house. He had bought a mansion on the beach at the other end of Grand Cayman from the port. He had a dock, but the bay was a little tight for a boat as large as his cruiser. The island was only seventeen miles long, about a half-hour drive. Land was at a premium on a small island, but he had acquired nearly two acres. This dining room was used for informal meals like breakfast. He also had a formal dining room, which was seldom used.

Brumley turned to Smirnoff. "I haven't seen anyone about, Kevin. Do we have any girls in the house?"

"Yes. There are currently seven upstairs, including the two new ones from Florida. They are still virgin. I was saving them for you."

"Maybe I'll look in on them later."

"Fine. They are in the secure room in the back."

"Have you ever thought about keeping some boys, also?"

"No. We've never even talked about that. Are you interested in obtaining some?"

"I've been thinking. It might be a good option."

"I'll look into it."

"Does that interest you, personally," Brumley asked.

"Not really. Could be good business, however. I don't even go for the girls, myself. I kind of like to watch them. I encourage them to entertain each other, you know, when we don't have clients here. I catch a good picture on one of the cameras from time to time, and post it on our internet front site."

When they finished, Brumley said, "Come down to the office a minute, Arnat." Brumley looked his security chief in the eye and said, "I have a delicate subject, Arnat. I've never asked you about your sexual preferences."

"Well, no you haven't, Mr. Brumley. It shouldn't matter, but I'm as straight as they come. I learned the difference in a woman and a girl a long time ago, and I like my women wild."

"Only women?"

"Yeah. You can have the girls."

"I was thinking about men."

"Hah. Not me. It's okay with me whatever you want, but I'm not interested. Don't mind my asking, Mr. Brumley, but I thought you only liked your girls. Didn't know you were bi."

"Well, several things have happened recently." He didn't say more.

"Well, boss, just don't be going too weird on us here. You could ruin the whole operation."

Brumley did not say anything else. He had been sure that Karackish felt a sexual attraction toward him, but he had denied it. He frowned. He wondered why the man would hide his feelings. Maybe he was wrong about him.

Karackish said, "I want to go to the port and check out the boats, if you don't mind."

"Just don't overdo. I meant for this to be a vacation for you and a chance to regain your strength."

"I'm fine. But thanks for asking."

Kevin Smirnoff entered the office when Karackish left. He said, "David, are you serious about adding boys to our stable?"

"Sure, why not? Could be interesting, don't you think?"

"Not to me, but I'm sure that some potential clients would be very interested. What if we attract women as clients? Some of the high-powered lawyers and business people who come down here are women."

"Get a second limousine and deliver them to the side door. We have unused rooms on the first floor, don't we? Put the boys there. It'll cost a bit to install plumbing for the rooms, but it'll be worth it, I think."

"I'm sure it will. Good way to expand."

"You know, Kevin, I've never asked you about your own sexual preferences."

"No, we've always treated that as private. Not that I have any secrets about it."

"So, is it alright to ask, then?"

"Sure. I like to watch the girls, like I said, but don't have any other interest in them My wife is enough sex for me."

"You aren't interested in men?"

"Not me. I'm far from that. You want me to have the girls ready for you?"

"Yeah. I'll be up in about half an hour." He usually took pleasure in any new girls, but today he resisted going, and did not know why.

Smirnoff called his matron, the woman who took care of the girls in residence. "Mr. B. will be in to see the new ones in half an hour. Put one in a white dress. The other – whichever has the best development up top – shorts and a skimpy top."

"They'll be ready, Kevin."

She took the clothes in to the girls and said, "Mr. B. will be here in a few minutes. You want to please him. The rest of your life depends on it. Put these on, and give me your robes." She handed the dress to one and the short set to the other.

The one holding the dress said, "No underwear?"

"No underwear. You won't need it."

She cocked an eyebrow at them. "Be quick about it. In case you haven't discovered it, there are perfumes and hair ribbons in the dresser. He likes for you to smell nice."

She checked them over when they were dressed, took the robes and left them. She shook her head when she was out in the hall. *Poor girls. They have no idea what they are in for.*

When Brumley walked into the room, the girls were sitting on their beds, nervously waiting. The shorter girl had short curly blond hair, and had developed early. She was quite pretty, with a round face and button nose.

The other girl was tall and thin, with straight black hair. She was acutely uncomfortable in the thin white dress.

David Brumley smiled and said, "Good morning." He sat in the only chair in the room. "My name is David Brumley, and you are guests in my house. Are you comfortable?"

They looked at each other briefly and then the blond girl said, "Yes, I suppose. Not uncomfortable, anyway."

"Good. What is your name, dear?"

"Sally."

"And yours?"

"I am Ruth Postins."

"Relax. I won't eat you. How did you come to be here?"

Sally said, "I don't really know. I answered an ad on the internet to become a model. Then I met with the agent and he brought me here, wherever that is."

Ruth said, "Same with me. I remember going down to a boat, and then being out at sea for several days. Then one day, I woke up in here. My parents will be worried to death. I thought I would only be gone for an hour or so."

"Yes, I understand. Modeling is hard work, though, and not everyone can do it well. We have several tests that we give, and it takes a few days. Give me your parents' names and I will see that they are notified that you are safe." He had no intention of notifying the parents: this was a ploy to take the edge off of their anxiety.

"You realize that modeling calls for the wearing of all kinds of clothing in many different poses?"

They nodded, guessing what was coming next.

Very good. Now, Ruth, let me see your legs. I don't know why they put a dress on you."

"She said that was what you wanted," Ruth said.

"Whatever. Stand up and let me see your legs."

She stood up and pulled her dress up just above her knees.

He worked with them for nearly an hour.

The next step would be to have sex with them, whether or not they agreed. After his initial handling, they usually did agree, again thinking that this was part of the job, their initiation process. However, when he stood and walked toward them, he found that he could not bring himself to touch either one. He thought it absurd that girls were so willing to follow his lead, a total stranger, but then he could not touch them. He wanted nothing more to do with them.

He did not understand his strong feelings. He had done this hundreds of times over the last 20 years, but today he could not make the move. He struggled with it for a few minutes, walking around the room, and finally said, "That's all. We accept you." He walked out and closed the door behind him.

He thought that boys would be even more fun. He would have Smirnoff recruit some right away. He found Smirnoff and said, "I'm finished. You can have a go at them or turn them over to Arnat and then customers."

"Didn't you like them? I thought they were pretty girls."

"They are, and they are fine additions to the stable. They just don't interest me."

"I would never have known. I like the way you talk them into thinking that all this is normal. They aren't so shocked when we send clients in to them."

"Well, I didn't always do it this way. I used to just throw them into it when I first started doing this. Didn't always work out. Sometimes the girls survived, but sometimes they committed suicide first chance they got. I lost some nice ones that way. So, I developed a patois to help them adapt."

Sharra had chosen that moment to listen in on his thoughts. She smiled and said, "That worked. I planted a suggestion that he could not stand the touch of a girl or woman. He just tried to break in the two new girls his agents brought to him, and found that he could not touch them."

CHAPTER 26

Mista called his broker the next morning. He had e-mailed a reply last night to say that he would call about 10:00, and to let him know if that was unacceptable. This morning he had an e-mail saying that he would expect a call.

The broker answered his call himself, "Good morning. George Roscoe. How may I help you?"

"Good morning, this is George Mictackic. Please call me Mista."

"Mista, is it? Let me make a note. All right, George, -- uh, Mista – if you have looked for boats on the Internet, you know that there are hundreds offered for sale. I look at every boat that I represent, and make a second inspection before recommending any boat to a potential customer."

"That's good, Mr. Roscoe. I know just enough about boats to be dangerous, so I am glad to hear that you are not just a paper pusher."

"The owner pays a commission. I like to earn my money, Mista. You also should inspect the boat before you buy. I will be glad to meet you at the boat and point out the things to look for."

"Good, I'll take you up on that."

"All right. The first boat is in Athens, Greece, and the other is in Izmir, Turkey. Ready for world travel?"

"Yes, that is not a problem. I don't speak Turkish, but I have a little Arabic."

Roscoe laughed. "That doesn't matter. These people speak English. Both boats were built in Turkey, by the way, and are of similar class. They are 82 feet and can sleep 8 to 16 people. When would you like to see them?"

"I am free to go any time you can set it up. I'd like to see both on the same trip, if that is possible."

"Probably. Let me contact the sellers and set up something. I will e-mail pictures of the boats."

Sharra was listening to his call and said, "Well?" when he signed off.

"You ready to travel? We're going to Greece and Turkey to look at boats."

"You still sure that you want to do this? That's an awful lot of money. Not that I mind seeing the world."

"The boats are in Athens and Izmir. We'll schedule enough time for you to see the countries while we are there."

Roscoe called back on Monday and said that the best he could do was Friday in Izmir and the following Monday with the seller in Athens. Robin said, "I want to go!"

Mista smiled. "Who would take care of Patches?"

"I'll find somebody. Or we could take her."

"No. We can't take a cat on an airplane, and can't keep her in a hotel room."

"I'll find somebody."

Mista said, "Janice I suppose you want to go also? If we like the boat, we'll sail it home."

"Yes. I want to go."

Mista told Mischal and Chandri what he had in mind and asked if they wanted to go. "I plan to sail the boat back if it is what we need."

Chandri said, "You will need me to navigate."

"You think I forgot already?"

"Yes. Old people always forget things."

"Thanks," Mista said. "I better tell Charly."

Charly said, "We already saw Athens, remember? Just a few months ago. But we better go, in case you get in trouble again."

Chandri said, "We only had an overnight stay. There has to be more to see."

Then Mista called his banker in Atlanta and told him what he had in mind. "Fine," he said. "Just let me know what you need and we'll wire the money to whatever bank they want to use. You are all set up for this and good to go."

They flew out on Wednesday so that they could spend most of Thursday and part of Friday sightseeing. Mista arranged a tour bus for them on Thursday. What he wanted to see most was the ruins of Ephesus, 50 miles down the coast, and their guide was glad to show off the countryside. "I would also like to see the site of Troy, but I'm sure that's too far."

"Yes, sir, too far to do in just one day. It's about 300 miles, and in Turkey … However, if you can spend several days, we could see it nicely. Or, you could fly to Canakkale and take a tour from there."

Mista looked around at the others. He appeared to be the only one interested in Troy. "No, perhaps we will come again and visit Troy."

The high point of the trip to Ephesus for Mista was standing in the ruins of the theater. The stage had an unusual feature: there were seven windows in the back wall. People had argued various uses for these windows, but the one that Mista remembered best was that they were used to hang different paintings that could be changed for different scenes. He mentioned one theory, "I read a theory some time ago that the book of Revelation was written with this stage in mind. The author believed that the seven series of scenes in Revelation were clues that the book was actually written as a play to be performed on this stage. I guess it was never very popular, but I found it a fascinating theory."

Sharra asked, "If it was so fascinating, why didn't it catch on?"

Mista shrugged. "I don't really know. I did some reading. By the end of the first century AD, the theater was probably like the stage shows in Las Vegas. Very popular among most people, and a primary entertainment for every city. However, just as today, most Christians seemed to avoid the theater. I found a few scraps of writing actually forbidding any Christian to attend theater. If that is a good summation of the situation, then it seems unlikely that a biblical book would be written for the theater."

Sharra shook her head. "Mista, we aren't in a classroom. Why didn't you just say that Christians didn't go to theater?"

"That would not be as accurate—"

"Forget accurate. That's close enough."

They met the broker and the boat's owner 10:00 the next morning. The boat was beautiful, paint and varnish in very good condition. He showed the operation of the sails, and the engine controls, and then took them to the engine room. They spent a long time in the master stateroom and in the salon.

"We use her many years in charter service. Tourist groups like to sail to several of the islands. She make good money."

"Lot's of time underway?" asked Mista.

"Yes, but that is good thing. Keeps boat alive."

Sharra listened in on surface thoughts as he showed the boat and talked about it. What he did not say was that the generator had enough hours on it that it was becoming unreliable. Sharra sent this to Mista, *Of course, the cost of a generator is quite small compared to the total cost of the boat. Still – might be a sign of other problems.*

He also did not mention that the electronics had become a little dated.

After two hours, Mista said, "Thank you, Mr. Kostokan. She is a beautiful boat, but not quite what I had in mind. Your price is good, and we will think about it. If I change my mind, we will contact you."

"Is something wrong?"

"No, not really. She has some age, but we knew that already. It's just not exactly what I wanted. As you can understand, when I spend this much money, it has to be right."

"Yes, true."

He offered a lower price, and they talked for a few minutes, but Mista had gotten enough clues from Sharra that he knew that this was not the boat he wanted.

They flew on to Athens that night, and arranged an all-day tour for Saturday. Their guide was a young woman who spoke fluent English but took her tour duties as just a day's work. They stopped first at the Parthenon, and she pointed out the details. She also told them that it had been intact until World War II. During that war, sixty years before, Greece had been controlled by Turkey until near the end of the war. The Turks had used the Parthenon as an ammunition dump, and blew it up when they had to withdraw, to keep the Greeks from getting the ammunition.

Mista switched to Greek and said, "No wonder you hate the Turks so much."

Her eyes widened and she responded in Greek, her eyes shining with unshed tears, "Yes. They just blew it up." Her whole demeanor changed when Mista spoke in Greek and showed his sympathy for the loss of a historical building. She continued to lecture in English, but made comments from time to time to Mista in Greek.

On Monday, Mista suggested that only he and Sharra go to inspect the boat. "The rest of you should visit the museum, and that will take you most of the day. We'll join you after we see the boat."

This boat was similar to the other in many ways, same size and type. The hull was built in Turkey, but it was only 10 years old and had been maintained in top condition. The electronics had been updated the year before, and the Caterpillar engines were in perfect condition. Again, Sharra listened to his thoughts as he talked about his boat. *He is not hiding anything, and seems sad to see her go.*

Mista dropped into Greek and asked, "Why are you selling, Mr. Papadokolous?"

He eyes widened at Mista's command of his language, "Milate Ellenika, Kerie Mictackic?" *You speak Greek, Mr. Mictackic?*

"Yes, not modern Greek, though. I have read classical writings and learned modern pronunciation. My language might be a little archaic."

"You do fine. I must sell because I am now too old to enjoy sailing. We once took family vacations, and I often took company executives on short cruises. With no distractions, we had time to think and plan strategies. Now, however, I must retire, and my family has no interest in sailing."

"You no longer sail, then?"

"Not for more than a year. My crew takes her out every three months, to keep systems active. If you like her, I will instruct my captain to take you on a familiarization cruise."

They argued about price and other issues for over an hour. Sharra was afraid that the Greek owner would resort to violence at one point. When they finally agreed on a price, Papadokolous broke into a broad smile. "You bargain like a Greek, Mr. Mictackic. I do not know when I have enjoyed a bargaining session quite so much."

"It has been a pleasure," Mista said.

As promised, the captain took them on a three day cruise, showing how she handled in various winds and wave conditions, and how to set sail for maximum benefit. He also gave them some pointers on rough weather handling.

They pulled out of Piraious – the port of Athens – a little before noon, under motor power. Once clear of the port, the captain showed Mista and Mischal how to raise and position sails, and then set a course southeast toward open sea. "Any place you want to go, Mr. Mictackic. I understand that you speak Greek. That name sounds almost Greek."

"*Parlo Elliniki* – I do speak Greek," Mista said. "The name is Serbic, but I am not sure of the exact origin. Some day I'll trace my roots. Could be Macedonia, or could be further north. Let me look at your charts. Chandri! You need to look, too."

"Yes. Two heads are better than one, as you say."

"True, but she is my navigator. She needs to see your charts and systems."

"Ah, yes. You will like the GPS system. You select your chart, and it plots your position and track automatically."

Chandri was impressed. "Looks like no work to do. What if it fails?"

"It does not fail. You understand the satellites?"

"Yes, I know it triangulates position from three satellites. The equipment here could fail, though, or we could lose power. Satellite transmission could be blocked. What is your backup?"

"Well, I have a sextant. Are you familiar with that?"

"Yes, of course. Are your star charts up to date?"

"Yes. But I never use it. I have a master's license, but … The GPS has never failed, Mrs. Yoeder. Besides, in Greek waters, where we mostly sail, one is never out of sight of land."

"I understand. Many people today depend entirely on the GPS. My teacher was a little more cautious than that, though. When we leave, we will sail back to the US, and we will be out of sight of land for a long time."

Mista said, "How long would it take to get to Rhodes?"

The captain pursed his lips. "About a day and a half, if the weather holds. That's a little far for a three day cruise, but I can probably get permission."

"No, that's all right. It would be interesting to sail by Thira, though."

"You believe that that is the site of the ancient Atlantis?"

"Probably not. But I would like to see it."

Chandri continued to study the chart of the Aegean, laid out on the chart table. After a while, she asked, "What's so special about Rhodes?"

Mista smiled. "Can you list the seven wonders of the ancient world?"

"No. I've heard of them. Was Rhodes a wonder?"

"No. But one was there. The oldest is the pyramid of Gisa. The last was the lighthouse at Alexandria."

"I've heard of them. And the Hanging Gardens. But what else?"

"You saw the ruins of the temple of Artemis in Ephesus. We didn't get to Olympus, where there was once a huge statue of Zeus. The people of Rhodes built a huge statue of Helios, the sun god, in one of the ports of Rhodes. It was about the same size as the Statue of Liberty, and the description probably inspired the design of the Statue of Liberty."

"I remember that. Didn't it straddle the harbor and was supposed to keep enemy ships out or something?"

"Legend was that it straddled the harbor. However, the harbor is several hundred feet across, and the statue was about 110 feet high. The math doesn't work. We'll sail by there on the way home. I'd like to see the harbor again."

CHAPTER 27

They spent Friday provisioning the boat and topping off all tanks. Mista, Sharra and Mischal stood near the stern of their new boat after she was ready for sea. Mista said, "We have to name her."

"She has a name already," Mischal said.

"Yes, but that's not our name. How about Sharon?"

"No. Not my name."

"I like the idea of having two women in my life with the same name," Mista said.

"I think one is more than enough for you," Sharra said with a broad smile.

"Well, I have two. I've been thinking about it. I want to use her for a base for our hunting. How about 'Wolfhound'?"

"Works for me," Sharra said.

Mischal said, "I like it."

They approached Rhodes early Sunday morning and sailed by. Mista looked back as they approached the Straits of Gibraltar several days later. "What if this straits were once solid rock at some point in the distant past?" he asked.

"What if it were?" asked Sharra.

"Like the Mithral Sea on Mindeshara. If this were solid, then this whole basin could have been a fertile valley."

"Maybe the source of the Garden of Eden story and/or the Atlantis story." Sharra said.

"There was a series of fantasy novels written some years ago with that as a premise. The whole valley would be below sea level. If that were history, and then the straits were somehow formed, then the valley would have flooded." Mista rubbed his chin and watched the waters recede behind them. "There are a number of rivers flowing into the sea from all sides," Mista continued. "They would have to drain somewhere."

Mischal said, "In the Mistral valley, that was all highlands, and the rivers drained naturally. I wonder how that would be possible in the Med. If it was."

"Well, we'll be in the Atlantic in a little while," Mista said. "You have our course plotted, Miss Navigator?"

"Sure do, Skipper," Chandri said. "I plotted it to go via the Canary Islands. Is that all right? We could take on fresh provisions before making the actual crossing."

"Fine with me."

The third afternoon after leaving the Canaries, Mista and Mischal sat in deck chairs on the forward deck discussing battle plans. Mischal asked, "When are you going to move on this guy?"

"What do you suggest that we do? Just walk into his house and cut his head off?"

"That might be the best thing. Get it over and done with."

"Unfortunately, we'd be arrested for murder."

"Yeah. Times like this I wish we were back on Mindeshara." They had spent years on a parallel world where the government was an absolute monarchy. Their duke would send them on a mission to capture and destroy a man like David Brumley.

"Even there, we had to collect evidence," Mista said. "Now, let me back up a little. Who would you kill?"

"Why, that's obvious. Brumley, of course."

"Why? What can you prove he has done?"

"Well, he kidnapped your girls, for one."

"I thought that was Sam Smith."

"One and the same."

"You're sure about that? Ever seen either one?"

"I saw him coming out of the house where we found the girls."

"Correction. You saw a man coming out of that house. Who identified him to you?"

"Well – no one. You called me and told me he was leaving, and I got there just as he left."

"No, someone was leaving when you got there. The girls identified a man as Sam Smith, and Smith did leave. He might be the man you saw, or Smith might have been in the car already when you got there. Next question, who is Sam Smith?"

"Brumley. It was his car."

"Yes, it was his car, but there were other people in the car. You do not know if Brumley himself was there."

Mischal sat fuming. He knew that they had fingered the right man and did not know why Mista was arguing this way. "Sharra identified him."

"Sharra identified Brumley, not Sam Smith. Sharra read his mind, some, and knows that he is the same man. But that is not acceptable proof in court. We know that we have the right man, but we have no way to prove it at this time."

"Yeah. Bummer."

"Here is something else to consider. What if he is not the brains behind all this? We know he has an appetite for girls – Sharra knows. We know that he picked up the girls and put them on the market, but he himself did not touch them. What if somebody else is calling the shots? There was a time once before when we took out the wrong –"

"Don't remind me. I have forgiveness for that." He referred to an incident in their past when an army captain under orders destroyed their home village and tortured a close friend to death. They had befriended a bard named Nadia and she had traveled with them for years until she was killed. Mischal had gone berserk, traced down the army captain and publicly executed him. This broke his vows as paladin, and he had sought forgiveness.

"I'm not holding a grudge. We just don't want to repeat that. What I am thinking is that maybe the chief executioner, AKA head of security, might actually be the boss. It was he who killed Sharra's father. It was he who tried to fry us in that B & B. It was he who actually put the girls to sleep and took them to Louisville. Maybe he was under orders, but maybe he acted in his own behalf, and Brumley is the one under orders."

"Does it matter? We need to take them both down, anyway."

"True, but if Brumley is only a minor player, we ought to take down the whole organization. Again, the trouble is, we need hard proof."

Janice and Robin walked up about then. "There you are!" said Janice.

"I'm bored," Robin said. "How long does it take to get home?"

"About another week or two," Mista said. "I remember a little girl demanding to come along."

"Yeah, but I thought it would be a lot more fun."

"Well, we could tie a rope around you and dip you in the water," Mista said.

Robin stuck her tongue out. "Not funny."

"Well, take a look at the world map. It's about 3000 miles from the Canary Islands to the Puerto Rico. That's two weeks at our best speed. Then we still have three or four more days to get to the Tampa area."

"That's too long."

"Well, we could start the engines. Then we could probably make about 12 knots, and it would only take us nine or ten days. Unfortunately, we only have enough fuel for five days, so we'd run out about halfway. We don't want to do that. No fuel means no generator, no electricity. That's not a good thing."

"What were you talking about?" Janice asked.

Mista and Mischal looked at each other. "Proof," Mista said.

"What does that mean?" asked Janice.

"That means that we need proof. You know we want to arrest David Brumley, but we don't have any real proof."

"He kidnapped us and tried to sell us," Janice said. "What more proof do you need?"

"Who kidnapped you? What was his name and social security number?"

"His name – oh. Sam Smith is what he said."

"As far as we know that person does not exist. Whoever he was, it was not Sam Smith."

"It was that old man, Mommy's dad. David Brumley," Robin said. "I'd know him anywhere, even though he dint look the same."

"How could you be sure?"

"I don't know. I just know. Like I knew that you can't lie, Mischal."

"How did you know that?" Mischal asked.

"I don't know. I just *knew*. And Daddy told me I was right. And I know Sam Smith the same way."

Mista said, "She is developing some powers. We don't know yet what they will be."

"I remember Sharra developing her powers," Mischal said.

"Yes. Remember the day I met you? I called you 'Bones' for no obvious reason. I had no idea that you had once been called that. Sharra was scared, because she somehow *knew* that I was going to say that."

"Yes. I remember that. How did you know?"

"I have no idea. It just seemed the right thing to say."

They sat in silence for a while until Robin rubbed up against Mista. "Daddy, I want to go home. Can't we go faster?"

"Sorry, Little Bird. Boats don't move fast. Ships don't move much faster. Wheels let cars move fast. Now, if you could invent a wheel that would allow ships to roll on top of the ocean, then they could go fast."

"Yeah, right. What kind of wheel would that be?"

"No one knows. That's why you would have to invent it."

"Can we listen?" asked Janice. "You were talking about getting proof."

"Sure, why not. You're part of this. You know, Misch, I'm pretty sure he's into drug importing. If we could identify the ships bringing it in …"

"And then do what?"

"Sidetrack it. Have it sent to a dead end, or to our house to dispose of."

"That would be stealing, wouldn't it," Janice said.

Mista looked at her. "You listened. Yes, I suppose it would."

"Of course I listened. I've tried to do everything that you said I should."

Mista shook his head. "Done pretty well, too. Proud of you. Still, he has no right to illegal drugs."

"But they're still his. He paid for them, right?"

"Yes, that's true. Rights or no, he did pay for them. The government could confiscate them, since they are illegal."

"But we aren't the government," Janice said."

"Right. We could divert them to a government office, or tip them where to find them. But I'll lay odds that they would never trace them to Brumley. I bet even the ships' captains don't know what they are transporting."

"Your theory that Brumley is not the key man becomes very possible here," Mischal said.

"Yes. I'm sure he knows, but I'm also sure that he keeps his hands clean. We have to force him somehow."

"I know," Mista said after a while. "I'll call our FBI rep." He punched in the number for Paul Ross and waited. Paul picked up on the second ring. "Ross."

"Paul. Mista. I've been thinking. We know that Brumley has to be in drugs."

"So? What else is new?"

"You already know?"

"You bet."

"You haven't done anything?"

"Not yet. We have to move slow on this one."

"How about if we find the stuff coming in and divert it to our house and destroy it?"

"No way! We don't catch it all, by any means, but we do find some of it. We are looking for his distributors so we can take the whole ring down. If you take the stuff, they'll think you are a distributor, and you're dead."

"I've got to find some way to tag him."

"You just do what you're supposed to do. Leave the drugs to us and the DEA. By the way, this is a secure connection, isn't it?"

"Yes. Always. We'll have to try something else." He clicked off.

Mista sat back in his chair and laid his chin on his chest. Robin sat on him and asked, "What's the matter, Daddy?"

"I've got to figure this out. We've been going around in circles. I know. I'll send any packages that we discover directly to the customs office. That ought to raise some eyebrows. It'll get Brumley's attention, too."

"What'd Ross say?" asked Mischal.

"Said they're tracking deliveries and trying to find all of his distributors."

"I wouldn't do it, then. You'll mess with one they're tracking and they'll get all upset."

"Yeah. I could have Sharra or Jeremy read his mind and see where he's going. If it is someone we already know, then I'll snag it. Losing the drugs will cost Brumley, and he won't have any idea what is happening. Sharra should love it. It'd be a good payback."

"Maybe. Try it."

"It should get his attention. But it's still not what we want. Hmmm. What would you girls do if he took you?"

"Took us where?" asked Robin.

Mischal leaned back and roared with laughter, slapping his leg. "Serves you right, Mista. A girl after your own heart."

"What's so funny?" asked Robin.

"You. Mista has a way of giving a literal answer to a question that he and everybody knows is not literal. You just paid him back."

"But where would he take us?"

"You don't get the real meaning, do you? He means take you sexually."

"Oh." Her face turned red. "I'd burn him up."

"I'd kill him," Janice said.

"You think you could?" Mista asked.

"You betcha. You wait. You'll see."

"Well. I've been thinking about some way to trap him. No, that's not a good word for it. The only thing is, it would put you at risk."

"So?" Janice asked. "We have been at risk ever since we started on this. What's new?"

"You were at risk, yes. But if we do what I have in mind, you will be at a really great risk. Too great."

"No, not too great. We can take care of ourselves."

"Well. If he captures you again, I would want him to try to use you himself. I don't want him to succeed, you understand, just try. I would also want some way to positively identify him. Pictures, voice admitting that he is indeed David Brumley. Think you could do that?"

"You betcha!"

Robin said, "Then can I burn him?"

"No, Honey. Only if you have to protect yourself. You girls are fighters. Maybe we can do it that way."

Chandri was at the helm and called "Mista come look at this."

CHAPTER 28

Mista went back to the wheelhouse and Chandri pointed to something in the water off the starboard bow. "I can't see it well from here," Mista said. "I'll go up to the flying bridge."

He climbed the ladder and looked out. Then he put his hand on the wheel at that station and called down, "I've got the wheel. Come on up."

Janice ran back and climbed up while Chandri was climbing on the other side. Janice got there first. "Can I drive, Daddy?"

"Not drive, Honey. Steer. Not right now. We'll take some time later and show you how. There's more to it that it looks like. Chandri. Take a good look. What do you think it is?"

"I have no idea. Looks like seaweed, but we're hundreds of miles from shore. Has to be deep here."

"It is. Look at your chart. If I recall, it is several miles deep at this point. That is Sargasso seaweed. You don't want to go through it."

"What? Will it slow us down that much?"

"Might. It could be thick enough to foul the screw. There are many tales of ships and boats lost in that area. That would slow us some, but more important, we would be dependent entirely on sail."

"So? We are under sail now."

"Ah, but there is more. Ever heard of the Sargasso Sea?"

Chandri pursed her lips. "Yes, but I don't remember what it was."

"Janice, do you know?"

"Nope."

"It is a huge area in the middle of the Atlantic covered with this seaweed. The seaweed has adapted to these latitudes and the deep water. This is also the center of the Bermuda Triangle."

"Oh. I know what that is. We went down last time we tried to go through it."

"Right. One of the things that happen here is freak storms that come up out of nowhere, like the one that sent us down. You remember the compass changes, also. Columbus discovered this area and assumed that he must be near land. He ordered soundings taken, but could not find bottom. The real danger to us is the wind, or lack of it. This area is bounded by ocean currents that circle it and winds that tend to circle it, often leaving the center calm or with very light winds. It is often called the Doldrums. If we lose the wind, and our screw is fouled by the seaweed, we would be stuck here perhaps for weeks. We could run out of food and water. Well, with luck, not water, since we can make water from sea water."

"Oh. 'The Rhyme of the Ancient Mariner'. That must have come from here," Chandri said. "'Water, water everywhere and nary a drop to drink.'"

"Could be. I don't remember if this was the setting. Seems like the albatross is a Pacific bird. If I remember correctly, they went to the Antarctic and then into uncharted seas. That would put them in the southern oceans. However, knowledge of the Sargasso Sea may have influenced the poem. Anyway, many a ship has been stranded here. It is also called the Horse Latitudes, since many Spanish vessels got trapped here and had to kill the horses to preserve water and food." He pulled the wheel over and settled on a new course fifteen degrees to the south. "You need to adjust your track. We'll skirt the southern boundary and then readjust course again."

Chandri said, "I'll go plot our new course. I also want to check the weather."

"All right. Janice, you want to learn to steer? Okay watch me. Notice, I don't just stand here and hold the wheel in one position."

"Be careful," Chandri said as she went down the ladder. "There is a tropical depression south of us and the wind is kicking up a bit."

"First, notice the sails. They have to be set at an angle to the wind that gives you maximum push, or speed. Any time you turn the boat, you have to readjust the sails. Always be aware of the state of your sails."

"Okay. But, won't they stay the same once you get going?"

"Basically, yes. But sometimes the wind shifts, sometimes the wind changes in other ways. It gets gusty, or dies off. Also, the water itself is moving. It is called a current. Both the wind and the current are going about the same direction that we are, right now, but that won't always be so. Because the wind and the current are the same, we have long high swells. You call them waves, but at sea they are called swells or seas. The wind makes the swells, but the current affects their size and shape. We are going faster than the current, but slower than the wind. So we ride up the swells and then down the other side."

"Okay. I can see that."

"But, notice. When we start up the swell, if I just hold the wheel steady, the bow falls off."

"Falls off what?"

"Oh. Falls a little to the left or right, depending on the direction of the swells. Watch the compass and I'll hold it steady on this one. See how it turns a little to the left? So I have to correct and get it back on course. Look back at our wake. See the curve it made when we turned?"

"Yes."

"You know this will happen, so you correct as you start up the swell. Just a little rudder, and the rudder balances the push from the swell, and you stay straight."

Janice tried, but either applied too much rudder or waited too late. She kept looking back at her wake and shaking her head. "This is a lot harder than it looks."

"Yeah. One thing, you can't steer by looking where you were. Keep your eyes ahead. The wake will take care of itself. You also need to be looking around the horizon all the time to see if another ship or boat is coming."

"Out here? There aren't any other boats out here."

"Sure there are. Ships cross the Atlantic all the time. Just like our highway laws, there are rules of the road that all ships and boats must abide by. There are international rules and Inland Water rules. Each country makes its own inland rules, but every country must obey the same international rules. They are mostly the same, but there are differences. Inland rules talk about channels and river currents, for example. International rules are mostly open water. You need to learn the rules."

"Okay. Am I doing better?"

"Yes, Janice. You are getting the rhythm of the boat and the seas. If you get good enough, we'll put you on the watch rotation a let you take a turn at the helm."

"At the helm?"

"Steering. Like you are now."

"Okay. I'd like that. I'd be something to do."

"Okay. First rule to learn. If you meet another ship, the basic rule is to pass on the left – that is, to keep the other ship to your starboard or right side."

"Unlike driving."

"Yes. But there are exceptions. You know … England is steeped in sailing tradition. Maybe that's why they drive on the left side of the road – to keep a passing car on their right side. A sailing vessel is defined as one under sail power alone. A powered vessel is required to avoid the sailing vessel. Why is that?"

Janice shrugged. "I have no idea."

"If a sailing vessel must turn, it is a major task. Depends on where the wind is. It might even shift from one side to the other. So the sailing vessel is required to maintain course, that is, make no changes, so that the other ship knows where it is going and can avoid it. However, reality is that many ships do not maintain a good watch, and might not even see us. Also sometimes they are reluctant to change course. If you see that they aren't going to change, you have to take action. So, if we were sailing close to the wind, for example, say we have the wind off our starboard bow. You have to turn right to avoid him. Always right, never left. Never cross his bow."

"All right. That makes sense."

"Right. But if you turn right, you turn right into the wind. You can't do that. You can, but you will stop or go backwards. You have to turn far enough that the wind comes on your port side, and shift the sails to the opposite side to catch the new wind. You see why the power vessel is required to change."

"Yeah."

"Secondly, if you get too close to him, he can block your wind, if he is to windward of you."

"Yeah, then we would stop."

"Yes, but not right away. The boat would slow to a stop, but could be drawn into the side of the big ship."

"Okay. I see."

"Now, there are special rules for two sailing vessels meeting. Their maneuvers depend on where the wind comes from. But enough for now."

Chandri stuck her head up and called, "Mista can you come down? You need to see this."

"Okay." He called Mischal. "Misch! Come stand with Janice a minute."

Chandri said, "Look at this." She showed him a chart of the Atlantic. "We're here. Hard to point to the exact spot on this scale, but we're crossing here. Now, down here we have a tropical depression. First of the year."

"Oh boy. Which way is it moving?"

"Stationary right now. It might develop into a tropical storm, and will probably move. Normal movement would be well to the south of our track, hitting the Caribbean at the Windward Islands, near South America, and then curving up wherever it wants to go."

"Hmmm. When it does move, it's forward speed could be anywhere from two or three knots to ten or twelve. If it does develop into a storm, it could be coming up toward Florida about the same time that we arrive. That'll be interesting."

"Yes. But as you say, interesting but not much fun."

"Well, we'll have to watch it. All we need is for it to trap us between it and Florida. The Spanish treasure ships found that's not a good thing. They found out the hard way."

CHAPTER 29

By the next morning, the winds had become erratic, and eventually died altogether. They had been in the Southeast Trade Winds, and these had failed. Chandri checked the weather map. The storm had been upgraded to a tropical storm and begun to move toward South America.

Mista went down to the chart room to check their position. "We are at 21 degrees north and 32 degrees west," Chandri said, "according to the GPS."

"You take a fix this morning?"

"No. Took one last night, and it agrees."

"Let's take a Local Apparent Noon sighting this morning. That will confirm the latitude. This puts us just within the Sargasso Sea limits, which we already know, having seen the seaweed. A little early to lose the wind, but I guess that's the result of that storm."

Mista went down to the salon to get some coffee and to consult with Mischal. "What do you think? Should we start the engines?"

"I don't think so," Mischal answered. "We only have fuel for five days. I'd hate to use it out here and then not have a cushion if we get into a storm somewhere."

"Yeah. I agree. Let's wait and see. Maybe the wind will come back up tonight or in the morning. That storm is heading for the Caribbean. I'd just as soon let it go and do its thing before we get there."

Mista looked around. Sharra and the girls were in the saloon, as was Charly. "Anybody want to go swimming?" he asked.

"In the middle of the ocean?" asked Sharra.

"Why not? We'll be here for a while."

Janice went topsides and the rest followed. She looked over the rail at the deep blue water reflecting the cloudless sky. "How deep is it?" she asked.

Chandri ducked into the pilothouse and came back a minute later. "It's 2,422 fathoms."

"Okay. What's a fathom?"

"Six feet," Mista said. "So how good's your math?"

Janice closed her eyes and thought. "I can't do that in my head," she said, finally.

Chandri said, "That's not a hard number. Do it either way. Six times 2 is 12, six times 4 is 24, so tack the two onto the 12, six times 22 is 132, and tack the 1 onto the last four. 14,532. Or do it from the right, if that's easier."

"That's the way they teach us in school," Robin said. "But that's too big a number to keep in my head. That's way too deep to swim in."

Mista grinned. "Anything over six feet doesn't count. Last one in's a rotten egg." He went below to change, Mischal right behind him. He was back a minute later and dived off the side of the boat. Mischal was seconds behind him.

"Hah!" Charly said from the water. She had taken off her shoes and jumped in, clothes and all. "Guess that's Misch, unless you count the chickens that won't come in."

"You cheated," Mischal said. "You never wear a bathing suit."

"Yeah. I don't like to show myself like that. I still beat."

Mista called, "Nobody else coming in?"

Robin got over her fear of the deep and jumped in, shoes and all. She reasoned that if something did happen, her daddy would save her.

Chandri looked down at herself. She was wearing shorts and a halter-top. She shrugged, pulled off her shoes and jumped in. No one followed. The rest were content to watch.

Robin swam over to Mista and said, "There's no bottom. Can I hold onto you?"

"Only if you take your shoes off. They're too heavy for swimming." He pulled her over to the ladder on the side of the boat and sent her up. She was back seconds later.

They played until they got tired and then came back aboard. Mista said, "Chandri check our drift. We should still be in the Canary Current."

"Let me wash the salt off and dry off." After a while, she said, "I marked our location. I'll check again in a few minutes. It'll take a while. At one knot, that's 200 yards every six minutes."

Half an hour later, she said, "We've drifted 800 yards to the west in thirty minutes."

"Mista said, "Good. That means we are now in the north equatorial current, and that will carry us to the Caribbean. At this rate, we'll be there in about 120 days. That's three times as long as it took Columbus, as I recall."

"One hundred and twenty days?" Robin said. "That's four months! We'll starve. Only I'll die of boredom first."

"We could catch fish, except there aren't any fish out here. No birds, either. Hmmm. That could be a problem. Better hope the wind comes back."

The next day they began to get light variable breezes as the tropical storm moved across the Atlantic toward South America. By evening the trade wind was back at normal. They raised sail and headed westward once more.

The storm that they were watching was moving a little faster than they were, but the next day it suddenly turned north. As it moved north and they continued westward, the winds became variable and light, and then dropped off again. The revolving circle of the storm was overriding the trade wind. A few hours later, the wind picked up again.

"Look at this, Mista," Chandri said. "I have plotted the storm's path and our path for the last six hours. Well, not our track, since we haven't moved in the last six hours, but the projected path at our normal speed. We're on collision course. But I don't understand why the wind changes like that."

"You've seen pictures of storm systems, like satellite views, right?" Mista asked. "A storm like this is a big circle of wind going counter-clockwise. If it were dead ahead, our wind would be coming from the south. The wind on the opposite side of the storm comes from the north. A huge circle. Now, since the storm is actually south west of us, the wind comes in from the southeast and the trades reinforce it."

"I see. It's just hard to visualize the changing directions of the wind."

"Think about this. The storm is moving north at 10 knots, right? The winds move in a circle around the eye. In the northeast quadrant, the wind adds to the forward speed. That is called the dangerous quadrant. All hurricanes are dangerous, but that is the most dangerous quadrant."

"Because the wind is stronger?"

"Partly that. But remember, the wind is not a straight line. The circular motion pushes things toward the center. So, if we were on the northeast quadrant, the storm is moving faster than we can go, so it is overtaking us and pushing us toward the center at the same time."

"Well, anyway, we don't want to sail into the storm, do we?"

"No, not at all. Set a course 25 degrees to the south and watch that sucker. We want her to go well to the north of us."

Chandri continued to monitor NOAA weather reports, even though the storm continued north. They had been known to double back. The storm eventually dissipated, however, and they felt safe as they continued across the Atlantic.

The next day the second tropical depression of the season popped up just off the coast of South America, directly south of their position. This one moved quickly up toward the Caribbean, almost seeming to deliberately pace them. Its course was northwest and theirs was south of west, a converging course. By the second day it had been upgraded to a tropical storm and named Bert.

They were just north of Puerto Rico three days later, and Bert had been slowed by the passage through the Lesser Antilles Islands as he crossed into the Caribbean. After entering the Caribbean, though, Bert had picked up more energy and was on the verge of becoming a hurricane. He also changed course and seemed to beheading up toward the east coast of Florida.

Mista asked Mischal and Chandri to meet him in the salon. Naturally, everyone else also came. "We have to make a choice here," Mista said. "My original plan was to put into San Juan and take on fuel and rations. With the storm coming this way, I'm not sure that that's wise."

"We haven't used much fuel," Mischal said.

"True, but the generator has been running the whole time. That takes some fuel. It's not critical to refuel, but it wouldn't hurt."

"Wouldn't we be safer if we stayed in port at San Juan until the storm passes," asked Charly.

"No. The last place you want to be is in port when a hurricane hits. You've seen pictures of all the boats washed or blown up onto the shore after a hurricane passes. We need to be at sea, but not in his path."

"Food is a little low," Sharra said. "Not dangerous – enough for five or six days. But if something happened, we could run out before we were rescued."

"Let's pull in," Mista said. "I would really like to have a full load of fuel while dodging old Bert. And I would also like to have a food safety factor.

To say nothing of fresh food. We don't want to waste any time, however. Misch, will you or Charly take Sharra and get food? I'll take care of the fuel. You'll need to call a cab."

The San Juan harbor is deep, but the entrance is long. It took about an hour to get in and tied up. Mischal and Sharra jumped off and headed for the store immediately. They were back before Mista had finished refueling.

"What'd you get?" Robin asked.

"Meat, potatoes and about twenty five pounds of frozen veggies," Mischal said.

"And ice cream?" Robin asked.

"And ice cream," Sharra said.

They were underway again in half an hour. Chandri watched her chart and the depth sounder while Mista steered. As soon as he cleared the channel, he raised sails and turned west. The wind was strong and gusty, coming out of the northeast. Chandri came up to the pilot house and said, "Course 295. Whew! This wind is stronger that I realized. Why is it coming out of the northeast?"

"Bert."

"Oh. He's behind us, isn't he? That puts us in the northwest quadrant. And with the wind forward of our beam, he will probably move faster than we do."

"Right. We have about five days before we get to Key West? What is his projected track?"

"It's heading toward Cuba right now. They are predicting that he will go up the east coast of Florida. Right across the Bahamas."

Mista pursed his lips. "I don't like this. If he stays on track, he'll be hitting Cuba about the time we hit the Straits of Florida. The Florida current there runs westerly, and it's about two or three knots as I recall. You can check that. Let's go look at your charts. CHARLY! Can you take the wheel?"

"Sure boss. What's the course?"

"Steer 315. Miss Navigator said 295, but I think we better turn upwind a little to compensate for wind drift. Especially with land to windward."

Mista and Chandri went down to the chart table. "Let's look," Mista said.

"Bert is just inside the Caribbean, here," Chandri said, pointing.

"Right. And you have his track laid out. He'll hit the eastern end of Cuba in about five days at this speed. We'll be just entering the Straits of Florida, and entering the current there, which will slow us down. And Bert will probably speed up as it picks up energy on the open water. He could cross Cuba before we get as far a Key West."

"And if he – it – does?" asked Chandri.

"As long as he continues north across the Bahamas, we're okay. If he veers west and goes into the Gulf of Mexico, he'll be chasing our tail. And gaining. We'll be trapped. We can't turn north – that's the keys. Can't turn south, that's Cuba. We can only continue west, and with him gaining on us. Not good."

"We could turn back east."

"We would be sailing right into the storm. And the more east we go, the more easterly the wind becomes, and we cannot sail into the teeth of the wind. Southeast is Bert, northeast is the southern Bahama islands. I think I know how those old Spanish galleon commanders felt like when they tried to sail up the Florida coast to escape the hurricanes. We can sail a lot closer to the wind than they could, and I still don't see any escape. We better just head west at best speed. I'll light off the engines when we hit the Florida Current."

As they went west Bert was upgraded into a hurricane and continued northwest, on track for the eastern end of Cuba. The further north it went, the more the winds shifted to the south. The seas became confused. The trade winds had been pushing them all the way across the Atlantic in a southeasterly direction, but the hurricane winds north of Puerto Rico, Haiti and Cuba were driving from the southwest. With the winds blowing in a different direction than the run of the seas, the seas became choppy and confused. The boat pitched and rolled, no longer rhythmically flowing with the seas.

The storm gradually closed the distance between them over the next three days. By the time it reached Cuba it had been classified as a category 2 hurricane. The winds shifted around to the south, and the boat heeled over and rocked with the gusts. Mista reefed his sails and then dropped the mainsail. He started the engines to get more speed and better control.

Chandri came up at 3:00 o'clock to tell Mista that Bert had hit the southern coast of Cuba and stalled. It was about 500 miles behind them, and winds at the center were estimated to be 90 knots. She looked around at the sky and sea. "Wow! It's almost dark already."

"Yeah. Send Charly and Mischal up. And ask Jeremy to take the wheel. I want to rig life lines. Should have already done that."

When they came up, Mista said, "Here's how we will do this. Two on deck to rig lines. We need something to hold onto besides the rail in case we have to go topsides. We will rig a safety line around our waists and looped around a cleat here. The third person holds the ends of our lines. If we get thrown over, you will be able to pull us back in." Since Mischal was strongest, he held the lines. Charly and Mista went out and secured lines fore and aft on both sides of the boat.

It took then a good hour to rig the lines. Charly carried the coils of line and paid them out to Mista who tied them off to strong points on the boat. Afterwards, Mista and Charly went down below to warm up and get dry. Mischal asked if Jeremy wanted him to take the wheel.

"No, I'm fine. Haven't done my share, I don't think. I just use the wheel to hold onto. It's easier for me to control the rudder with my mind. Wish I could control the winds that way."

"How long can you keep that up?"

Jeremy grinned. "Not long. Actually, it's more work to do it that way. I'm just steering like anyone else would. But, I'm okay. Take a break and get some dry clothes on."

With Bert stalled on the southern side of Cuba and losing energy over land, the winds dropped a little in intensity began to shift back to the southwest. The boat settled down some. It was still a rough ride, with the current pushing the seas toward the east and the wind coming out of the southwest.

Mista looked around at the group huddled in the salon. Sharra and Janice were both a little green and had decided not to eat anything for a while. Mista carefully pumped coffee into a Styrofoam cup and drank some. "Ugh. Warm, at least. But it's coffee. The good news is that the storm has slowed down and weakened. Looks like it is still on track to go up the east coast of Florida. The bad news is that it's going to be rough for at least another day. Might be hard to cook."

"Hard?" asked Sharra. "I'd say impossible."

"Yeah. Well, I'm hungry. I think I'll make a corned beef sandwich." He started to set his cup down and then grabbed it before it could escape. Robin ran over. "I'll hold it for you, Daddy. Can I have a sandwich, too?"

"Sure, Robin. Glad I'm not the only one hungry."

"What is a corned beef sandwich?"

"I'll show you." He opened a cabinet carefully just a crack and looked inside. Cans had fallen everywhere. He made a face and reached in and snagged a can of corned beef and then refastened the cabinet door. Robin stood watching as he unsnapped the key and opened the can. When he had it almost opened, he remembered that he did not have a knife out or any bread. "Hmmm. I'm out of hands."

Robin stood in front of him with her legs spread, easily swaying back and forth as the boat rocked and pitched. Mista said, "You've got your sea legs, haven't you?"

"What are sea legs?"

"The ability to stand or walk and sway with the ship or boat. Like you are doing. I bet Janice can't do that."

"I'm not even going to try," Janice said.

"Can you hold this can in your other hand while I get the bread and a knife?"

"Sure."

He got the bread first and dropped it into the galley sink to trap it. Then he got a paring knife, took out two slices of bread and gave them to Robin, taking the can of corned beef back at the same time. He cut two slices of the meat while it was still in the can and then took the top piece of bread in one hand and laid the slices of meat on the other piece, and then put the top back on it. He took another slice of bread. "Can you hold two?"

"I think so."

He cut two more slices and laid them on the bread. Then he dropped the can into the sink and got another piece of bread and finished his sandwich. "It's better with mayonnaise. I wonder …"

"I think you have enough to juggle," Charly said. "I wouldn't have believed that if I hadn't seen it with my own eyes."

"Well, you shouldn't let a little weather keep you from eating," Mista said. "How are we doing?"

Nobody answered.

"Like I said, at least another day of this. Hopefully, with the wind at a more favorable angle and the storm stalled, we will be able to leave it behind. Still, until we do, nobody goes topside unless absolutely necessary. All portholes closed and dogged down tight, all doors and hatches stay closed."

"It's getting stuffy down here," Janice said.

"Well, it won't be forever. Just keep them closed."

Chandri came in and said that Bert had been downgraded to category 1. "Looks like we made the right decision."

CHAPTER 30

After supper – which was sandwiches for some and nothing for others – Chandri took the watch. Mischal relieved her after two hours. They were all rotating every two hours while the helm took so much work. Like everyone else, she only slept fitfully, rolling from side to side. She wished that she had a hammock.

Mista was on watch when she got up at 5:00 the next morning. She wanted to check her position and the storm track before she took the wheel at six. Her GPS track showed that they had averaged 5 knots during the night and were just entering the St. Nicholas Channel south of the Cay Sal bank. She shuddered. Mista had told her to watch for that, that more than one ship had foundered on the rocks there. Hopefully, they would be clear of the bank by nightfall and could turn more to the north, heading for home.

Then she checked the storm plot. Her face went white, and she wished that she had gotten up and checked it earlier. Bert had turned back out to sea and was going due west along the south coast of Cuba. It was building up fast and was already nearly to category 3 – 94 knots. Not only that, it was moving fast across the water. She checked the wind and found that it was coming from the east as it circled the center, but blowing to the west, so it would be called a west wind. That meant that Bert was nearly due south of them.

Well, maybe that's not all bad. If it keeps up it should be ahead of us by night, giving us a northeast wind. Then we can turn and run before it, rounding Key West about first light. Current will set us to the east, though. Have to make sure we don't run into Key West.

She plotted their position and track and then plotted the storm's position and track. Then she went up to relieve Mista and give him the bad news.

They picked up a little speed during the day, with the wind on the port beam and the seas broken some by the passage over the rocks and cays of the Cay Sal Bank, and Mista stopped the engines to conserve fuel. Bert had almost overtaken them, but then slowed as it crossed the Cayman Islands. Then it turned north again and headed for Cuba again, toward a point about 60 miles east of Havana. Mista looked at the track and shook his head. "We don't know if it will continue up the east coast of Florida or the west. All we can do is run before it and hope."

Chandri laid a course for a point about 50 miles west of Key West, assuming that the current would set them 25 miles eastward during the night. She came up twice during the night to check the course and the storm. She also checked the radar. She knew that there were several keys west of Key West and did not want to run aground.

The next morning Bert made landfall in Cuba again and slowed down. They passed about 75 miles west of Key West, within sight of Dry Tortugas, and entered the relatively shallow waters of the continental shelf. Mista called the Coast Guard station in Key West to give them their position.

"Hey, you guys ought not to be out there, you know," came the answer.

"Tell me. It's like this storm is chasing me. Every turn I make he comes right behind me."

"Well, it's too late to turn east. You need help?"

"Not at this time. I don't want to put into port at any place Bert is going to hit."

"That's wise. We've sent all our cutters to sea."

"You can run. I'm mostly sail, max 12 knots. My last hope is that Cuba will slow him down enough that I can get out into the Gulf. And that he doesn't follow me there."

"You talk like it's a person. It goes where the wind drives it. Looks like it's going up the Florida west coast."

"That means my house near Tampa. Well, it's better equipped to withstand a hurricane that the boat."

They ran before the storm all day. Mista started the engines again to get as much speed as he could sustain. Shallow water meant that the seas were much bigger and longer, but not as confused. He meant to turn to the southwest before dark, if the storm stayed on its northern track.

By mid afternoon, it was obvious that the storm was going north. He was out of sea room and could no longer run before it. He could not turn northwest, because that would put the wind on his beam, and likely capsize him. He ordered everyone to don life jackets. Then he ran the engines up to maximum speed. He dropped the main sail and prepared for his turn. At the bottom of one long swell, he put the rudder hard over and swung the mizzen sail to the starboard side. The boat turned in the trough, the wind caught the sail and the boat started back up the swell it had just come down. It was done. He had been afraid that the mizzen sail would snap when the wind caught it, but it had held. He breathed again.

He sent Charly and Mischal out to man the mizzen sail. They were running before the wind, and it was time to drop all canvas but the jib. The rigging and body of the boat were enough for the wind to drive it at a good speed, and the jib would keep the stern to the wind. This was called sailing with bare poles. Sails were hoisted by winch, but in this wind, he wanted someone on the sheets. Jeremy went with Charly to see if he could help. They manned the port side and Mischal the starboard. They centered the boom and secured their lines on cleats, and then Mista hit the switch to lower the sail. Charly pulled the beam toward her, and Mischal gave her slack and they secured the sheets so that the boom was positioned just over the port rail. Next they moved up to the mainmast and pulled its boom over to the starboard rail and secured it. Mista flashed his light three times, and holding the lifelines they all worked carefully back to the pilothouse. Mista turned to Chandri, who had just come up. "Take the wheel. I'm going down and get some coffee."

"You can't make coffee in this storm!"

Mista grinned. "A sailor always has coffee at hand."

"Yeah, right. I'll believe that when I see it."

"I'll be right back. I filled the thermos jugs before the storm got bad. Hope it's at least still warm."

He went down the hatch to the main salon, making sure that the hatch was secure behind him. There were a total of eight people on board, including his wife and two daughters. When it became obvious that they would experience severe weather, he had called them all into the salon and laid down the safety rules for them. "Make sure that all the portholes are closed and dogged tight. Make sure that every door and hatch stays closed at all times. If you go through one, close and secure it behind you. We are going to rig safety lines inside the rails for those that have to go topside, but nobody goes up unless they absolutely have to. If it gets too bad, I want everyone to put life jackets on."

"Those smelly things?" asked Janice, his twelve year old.

"If you happen to go overboard, you won't have time to grab one on the way over."

Robin, his eleven year old, said, "It's hot down here with the windows closed. Besides, I want to see the storm."

"Portholes," Mista said. "If you open one you'll be breathing water instead of air. You want a little hot or a boat full of water?"

"All right. But it's stuffy down here."

Mista filled a Styrofoam cup with coffee. It was just a little more than warm, but it was coffee. "The wind is kicking up. I'm getting about 40 knots now. Time to put the life jackets on." He already had his on, since he had been topside. He made sure that Janice and Robin had theirs on and that they were tied securely, and then he went back up.

Charly and Jeremy had just come into the wheelhouse. Mista said, "You two better get below and get warm."

Just then, Robin opened the hatch and climbed up. "I want to stay with you, Daddy." The boat took a sudden lurch and she lost her footing, slid across the deck and out the open door and over the side.

Mista did not hesitate, but jumped over after her. Her life jacket had inflated automatically when she hit the water, and Mista swam to her and held onto her; then turned and looked for the boat. He pulled Robin into a life saving hold and swam for the boat, not believing that he had a chance to get there; but he had to try.

Mischal throttled the engines down as much as he dared. He had to keep enough speed that the boat kept steerageway, or the waves and wind would turn it and swamp it. Jeremy stepped out and called, "Hold me, Charly!" She grabbed his belt in one hand and hung on to a rail in the wheelhouse with the other. Jeremy snatched a life ring off the bulkhead and threw it at Mista. He used mind power to send it directly to Mista, and then sent a mental message, *Grab the life ring and I'll pull you in.*

Mista sent, *Where?*

Coming your way. It bumped Mista on the head.

Got it. You better take the wheel and let Misch pull me in.

Roger. Hang on.

Charly said, "You get back in here. Can't lose you both."

Jeremy handed her the lifeline. "He has the ring, just pull him in."

162

Charly said, "Take the wheel, Jeremy. Misch, come help me pull them on deck."

Mischal stepped out to the safety line and waited. When Charly had pulled Mista up to the side of the boat, he lay down on deck, held the rail with one hand and reached down. Mischal tried three times to grab Mista's hand when he rose on the swells, but could not get a grip. Chandri heard or sensed the commotion, and stepped into the wheelhouse. She yelled, "Make a bight!"

"What do you mean?" asked Charly.

"Here. Give me some of the free line."

Charly picked up some of the line that she had used to pull Mista in and handed it to Chandri. Chandri quickly doubled the line, making a loop, or as she had called it, a bight, and then passed the line back through the loop. She yelled, "MISCH!" When he looked back, she pushed the line back and forth through the loop, and then handed it out to him.

Mischal showed the line to Mista, and he reached up for it. Mischal dropped it to Mista, and Mista put the loop around Robin. When Mischal pulled up on the line, it tightened around her and he pulled her up. He held a fistful of her shirt and life jacket in one hand and looked back at Charly. "Now what?"

Charly passed the life line that Mista was hanging onto to Chandri and said, "Give her here. I'll hold her. You pull Mista up."

Mischal dropped the line back down to Mista. He put the loop under his arms and tightened it, and Mischal flipped the line around his wrist and heaved. Mista grabbed the rail and pulled himself on board. Mischal called "Get the engines up to speed, Jeremy!"

"Roger."

When Mista came inside, Robin leaped into his arms. "Don't yell at me, Daddy."

Mista said, "I know you like to get wet, Honey, but this is not the time or place."

"I didn't do it on purpose!" She hung on and cried.

"All right, Little Bird. I was afraid I'd lost you. You're all right now." He looked out at the rigging. "Bring her a couple of degrees to starboard. Watch your helm, the wind will try to push her back around."

Jeremy eased the wheel over and the boat changed its motion as the relative direction of the wind and swells changed. "Okay, that's good," Mista said. "With any luck, we'll be out of this in a couple of hours."

Mischal said, "Want me to take the wheel, Jeremy? Good thinking, throwing that life ring. We couldn't have turned back."

"Well, I knew it was right out there and already had a line on it."

Mista took Robin down below to get her some dry clothes. Her stateroom was aft, so they went there first. "Get some dry clothes on, Hon."

"But …"

"I'll turn my back."

She came to him a few minutes later, dry, and said, "Thanks, Daddy. I thought I was losted."

"Well, you remember, sometimes you need to obey without question. It could save your life. This was one of them. You stay below, now, okay?"

"Yes, Daddy. Are you mad at me?"

"No, Honey. I can't get mad at you. Maybe I would have been mad if I'd lost you though." He took her hand and said, "Let's go to the salon. I can't carry you; I'm still wet."

CHAPTER 31

Their nemesis, Bert, turned eastward across Ft. Myers and continued across the state of Florida. As it moved east it also lost energy while crossing the land and the winds diminished rapidly. As they sailed out of the danger zone, the wind shifted to the north and the boat's motion grew much less spastic. By morning the hurricane clouds were a dark blur on the eastern horizon.

Chandri came up to the pilothouse and gave Mista their position and the latest report on the hurricane. "We didn't make many miles during the night, but you probably expected that. Anyway, the storm is on the way to his death. It's be reclassified as a tropical storm."

"Good. Of course, it could revive once it hits the water again."

"Yes, but it's on the way north and east."

"Right. Let's head for home. Call Mischal and Charly up, if they're awake, and lets come about and get some sail on."

Chandri went down and then climbed back up a few minutes later with Mischal in tow. "Charly's asleep. I'll take the port side," she said.

They came into Tarpon Springs the next morning. Mista called ahead and made arrangements for repairs and refitting at the boat yard there. As soon as the boat was repaired and updated he intended to install an Internet server on board and add an automatic searching satellite antenna. They would have been able to use the Internet connections on the trip, had there already been an antenna and server.

They spent the rest of that day and the weekend doing nothing but resting and catching up on sleep. No one had slept much while running from the hurricane. Monday morning, Mista called a planning session.

"I want to use that boat," he said, when everyone had gathered. I want to cruise in the Gulf of Mexico off Key West and Dry Tortugas – that's about 60 miles west of Key West."

"Yes," Mischal said. "Used to be a prison, but now it's a tourist site. I'd kind of like to see it."

"Well, we can take a day and do that. No reason why we can't relax once in a while. We ought to pull into Key West one day, too. I'd like you girls to get back active on the Internet and see what you can catch. Since you will be at sea, they won't be able to come see you until some future time. Gives us a little control."

"Let 'em come," Janice said. "I'm ready for them this time."

"Me, too," said Robin.

"Good. I assume you are ready, too, Shawnah? You don't have to do it if you don't want to. Specifically, I want to trap Brumley. We know that he's clever, and that he basically keeps his own hands clean. We have to push him into something."

"That constitutes entrapment," Jeremy said. "If we set a trap and he falls for it the courts will not allow it. All our work –"

"You aren't a lawyer yet, but you already talk like one," Mista said. "I am not interested in what the courts think." His eyes had turned steely gray. "I want that man dead. Unfortunately, we live in a civilized country. They don't believe that we know what we know, and we cannot prove it in a way that they will accept. So we have to do our own thing. I understand that the courts interest is protecting the innocent. They would rather a guilty man go free than for an innocent man to suffer. I applaud that sentiment. But we *know* that this man is guilty."

"Hear, hear," Mischal said. "About time."

"Sharra, are you willing to go into his mind and push him in the right direction? I don't think he will make a move against us without a little help."

Sharra shuddered. "No. I don't think I can go there. I have no compunctions about doing harm to him, but I don't want to have to go into his mind."

"All right. Jeremy?"

"I have some reservations about forcing a man to do something that he would not ordinarily do, and then whack him for it."

"We can be sure that he is doing his thing with other girls. We just don't know who and when. About the only way we will catch him is if he tries something with one of ours. That's the reason for the push. Not to make him do something he would not ordinarily do, but to make him do it to us."

"Still, …"

"Okay. Contact Molly. Ask her if she will help. Now, the reason I want to be at sea is that I want to see what ships Brumley has coming into Tampa. Once we identify them, I want to know what contraband they are carrying."

"You don't know if they are," Jeremy said. "Yes, we do know some of the things he had done, but we do *not* know if he is importing drugs."

"That is true. Even if he is, the captain or bursar of his ships might not themselves know. But if they do, then we have reason to act. Whenever we can, I want to find out who is taking delivery of the drugs and force him or her to turn them over to the customs office. Even if it screws up some DEA sting. We won't find them all, and there will be enough to give them what they want. Once he starts losing product, we will have his attention. We'll just have to wait and see what he does."

Jeremy said, "I contacted Molly. She'll be here tomorrow night. She asks if we have a place for her to stay."

"Hmmm," Mista said. "Njondac, could she sleep in the back of your truck?"

"Sure. Long's she's got a car ta get here in."

"Jeremy?"

"She's driving. Says maybe your truck won't be any worse than sleeping on the ground."

"Don't tell her, but I had planned to partition off a couple of rooms in my lower lever. One for Em, and one for whatever or whoever. If you guys can help me with that, we'll have it ready and furnished for her by tomorrow night."

"I'll help, Daddy," Janice said.

"Me, too," said Robin.

"I have an idea how you can help most," Mista said. "Sharra, would you take them and go pick out the furnishings we will need? You also need about five student desks, since Em wants to hold school there also."

"Sure. You girls want to go shopping?"

"We need at least the bed here by tomorrow night," Mista said. "If they can deliver that fast, then fine. Otherwise, we might need to ask Njondac to borrow his truck. Better think double or queen bed, in case her husband comes with her, or comes to visit." He did not expect Karl to come with her, but did expect him to visit.

"Sure, I'll get it fer ya. But ya needs some lumber, too, don't ya?"

"Yes. We'll need studs and dry wall. Guess we better get doors for the rooms, too."

The men went down to lay out the new rooms and figure out the materials that they would need, and Sharra went to get ready for her shopping trip. She paused at the door and said, "You might think about painting the walls, too. If you do, you'll need paint."

"Yeah, that's probably a good idea," Mista said.

It took the rest of the week to make all of the arrangements, but they headed out to sea early the next Monday morning. Mista had paid a technician to run wiring to all staterooms and the salon, and then he set up his server in the master's cabin. He set up computers for the girls in their cabin, and computers in each of the other cabins plus the salon. The boat had two masters' cabins and four guest cabins, plus two crew cabins. Mista put the girls and Em in one of the masters' cabins. Njondac chose not to go to sea. Sheila also did not want to go, at first. But then she said, "I better go. I can cook for you all."

Mischal said, "Njondac, you should go."

"I don't got no need ta be on tha ocean."

"Sure you do. Nobody knows engines better than you."

"Ya gots a sailboat."

"We have two diesel engines, too."

"Oh. Nobody told me that. Sure, I'll come."

CHAPTER 32

They had a list of ships owned by Brumley and had gotten a list of scheduled arrivals from the Port of Tampa, so they knew what ships to expect and when. They were waiting for the first Brumley ship to come into port on Wednesday morning. It was a banana boat, not much larger than their sailboat.

Mischal hailed the ship when it came within hailing distance. "Ahoy the ship. We're heading south. How's the weather?"

The captain was puzzled. Didn't everyone have radios? "Weather is fine."

"Well, we just wanted a personal report. We got caught in Hurricane Bert last week. I'm just curious, but are you carrying bananas?"

"Yes. We always carry bananas. Why do you care?"

"Well, sometimes we need something special moved, and wanted to know if you'd be interested."

"No. We are a banana boat. Good day."

Molly had been listening to his thoughts. She did not want to go deep, but the surface thoughts were enough. When Mischal mentioned carrying special things from time to time, his mind jumped to the box in the ship's safe. He did not know what was in it, but the owner had asked him to carry it to Tampa from time to time. He was to deliver it to a courier who would be waiting. The man's face flashed in his memory. He was always the same courier.

Molly came out of the pilothouse, where she had been watching. "If Karl knew what I was doing, he'd shoot me."

"I wouldn't tell him, then," Mischal said.

"No, I don't think I will. He knows we are right, but he's just a stickler for procedure."

"You ought to talk to Mista about it. Have you talked to him?"

"Since I came down? No, not really. But if I'm going to redirect that courier, we need to go into port so I can see him."

"Why don't you just tell that captain to tell the courier to take it to the customs office?"

"Not that simple to make someone do something he would not ordinarily do. Of course, that's true about sending the courier to the customs office, too, but in that case we are simply redirecting him. Besides, the captain might not have the authority to send him somewhere else, and even if he does, the courier probably would not obey that kind of order."

"Okay, okay. Mista's on the helm. Tell him."

Molly climbed up to the flying bridge and told Mista that the boat was delivering a package to a courier when it docked, and that the captain did not know what was in it. "I'll need to see the man getting the package to be able to influence him," she said.

"Okay. I hadn't thought about that. Guess it would have been better if we had been heading into port when we hailed him, instead of turning around and following him. Well, the wind is favorable. We would be on a close reach, and that's our fastest sailing point. I'll light off the engines, too. We should be able to overtake him before he reaches port, and then be pier side when he comes in."

Mista called out, "Standby to come about!" and then put his rudder over, letting the stern fall through the wind. When the boat turned so that the wind was on the other side, the booms swung across the deck. Then Mista sent Mischal up to pull them in closer to the centerline, since they would be sailing closer to the wind on their new tack.

They tied up to a spot well away from their target ship's berth, but close enough that they could see people coming and going. Mista told Mischal to walk down the pier in the opposite direction to allay suspicions. They had not seen Molly, so she sat in a chair on the flying bridge where she could observe.

After the customs inspectors had left, another man went aboard the banana boat. He reappeared a few minutes later carrying a small duffle bag. Molly sampled his thoughts. He knew where he was going and he knew the man he was to meet, but he had no idea what was in the bag. She went a little deeper and left a strong suggestion in his mind, similar to a post-hypnotic suggestion, that he really should go to the customs office and show them his duffle bag. He did not know why he did it, he was simply convinced that it was the right thing to do. He was well out of sight when Mischal came back, carrying a sack that appeared to be groceries. As soon as he was on board, they cast off and headed back out to sea.

An hour later, another man came to the banana boat. He was obviously familiar with the docks, but was not a seaman or stevedore. He looked more like a buyer, or perhaps a ship owner. He asked for the captain and then asked if he had seen a man named Joe Smollock.

"Yep. Come and gone. Why?"

"He was supposed to pick up something."

"He did. What is it to you?"

"Never mind. You have proof that he was here?"

"Yep. Not that it's any of your business."

"Well, it could be, but you wouldn't know. Have a nice day."

The man walked up the pier, got into a late model car and drove off. He knew that the captain probably did have proof, but he was not supposed to know what he had delivered nor to whom it was going. He had to assume that the courier had either been waylaid, or had turned. Either way, he was a dead man.

He called Brumley and reported that his man had not showed.

"No sign of him?"

"No, sir. None at all. I visited the ship, and the captain said he had come and gone."

"You should not have made contact with that ship. I want to keep you an unknown. You know what to do next. Unless he has the item with him and was just delayed, eliminate him. No leaks. But find his package and retrieve it."

The man called two men that he had on retainer, described Joe Smollock, and told them to find him. It did not take them long to find someone who had seen him going into the customs office.

The man called David Brumley. Brumley shouted, "He did WHAT? Took it to the customs office? Why?"

"I didn't want to ask questions like that. It was risky even knowing about the man. They wanted to know what my interest was."

"That was a million dollars! One million dollars!"

"Yes. How do you suggest that I meet expenses, now?"

"Surely you have some reserve. I pay you enough. I'll send another package, but it will take a week to get it there."

"I can hold out for a week. But this one better get here."

"We will have to arrange a secure transfer. The Jessie Bell is coming in next Tuesday. She is a charter sailboat, taking a group to the Caymans next weekend. Have someone meet her. You set the password and the role play."

The man waited a beat. Then, "Okay. I'll have a woman come to talk about a charter. Her code word will be that she is on a ricochet romance. She will bring a briefcase with her to swap, or load."

"Swap. The captain will not know what is in the case."

Molly looked back at the harbor as they headed out to sea. "I sure would like to hear what he says when he hears about this."

"Listen in and see," Mista said, only half listening. He was concentrating on staying in the channel.

"I've never met the man," Molly said.

"Talk to Jeremy," Mista said without looking at her.

"Well!"

"Sorry. I'm busy at the moment."

Molly raised a shoulder in pique and climbed down the ladder to the main deck to go find Jeremy. Mista was so maddening. Sometimes he seemed to be totally interested in her, and other times he might not even know she was there. There were very few men who could ignore Molly's presence. Mischal was the other one. Mischal did pay her no mind. Jeremy would notice her.

Jeremy was in the salon, studying. He smelled her perfume the moment she opened the hatch, but did not look up. Molly walked over to the table and stood a minute, waiting for Jeremy to notice her. After a full minute, she said, "Jeremy."

He looked up. "Yes?"

"Are you busy?"

"Well, yes. What can I do for you?"

"If you're not too busy, I need some help with our project." She was beginning to wish she had not come. She missed Karl. Karl paid attention to her. Here everything else seemed more important than what she was doing for them.

Jeremy closed his book. "I was just studying. That can wait. What do you need?"

"I'm working on diverting the drugs that this guy Brumley is sending to Florida. I diverted one package and wanted to know how he reacted."

"Oh. Oh, you haven't met him, have you? By the way, we are not sure that he is sending drugs in. He is Sharra's stepfather."

"Oh. That's why she wouldn't do it. And you?"

"You know I'm studying to be a lawyer. I'm not sure that I agree with the actions we will have to take."

"But, we want to trap him."

"Trap is the operative word. I understand what this is all about, and I know that we know that he is guilty. I just don't like the methods we seem to want to use."

"Well, tell me what it's about. I've been kind of out of the loop."

"Yeah, I understand. Well. You know that we are pretty sure that Brumley is the man who kidnapped Mista's sister Sheila when she was eleven, and that he has continued to take girls that age and put them into prostitution."

"That's why Mista adopted his girls. They are bait."

"Yes and no. Yes, they are bait, but he did not have to adopt them. He just got attached to them and wanted to keep them. And they had no parents, so he became their father."

"Sharra's not so keen on the adoption, is she?"

"No, she's okay with it. It just wasn't her idea, and she is a bit slow to warm up to it. Let's see if Brumley has heard."

Jeremy let his mind search. Once he had made contact with the man, he could find him again anywhere on the planet. After a minute, he smiled and said, "Listen in." Molly made contact with Jeremy and shared his connection with Brumley. He had just signed off with his man in Florida and was fuming about his loss. The million was affordable, but there were consequences. People would want to know who smuggled that much cash in and why. They would surely question his captain, who knew nothing. They would be watching all his boats. They would surely look hard at the Jennie Bell when she came in next Tuesday. The fact that she was a charter boat would help, but they would surely look. The woman carrying a case in was a good plan. He'd have to be sure that the case matched the one he would send. Next thing they would begin to impound his boats.

Jeremy backed out. He had heard enough. "Well? What do you think?"

"Still think it's entrapment?"

"No. Entrapment is setting a trap that provokes someone to do something that they would not ordinarily do. He has already done this, and is planning more. All right. I'll help."

CHAPTER 33

Mista and Jeremy talked to the harbor master of the Port of Tampa and told him what was happening and what they were doing. He told them the berth assigned to the Jessie Bell. They asked for a temporary berth near enough that they could observe the Jessie Bell when she came in, promising to do nothing to interfere with the operation of the other boat. They did not talk to the customs officials.

Mista called FBI Agent Ross and briefed him. He said that Brumley was planning another delivery the following week.

Ross said, "You need to stay out of it. Let us do the investigation and arrest."

"You won't be able to. If he repeats what happened last week, he will have cash with him, but neither you nor I can prove that it was ever on that boat."

"We'll be there, anyway."

"Fine. If we can't make him give it up, we'll spot him for you. It is illegal to carry large amounts of currency into the country, isn't it?"

"Yes, but you have to prove it."

Molly was stretched out on a blanket on the flying bridge, sunbathing, when the Jessie Bell came in. Jeremy was working on the anchor capstan. Neither one seemed to be paying attention to the Jessie Bell. Molly raised up and watched her pass and then lay back down.

Customs agents made a much more thorough search than usual. They inspected packages carried by the passengers and compared the declaration lists with the products. They searched obvious places in the boat for concealed packages, but did not have a search warrant for an invasive search. The agents left after nearly an hour, and the passengers were not far behind.

After another half an hour a woman walked down the pier to the boat. She was dressed in a revealing sundress and high-heeled sandals. She had a black briefcase chained to her wrist. Her blond hair fell loose around her shoulders. Every man on the boat stopped work to stare.

She stepped lightly aboard and asked for the captain. When he came out on deck, she said, "I'm interested in chartering a trip to Grand Cayman with my new boyfriend."

"We just got back, ma'am. Won't be able to go again for another week."

"You sure? I just busted up with my husband, and I guess this is what you'd call a ricochet romance. I just want to get away with him for a week."

"Hmmm. Come down below, and we'll talk about it."

They went down and then came back up a few minutes later. She said, "I like your boat, but I need to sail today. I want as much of the week as I can get. Goodbye."

Molly lay on her stomach with her head turned away from the other boat, but she had a mirror set up so that she could see people coming and going. As soon as the woman left the Jessie Bell and turned away, Molly leaned up and made mental contact. She began immediately to try to persuade the woman to go to the customs office. However, she was not open to the suggestion. She had been warned that a man had gone to the customs office last week for no apparent reason, and warned that she had better not repeat that.

Molly sensed her resistance. The woman reached the head of the quay and hesitated briefly and then turned toward the customs office. Molly kept a light touch. The woman wondered idly what was in the case she was carrying. None of her business, but she couldn't help wondering. She stopped at the door of the customs office. *What am I doing? This is what Masters said happened last week. The guy just went into the customs office for no reason. That's what I was about to do. Good grief! I'd be dead.* She turned and walked quickly back to where she had parked her car.

Molly sent to Jeremy, *She broke the suggestion. You want to try?*
Sure.

Jeremy worked his way around the capstan to a point where he could see the woman and sent a mental probe. She had just unlocked her car and was about to get in. He laid a gentle but strong suggestion in her mind, *The best thing I can do is leave this in the customs office. They'll thank me for it.* She closed her car door without getting in. *I really should leave this at the customs office. It must be for them.* She started back up the street, went half a block and stopped suddenly. *Whoa! Masters will kill me. Why am I even thinking about it?* She turned and walked quickly back toward her car.

Molly called Mista. "No luck. Give her to the FBI."

Mista called Ross, and he sent two agents to arrest her. One of them showed her his badge. "I am James Fitzhugh, FBI agent. May we see what you have in that case?"

"Certainly not," she said. "I have private papers in here and you have no right to demand to see them. I don't even have the key."

"I'm afraid we will have to arrest you, then."

"For what? I've done no wrong."

"Where did you get that case?" they asked.

"I brought it from my office. You can see that it's chained to my wrist."

"You brought that case from the boat up there. Please accompany us to the customs office. If it came in on the boat, it must be declared."

"This case was never on that boat. I went down to charter the boat and now I'm going back to my office."

Ross spoke in their ears. "Leave her. We have no probable cause."

"Sorry to bother you, ma'am." They turned and left. Mista watched, and then called Robin up on deck. "See that lady there, walking toward a car?"

"Yes."

"Can you burn the case she's carrying?"

Robin looked up at him. "Yes. You want me to?"

"Yes."

Robin concentrated on the case and a few seconds later smoke began to curl out of its seams. A few seconds later flames began to leak out of the case, just as she opened her car door. The woman dropped her car keys, opened her purse and fumbled frantically for the key. Suddenly, she remembered that she did not have a key to the chain, and the case was burning fiercely. She had had a key to the chain on the case she took aboard the boat, but she had left that with the boat. The chain was hot enough to burn her, and flames were threatening her dress. She looked up and down the quay. No ladders close by, going down to the water, and the water was too far below the dock level for her to dip the case in the water. She tried, anyway, but she could not reach it, and she was getting serious burns on her arm. Her dress caught fire. Out of options, she turned and jumped into the harbor.

One of the men on the boat saw her jump, and he jumped in and swam to her to pull her out. She gave him a terse 'thank-you', and stomped up the quay back to her car, the burned-out case swinging.

The agents ran over and asked if they could help.

"No. Leave me be. I don't know what's in there to made it burn so."

"I thought you said it was papers?"

"I thought it was. That's what I was told. I don't have a key to it. I just took their word."

She got into her car and drove away. Jeremy followed her mentally as she went to the rendezvous with her boss, and gave the FBI the location. They had the name that the man had given his courier, Jake Masters, but had no way to know if it were really his true name. They did have a good mental description.

Ross drove to the location given and took a picture from half a block away. Then he called Mista. "I see the man, and took a picture. We'll ID him. What is his relationship in this?"

"I don't know, exactly. He called Brumley and told him that the first money shipment went astray. Brumley arranged to send him another bundle. He seems to handle business for Brumley here, but I have no idea what. He sent him a million dollars, though, and that's serious business."

"How did you know that? The customs people would not have told you."

"No. We have our own way of finding out."

"Of course. I should have known. Well, we will put a watch on him."

Once again, Brumley said "WHAT? What happened this time?"

"Well, Mary – my courier – says that the FBI tried to arrest her and then suddenly the case caught on fire. Caught on fire while it was chained to her wrist. "

"So now I have another million gone, this one burned up?"

"Right. Now what do we do? I have to make some payments. They're holding up product. I guess you'll have to bring it yourself. Or wire it to me."

"Can't wire that much without attracting attention. Can't bring it in legally. You could come get it."

"No way. I'm not taking that risk. We've never had trouble with this before. What's happening?"

"How would I know? Maybe your couriers have been bought."

"No way. Maybe Joe, but not Mary. I have used her for years. I pay her well, and she knows not to ask questions. I always chain the case to her wrist, and she doesn't have a key. She's never failed me."

"Maybe she thought she was carrying cash, and could just take it and run."

"No way. She knows that I'd find her."

"She could hide pretty well with a million dollars."

"Yes, but she would not suspect that she had that much, even if she did think it was money. No, somebody knows."

"Somebody knows who your couriers are?"

"I don't know. They know something. Maybe they have made the couriers."

"Was anyone watching," Brumley asked.

"No. I drove by before she went aboard. Nobody was around except one sailboat, and they weren't paying attention."

"How can you be sure?"

Masters said, "There was a girl asleep on the flying bridge, or at least sun-bathing. There was a workman painting something up in the bow, but he had his back to the boat. Anyway, another crewman came back and they got underway before Mary got back to her car."

"They could have been spotting for the FBI or somebody. That doesn't explain how the case caught on fire, though. Your girl Mary must have set it on fire."

"No, I don't think so. She got burned pretty bad, herself. Remember, she didn't have a key, so couldn't get it off. Ended up jumping into the harbor to put out the fire. She was mad as a wet hen. I had to promise her a new dress and shoes, and pay her medical bills."

"Well, I still don't trust her. I'll bring you the cash. I'll have to get the Jessie Bell back to pick me up. It'll be ten days. But I don't have another boat that I can divert, and I can't go through customs, so I'll have to come in on the boat."

Jeremy and Molly listened in to that conversation, and when it was over, they looked at each other for a minute. Molly said, "They made the boat. If it's there next time, they will know we are involved."

"Yeah. I better hide on the pier and wait."

"You can make yourself invisible, right?"

"Yeah. They won't see me."

"We better be near. We can have Mischal come over in the dinghy and pick you up after."

Jeremy said, "That's an interesting development. Maybe we can get our hands on the big guy himself."

"Is it illegal to bring money into the country?"

"There are some rules. There is a limit on how much cash you can carry in or out. Less than a million dollars. It's actually $10,000, if I recall correctly. You can wire money from bank to bank, of course, but then you have to get it out of the bank. If he is talking about large payments, though, he has a problem. Banks have to report deposits and withdrawals of $10,000 and over."

"So," Molly mused, "he brings cash in directly. But where does he get it?"

"Well, that's the question, isn't it? He probably has an account in an off-shore bank where he keeps his money that he doesn't want the United States government to see. Then he can take cash out, transport it to this country, and use it however he wants to, without arousing suspicion."

Mista walked up and said, "You have learned a lot about our country already, haven't you, Jeremy? Hard to believe you came here for the first time just a year ago. I hear that Grand Cayman is popular for keeping illicit accounts. Some of them are not actually illicit, but a place to keep money without having to report it to anyone. If he is into drugs, as we suspect, and prostitution, which we know, then he doesn't want Uncle Sam to know about that money."

"Who is Uncle Sam," Molly asked.

"Sorry, just slang," Mista said. 'Uncle Sam' is slang for the United States government. I'm not sure exactly where it came from, but the story is that the initials, US, were expanded to 'Uncle Sam' during an early war. The war of 1812."

"Interesting," Jeremy said. "But if you are right about his drug and prostitution business, that has to be a cash business, then. So he must also take cash out."

"Yes, probably the same way, by courier. He could do some money transactions under the cover of his freight businesses. They would normally handle large amounts of money. We'll probably never know what all he uses for bookkeeping. But if we can trace even a few things to him, we can nail him."

"Well, to bring you up to speed," Molly said, "he is coming in himself in a week or so with more money. Since we busted the last two of his couriers, he is running a little scared. Maybe we could have the FBI arrest him when he takes the money off the boat?"

"They would not have any reason to suspect him," Mista said.

"We could tell them."

"Yes, but they need to have provable cause," Jeremy said. "We know what is happening, but the courts would never accept our evidence. So, even if they did arrest him and search him, the court would throw it out as an illegal search."

"So the criminal is protected and all those girls are at risk?" asked Mista.

"The basic idea is to protect ordinary citizens from harassment," Jeremy said. "I have no quarrel with that philosophy. However, it does make it harder to catch a thief."

"Well, we will need to be here when he comes in," Mista said. "We'll do something. Maybe just burn his own money case."

"They saw our boat this time. Didn't connect us with the accident, but if we are there again, they probably will," Jeremy said.

"That's okay," Mista said. "I don't mind if he knows that we are onto him. I think we'll stand out to sea while we're waiting."

CHAPTER 34

As soon as they were clear of the channel, Mista raised sail and set a course a little west of south. His intention was to sail up and down the Florida coast just out of sight of land. He wanted to get a feel for the flow of traffic into and out of the harbors along the coast. Tampa, he knew, would be the primary freight harbor, but he expected to see other boats coming and going as well. Fishing boats, as a matter of course, but also private cruisers and sailboats. He had had the radar checked and calibrated while in the dockyard, but it did not need any adjustments. The seller had told the truth about his electronics upgrade. They could see large ships on the radar screen up to 25 miles. Boats were a mixed bag. Most small boats were either wood or fiberglass and could not be seen more than a few miles. Larger boats tended to be steel construction, and, depending on the size of the boat, could be seen much further. Mista kept in mind that not all large boats were steel – his own was wood.

Had he been looking just for maximum boat traffic, he would have looked on the east coast. Miami and West Palm Beach had many more boats and boatyards than the area around Tampa. However, he knew that his quarry, David Brumley, had a base in or near Tampa, and he expected his shipping to come into that port.

As soon as the boat was steady on course, Mista called Molly and asked if she wanted to take a turn on watch.

"I don't mind, but I have absolutely no idea what I'm supposed to do."

"Basically, steer the boat, keeping it on course. Keep an eye on the direction of the wind so that the sails are in the right position."

"I wouldn't know how to change them."

"I wouldn't ask you to, since you are new to the boat. Just call me or Mischal if you have a question. The most important thing is to be on the lookout for other ships and boats. We have radar watching, too, but I like to actually sight any contacts. We might have to change course to avoid another boat. Ships should avoid us, but if they don't, then we need to take evasive action."

"Sounds complicated."

"I'll stay with her and show her everything," Charly said.

"Good. Once she gets used to it, put her on autopilot. The navigation system installed in this boat is really more than I expected. It is tied into a computer that displays charts on command and plots our position and track on a large computer screen. The radar is also tied in and the computer plots the position and track of any ships it picks up. If it looks like we are going to pass too close to the other ship, the computer sounds an alarm. Still, I like to have human eyes up there."

Mista went below and logged onto his computer. He had already tested the installation and knew that it worked, but now he wanted to see just how well it worked. He had had his satellite antenna installed on a short tower on the flying bridge, The antennae itself was inside a fiberglass hood and mounted on gimbals, keeping the antenna platform horizontal at all times no matter how the boat rolled or pitched. He also had a gyroscope attached which kept the antenna platform always pointing north. The antenna itself could be rotated and raised or lowered to line up with the satellite. Once locked on, the platform remained stable, keeping the antenna always pointing at the satellite. This was the same basic system used to create ships' gyrocompasses.

Mista called up Google Earth. He had a paid subscription that gave him faster access and better resolution than the free version. He scanned up and down the west coast of Florida, taking a close look at the harbors of Tampa and St. Petersburg, and then Ft. Myers. He could clearly see the boats and ships docked, but also all traffic on the gulf. Sharra and Chandri watched over his shoulder as he worked.

"He leaned back after a while and said, "Let's look at West Palm Beach." He adjusted the view to show the east coast of Florida and then zoomed in for a closer look.

"Wow!" Chandri said. Look at all those boats."

"Yeah. All shapes and sizes. There are only a few on this coast as large as ours. But that makes it easier to spot one we might be looking for. Too bad this picture is not real time. We could follow the boats or ships he uses wherever they go."

Chandri asked, "Can the government track ships in real time?"

"I'm pretty sure that they can," Mista said. "However, I have no way of really knowing. I'm sure that information would be classified. What we should have done was put a GPS bug on that boat. Then we could get it's location at any time, and plot it ourselves. Well, next time."

Mista said, "Play around with it if you like." He went back topside to talk to Molly.

He watched her at the helm for a while, and then said, "How are you doing?"

"Got the hang of it. Not hard. Boring, though. Just stand here and turn the wheel back and forth."

Mista grinned. "More boring than lying on deck improving your tan?"

She smiled. "No. But I can sleep while sunning. Hard to sleep here."

"Well, put it on autopilot. We aren't really going anywhere, just hanging out to observe traffic and then to be in position when Brumley comes in."

"Okay. Done. Now what do I do?"

"You still need to stand on watch. I don't entirely trust machinery to keep us safe. Even though I am a computer person, I trust people to make decisions more than I do a computer. And sometimes the computer gets off track, or the radar is a little off, and it takes a person to take charge. Some of the worst maritime accidents were caused by trusting radar and not putting an eyeball on the scene. Next. You still have contact with the captain of that boat? Has he been informed of our little interference?"

"Yes, and yes, he has. Well, not directly. He was given orders to go back to Grand Cayman as soon as he could resupply and get underway."

"Good. How about Brumley?"

"I don't have any contact with him. I've never seen him."

"Oh, that's right. That's what you were trying to say earlier, when I was too busy to listen. Well, with any luck, you'll see him soon, and then you can start working on him."

"Working on him? What do you have in mind?"

"I want to implant a suggestion to kidnap my girls again."

"Again? Wasn't once enough?"

"I've talked to them. They are hyped up about it. For them, it is a chance to get back at him for taking them the first time. Robin's talent has progressed quite a bit, and Janice has improved her skill with a sword. And knife. She's not likely to have access to a sword. We'll have to be sure to get Misch to equip her. I want to catch him in the act and then take him down hard. If he has possession of my girls, and is attempting either to rape them or sell them, I'll have him by the short hairs."

"Oh. I'm not sure I'd want my daughter to be bait for a man like that."

"If she were older and trained, you might. Would you be afraid to go into his den yourself?"

"Hah. Not me. But I've been around, you know. I can take care of myself."

"I know. So can my girls. But I intend to be right behind them. You and Jeremy can monitor them and also listen in on Brumley."

"Yes, but we can't keep that up for very long at a time."

"No, but you can take turns. Just check in on him from time to time. And you can set a link with Robin or Janice so that they can call you if something happens. Keep an eye out. Call one of us if you need a decision."

"What if I meet another boat?"

"If it's a ship, they are required to avoid us, because sail is not as maneuverable as a powered ship. If it's another sailboat, then the one to windward has to avoid the other one. Same reason – the boat to windward has more room to maneuver."

Mista picked the phone at the helm station and called Jeremy's room. Jeremy answered after several rings. "Yes?"

Mista said, "I need to do some planning. I'll be down in a minute."

"Right. I'll be here."

Mista walked down the passageway to Jeremy's stateroom and dropped into a chair. The boat was heeled over slightly in the light wind, but Mista was used to being at sea. The boat had handholds everywhere, but he prided himself on not needing them.

"What's up?" asked Jeremy.

"You can contact Brumley?" It was more a statement than a question.

"Yes, of course."

"What are his plans now, can you tell?"

"Just a minute." He sent his mind out. Brumley was talking to the captain of the Jessie Bell.

"I need you to return to Grand Cayman immediately," Brumley said.

"But, we just came in, sir."

"I know. But I must come to Tampa immediately, and I cannot come in any other way."

There was silence for a moment. Then the captain said, "Very well. I need to give my crew a little time on the beach. We'll leave tonight. But, don't forget, it's at least five days to get there and five to get back. I'll also need to pay a bonus to my crew for leaving again so soon."

"Oh, all right. I'll pay them. Can't you shorten the time? Run on engines and sail?"

"We can make a little more speed by running the engine all the way, but that is a lot of fuel. We'll pick up the trade winds once we get past Key West, I can probably get there in four days."

"Well, just do the best you can. It's important."

Then he called his security chief. "How soon can you get here?"

"I've got to rendezvous with a contact tonight and take on cargo. I'd say six days."

"You've got that fast cruiser, what takes so long?"

"I'm at the other end of the Caribbean, that's what. What's happening?"

"I've lost two shipments in as many days. I'll have to take cash payments in myself. Banana boats are too slow, the Jessie Bell is in Tampa, and I can't risk going in commercial."

"You have your own plane."

"They will be watching that like buzzards circling. No, I have to go by boat."

"Well, we'll be heading for Tampa for the delivery. I'll meet you there."

Jeremy told Mista what he had heard. "Looks like we shook him up good."

"Yes. I'll head south and try to pick him up at sea and shadow him I'd also like to see what kind of cruiser he has. I'll bet that is where the drugs come in. Assuming that he does deal in drugs."

"I didn't get any indication of what the cargo was, but I suspect that you are correct."

Mista walked back to the salon to get some coffee. Sharra was there, talking with Sheila. "What's up?" Mista asked.

"Nothing. Just talking about what's for dinner."

Sheila said, "Did you know that this stove stays level no matter what the boat does?"

Mista smiled. "No, but I'm not surprised. Must be mounted on gimbals. Otherwise it would be pretty hard to cook."

"Yes. I didn't know if I'd be able to actually cook anything or not. But it works well."

"The only problem is," Sharra said, "we have used up most of the good stuff. We've got hamburgers and peanut butter."

"Any corned beef left?"

"Oh, yes. Plenty of that. But, like I said, we've used up most of the good stuff."

"Well, I was heading south, but we've got a couple of days before we have any action. Why don't we pull into Clearwater and restock. Also, I've been thinking. Maybe we would be advised to buy health insurance."

"We have always paid our own bills," Sharra said.

"I know. But I think maybe we would save some by buying insurance. Also, we always have trouble getting into a hospital on just our promise to pay. I'll go ashore and arrange it while you all do some shopping."

CHAPTER 35

They were ready to leave again by 4:00, but Mista said, "Why don't we eat out tonight? I'm in the mood for some good seafood."

Robin jumped up and down, clapping her lands. "Yes! Let's go."

Janice was already more grown-up than that, at twelve, and she simply smiled and said, "Sounds good to me."

Mista asked the dock master if he knew any good local restaurants specializing in sea food.

"Sure. Two blocks up and turn right. Two more blocks. Can't miss it. Better go early, though. There's always a line."

"Okay, thanks."

After the meal, Mista ordered coffee for himself an deserts for any who wanted one. Then he pulled out the receipts from the insurance company. "I have contracted health and accident insurance for our entire group. I didn't see any sense getting maximum coverage, since we are all healthy. I don't know yet if they will cover Samantha. But we have a doctor's co pay of $20.00 and 20% of any hospital stay."

"Why don't we just pay as we go. That's what we've been doing," asked Mischal.

"For average users, the insurance will cost more than direct payment. It seems to me to be like paying for your medical care over time. But it also covers catastrophic events and major diseases, like cancer. An emergency room visit can easily cost five or ten thousand dollars. More if they have to do surgery. When Charly got shot last year, it cost $10,000, and all they had to do was check her. When Jasmine was shot, I think the bill was something like $100,000. You remember, Sharra? It would have been paid by the insurance provided by Biotech, since we were working for them at that time."

"I think that was right, Mista."

"So for routine, it just spreads the cost out, and pays for major emergencies. But also, it solves the problem of admission to a hospital. They like to see an insurance card. Here is the group number we are covered under. This receipt is enough for temporary coverage. We will all get cards in a week or so. If we happen to be home."

"Just what we need. A card to carry," Mischal said.

"Well," Mista continued, "it also covers accidental death, so if someone should be lost overboard, they will pay for her. Depending on who it was, probably more than she was worth."

Robin stared at her empty plate, blushing slightly, and refused to look up or speak. She knew who he meant.

"Hmmm. It says it pays $50,000 for accidental loss of life. I could probably save some money if I could get it to just pay what people are worth."

Robin continued to look down.

"You think you are worth $50,000, Robin?"

"Yes. I'll be worth more when I'm grown. I don't care what anybody says. I didn't mean to go over the side."

Sharra said, "He's just teasing, Honey. We know you are worth more than just money."

When they walked back to the boat later, Robin took Mista's hand and walked beside him. "You do think I'm worth more than $50,000, don't you, Daddy?"

Mista said, "Of course, Sweetheart. I was just teasing. If it is alright with everyone, we'll spend the night in port and get underway in the morning."

"All right with me," Sheila said. "Be nice to be able to sleep without worrying about rolling out of bed."

Robin said, "You need to get a big chair, Daddy. I miss not having one."

"I'm afraid it would crash through the side of the boat in heavy weather," Mista said. "However ... I miss it too. Maybe there is a chair made for boats that can be bolted in place. I'll check. Meanwhile, I guess we could stretch out on the bed for a few minutes before you go on to your room."

Since there was no hurry, they ate breakfast first and waited for the morning traffic to slow before getting underway. When they cleared the harbor, Mista set his course due south. Since the wind was from the northeast, it would set them a little to the west. He asked Chandri to plot a course for Key West, taking into account the wind offset.

She came up a few minutes later and said, "Why don't we go to Dry Tortugas, since all we have to do is wait around anyway?"

"Sure. Make a course for Dry Tortugas." He knew that the tiny key with the old prison on it was about sixty miles west of Key West, so his current course would not be far off.

"Okay. Already did. 184 degrees."

"Hah. Ahead of me?" he put the rudder over and settled on the new course and then checked the tell-tales on his sails. They were small tassels on the sails that told him if the sails were in proper trim for best sailing. The small correction left the sails in trim, so no adjustment was required. He noticed Janice following his gaze. "You know what I'm checking?"

"No. I don't see anything."

"See those little tassels? They hang straight down if the sail has the wind just right. You can't preset a sail, because so many little variables happen all the time."

"Okay. Can I steer some?"

"You remember your rules for meeting other ships and boats?"

"Yes. Want me to say them?"

"No, just keep them in mind, and be sure to take action, or call somebody in plenty of time. You know your sailing points?"

"Some of them. This is called a broad reach, right?"

"Right, with the wind from behind the beam. Or, properly, abaft the beam. What is 'in irons'?"

"I guess when you don't have room to turn."

"Not exactly. It means when you are heading straight into the wind. We can't sail, that way, of course, so the boat would come to a stop. If you get cornered somewhere, like off a coast, or near rocks and the wind is setting you onto the rocks, you might have to turn into the wind, and then you would be in irons. You can't move. I guess that's where that expression came from. You might find yourself aground before you can find a good course out. Lesson: always be aware of anything to windward of you."

The boat had a four-foot mahogany wheel, almost bigger than Janice. She felt dwarfed by the wheel, but she had her sea legs by now, and this gave her something solid to hold onto. She relaxed after a few minutes, and the boat settled on a steady course.

Charly came to relieve her after an hour. "I thought I would be here all day," Janice said. "My arms are about to break."

"You should have put it on autopilot," Charly said. "You don't have to actually steer this thing all the time. Let it steer itself. You need to be here, though, to look out for traffic. I'll take over for a while."

The wind was light, and the seas low, so the Wolfhunter fell into an easy rhythm. Mista checked with Chandri on their progress. She showed him the track and the course she had plotted. "We are steering a little toward the east to compensate for the wind. As you can see we are pretty well on track. I guess I figured the wind offset about right."

"Yep. You did. Only making a little over five knots." He studied the sails. "Sails look right. I guess that's pretty good for the light wind we have. Take us a good two days to get to Dry Tortugas."

"Yes, about 120 miles a day at this speed."

"We don't want to come up on it in the night. There are other rocks and little keys in the area. If we get too close, we need to turn out into the Gulf and come back later."

"Okay. I'll be up for the morning watch, so I'll check our position then."

It became obvious toward the end of the next day that they would get to Dry Tortugas during the night, so Chandri changed course to the southwest, and then back to the east the next morning. Mista dropped sails when they got close and came in under power. They spent half a day exploring the old fort, and then headed back to sea.

Mista set just enough sail to maintain steerageway and then asked Jeremy to check on Brumley and his captains.

Jeremy reached out with his mind and then reported. "Can't tell much from the captain of the sailing boat. I think he must be just rounding the western end of Cuba. Another day to get to Grand Cayman. The other boat, the cruiser, just pulled into Grand Cayman, and Brumley is aboard, demanding that they get underway. That's the boat that his security chief, Karackish is on. They were taking cargo, but were not saying what that cargo was. I think that's the one to watch. She's a fast cruiser, should be here in a couple of days."

"I agree. I was thinking of visiting Key West, but I think we better not. Let's head north. I'd like to be in or near Tampa Bay when he comes in. I suspect that this is a drug delivery, and I'd like to see how he does that."

Mista put the rudder over to turn right onto a westerly course. The booms swung across the boat to the opposite side as the apparent wind shifted. Mischal took the sheets on the mainsail, and Charly took the Mizzen. They let the sheets out to set the sails properly, relative to the wind. As soon as he was clear of the rocks around the keys, Mista turned north, and they adjusted sails again. Mista said, "You catch all that, Janice?"

"I see how you set the sails, and the little telltales are just hanging, like they are supposed to. We are sailing kind of into the wind, now, that's … uh, Oh! That's a close reach, right?"

"Right. That's the sailing point. We make our best speed on a close reach."

Janice said, "How can we make better speed sailing almost into the wind?"

"Look at the sail. See how it bows out in the front, like an airplane wing? That creates a low-pressure area and pulls the boat while the wind also pushes on the back side. The same way an airplane wing works."

CHAPTER 36

They planned to hold their north course until they were just off the Tampa harbor entrance. However, just short of their goal, the wind died to a dead calm. Mista was in the salon and felt the change in the boat's motion, so he came up to see what was happening. Chandri was on watch, and she said, "We lost the wind."

"Yes I see. He looked around and saw a squall line approaching from the west. "There's the reason. Let's get sail down and engines running." He hit the alarm klaxon to call everyone on deck. The last thing he wanted was for that wind to hit the boat with all sails flapping.

Njondac dropped into the engine room and started the engines, while Charly and Mischal manned the sheets. Mista said, "Head directly for the squall line as soon as you have steerageway, Chandri." He dropped the sails as soon as Mischal and Charly were in position, and then told them to secure the booms on the centerline with a sheet fastened to a cleat on each side of the boat.

Then Mista told Molly to stand by to help Chandri if she needed help, and he and Mischal ran to the bow to lower the jib. However, the squall hit before they got there. The boat felt like it had hit another ship. A wall of water crashed on the bow, sending a sheet of spray down the length of the boat. Then the rain hit. It passed in just a few minutes, leaving everyone on deck soaked.

"Wow!" Mista said. "Good thing we didn't take that wind broadside. Many a boat has been capsized by squalls like that."

"We'd have been better off at a pier," Chandri said.

"Actually, no," Mista said. "As long as we were ready for it, which we were, we were safer out here. I'll never forget a squall like that one day when I was in the Navy. We were tied up in Norfolk. You understand, the Navy uses six lines to secure a ship to the pier, and each line was doubled. I saw that squall coming across the Chesapeake Bay, and called my Chief Boatswains Mate. He called all hands on deck, and doubled the lines again. That wind moved us six feet forward against all those lines. Well. That puts us pretty far out. Let's leave the sails down and the jib up and head into port on power."

Chandri said, "You want to take her in, Mista? I'm not all that comfortable in close quarters."

"You'll be okay. Just remember the old rhyme: 'Red Right Returning.' Keep the red buoys or lights on the right when coming into port."

"Okay. But you better stay up here with me. Look! There's a cruiser coming up fast from behind. Looks like he's heading right for us. Isn't he supposed to avoid us?"

"If we were under sail alone, yes. Ooops. Forgot to raise the cone. That tells others that we are under power as well as sail. Not that it really matters, in this case. An overtaking vessel is required to avoid a boat or ship he is overtaking. Looks like he is not obeying that rule, however. Let me take the wheel. Plot his course on the radar scope."

After two minutes, Chandri said, "He's heading straight for us."

"Wonder what his intentions are?" Mista said. I don't know if he is not looking, or what. He certainly should be looking, coming into port."

"He is supposed to have a lookout anyway, isn't he?"

"Yes, but sometimes people ignore that rule. We aren't in the channel, yet." Mista turned directly into the wind. Since he still had the jib up, the boat slowed immediately. He also cut the engines to an idle and put the propellers in reverse, and then sounded four short blasts on his whistle. The other boat made no change, but continued on its course.

Molly came up as the other boat cruised past, still making high speed, heading directly into the channel at what looked like about 24 knots. She said, "That's Arnat Karackish at the wheel. Brumley must be in a hurry."

With the other boat safely past, Mista ran the engines up again and turned toward the channel entrance. He said, "Brumley is in the wheelhouse with him. See him? Now's your chance to make contact."

Molly nodded and sent her mind out. "Yuck. That's a truly evil mind."

"So I've heard."

"I got enough to know what they were doing. He told Arnat to cut us off, he didn't want to have to trail behind a slow sailboat."

"Hah! He didn't recognize us. We need to tie up somewhere near him, so we can observe. I had to take what I could get from the harbormaster. If that's not hear him, we'll just cruise up and down the channel and watch."

It turned out that their berth was one pier over. The customs inspector cleared them after a cursory look at their declaration. He checked the boat's log, which showed only one call at Dry Tortugas, which was a part of the United States. The other boat was cleared a few minutes after, and the two inspectors walked down the dockside together.

Molly and Sharra watched together from inside the pilothouse. They could not be seen through the windows at any distance. Molly said, "You've been awfully quiet on this trip, Sharra."

"I'm not real happy right now."

"Why? Don't you want to see him fall?"

"I do. I want him to fall *hard*. But I don't want to be the agent that makes him fall. It's enough that I am part of it. Besides, what will happen to my mother? And what else will I learn about my father. He might have been up to his neck in their little operation."

"Yeah, I see. It's probably best if you don't have any direct action here. You're too close. Just as long as you really want us to take him down. I'd hate to do the job and then have you mad about it."

"No, I want it done. It needs to be done. Look. There's a man leaving. It's David Brumley."

Molly reached out and *touched* his mind. First she reinforced her earlier suggestion that he wanted Sharra's two girls, wanted them for himself alone, not to share with others. Then she listened for his response. Carefully done, he would think he was feeling his own desires, thoughts that just naturally occurred to him.

Since she denied me when she was their age, it would be payback to take her daughters. Mess with them a lot and then send them back to her all messed up. Serve her right.

As he approached the main dock, Molly sent another thought, a desire to go to the customs office and give them the bag he was carrying. He started to turn and then stopped abruptly. *Now why did I do that? Masters is supposed to be waiting for me down the main street. I certainly don't want to turn in my own money to customs.*

Molly called Mista. "Better get up here and get ready to burn his money again. He resisted my suggestion."

"Be right up."

Mista and Robin climbed up on top of the pilothouse so that they could see better. At this point, he did not care if they recognized him. "See that man? Can you focus on the bag he's carrying and get ready to burn it?"

"Sure."

Mista moved in front of Robin, blocking her vision. Can you still burn it?"

"Of course. I have a focus on it. I don't have to continue to see it with my eyes."

Brumley passed out of sight down the street. Mista said, "Molly, can you follow him and tell me when he meets his contact and is ready to hand over the money?"

"Sure. Let me come up there. Or you come back down to the main deck."

"Okay." Mista and Robin climbed down and waited.

Molly said, "I can't actually see and hear what he does. But if he thinks about it, like if he says something, then I hear his thoughts.

"Okay. He just greeted a man named Masters. He must be in the car. He just said that he brought two million this time."

"Okay, Robin. Burn it. Burn it hot. Maybe we can also do some collateral damage."

Brumley greeted Masters and got in the car. He looked around to make sure that no one was observing them and started to open the bag as Masters pulled out from the curb. The money inside burst into flame just as he started to reach inside. The fire was intense enough to sear his hand and catch the bag on fire instantly. The seat covers caught on fire and their clothes began to burn. Both men opened their doors and jumped out, leaving the car to fend for itself.

It wandered into the opposite lane, the fire spreading rapidly inside the car, and crashed into an oncoming gasoline truck. The truck was not seriously damaged, because neither vehicle was moving fast, but the flames were dangerous. The driver slammed on his brakes and reversed the truck. Unfortunately, the car behind him did not have time to move, and the truck backed over it.

Brumley and Masters were dancing around and swatting their clothes, trying to put out the fires. The truck driver jumped out with a fire extinguisher and ran to the car he had crushed. The woman inside was alive, but unable to move. He did not know how badly she was hurt. The driver could do nothing to help her, but he did call 911. Fire trucks and an ambulance were there in minutes, being housed on the port.

Firemen hosed down the front of the truck, to keep it cool and then foamed the burning car. Two more firemen brought their Jaws-of-Life and began to cut the woman out of the car. It seemed to take forever to cut her out; when they did, she was still alive, but unconscious. The EMS crew rushed up with a gurney, checked her for broken bones and bleeding, and loaded her onto the gurney.

Masters suddenly recognized her. "Good God! That's Mary! Hey! Where are you taking her?"

The ambulance driver said, "Stand back, sir! Give us room here."

"I knew her. Where are you taking her?"

"Central Hospital. Please stand back."

"I didn't know she was down here. Wonder what she was here for? I don't guess it matters."

"Come on back to the boat and we'll get you some clothes. You need to have your car towed, too."

"Yeah. The Lexus is a total loss."

Police had arrived by this time, and one of them stopped the two men. "Excuse me, gentlemen. Were you involved in this accident?"

Masters and Brumley looked at each other. Masters shrugged and said, "Yes. That was my car. The one that burned."

"I need to fill out a report, sir. Where do you want your car towed?"

"The dealer. Maybe he can salvage something."

"Roger. Can you tell me what happened?"

"I was pulling out into the street when the car suddenly burst into flames. I have no idea why."

"The car? What part of the car?"

"The seat between us."

"Hmmm. Car seats don't usually burst into flame for no reason. What was on it or in it?"

"Nothing. I don't understand it."

"Well," Brumley said, "I had a small overnight bag. But just clothes in it."

"What caused it to hit the truck?"

"I don't know. Our clothes were starting to burn and we both jumped out."

"Leaving the car running?"

"I guess. I never even thought about it. I just wanted out."

"You should have stopped the car, sir. You might have a death on your hands, and if that truck had caught on fire …"

It took an hour to finish the local investigation, have vehicles towed and to clean up the streets. The police officer gave Masters a ticket for failing to have his vehicle under control.

When he released them, Brumley said, "Let's walk back to the boat and get you something to wear. We need to make some plans, too."

"I'll say. What are you trying to do to me? That's three firebombs you've sent me."

"Me? Do to you? I wouldn't burn four million dollars of my own money!"

"I don't even know if there was any money in any of those packages. Our business is not based on trust, you know. You need to show me some hard cash real quick."

Brumley sighed. "How much do you need right now?"

"I need a million right now. I need it two weeks ago."

"I can't move that much cash all at once through normal channels, and you know it. I could take it out of a local bank account, but anything over $10,000 gets reported to the government. I can put it into an overseas account for you, and you can covert it to cash yourself."

"I don't have an overseas account. Wouldn't do me any good. I deal in cash. Checks have handles on them," meaning that his purchases and sales had to be untraceable.

"All right. That boat is worth $7,000,000. Will you take that as security?"

"Security I don't need." He rubbed thumb and fingers together. "I need cash money that I can spend. You can start by buying me a new car. And covering Mary's hospital bills and a new car for her. Then give me whatever cash you can as earnest money on the rest."

"I can do that. Let's get cleaned up and then go buy you a car. Why don't you come back to Grand Cayman with me and I'll give you the money there. Then you can bring it back in. I just wish I knew what was happening."

"Right. You'll send me back in the boat?"

"Correct."

"Deal. A little partying with some of your little girls would be icing on the cake."

CHAPTER 37

Mista stood in the bow with Sharra and Robin watching the two men return to their boat. Mista said, "You done good, Robin."

She grinned. "That was fun."

"Just don't let it get to be too much fun. Hurting people, even if it is necessary, should not be fun."

They saw Brumley pointing at them. "You think he recognized us?" Mista asked.

"Looks like," Sharra said.

Molly tuned in and reported later, "He saw you and said he didn't know how, but you must have something to do with this."

"He remembers when he tried to rape me when I was thirteen. I did not know then that I had any psionic power, but I unconsciously focused on him and he ran from the room holding his head."

Mista said, "He might also be remembering the fires when his men tried to ambush us in that Bed-and-Breakfast. That's okay. I don't mind him knowing that we are closing in on him. I think we might just have his attention, now."

Molly said, "You do. He is fuming. He knows that you must have something to do with the loss of his money, but has no idea how you could. If he could get his hands on you right now … he'd choke you to death. Or so he is thinking." Molly sent another reinforcement to his desire for the two girls and then monitored his response again.

If I could get those girls of hers. That would indeed be double pleasure. Maybe it's time for Sam Smith to appear again. No. They would be afraid of him this time. I'll think of something. Has to be a way. If they don't set a watch, and I bet they don't, in port, then maybe somebody can sneak aboard and carry them off.

Molly said, "He is thinking about having someone sneak aboard tonight and carry you two off."

Robin looked up at Mista. "Is this it?"

Mista nodded. "You ready for it?"

"I'm ready. So is Janice. He'll wish he'd never seen us."

"All right. Go get Janice."

The two girls came back just as Brumley and Masters left the boat again. They could see a taxi waiting for them. Brumley glanced over his shoulder and stared hard at the girls. *Yes. They've grown up a bit. This will be even better.* He said, "Masters, see those two girls on that ketch down there?"

"Yeah. They yours?"

"Not yet. They are my step-daughter's daughters. I'm going to take them and have a gay time with them. With any luck, I'll snatch them tonight, and then we'll make for the islands at first light."

"Your own grand-daughters? That's cool."

"Not really mine. Their mother is my step-daughter. No blood kin. I would have had her when she was their age, but she somehow managed to fight me off. Then she ran off right out of high school. Never saw her again till this summer. Ten years. She must have been pregnant with the oldest one when she ran away. Said she was going to college, but never got there. This will be payback for their mother being so stupid."

"You will share them won't you? Could make this trip much more fun."

"After I've taken their cherries you can have a go."

Mista watched them get in the taxi and leave. Molly said, "He promised to share them with his man there. He's taking him to Grand Cayman first thing in the morning, so he plans to steal you tonight."

"Okay," Mista said. "Here is what we do. I've got two chastity belts for you, an—"

"Chastity belts?" Janice asked. "What is a chastity belt? Is it what I think it is?"

"I don't know what you think, but it is an iron belt that we would bolt around your waist, with an iron strap that goes between your legs. Actually, we should weld them on."

"Iron belts? Wouldn't that hurt?" Robin asked, eyes wide.

"Maybe a little. You'd have to be careful not to grow while you are gone."

"I can't keep from growing!" Janice said.

"Well, that could be a problem. You know, we spent a lot of time in a place where they had knights and kings and things. That's what they did, where we got the belts. When they went on a long journey, or went to war, they might be gone for months or even years. So they'd put one of these belts on their wives, so she couldn't sleep with someone else if she got too lonely while they were gone."

"Daddy, that's terrible!" Robin said. "I don't want to wear an iron belt."

Sharra said, "Mista if you don't quit teasing those girls they won't know what to believe."

Mista grinned.

Janice said, "You're teasing! Aren't you?"

"Yes, I'm teasing. Aren't you glad that I trust you? Men really did put chastity belts on their wives if they didn't trust them. And many did not trust their wives. Or the men they left to guard their home castles. I don't really have one, and wouldn't put it on you even if I did. I do trust you."

"Thanks, Daddy," Robin said, putting her arm around him. "We don't want to have sex with that old man, anyway."

"Well, there is danger here. It's not so much that you don't want it — and I do believe that you don't — but he will surely try to force you. Now, here is what I really want to do. Molly you enforce his desire, you and Jeremy. Make him want them so bad that he can't wait to get them into a room alone."

He turned to the girls. "He'll be looking at you like he can see right through your clothes."

"I've seen men like that," Janice said.

"Yes, I guess you have. With many men, it is just looking. In this case, it could be danger. Now, Molly, can you flavor his desire so that he wants them only for himself? So that he will let no one else have them?"

"I can try. I believe I can. There is always a chance that he will resist successfully, as he did this afternoon. But I think I can."

"Okay, good." Mista sat back against the anchor capstan, bringing his face level with the girls. "Now I really do not want you to be hurt in any way. I do not want him to rape you. I realize that I am putting you in harm's way."

"You aren't doing it, Daddy," Janice said. "We volunteered for this. We know the risks, and it will be our first real fight for you."

"Thanks, honey, but I am still responsible, and it scares me. I don't want you hurt. However, you can expect that he will take action. You know he will. He'll probably want your clothes off, first. That's not something I look forward to, and I'm sure you don't either. Fight him off, put him off, whatever you want to do. Janice, you are my tanker girl. I wouldn't be surprised if you put on a show for him. Not that I'm asking you to, you understand."

Janice grinned. "Worse things have happened to me. So he sees me. So what? It's just looking."

"Well, I don't want him seeing me," Robin said.

"Yes," Mista said, "you two are very different about things like that."

"Don't worry, Daddy," Janice said. "It's just part of the game. That's as far as he will get, though. I'll kill him first."

"You probably won't have a weapon."

"With my bare hands, if I have to."

"And I'll burn him."

Mista grinned. "Don't lose your courage when it starts to happen and you'll be all right. Robin, you can control your fire, right? Make is little or big?"

"Yep."

"Okay, when he starts to get serious, that is, when he starts to take you, put a little fire in him somewhere. Between his legs, in his belly, on his face, wherever you want to. Just a little. Don't kill him, but just hurt him. What will happen is that he will have a driving desire to take you, but every time he tries, he will burn. He'll back off. I don't think he will give up, but will back off and try again later."

Robin grinned. "Yeah. That'll be fun."

"Okay, just enough to hurt him and prevent him from actually raping you. Same with Janice. When he comes at her, you burn him a little in a place that hurts."

"What if she's not in the same room?"

"Hmmm. Molly set a link with them so that they can call you at will. I realize that that is an energy drain. Maybe you and Jeremy want to take turns with the link. Sharra, you might want to help with that."

"That I'll be glad to do. I don't want them hurt either."

"Okay. One of us will always have a link. Not an active contact, that takes too much energy. But the link so that you can call, or if you are threatened directly it will activate automatically. Then whoever has the link with you will call Robin and let her know when to burn him."

"That will be great," Janice said. "I love it."

"All right, now, if he gets too frustrated, he might just tell his man to have a go at you. Same thing. Burn him. Don't kill him, but you might want to do some serious hurt on him."

"Okay," they both said at once. Mista shook his head. They saw this as an adventure, ignoring the danger. He desperately hoped that they would survive intact.

Mista said, "Now I need to find Mischal and Charly. We need to set a watch to see when and how they offload their special cargo."

He found Njondac supervising the fuel top off and talking with Mischal. Mista walked up and said, "You going to set a watch tonight?"

Mischal said, "Yes, I think we ought to. It seems safe, here, but you never know."

"You might want to watch that other boat also. You know that they have some kind of cargo that they don't talk about."

"Meaning drugs, I suppose."

Mista shrugged. "They don't talk about it, so we don't know. We do know that they were in South America somewhere taking a transfer from another boat. Could be anything. I assume that it is probably drugs."

"Oh, yeah. That makes it more interesting. I'll put Charly on the mid and Chandri on the morning watch. She likes to get up early anyway."

"Ya don't need me in the rotation," Njondac said, "but if something happens, ya be sure to call me. I'm tired of settin' around doin' nothin'."

"Let's go see Jeremy."

Jeremy and Charly were together in the salon. Chandri was also there, as it happened. Mischal first asked Charly to take the mid-watch and asked Chandri to take the morning watch. "Yes," he said, "we need to stand watch tonight."

Mista said, "Not just for security. I expect them to offload something that they don't want to go through customs. I don't want it to get to its destination."

Charly grinned. "Finally! Some action."

Mista said, "I think it would be foolish to attack them."

"Hah!" Mischal said. "We could take them."

"Probably," Mista said. "But we'd have the police down on us and they'd still get their package where it is supposed to go. Wherever that is. Jeremy, are you good for a sleepless night?"

"If that's what it takes."

"Good. When whoever is on watch sees them taking something ashore, call Jeremy. Jeremy, you check them out. See inside the package if you can. Read their minds. They might not know what they are carrying, and might not even care. You might not see anyone who knows what it is."

"Probably drugs," Chandri said.

"Probably, but we don't know that. They should have instructions for delivery, though. Try to get that name and/or place. Then destroy the package."

"How?"

"Any way you like. I think fire would be too much like a coincidence."

"Hmmm." Jeremy steepled his hands and rubbed his forefingers on each side of his nose, thinking. "I could crush the box or bag and spill the contents. Or I could make them drop it and then burst it open. If it's cocaine, I could *move* some gasoline onto it and saturate it. Wouldn't be much good after that. I could *push* it into the bay."

Mista said, "Well, be thinking about your options. You want it to look as near natural as you can. They'd have a hard time explaining how they dropped a bag of cocaine on the dock."

"That's their problem. It would just slide right out of their hands. Okay. I'll turn in now and get some sleep. Call me when you need me."

"You can do that?" Charly asked. "I've never seen you put yourself to sleep just like that."

"You warriors do it all the time. You train for it, and learn to sleep when you can. It's a good trick to have. I can do it, but don't usually have the need. Now I do ..."

Nothing happened on the first watch. Mischal called Charly at 11:30, and she came up a few minutes later. "Like old times," she said. "Watch-standing is a chore, but at least we are doing something that we are trained for again."

"Yeah. Feels good to be in action. Call me if you need me."

"Like I would? I know. It's good to have backup. I will."

Light flared from the salon windows when he went down. Charly closed her eyes and opened the door. "Mitch! Don't we have red lights in there?"

"Oh. No. Sorry." The lights went out. "They didn't think military when they built this boat. There's enough light from the dock lights that I can see where I'm going after my eyes adjust again. You have a red flashlight?"

203

"Yes." Mischal knew from his military training that red lights do not destroy a person's night vision. He had told Charly some time ago, and she had a flashlight prepared.

Mischal had been gone only a few minutes when a clock somewhere in the pilothouse struck eight times in groups of two. "Ding-ding, ding-ding, ding-ding, ding-ding." Charly started and then laughed. *Mista and his Navy. Didn't know he had a ship's bell clock. Wonder how long they've done the eight-bell thing. One bell at 12:30 and then keep adding a bell till you get to eight. Four hours equals one watch. Then start over. I guess it goes back to hour glasses. Turn the glass every half-hour and strike the bells. I have to figure out what time it is by the bells, but I bet Mista just knows exactly what time it is without even thinking about it. At least I can keep track of time without needing a light.*

Just after the clock struck four bells and Charly thought, *Four bells -- That's 2:00,* she saw movement on the deck of the other boat. It was too far away to see much, but as she watched, she was sure that someone was moving about on the deck. She clicked on her flashlight and dialed Jeremy. "Somebody's moving."

"Right. Be right up."

Jeremy was careful not to turn on any lights. He bumped a couple of chairs, but otherwise made it safely to the pilothouse. Charly pointed out the men who had just gathered on the dock. Jeremy studied them for a minute and then said, "Each one has something. Looks like a small box. They are to leave them in 'the room' in 'the warehouse'. It must be nearby. We could just let them deliver and then call the FBI and let them come pick it up. Once they take it there, I'll know where it is. They've done this before, so they just think 'the room' and so forth."

"Yeah, I figured that," Charly whispered. "It'd be fun to stir them up, though."

"Well, I could bust one and let them deliver the other two. I wonder how much money that stuff is worth?"

"I have no idea. I don't even know the street prices for a little pinch of it. I know it's expensive, though. Must be more than a million dollars there."

"Much more, I bet." Jeremy concentrated. Suddenly the man in the middle dropped his box. It hit the dock with a thud and burst apart with a little help from Jeremy. White powder spilled out and flew in all directions.

All three stopped short. They could hear one man saying, "My God, Charlie! How did you do that?"

They couldn't hear his reply, but they heard another voice say, "He'll kill you!"

Jeremy listened to thoughts. The man who had dropped his box was in a panic. He could not understand how he could have dropped it, but the fact was that he did. There was a little wind and the powder was beginning to blow down the pier. He called his buddies and they began to try to scrape up the remainder, but then had nowhere to put it except in the broken box. That gave Jeremy another idea. They called it 'Blow'. He stirred up a little whirlwind and began to blow the powder all over the pier. It picked up enough that the men had no choice but to breathe it, and soon they were too high to care about the spilled powder. It was blowing away faster than they could clean it up, anyway. Finally they picked up the other two boxes and went on to the warehouse.

Jeremy followed them mentally until they got to the warehouse and then get a mental picture of the building. Then he went down and woke Mista and told him to call his FBI contact and tell him where the powder was stored. Two hours later, two cars pulled up beside the building, lights off. Eight men piled out and entered the warehouse. They searched until they found the cache and took it with them.

When they left, one of the men asked his boss, "Hey, Mr. Ross, what are we going to do with this stuff?"

"Put it in the evidence locker. I don't think we can prove where it came from, but at least it's off the street."

Chandri had only been on watch half an hour when she saw someone walking up the pier. He shuffled and stumbled like a drunk, and was singing loudly to himself. He stopped opposite the Wolfhunter and looked it her for a minute. Then he shuffled over and started up the gangplank. Chandri stepped out of the pilothouse and said, "Go away, old man. Find some other place to sleep."

"Who sez?" he asked, slurring his speech.

"I do. Beat it."

"Okay, okay." He started to turn away, and then whirled quickly and fired a pistol at Chandri. It made almost no noise, just a click and a puff of air. She felt a sting on her chest, and then slumped to the deck before she could raise an alarm.

He waited a minute and then walked on board. When he was on deck, he raised his hands and beckoned. Two more men moved out of the shadows and joined him. Charly was not asleep yet and felt the boat rock. She woke Jeremy and whispered, "They're here."

He used mental speech, *Well, let them. Just be ready in case of trouble. Wonder how they got past Chandri?*

Don't know. Didn't hear anything.

Sharra was also not sleeping. She had strong reservations about letting the girls go, but Mista had insisted, and the girls wanted to. Still, she could not sleep. She felt the boat rock and then heard footsteps above. She heard them going down into the salon, not knowing where the girls would be sleeping. They did not turn on lights and they did not stumble, so Sharra assumed that they were either using red flashlights or had night vision goggles. After a few minutes she heard them come back up on deck and then move aft. Their stateroom and the girls were separate from the rest, and the entrance hatch was aft. She cracked her door slightly and waited. The first man came down the ladder face first. The only safe way to come down a ladder on a ship was to back down. He seemed quite familiar with boats, and walked quickly down, holding the handrails. When he was halfway down, she reached out and held his feet in place. He had only a light hold on the rails, and pitched forward, falling to the deck below with a crash. One of the other men said, "God, Jimmy, you'll wake the dead!"

The second man was more careful, but Sharra sent him an illusion of the last two steps disappearing. His foot was already out and he was off balance. Not seeing a step, he tried to step all the way down to the deck, and sprawled on top of the first man, who was just getting up. The third man made it with no incident, mainly because Sharra was getting back into bed.

The girls were awake, too excited to sleep. They heard the commotion in the passageway and knew that their mother must be messing with the intruders. Janice covered her mouth to suppress a giggle. It wouldn't do for the men to see that they were awake and laughing at them.

They looked into Sharra's room first. When they saw Sharra and Mista, they turned and looked into the girls' room across the passageway. They fired two tranquilizer darts into the girls and then one man picked up each girl, threw her across his shoulder in a modified fireman's carry, and started out. The third man stood in the doorway, waiting. Sharra moved the door, making it slam into the man as he stood there and knocking him across the passageway and into their room. One of the other men whispered hoarsely, "Come on, Jonesy. Stop messing around."

The men carrying the girls went up first. When Jonesy started up, Sharra held his feet at the first step, causing him to pitch forward and strike his head on a step, drawing blood. *Good! I've bloodied all three of them. We'll take that for DNA analysis.*

Jonesy hurried up the ladder and said, "Let's boogey! This is a ghost ship."

Sharra listened to their steps on the deck above, and then went to the hatchway, climbing up enough to see them leaving. When Jonesy was about halfway across the gangplank, she jerked it to one side with a mental push. Not expecting the sudden movement, he was dumped into the water between the boat and the dock. He could not find a ladder on the dock, so had to climb aboard the boat again, and make his way forward. This time, he did not trust the gangplank, and jumped across the water gap.

Sharra came back to bed and lay on her back, eyes open but seeing nothing. Mista rolled over and put his arm around her, drawing her close. "They'll be all right," he said.

"I hope so. But I can't help worrying."

"They know what they're doing, and we'll be monitoring."

"You hope. They're just girls."

"Nearly as old as you were, and they have had some training. You hadn't."

"I know, but … What if you lose them?"

"Can't. They have their GPS watches so we will know where they take them, and we can always know what is happening to them. They'll be all right. They'll be getting underway at first light, and we won't be far behind."

"But they have more speed than we do."

"Yes. That boat is capable of 25 or 30 knots, or I miss my guess. But we know where they're going. We'll be right behind them."

"You hope. OH! Chandri! I hope they didn't hurt her." Sharra jumped up and ran to the ladder. Mista followed. They found Chandri slumped by the door to the pilothouse. Mista found the tranquilizer dart. Mista carried her down to the salon and then called Njondac to take the rest of her watch.

Sharra looked at Chandri and shook her head. "I don't know what we are dealing with here. Capable of murder, that's for sure. At least they didn't hurt her. By the way, Mista, I tripped those men up last night. They all left bloodstains back there somewhere. We should get that analyzed for DNA so we can prove who kidnapped the girls."

"Yeah. At last we have more than just our word. Of course, the man we are really after will probably still have his hands clean. I think the girls will get them dirty for him."

Sharra slept fitfully and was up with the light. She was standing on deck when the other boat passed them on the way out to sea. Arnat Karackish was steering, with Brumley at his side. Brumley said, "That's her," pointing to Sharra. "She is the cause of all my trouble. Nothing has gone right since she came back."

"Well, I can take care of that," Karackish said. He took a silenced assault rifle from hooks on the pilothouse bulkhead, raised it and fired one shot. The boat rolled a little as he fired, so instead hitting her just above her ear, his shot grazed the top of her head. She collapsed, unconscious. The cruiser put on speed and was soon out of sight.

CHAPTER 38

Njondac watched the boat pass and saw Sharra fall. He did not see the shooter or hear the shot, so he did not know what had happened. He ran back to where she had been standing. He saw the blood and looked up at the boat that had passed, but it was already out of sight. He called, "MISTA! Get up here."

His shout was loud enough that everyone on the boat heard it and they all came running, crowding around Sharra and Mista, who was kneeling beside her. Mischal pushed his way through the small crowd and knelt beside Sharra, feeling for a pulse. He looked up. "Move back! Give us room. She is alive."

Molly was the first to take any other action than to look. First she contacted Jasmine. *You need to get to the boat. Sharra's been hurt.*

What happened?

I don't know. We found her on deck with blood everywhere. We're somewhere in the Tampa Bay Port. Head this way, and I'll update you later. Hurry.

On the way. Em will come, too.

Next Molly called 911 and told them to send an ambulance. She did not know the area, but knew that Jasmine must be at least half an hour away. She did not know if they could wait that long.

Mischal was also in action. Memories came back to his wartime medical experiences. He searched for the source of the bleeding and found the wound on her head. It was more than a scratch or simple groove. It had hit low enough to crack bone. Sharra was unconscious, but her pulse and breathing were steady. He looked over at Mista. "It's bad, Bro. Feels like a bullet wound, but I didn't hear a shot. We need to get her into a hospital *NOW!*"

Mista nodded and looked up. He did not have his phone with him, against his own rules. He had jumped straight out of bed and come up when Njondac had called. Molly said, "I've already called 911 and Jasmine. They'll probably have her in a hospital before Jasmine can get here." She could already hear the siren. "Oh. What pier or wharf is this? They need to know."

"Pier 2," Mista said.

The 911 operator was still on the line, and Molly passed that to her. A minute later the ambulance squealed to a stop at the gangway and two medics jumped out. Molly said, "They're here. Thanks for staying with me." The two men had gotten a stretcher out of the back of the ambulance and were running for the gangway. Molly waved them to their location on the fantail.

Mischal, meanwhile, was feeling for broken bones and any other bleeding. He found no other injuries. "Thank God for small favors," he said. "The head wound is bad, but at least there's nothing else."

While the medics were checking Sharra, Molly contacted Jania. *Honey, can you come home right away?*

I guess I could, but why?

Your mother's been hurt. Mischal said she was shot. It looks bad.

How bad? Molly could feel her panic.

I don't know. She's unconscious.

Can you patch me through to her? I can't contact her direct.

Sure. Hold on. Molly tried to contact Sharra, but could not find her. Then she knew that it was bad. Even unconscious, she should be able to at least feel her presence. *Hon, you need to get here. I can't even find her mind.*

I'll come right now. I don't care what they say at school. Tell me what to do.

Go to the airport. We'll arrange a flight for you and I'll let you know where and when.

I'm on the way.

Molly said, "Chandri, can you get Jania an e-ticket? I just talked to her and she's heading for the airport."

"Sure. I'll get on it."

Then Molly contacted her husband, Karl. *Hey! Can you pull strings and get an airplane to San Juan?*

Probably could. What's up?

Sharra's just been shot. Looks pretty bad.

She's alive, right? You're in San Juan?

Yes, she's alive but unconscious. They're taking her to a hospital as we speak No, we aren't in San Juan. Jania is there. I want her here. If her mother has a chance Jania can save her. I'm not sure anybody else could.

If you say so. I didn't know she was that good. I can probably get a plane down there, but look, see what you can get commercial. Figure it'll take an hour to find a plane and pilot ready to go. I know a couple of guys at Cobb Air Force Base. Maybe they have somebody wanting to fly a cross country for training. Anyway, give me an hour. Then figure two hours down there plus the trip back. I'll see what I can do, of course. But if you can get a flight out soon, that would be quicker.

Okay. Thanks for helping, Darling. Chandri is already working on a commercial flight.

Chandri came up from the salon and said, "I've got her on a flight at 11:00. First available flight. I convinced them that it was a medical emergency. It'll be here at 1:14."

"Great. I called Karl. He's trying to see if he can get somebody down to pick her up. If he can get a faster flight, can you cancel that?"

"After them making arrangements? They might charge us anyway."

"Let them. I'm sure Mista would pay it in a heartbeat. He's not thinking right now, you know."

"I know. I remember when she was captured. He thought she had been turned against him, and he was devastated. Didn't even want to live. She's not against him, now, but she might not live. And I know he's blaming himself. Should blame me. I let them on last night."

"You let them?"

"Well, I wasn't cautions enough. They got close enough to shoot me with a tranquilizer gun. So, yes. I let them. I'll never forgive myself."

"Why? They were expecting them."

"I know, but still…"

Molly shook her finger at Chandri. "Don't be blaming yourself. They were ready for the kidnapping. The girls are primed for it and we have support all planned. They did not expect them to take a potshot at Sharra when they left. Your letting the men on board had nothing at all to do with that. Okay?"

"Yeah, I guess. I still feel bad about it."

Molly's cell beeped. "Yes?"

"Karl. A Colonel Ben Evans will be in San Juan airport in an hour an a half. He was just looking for an excuse to fly. He's taking two planes – they will fly formation all the way down and back. He will have a flight suit and oxygen mask for Jania. Tell her that he will taxi to the terminal and she is to meet him there. She'll have to pull the flight suit on over her civvies. He'll have flight boots for her also."

"Great! Thanks, Darling."

Molly turned to Chandri. "Cancel the reservation. Tell them that the Air Force is going to pick her up. Tell them we'll pay for the ticket anyway, or a cancellation fee. Whatever they want. And thanks for being so quick."

The medics started for the gangway with Sharra on their stretcher. Molly called, "Where are you taking her?"

"Central Hospital."

"Okay. We'll be there as soon as we can. Can her husband ride with you?"

"No. We will need room to work. Sorry."

Molly called a taxi. "Better send two. There's a bunch of us."

When the taxis came, Mischal said, "I'll stay with the boat. No point in leaving it open."

Njondac said, "I'll stay wit ya, Bigun."

Molly and Chandri walked on either side of Mista when they went down to meet the taxi. He was not in a daze, but his thoughts were far from the here and now. The last thing that he had expected was for Brumley to shoot his wife when they left. His own step-daughter. Now he had Mista's daughters, and Sharra might not live. And he was the one who had set it all up. Whether Sharra lived or died, that man was a dead man. And if he hurt his daughters – then he would suffer before dying. He did not sound like a philosopher. He did not feel like a philosopher. He was a man who had been wronged, seriously wronged and he would not stand still for it.

They bustled him into the taxi, sitting one on each side. Sheila followed with Charly and Jeremy in the second taxi. Molly called Jasmine to tell her that they were going to the hospital. *You know where Central Hospital is?*
No idea.

Just a minute. She got directions from the driver and passed them on.

Karl called a minute later. "Forgot to tell you that they will be landing at McDill Air Force Base. Somebody will have to meet her there. You know where it is?"

"I have absolutely no idea. I'll take a taxi."

When they got to the hospital, Jeremy headed straight for the emergency operating room. An orderly blocked his way. "You can't go in there, sir."

"Watch me. You need me in there."

"Just a minute, sir." He opened the door slightly and said, "Dr. Baskins? Could you step out a minute?"

"What is it?"

"This man insists on going in there."

"You can't come in while we are operating."

"You need me to help. Trust me."

Mista said, "You *will* let him in. He is the best chance my wife has."

"It is against policy. We have one of the best neuro-surgeons in the state here."

"I respect that," Mista said, "but I also know what my son-in-law can do. Gown him and let him in."

"I will not be in your way, and I will not touch anything," Jeremy said.

They had already cut her hair and prepped her scalp. They were just peeling it back from the wound when Jeremy stepped in. The assisting doctor said, "Have you seen wounds before?"

"Yes. I've been in a war zone." Jeremy checked Sharra's mental state. He assumed that they had her under sedation. He was surprised and worried when he could not find her. He said, "Is she sedated?"

"Yes, of course."

"Good. Is she in a coma?"

"Probably. We cannot know that as long as she is under."

Jeremy nodded and checked the monitors for her life signs. He watched as they cleaned the wound and began to pick out bone fragments and metal fragments. They worked slowly and carefully. An hour later, they had most of the fragments out. The rest lay embedded in the skin that Jeremy could see in the wound. He also saw that the membrane was cut or split. He asked, "Is that her brain that I can see?"

Dr. Baskins stepped back in exasperation. "You are distracting us. Yes that is brain."

Jeremy said, "The membrane will have to be healed."

"It will have to heal itself. Now may we continue?"

"No. I assume that you are about to pick the rest of the fragments out? Those partially imbedded in that membrane and her brain itself?"

"Yes!"

"You will not. I assume that there is risk that your instruments will touch and scar the brain?"

"Of course. It is a risk we must take."

"I will do it. Where do you want them?"

"You cannot touch her."

"I don't intend to. Where do you want them?"

A nurse held up a bowl. Jeremy studied the first fragment that he saw and then *moved* it to the bowl with his mind. The doctor gasped. "How did you do that?"

Jeremy smiled tightly. " It's a little trick I learned. Comes in useful sometimes." He looked at the next one and moved it.

It took him half an hour to move the pieces one by one. Then he said, "Are there any more?"

Dr. Baskins said, "No I don't think so. We close her up now and hope that she comes out of it."

"You think that there might be more shards still inside?"

"It is possible. Likely, even. I don't want to cut any deeper."

"Then wait for her daughter to come. She will finish the operation."

CHAPTER 39

Jania was standing by a window watching as two Air Force jets landed in formation and taxied right up to the door of the terminal. She was wearing a short white dress and loose sandals, the clothes she had been wearing when Molly called her. A woman climbed out of the back seat of the second plane and ran toward the door, carrying a box. Jania went out to meet her. The woman said, "Here put these on. Quickly."

The flight suit was not hard. Then the flight boots. "Boots?" asked Jania

"Yes. Everything."

She shook off her sandals and slid her feet into boots that were about six inches too long. Well, she didn't really have to walk in them. Then the gravity harness and the helmet. "Okay. Climb up, belt in good, and then plug this into the hole that says 'oxygen'. Let's roll."

She ran back to her plane, and Jania awkwardly climbed into the lead plane. She got herself strapped in and found the oxygen plug. As soon as she did, the pilot said, "Welcome aboard, Miss Christmas. Ever flown before?"

"Not in one of these."

"You'll do okay. Put your hands in your lap and keep them there till we are straight and level. I don't want you touching anything accidentally."

"Okay."

"We'll give them a little show when we take off."

Jania looked back at the terminal. People were lined up on the roof watching them.

"We'll take off fast and hard. When the afterburners kick in you'll think it's going to push your tummy right through your backbone."

"Okay."

He radioed the tower to get permission for immediate take-off. He had already declared an emergency situation, and they were holding traffic. Not that there was much to hold in San Juan at 9:00 in the morning. They taxied out to the center of the runway, turned into position and pushed them to full power with brakes set. Her pilot said "go" and they both released their brakes ats the same time. And rolled down the runway. "Rotate." The first plane rotated and leapt off the ground, and the second locked into place on his wing. To the people on the ground it looked like they leapt straight up, and Jania felt like they were going straight up. The colonel said, "Afterburner." And they both lit off the afterburners and disappeared in a burst of smoke and flame and a roar of thunder.

"Afterburner." They both killed the afterburners to conserve fuel and continued to climb to their flight altitude.

When they were straight and level, he said, "Well, how did you like that?"

"Jeez! It was scary at first, but I figured that if you could take it, so could I. Then it was fun."

"You don't scare easy, do you?"

"Nope. I've seen things you wouldn't want to know about."

"Try me. I've been in this Air Force for a long time. I've seen a few things."

"I nearly killed a man once, with a mace. Maybe I did."

"With mace or a mace?"

"A mace. He was going to rape me."

"Oh. Is that a warning?"

"No. You asked me."

"I did. What else?"

"My uncle is a paladin, and so is my half-sister. When those two go to war, nothing slows them down."

"They killed a couple of people?" He was half-amused and not quite believing her stories.

"I saw them cut down 25 armed guards one night like they were cutting weeds."

"Wow. You have seen a few things."

"Yes. I've been to war. Some things I can't talk about." She had been raped and beaten and left for dead two years ago. She still could not talk about it.

"Are you a killing machine, too?"

"No. I'm a healing machine. I can kill if I have to, but I'd rather not."

"That's why they sent me to get you. You must have some connections."

"I don't know about that. Molly arranged it. She is married to Karl Spicewood."

"Ah! That's the connection. Karl called in a favor."

"Was it a problem?"

"Oh, no. I was looking for an excuse to fly a cross country."

"Well, thanks for coming after me."

"You want to fly it awhile?"

"Can I?"

"Sure. Let me warn off the wingman. Jenny, break away. Miss Christmas is going to fly for a while."

"Where is the accelerator?"

He laughed. "Not one. There is a power lever, but don't touch that. We want to keep the same speed. Just keep your nose level and wings level. Just a touch on the stick will change it. And keep the altitude at 30,000. See the altimeter?"

"Okay."

It took a few minutes of over-corrections, but after a while, she got the hang of it. "This is fun."

"Well, let me have it, now. Time to come in to MacDill. Hands off the stick."

"I have it, Gary. Form up."

On the way down, he asked, "Are you in college?"

"Pre-med. I'm going to be a brain doctor."

"Uh, brain surgeon."

"No, doctor. I don't want to cut people up, just heal them."

"As you like it."

They rolled to a stop by the hangar, and climbed out. The chocks were already in place by the time they hit the ground. "Somebody meeting you, Miss Christmas? I'd be glad to take you to the hospital."

"Yes, Molly is meeting me. I see her." She started to run to meet her, but tripped on her oversize boots. "Oh!"

The colonel helped her up. "You all right?"

"Yes, I'm not hurt. Forgot about the boots. I hope whoever owns them doesn't mind my wearing them."

"Oh, I'm sure Jack won't mind a pretty girl wearing his boots. He'll probably talk about it for months."

Molly came over. "I'm Molly Gre – Spicewood. Thanks for bringing my girl, colonel."

"My pleasure. Have a nice day."

CHAPTER 40

Dr. Baskins said, "Another civilian? I don't think so."

Jeremy looked at him coldly. "She is studying to be a brain surgeon. Even now there is no one who has a better chance to heal this woman. You will wait." He sent a call to Jania. *Hey. Where are you?*

Just landed at this air base. I see Molly waiting for us.

Good. You need to hurry. You need to finish the healing process before the doctors here finish killing her.

Fast as I can.

Jeremy looked at the surgeon and said, "Jania, her daughter, is at MacDill. She will finish this."

"If you are going to do the job, we might as well leave."

"Go ahead. We won't miss you."

The surgeon said, "Get the chief surgeon. Now!"

Nobody moved until the chief surgeon walked in ten minutes later, gowned and gloved. He said, "What is going on here?"

"This man is interfering with our patient. He refuses to leave."

Jeremy said, "They must not close her up until her daughter sees her. She will be here in a few minutes."

"I don't want her daughter to see her like this," the surgeon said.

Jeremy said, "You *do* want her to see her. She has seen wounds before. She is a healer."

"You mean doctor?"

"No. I mean healer. She is studying to be a doctor, too."

Just then they heard a commotion at the doors. Jania said, "Let me in there!"

Then, "All right put the gown on me. Booties too, I don't care. Just let me in there."

The door burst open and Jania ran to her mother. "Oh, my. What have you done to her?"

"We didn't do it, miss. We are trying to save her life."

"Well, move out of my way. She put her hands on the sides of Sharra's head.

The surgeon immediately tried to move them. "You can't touch her."

"Move! I have to touch her to heal her."

Jeremy sent, *We have cleaned out most of the fragments of bone. There might be more that we can't see.*

Let me see. Link in and move them if I find any. She looked inside. After a little she said, "Here's one. Move it." A little later she said, "Here's another." Another minute passed, and then she said, "Here's a big piece of metal." It clinked on the dish.

"Okay, that's all I see." She moved her hands over the wound and prayed while studying the tissue under her hands. *Push these together, here, Jeremy. Okay. See that red line? Connect it. Okay.* They worked for an hour, mending tissues bit by bit.

Then Jania leaned up. "Okay. Close the membrane, there, Jeremy." Jeremy did, and she prayed for healing. "Now the bone." "Now the scalp."

She studied the results and then said, "Okay. That's all I can do. We just have to hope and pray now. You all can have her. Don't lose her."

The three doctors watched her go, openmouthed.

The chief surgeon said, "How did you do – whatever you did?"

"I don't know. I pray for healing and God heals. I don't know how it happens. But I mended the damaged brain cells. We don't know what is in those cells, but I don't think it is too important. Just mending the flesh might not restore the brain functions."

"You are right, those cells are not important."

"You don't know that," Jania said. "That is an assumption. It is probably correct, but I do not assume anything."

"We do know what is in brain cells," the neurosurgeon said.

"No you don't. You know what happens in some of the areas of the brain, but you do not know what is in any given cell. That is one thing I intend to find out."

"No can tell what is in a certain cell."

"Like I said, I intend to find out."

She turned and walked out, Jeremy on her heels.

The chief surgeon said, "I want that girl!"

"She did good," Dr. Baskins said.

"I know. That's why I want her. On my staff. Get her name."

Mista was sitting in a big chair in the corner of the waiting room, staring at nothing. Jania ran over and jumped into his lap. She threw her arms around his neck and cried. "I've done all I can, Daddy. Just pray that it's enough."

"Thanks, Kitten. We'll just have to wait and see."

After a few minutes, Jania sat up and kissed Mista, and then got up and sat in the chair beside him. She took his hand in both hers. "Daddy. It's scary."

"What is, Kitten?"

"I couldn't see Mom."

"What do you mean? I thought you went in there."

"She's not there." She looked over his face, her eyes wide. "I could see her brain and everything. It all looks normal, but like she is in a really deep sleep or unconscious. But I couldn't see *her*."

"Do you mean that she is brain-dead?"

"No. The brain is active, doing it's automatic things. I can see synapses firing and the little currents flowing. See? I've leaned some new words. I know what these things are called, now. But the soul or spirit – MOM – is not there. Maybe she is already gone, and her body will eventually die. Maybe she just withdrew to a safe place until the body is healthy again."

"How would she know that?"

"Maybe she wouldn't know. Maybe that's why some people come out of a coma – and they will call it a coma – after just a little time, and some take weeks or months. And some never come out. We don't really know what is happening with a coma."

"Sure we do. The person cannot respond."

"Yes, but why? Maybe they just aren't there. Maybe they can hear but can't answer. Maybe they can't hear or see, so don't know anyone is talking to them. All I know is that Mom is not there right now."

To Mista that meant that she was probably dead and it was just a matter of time until the body quit.

But Jania said, "That doesn't mean that she is already dead. It might just mean that God has her somewhere safe until he is ready to give her life back to her. Or he might decide to take her on home. Will you be all right, Daddy?"

"I'm all right. But I'm not very happy right now."

"Of course you aren't. I did the best I could in there, Daddy. You know that, don't you?"

"Yes, Kitten, I know that you did. You've grown up."

"I'll stay with her until she comes out of it. Or …"

"Thanks. She'll be glad that you did."

"I might have to take this quarter over again, but I have to stay. Somebody has to tell Don Miguel what happened to me. He'll be worried. And I don't have a stitch of clothing except what I have on."

"Well, when she comes out of recovery we'll go get you some clothes and things. They'll probably put her in intensive care at first, so we won't be able to stay with her anyway."

Jasmine came over and sat beside Mista. "You all right, dear?"

"Yes, I'll be all right," Mista said. "Not too happy with David Brumley right now. If I could get my hands on him I'd like to barbeque him from the inside out."

Jania smiled. "You don't live on a world where you can do that any more. But I bet little Robin would do it for you. Where are the girls?"

"Brumley kidnapped them last night. They're on his boat on the way to Grand Cayman."

She clapped her hands to her face. "You let them kidnap the girls?"

"Yes. It's a trap about to be sprung on him. They volunteered and are all ready for it. Molly, have you contacted the girls lately?"

"No. Let me try." After a minute, she said, "They are alive, but I cannot contact them. Feels like they are unconscious. Maybe they are still under the tranquilizer."

CHAPTER 41

They all went down to the cafeteria for lunch. No one was hungry, but they needed to eat, and they needed to walk around. When they came back, they found that Sharra had been moved to the ICU. She was out of recovery, but had not regained consciousness. They were told that she was in a coma.

Jania looked at Mista. "Told you."

Mista said, "Well, we could go get you some necessary things and then check back."

"Charly said, "We should go on back to the boat. There is nothing we can do here."

Em said, "I don't care. I'll stay."

Sheila said, "I'll stay with you."

Jasmine took Charly, Jeremy and Chandri back to the boat while Mista and Jania went shopping. Molly could never resist a shopping trip, even though she did not need anything.

They returned several hours later and found everything the same. Mista said, "Sheila, you and Em might as well come back to the boat for the night."

Molly said, "I can monitor her from anywhere. We don't really need to stay here."

They moved Sharra into a private room the next day. All of her body signs were normal, temperature, blood pressure, heart beat, and brain waves. Mista readily agreed to pay extra for a private room and to have a room with monitoring equipment. They visited during the day, but there was no change. They returned to the boat for the night and Jasmine took Em back to Crystal Beach to check on the children.

After supper, Mischal said, "What are your plans, now, Mista?"

"Wait and see what happens. What else can I do? I don't want to leave her, and the girls won't be in Grand Cayman yet. Molly, can you check on the girls?"

"Sure." After a minute, she said, "I can't reach them. Something is blocking contact with them."

"Let me check the GPS monitor," Mista said. As suspected, they did not have a GPS location for them. "If they are inside the boat, and surely they are, then the satellites can't reach them."

Molly said, "Leave it on trace. Surely they'll let them up for air and then they will show up. I can't maintain a search for that long, but the computer can."

"Right. Good idea."

"I meant more than just immediate plans, Mista. Seems to me like we are stalled out here."

"I don't know what to do. I don't want to leave Sharra."

"Yeah, I understand that. Look, I'm not a sailor. I don't mind using the boat to go somewhere. But I've had it with just sailing around aimlessly in the Gulf of Mexico waiting for something to happen. I've got family and don't like to be gone for days at a time. I'm going back home. Chandri loves the boat. She can go as navigator IF you are going to a particular place with reason to go. Not just idling around, though."

Njondac said, "I'm goin' too. It's okay if you needed me, but not jes ta laze around on tha sea."

Mischal said, "If you decide to make a frontal attack on old Brumley's fortress, call me. I'll be glad to go to war with you. I'm just not a sailor."

Mista said, "I understand. I have never asked you to do something against your better judgment. See to your family. I'll make sure that the boat is secure here. It's as good a place as any to stay while we see what is happening. Anyone else wants to leave, go ahead." Although he said that he understood, everyone knew that he was disappointed. He did understand their reasons, but was sorry to see them go. Nevertheless, he would do nothing to try to make them stay.

Charly said, "I'm not leaving you. I'll get Jasmine to take me to get Charles tomorrow. And my car. Jeremy, will you stay with us? You can continue to study."

"I'll go wherever you go, dear. I have no other home."

Molly said, "I think I'll fly back home to see my husband, as long as you aren't doing anything. I can monitor Sharra and the girls from Atlanta as well as I can from here. Call me if you need me."

Sheila said, "I'm not going anywhere."

No one needed to ask Jania. She did say, "Since I'm staying on here until Mom recovers, you need to ask Don Miguel to send my books. I'll use the time to study and experiment."

Mista checked his computer, but there had been no sign of the girls. "I'm going to turn in. I'm not very talkative tonight."

"Like you ever were," Charly said to herself.

Jania followed him up to the main deck and then down. She was sleeping in the girls' room. Mista sat down in his lounge chair and called Don Miguel. He had not talked to him in a long time, and was not looking forward to this conversation, under the circumstances. Don Miguel owned a historical coffee plantation on Puerto Rico, and Jania had been staying with him while she was in college. Mista and he had become friends while Mista was on a project that took him to Puerto Rico.

The Don's secretary answered, and when Mista identified himself, he put the don on. "*Buenas tardes*, Senor Mista! Good evening. It is good to hear your voice. But I have terrible news. Jania has gone missing. She was in classes day before yesterday, and suddenly disappeared. I have been wanting to call you, but tried to find out something first."

"Not to worry, *amigo mio*, my friend," Mista said in Spanish. He liked to practice his Spanish, and Don Miguel liked to practice his English. "Sharra has been shot and we sent an airplane to pick Jania up. We should have told you, but we've just been too busy. She is with us, and will be here for a while."

"Oh, I am so sorry. She will be all right, no?"

"We don't know. That's why we sent for Jania. Sharra is in a coma."

"Oh, I am sorry to hear that. Yes, she must stay with her mother. Is there anything that I can do for you? Do you need me to pay for the hospital?"

"We do not know if she will live or die. Thanks for asking, but the hospital is covered. Jania needs for you to send her books so she can study while she is here."

"Ah, that girl will be a wonderful doctor. She studies all the time. Yes, I will send them in the morning. Is everything else okay? You still getting the coffee?"

"Oh, actually I have a new address. I bought a house in Crystal Beach, Florida."

"Give me the address and I will send coffee with the books. Don Miguel had sent ten pounds of his best coffee to Mista every month ever since they had met He sent a dark strong bean for Mista and a lighter mix that even Sharra had liked.

"Don Miguel, Jania says that her car is still on campus. Could you send someone to pick it up?"

"Of course. We will pick it up when we take the coffee to be shipped."

They talked on about one thing or another for fifteen minutes and then signed off. Mista put the phone back on his belt and sat staring at nothing. He was not given to depression, but at that moment he felt like the world was caving in on him. Jania sat on the bed across the room, watching him. After a few minutes, she got up and came and sat in his lap. She put her head on his shoulder and put her arms around him.

"You must feel terrible, Daddy. You wife in a coma, your little girls captive and lost, and now all your friends are leaving you. Let me help."

Suddenly, Mista realized that Jania was much warmer than just another person should be. She was giving him healing, and he felt the energy flowing. He was no longer tired, and felt like a weight had been lifted off his back. The depression he would have to solve himself, due to the very nature of depression.

He said, "Thanks, Kitten. I needed that."

She smiled. "You knew what I did? Of course you did. I'd sleep with you and make you feel even better, but I know you would not let me."

"You're right. That would not be a good thing."

"I mean, just sleep."

"I know. Still not a good thing. Sleep in the girls' room and let me go to bed now. No. Wait. Get my Bible, Hon."

Jania stepped across the room and brought it to him. "Would you read to me? You know the story of David, don't you? King of Israel?"

"Yes, I remember it. What does that have to do with you?"

"Read me I Samuel, chapters 19 – 24, and let me just listen and meditate."

The story she read was remarkably like Mista's present condition. David had been anointed king while the old king still lived. He even married the king's daughter. But the old king Saul had tried to kill David. His wife warned him, but when Saul asked her why, she said it was because

David threatened to kill her. He went to the priests, and Saul killed all the priests in that village. He went to an old prophet but Saul tried to kill him there. He sent his family away, and tried to escape to a foreign land, but they would not help him. Mista felt very much like that. David had lost his marriage, his friends, his job, his priestly support and his family. He must have felt that God had deserted him, too. But then he realized that God had not, and he renewed his spirit.

Mista sighed when she had finished. "Thanks, Kitten. That is what I have to do. I have to go to the desert and renew my spirit. The question is, how? I'll figure it out. I'm going to bed, now. Good night."

Jania gave him a goodnight kiss and left. When Mista turned to go to bed he discovered that the kitten was curled up in the middle of his bed. He stroked her, listening to her purr. "Like me better than the stranger girl? We'll get your mistress back soon enough."

CHAPTER 42

The next morning Sharra's condition remained the same. Jasmine came up with Em, and decided quickly that there was nothing she could do for Sharra. Em had brought the books and coffee. "It came this morning by FedEx, overnight. That cost him a bundle!"

Jasmine took Charly and Mischal home to get their cars, but Em wanted to stay with Sharra.

Molly took a taxi to the airport. When she left, she said, "I still can't see the girls. I hope they are all right. I'll keep trying."

Eventually, no one was left but Mista, Jania and Em. Mista said, "You don't need to stay, Em."

"I'll stay. She needs someone to stay with her. I brought my car, so I can leave if I need to."

"I'm staying," Jania said.

"Well, we don't all need to be here all the time. You want to set up some kind of rotation?"

Jania said, "No. I'm going to stay here. I've got books and I can watch TV. Em can stay with me if she wants, but I'm not leaving until she wakes up."

Em said, "I used to be a nurse. Well, I guess I still am a nurse. I'm used to long vigils. I'll stay with you."

Jania laid her hands on Mista's chest and pushed. "You go do what you have to do, Daddy."

"But ..."

"Leave us. You have something to do. I'll call you if she wakes up."

He walked over and stood looking down at Sharra for a few minutes. *Fourteen years. We've seen a lot in fourteen years. Come back to me, Sharra. I need you.*

He leaned down and kissed her lips. He half expected them to be cold, but of course they were warm but totally unresponsive. He pulled $200 out of his pocket and gave it to Jania. "In case you need it." He kissed her and then turned and walked out, feeling like he had closed a chapter in his life.

"Where did you send him, Dear?" Em asked.

"He said he had to go to the desert to renew his spirit."

"But there aren't any deserts here."

"I know. I think he meant he had to be alone for a while."

"Oh. I heard that he did that once last year up in Georgia. Went up to the waterfall and spent a whole day sitting and watching the water. He came back a new man."

Mista walked back to the boat. It was only a few miles, and he was used to running 15 miles a day. He let his mind drift, not really thinking about anything; just letting thoughts come and go as they wanted to. He still did not know what he was going to do when he arrived back at the boat. Charly and Jeremy were back, with their baby, and Jasmine had come with them.

Jasmine hugged Mista when he came aboard. "I was worried about you."

"Don't be. I'll be all right."

"Yes, you will. I'm to make sure of that."

Sheila had supper ready. "I got a little corned beef point and made you some corned beef and cabbage, Mista. I know you like that."

"Thanks, but I'm really not hungry."

"Eat anyway. You need to eat."

Mista ate a little. It was good, and she had prepared it especially for him. Then he went to his computer to check the girls. It had traced their location briefly that afternoon on Grand Cayman, as he had thought that they were going. The trace lasted only a few minutes.

"Must have been in the open going from the boat to a car," Jeremy said. "I should have been listening for them." He checked. "I have contact, of a sort. They are unconscious. Probably another tranquilizer dose so that they won't know where they are. At least they are alive and appear to be unharmed."

Mista checked the location of the reported position. Had it been an active trace, he could simply plot it on his mapping software. "Well, we knew it was Grand Cayman. They were in the main port there,

Georgetown. Now we don't know where they are. At least they must be on the island somewhere."

"Why don't you keep the screen open and hope to spot them when they arrive at their destination?"

"Good idea."

They did not get another report, however, and when Jeremy checked later, he could no longer get a contact. "I don't know how they do that," Jeremy said. "I should be able to at least feel their minds."

Charly said, "Is that the same sense you get when you try to contact Sharra? That they just aren't there?"

"Yes. But Sharra's in a coma. I can understand that. You think maybe … No. I don't want to think that something has happened and that the girls are also in a coma state."

"You better think it," Charly said. I wouldn't put it past those men to knock the girls around some."

Mista said, "If I knew that was what was happening … we should be on the way there. Why don't you try Brumley? See what he's thinking."

"Sure. Hold on." A minute later, Jeremy said, "That's really odd. I can't see him, either."

"Maybe they have some kind of shield," Charly said.

"They don't even believe that mental telepathy is possible," Jeremy said. "How could they build a shield? And why?"

Mista said, "Remember when they held Jania captive? They put her in an unused walk-in freezer. The wire and piping in the walls made it into a shield."

"Oh. Forgot about that. It's possible. We can hope." Mista stared blankly at his computer screen for several minutes.

Jasmine came over and sat beside him. She picked up his hand and held it in both of hers. "Are you sure you're all right? You act like you're in a daze."

Mista smiled. "Just thinking. You know I'm not all right, but I'll survive. I don't want to lose either Sharra or the girls. Losing them both at once – that's almost too much. And to the same man. Makes me want to go stuff him into a hole or something."

"Be careful, dear. Don't let your anger turn into rage."

"I know. I'm the philosopher. How many times have I said to someone else, 'don't focus on your anger. Holding rage against your enemy only hurts you and he just laughs at you'. Now I know why people tell me that they can't help it."

"You can help it, you know. You, of all people, know."

"I know. And I know that it is a lot easier to *rage* against him than to let it go. I will let it go, but it takes time."

"Will you also forgive him?"

Mista turned and looked at her for a full minute, turning that idea over in his mind. He knew that forgiveness was required. But could he do it? "It's easy to tell someone else to forgive. It's excruciatingly hard to actually do it. Does it mean that he gets away with it?"

"No, you know it doesn't mean that. Forgiveness has nothing to do with that man. It has everything to do with you."

"Yes, of course." He gripped her hand. "I'll need help. You still have the ear of God?"

Jasmine smiled gently. "Everyone has the ear of God. He listens to all of his servants."

"Yes, but I think he likes you best. No, I shouldn't be flippant. But you do get answers when no one else does. I'll need help."

Jasmine closed her eyes and said, "Dear Lord, cleanse this man, your servant. Help him to do what he must do, and don't let him go under in this deluge of sorrow."

Mista said, "Thanks. "I'm going to bed now. Good night all."

The next morning, Charly woke up with the light. The boat's motion felt different. They were not underway, but something was different. Then she realized that she felt and heard the boat's engines running. She jumped up and pulled her shorts on, and ran to the ladder to the main deck. She slept in a knit sleeping shirt, so she felt mostly dressed.

Mista had undone all the lines tying the boat to the pier except the one line by the bow. He was standing by it, as if ready to throw it off, also. Charly said, "What are you doing?"

"Getting underway. You can get off if you want to. I was waiting."

"I'm not getting off. You can't sail this boat by yourself."

"Yes I can. Once I'm clear of the harbor, I'll set the mizzen sail, secure the engines and set the autopilot. I don't need a lot of speed."

"You can't do it all by yourself. I'm not leaving anyway."

"Suit yourself. How about Jazmine and Jeremy? Better give them a chance to leave."

"They won't leave, either. Are you crazy, Mista?"

"I don't think so."

"I think you are."

"No, I 'm not. But I have to go out. If you want to help, then come cast off this line. First, let me push forward on it a little to spring the stern out into the channel, and then cast it off."

"All right. But this is crazy."

Mista engaged the engines and pushed forward slowly. The line held the bow against the pier, but the thrust of the engines pushed the stern out. Then he put her into reverse, and backed slowly. Charly cast off the line, and he backed on out into the channel. When he was clear, he went forward, and turned out into the channel.

When they had cleared the last channel buoy, he hoisted the mizzen sail, set it for proper angle to the wind, and secured the engines. He made sure that there was no traffic near, set a course of 200 degrees – slightly southwest – and set the autopilot. Then he took a deck chair up to the bowsprit, sat down in it, and closed his eyes. The wind was light, and he only had one sail up, so they did not move fast.

Charly went up and asked him what he was doing.

"I'm thinking. Leave me be."

She went down and called Jeremy and then Jasmine. Jasmine went to Mista and asked him what he was doing. He said, "Thinking. Let me be."

She stared at him for a moment, and then went back to the pilothouse. Charly said, "What did he say?"

"He's thinking. Meditating? Praying? I'm not sure. But I think he knows what he's doing."

"What should we do?"

"Nothing. Eat breakfast, make sure the boat stays on course, watch for traffic."

"Should we put more sail on?"

"How fast does he want to go?" Jasmine asked.

"I don't know. I don't even know where he's going."

"Nowhere, I think."

"I think we should put the jib up, Jeremy," Charly said after a moment. "That seems to steady the boat a lot."

"Okay. You think we can do it?"

"I don't see why not. I've hauled the sheets many times. When I say, you hit the winch button and raise it. I'll get it in the right position." The boat did steady up and picked up a bit of speed. She was still not making more than 2 knots, but if you are not going anywhere, two knots is fast enough.

Mista sat in his chair all day and all night. A rain shower came up mid-afternoon, washing everything, including Mista. He did not seem to notice. After the rain, Patches came up and curled up under his chair. Charly was afraid that she would fall overboard, and went up to get her. She raised her head and growled, then hissed at Charly. "Okay, okay. If you fall in, it's your life."

Charly went back to the pilothouse. "Mother, how does she know? It's like she knows that Mista is thinking about Robin and thinking about rescuing her."

"Maybe she does. Cats have a strange sense of perception. They seem to know what you are thinking."

Mista was not thinking about anything at all, in a logical sense. He was not using words. He blanked his mind and went into a meditative state. His goal was to be in communication with God, and that did not require words. His boat was the perfect place for him, in his present state of mind. The gentle sound of water and wind, the sails flapping and lines humming were all background noises that he heard but ignored.

He had three things to work out. He did not know what to do about Sharra. If she were lost to him, he would be hurt deeply, but he would go on. He remembered his instruction in meditation from a psychology professor who was deeply religious. One possible goal of meditation was to block all irrelevant thought and let the mind be free of distraction. Then when he felt the presence of God, he prayed the 'prayer of the heart'. That prayer, again, was not words, but just a reach for something that he wanted desperately. His prayer was for Sharra. *I want her back. I've neglected her, but I need her. I want her more than anything else in this life.* There was no sense of answer, nor did he expect any. It was just a cry from his heart.

Then the girls. He had put them in harm's way. *I cannot allow them to be hurt. I cannot. But what can I do. I can't even find them. Please give them back to me.*

As time went on, he began to think about Brumley. He had to forgive. *Help me forgive. Cleanse my heart of hatred and restore my soul. I don't have to hate him and I must not. He is not an item of interest. But I cannot allow him to go on destroying lives. He must die. Not from revenge on his shooting of Sharra or kidnapping my girls. For all the lives that he has destroyed. All the girls he has put into slavery. All the lives he has ruined with his drugs. He will die.*

With that a sense of peace flooded him. He revisited each of his prayers several times. Each time he received the peace that all would be well. He did not know if Sharra would come back, but he would be in peace either way. He sincerely hoped that he could rescue his girls, and that peace was hard to achieve. What if he failed? He had to do his best. If he did all that he could, would he be in peace? Yes, he would. And Brumley must die. Not by his hand, and not from vengeance. But he must die.

At exactly 3:00 the next afternoon, Mista sat up. He took a moment to come back to full consciousness, and then he walked back to the pilothouse, Patches at his heels. He took the wheel and disengaged the autopilot. "We're going back. Standby to come about. He put the bow into the wind and then swung it on to a reverse course. The boom swung across the stern and the sail filled. Then he sent Charly to man the mainsail sheet. "Let her fall into the wind and then position her for best speed." He raised the mainsail, and it filled eagerly. The wind even seemed to pick up in intensity.

After a minute, he started the engines, running on both sail and power. They had spent a day and a half at two knots. Now they were making about 12 knots, and would be back in about two hours.

Jeremy came up from below. "Mista! I just talked to Jania. Sharra is awake! She's calling for you."

"Mista smiled. We're on the way."

"How did you know? Oh, she talked to you."

"No, she hasn't called me yet. I asked to have her back, and I just assumed that I would find her."

"What if you hadn't?" Charly asked. "What if she had not come back?"

"Then I would have had to do something else."

Sharra called. *Mista?*

Coming, Darling.

Where are you? Where am I?

I'm at sea. I'll be there in two hours. You're in the hospital.

Oh. Hurry. I love you.

I love you, too.

Jeremy called Mischal. *Pack up. Bring your guns. Meet us at the pier where we were. We're going hunting. Be there in two hours.*

What happened?

I don't know. Mista just suddenly jumped up and said we're going after the girls. We don't even know where they are, yet.

Hope it's not a wild goose chase.

I don't think so. Something happened. Sharra came to at that same time. We're picking her up, too.

All right. We'll be there. We need to bring food? I'm bringing the kids, too.

Wow. Better bring hammocks. If you have anything frozen, bring it. Don't take time to shop.

Next Jeremy called Molly. *You want to be in on the kill?*

What do you mean? Has something happened?

Yeppers. Sharra's back, and Mista is going to get the girls. We haven't found them yet, but we're going hunting.

I'll be there. When are you leaving?

In about two hours. Hey, meet us in Georgetown, Grand Cayman. That's where we're going. We know that they were there. Got a sighting for just a few minutes.

I'll fly down. When? And do you need wheels?

I'd say three days. Yes, rent a car, a big one. Suburban or Range Rover. Does Karl want to come? Maybe he could act as liaison between us and the local police. We might need it.

I think Karl wants to stay far away from this one.

CHAPTER 43

Janice woke up first. It was totally dark in her room, but she could still feel the boat's motion. She thought she had gone to sleep after all. She had meant to stay awake until the men came for her, and both she and Robin had slept in their clothes. Then she remembered hearing the commotion the men made, falling around in the passageway outside her room. And then she realized that the boat's motion was different. It rolled from side to side, like they were underway. Then she realized that she could hear, or feel the vibrations, of boat engines. They were underway. She did not remember anything after hearing the men outside her door. She had held her eyes closed when she heard them so that they would think that she was asleep. How did she get here?

She tried to look around, but the room was totally dark. It could not be her room. She had two little portholes, so there was always some light, even at night. The bunk felt the same, but then probably all boats' bunks were pretty much the same, a mattress and a little rail built in to keep you from rolling out of bed. She felt her way to the wall —*I should learn to think like Daddy, since we spend so much time on boats. He would chide me and say it is a bulkhead. Oh, well. Wall.*

She moved along the wall until she bumped into something. She felt down. Another bunk, and Robin still asleep in it. "Robin! Wake up!" She shook her.

Robin stirred and opened her eyes in the dark. "Is it time to get up? Oh. Hey! We're underway. Didn't they come and capture us after all?"

"I think they did. This not our room."

"It's too dark. I can't see anything."

"I'm trying to find the light switch." Janice moved on. She found the switch and turned the light on. Then she tried the door. "Locked. Not surprised."

Robin said, "I don't remember anything. What happened?"

"I don't remember, either. Maybe they gave us some kind of sleeping pill."

Robin said, "Maybe they shot us with a tranquilizer gun, like they do wild animals."

"Yeah. Wonder what time it is. I'm starving." She looked at her watch. "Six o'clock. Only been a few hours, but it's about time for breakfast. I hope they feed us."

Robin said, "It's been longer than a few hours. I'm starving. Maybe it's six in the evening?"

Karackish heard the movement and conversation over his monitor, and pushed a button. A man opened the door and stepped in. "Yes, sir?"

"Our guests are awake. Take them some dinner. And be sure it is heavily laced, so they go back to sleep."

"I ain't even seen them. They good lookers?"

"Like all of them. If you like them that young. Don't get yourself in trouble."

"I won't touch them. I do like to look, though."

"Well, just do your job. Put a double dose in their food. I want them to sleep all the way."

Two nights later, Karackish called another man. "Come. We need to move our guests."

They picked the sleeping girls up and carried them to a room that had been secured against electronic interference of any kind. No cell phones worked in that room, no beepers, and no outside surveillance could pick up sounds or visuals. It had one bed in one corner and a desk with a computer bolted onto it in another corner. They put both girls on the bed.

Karackish said, "That's all, Joe." The man left, and Karackish sat down to wait for the girls to wake up. He had brought them here in case they had some kind of transmitters embedded in them. He had respect for the capabilities of Mista's group, even as he plotted against them.

Karackish waited patiently. He was military man, used to standing long watches, waiting for nothing to happen. Or something. The girls stirred an hour later. Janice woke first and sat up. At first she was surprised to find the light on, and then she saw the man sitting across the room, watching her. "Oh. Haven't seen you before. Where's the bathroom? I have to go."

"On a boat it's called a head. There isn't on in this room. You'll have to wait."

"I'm dying."

"Too bad. Wake your sister."

Robin stirred and sat up in the middle of the bed. Then she saw the man across the room and quickly pulled her skirt down. "Where's the bathroom? I have to go."

"You'll have to wait," the man said. "Listen up. Do you know why you are here?"

"I don't even know where I am," Janice said. "Seems like I've been asleep forever."

"Only a few days. Your grandfather is bringing you here to his house. He will provide your every need. Far more than your mother was ever able to do. In return, you will give him pleasure."

"I don't want to be here," Robin said. "I want to go home to my daddy."

"You will never see your daddy again. If he is your daddy."

"What do you know about anything?"

"I know just about everything about you. I know that your daddy didn't marry your mother until long after you were born. Not that it matters any more. You are here to give men pleasure. I tell you this for your own benefit. If you cooperate you can have a good life. If you don't, it will be filled with pain."

"He must be a mean old man," Robin said, "to make demands like that. It's not even right."

"Mr. Brumley will decide what is right for you. Do you understand me?"

"Janice said, "Mr. Brumley is God, now?"

"As much god as you will ever know. His word is law. I do what he says. You will do what he says. If you fight, you will be sorry."

"Well, I –" Janice tapped Robin on the leg before she could finish.

"We will not be happy as long as we are prisoners. That's all I have to say to you."

"Suit yourself. You're here to stay, so you might as well accept it and make the best of it." He got up and walked out. The door clicked behind him.

Janice ran to the door. "Locked."

"Where is the bathroom?"

"It's a head, and there isn't one."

"Well, if they don't let me out pretty soon, I'll wet his bed."

"It might be our bed."

"No, this is some kind of office. See if you can use that computer."

Janice went over and turned the computer on. Robin acted on her threat. She pulled her skirt up and her pants down, and proceeded to wet the bed. The computer screen lit and after a minute asked for a password. Janice tried several things, but nothing worked. After the third try, the screen changed and posted a message: "You have tried three passwords. You are locked out."

"Oh well, I didn't think they'd leave us a computer." She sniffed. "You didn't?"

"I did."

"We probably have to sleep here tonight."

"I'll sleep on the floor."

"I guess I will, too. If they don't let us out of here soon, I'll have to use the bed myself."

"If they don't let us out pretty soon, I'll pull the covers down and leave a deposit there."

The door opened and a woman stepped in. "Come."

She led them down a passageway to another door. "Head." She opened the door and stood in the doorway while the girls used the toilet. Then, "Back."

"Phew!" Janice said, when the woman had closed the door behind them. "Scheduled head breaks. At least we had a head in the other room."

The same woman brought supper to them a few minutes later. They were left awake the rest of the day and the night. The woman appeared at midnight, according to Janice's watch, for another head break. She brought them breakfast the next morning, and gave them another head call. They began to stumble with drowsiness on the way back to the room, and fell on the bed, asleep, before she had closed the door.

A little later, two men picked the girls up and carried them to a waiting car. Brumley and Masters were already in the car, and Karackish got in after the girls had been placed on the floor. Brumley said, "Home, Adams."

"Yessah, Mr. B."

After a few minutes, Brumley said, "Arnat, these girls smell like they wet themselves."

"I had them taken to the head every six hours. That's enough for anybody."

"Apparently not. Why did you have them in my office?"

"The only room that I could be sure was secure. In case they woke up and tried to give out their location."

"You didn't have them there the whole trip."

"No, it didn't matter if they sent out a location while we were at sea. But if they sent it on our approach, they their father would know where we are."

"How could they do that, anyway?"

"I don't know. Maybe they have one of those locator chips implanted, or some kind of cell phone. You remember when you took them in Florida, before. No one knew that you had them, and you took them straight to Louisville. But they were outside your house an hour later. I don't know how they knew, but I wasn't taking any chances."

"Well, I guess that was wise. But you'll have to put a new bed in my office. And get these girls cleaned up first thing."

"As soon as it wears off and they wake up."

"No. Have someone wash them right away."

CHAPTER 44

When the girls woke up several hours later, they were in a new, well-lighted room. One wall had four large windows, covered with light curtains. They could also see that the windows were covered with a fine wire mesh. Janice tried to open one, but it seemed to be bolted shut. Janice looked outside, trying to figure out where they might be. All she could see was trees.

Robin sat up on her bed. They were both wearing thin white cotton robes. Robin said, "Wonder where our clothes are?"

"No telling. They probably threw them away."

"After all that work Mischal did."

"Yeah."

Mischal had embedded a thin knife blade in the sole of a shoe that each girl would wear. Then he had opened the bottom seam of Robin's skirt and put an Exacto knife blade in it, a long piece of wire and a pencil stub. He had done the same in the hem of Janice's shorts. "You never know what you will need," he had said. "The knife can cut you free if they tie your hands, the wire can become a lock pick. You can do a lot with simple tools."

However, they had left their shoes behind in their haste to get the girls and get out. And now the clothes were gone, too. Janice said, "I guess we'll just have to depend on our brains."

A woman came in a few minutes later, carrying two sets of clothing. She had a dark red mini-dress for Janice and a light blue mini-dress for Robin. No underwear. She said, "You will find perfume and hair brushes in the dresser."

"What about underwear?" Janice said.

"You will not need underwear. Dress now and give me your robes. Mr. B is waiting."

Robin asked, "What about our own clothes? And we don't have shoes."

The woman said, "We will burn your old clothes. And you will not need shoes. You will not leave this room."

"Aww. Please? That is my favorite skirt."

"Well. All right. I will wash it and bring it back to you. I suppose that those were your favorite shorts?"

"No, not really. But I would like to have them. It was a favorite top."

"Okay. But you must not let Mr. B. see you wearing them. He will send clothes for you to wear when he visits or when he sends a client to you."

Robin said, "We probably need a bath. We've been on a boat for a long time. I don't how long, but it seems like forever."

She smiled. "How can you not know how long? Where did you come from?"

Robin said, "We came from Tampa, but we were asleep the whole time. They must have given us something to make us sleep."

"That would probably be three or four days. Most people come here by air. Doesn't take so long. You did need a bath, and I already bathed you. Did I miss something?"

"Oh, no. I don't feel dirty. I just assumed that we would need one." She looked at the dress. "I don't like not wearing underwear. And I definitely need a training bra."

"Mr. B. did not send underwear. He likes you without it. Get dressed now, we don't have all day."

The woman combed and brushed their hair. She pulled Robin's hair back and looked at it critically, then let it hang. She tied Janice's hair back. "Don't forget the perfume." She tapped on the door and it opened. She scooted out quickly, and the door shut again.

"Guards?" Janice said.

"Well, remember, we escaped the last time." Robin picked up several of the bottles of perfume, one at a time, and smelled them. She chose one that smelled like flowers and dabbed a little on her wrists. "I never wore perfume before."

"Well, I'm not going to now. Not for this creep.".

Brumley came in a few minutes later. He did not look like the man they remembered as Sam Smith, but he did have gray hair. He sat on the only chair in the room and smiled. "I'd like you to get to know your grandfather. You will be living with me, now, so we should become friends."

The girls sat on their beds, turning their knees away from him, highly conscious of their short skirts and no underwear. Janice said, "Not in this lifetime."

Brumley said, "I know that my method of bringing you home was a little unorthodox, but I don't think your stepfather would have released you otherwise.

Robin said, "He wa—" a glare from Janice stopped her.

Janice said, "You don't know anything about us."

"On the contrary, I know everything important. My step-daughter was always a willful child. She ran off right after she finished high school, and you were born while she was in hiding. Now that she has chosen to reappear, and with two beautiful girls, I intend to take you off her hands and raise you properly."

"You want to raise us?" Robin asked.

"Why would I take you otherwise? Oh. Your mother must have a distorted view of the kind of man that I am. I will put you in the best schools and buy you whatever you want."

"In return for which, you get to rape us," Janice said.

"Oh, come now. I don't intend to rape you. Not my own granddaughters. I see I must overcome a great deal of mis-trust. Just another reason why she is not the one who should raise you. Your grandmother was very impressed with you when she met you this spring. She wants to get to know you, too."

"If you are interested in raising us properly, why did you have us dressed like little porn queens?" asked Janice.

"Oh that. Well, you must know, I don't have much here in the way of girls' clothing." He lied. "We'll take you shopping for whatever you like, as soon as I can trust you not to try to do something foolish."

"Like running away?" asked Janice.

"Among other things, yes. Now. What would you like as a proof of my good will?"

"I miss my kitten," Robin said.

"Then you shall have another."

"But she won't be Patches. And Patches misses me."

"I just want my Daddy," Janice said. "And my computer."

"Forget the daddy. But we might be able to get you a computer."

"I'd like some books, too," Janice said. Having learned to read, she was finding great pleasure in reading. She had discovered the Nancy Drew mystery series, and was reading them as fast as she could, which was still not very fast. But, as Mista had told her, every book she read increased her reading speed.

"I like to read, too," Robin said. "Could we have some Nancy Drew books?"

"That's an easy request," he said.

Brumley spent another half-hour trying to draw the girls out. Robin softened a little. He did seem like a nice man. Janice was skeptical. She had grown up on the streets and knew a con act when she saw it. She was also cunning enough to try to play him. He had promised a shopping trip. She knew that that might be only a false lure, but still, if he did take them out she could call Mista. She couldn't talk to him, but the call would alert him that they were still all right, and would tell him where they were.

Her final attempt that day was, "When you take me to pick out the clothes that I like, then I might start to believe you."

He smiled. "We will need a day or so to see how you adjust. My staff will keep me informed."

"So why is the door locked and a guard outside? Because we ran away last time?" Janice asked.

"I don't know what you mean. You did leave almost as soon as I came home that night that you were at my house in Kentucky, but I did not think that was running away."

"We know –" Robin began.

Janice stopped her with a glare. *Let him think we don't know.* She knew that Robin was not a mind reader, but Robin did pick up things from time to time.

Brumley said, "I'll have some chairs brought in for you. Would you like a desk and some drawing paper and crayons?"

"Colored pencils, water colors and drawing pencils," Janice said. "Not crayons, please. We are grown up."

Brumley smiled. "Not quite grown up. But I guess you have outgrown crayons."

As soon as Brumley left, Janice said, "I have to go wash my hands." She headed for the bathroom and jerked her head fiercely at Robin. In the bathroom, she turned on the water all the way. Then she whispered fiercely in Robin's ear, "This room is probably bugged. Careful what we say. I think that screen wire we see keeps them from contacting us. Have you heard from Mom or anyone?"

Robin shook her head.

"We're on our own. Remember to burn him if he gets too close."

"But he seems nice."

"Seems to, right. You'll see. Try to get outside the room, though, so we can contact Mom."

Janice flushed the toilet, just for good measure, and let the water run a little longer.

When they left the bathroom, Janice said, "Don't worry. Daddy will be here soon to rescue us.

"But he doesn't know where we are."

"Oh I don't know. He's pretty smart. I bet he is already on the way. But his boat is a little slower, so it might be a day or two."

"I hope he comes soon."

CHAPTER 45

Brumley walked down to his library and pulled a bell rope. Masters was waiting for him, but did not say anything, since the butler appeared almost at once. "Yessuh, Mr. B."

"Have some easy chairs put in their room. Put two desks and chairs in it. Then go to town and buy a box of art supplies. Everything. Paints, paper, pencils, watercolors, chalk. Whatever they have. And get some books. Get the whole Nancy Drew set. And horse stories. Girls like horse stories."

"Yessuh, Mr. B. Anything else?"

"No, that's all for now. Make sure that they are comfortable, and instruct the staff to be friendly. But do not let them out of that room."

When he left, Masters said, "Why only that room?"

"It's shielded against electronic surveillance and cell phones. Arnat thinks that they have some way of communicating."

"Oh. I just wondered. Is it my turn now? You going to leave them together?"

"I think I will leave them together. It could be fun having the other one watch. Besides, it is the only room that is shielded. But, no, it's not your turn. I haven't even had them yet. You know, it's one thing to take a girl who hates you, but does what she has to. It's quite another to take one that likes you."

"I wouldn't know. But I can't stay around much longer. You owe me cash money. And I need to try to find some more product immediately. The last shipment? Someone found the stash and lifted it. It was gone when my agent came to get it. We'll find another hiding place, or do something different."

"Well, we don't want the delivery boy and receiver to see each other. What they don't know, they can't tell. Does anyone have more than they could be expected to have?"

"Not that my agents can tell. It doesn't seem to have made it to street yet."

"Well, we need to monitor that. Maybe whoever it was is smart enough to hold back. Maybe it's just an accident. I still can't figure out how that one dropped his into the bay."

"Maybe that was not an accident. Maybe he did that as a cover, and he came back to get the rest later."

"No. He was dead later. Of course, he might have had a contact. Well, do what you have to do. We'll go get you some cash whenever you are ready. Come back later to have your go at the girls. It will take me a few days to charm them, but I will enjoy it – if it doesn't take too long."

Jeremy had chosen that moment to check in on Brumley. He had not been able to contact the girls, and now he knew why. It also gave him an additional weapon. He pushed a little on the charm idea that Brumley had mentioned, making him want the girls more, but also making him want to charm them more.

He reported to Mista. "Well, I still can't find the girls, but I did listen in on an interesting conversation. They think a rival dealer found their shipment. That's a good thing. Maybe it will stir up some dealer clashes. The girls are in a secure room, one that is shielded from communication devices. Apparently that also blocks our mental links. They are unharmed. Now, here's a new wrinkle. Brumley is trying to make friends with them."

"Oh, now he loves them?"

"Not at all. It enhances his pleasure if they like him a little and put out from pressure rather than a direct rape."

"I guess that makes sense, in a twisted way."

"I reinforced that idea. He will want them more and more, and will try even harder to befriend them. If nothing else, it will buy us some time. It will also increase his frustration level, wanting something that he cannot get. I think he is used to getting whatever he wants, even to pretending friendship."

"Good. I think Sharra had already started him down that road. She made it impossible for him to touch a girl. This ought to be interesting."

CHAPTER 46

Brumley visited the girls twice a day for several days, morning and evening. As time went by, he found it harder and harder to wait until they came around. He had a TV and DVD player put in their room the second day. Robin liked to watch movies on the set, but Janice preferred to listen to music. The third day, she asked for a radio so that she and Robin could listen to different things. She would follow along with the music under her breath until she learned all the words.

Robin began to cave in under the constant pressure. She was beginning to believe that she would never see Mista again, and Mr. B. was being very nice to her. She was beginning to believe that the talk she had heard was mis-informed.

At the same time, however, she missed her daddy. She had come to love him deeply. Now, he was gone and she missed him. Then her childhood fears returned. Everything that she had ever loved had been taken from her, sooner or later. Now, even Mista was taken. It made her sad and angry. She began to think that she was destined never to have anything she could call her own.

Brumley saw her weakening, and was even more anxious to convert her. He did not suspect that at least half of his feelings and thoughts were programmed by the step-daughter that he thought was dead. In spite of her rejection, he had always felt drawn to Sharra. Somewhere deep inside he held to a hope that he could win her over to him. His handling of the girls was known to psychologists as conflicted motivation. He wanted to have sex with both girls, believing them to be Sharra's daughters. He knew that this would tear Sharra to pieces, and that, in his mind, was a worthy goal.

At the same time, an unconscious motivation was to have sex with them in her place – since Sharra would not consent. It was not quite the same, but at least they were her flesh and blood. He would not have been so interested had he known that they were adopted. He knew that Mista had adopted the girls, but assumed that they were born to Sharra. So he continued to redouble his efforts with Robin and paid scant attention to Janice.

Something happened on the third day. Janice began to sing one of the songs that had appealed to her, a song of loneliness and courage, courage that conquered her fears. Robin was drawing a water color picture of a girl drowning. She was not consciously thinking about what she was drawing, just letting her mind and fingers wander. The song penetrated her consciousness. She stopped drawing and said, "What are you doing?"

"Just singing. Does it bother you?"

"NO! I suddenly feel all better. Sing some more."

So Janice sang for half an hour, and Robin was whole again. Neither girl realized what had happened. Janice sensed Robin's loneliness and despair and wanted to somehow lift her spirits, but did not know how. So she sang. She sent her own emotions with the song. Robin picked up her emotions without even knowing it and began to share Janice's upbeat mood. The last song she sang was "Danny Boy".

When she had finished, Robin had tears in her eyes. She came over and hugged Janice. "I've never heard that song sung like that. I didn't even know you could sing."

"I guess I didn't either. I just wanted to sing. You know what that song says to me? Daddy will come. He will. Remember what he told Aunt Sheila? That he would not stop looking until Hell froze over. He'll be here."

"I hope we don't have to wait 25 years."

"Oh, no. I bet he already knows where we are, and is just figuring out a way to get us free."

By the fourth day, Brumley's patience had worn thin. He had been told what Janice said about Mista finding them, about already knowing where they were. He did not believe that he could know. Just to taunt Mista, Brumley sent him an e-mail with a photo of the girls smiling and wearing clothing that Brumley had provided them. He had said, "Your wife is dead, and I have your daughters. The next picture they will be naked and making love to me. Do not bother to try to trace this e-mail. It was sent from a temporary pre-paid account."

He had turned the phone off and tossed it into the garbage after sending the message, so that even the phone's location could not be traced.

Then he told Smirnoff to have the girls dressed in what he called 'modeling dresses' – mini dresses and no underwear. When Smirnoff said that they were ready, Brumley went to see the girls. "I think we have danced around long enough," he said. "You are both pretty girls and I can put you into position to become models."

"You just want to rape us," Janice said.

Brumley bristled. "If I had wanted to rape you, I would have by now."

"You might have tried."

"Don't make me angry. Robin, let me see you walk. Prance a little, like you were wearing high heels."

Robin looked at Janice. Janice shrugged. She saw no harm in walking. Robin walked across the room. Even at eleven, she already had a natural grace and a small sway.

"Good. You have some promise. Now, pull the dress up on one side and do it again."

"No! I don't think so!" Robin went to a corner chair and sat on her legs.

"Humph. I thought you were a little more obedient than that. Janice, let me see you walk."

"I'm not interested."

Brumley glared. "I want you to walk!"

Janice stood up and stomped across the room, and then sat back down, careful to turn her legs sideways and pull the dress down as far as it would go.

Brumley glared at her for a moment. "I could rip that dress right off of you."

"Go ahead. You wouldn't see much grace and charm that way."

"What's it going to take? Threaten you with your life?"

"What have I got to lose? Well." She softened her face and appeared to study him. "There is one thing. I haven't been outside in days and days. I bet you have a pool here. I'd like to go swimming, and so would Robin. She loves the water. If I could go swimming, I might be interested in your little game."

Brumley waited a beat, thinking about that. What harm could there be if he were with them the whole time? "You'd have to swim in your birthday suit, since you have no swim suit."

"And I have no underwear. It might be worth it to see the sun again."

Robin gasped. "Not me! I'm not going naked."

Janice said, "Nobody else will be there? Just you. I promise not to try to run away."

"Just me." *And the guards in the trees, of course,* he did not say.

"All right. What's to see, Robin? Just skin. I just want to get wet again. You will too. Let's do it." She crossed her hands in her lap and turned toward Robin so that Brumley could not see her left arm, and pointed to her watch.

Robin's eyes widened. She could do that. "I'm scared. I don't want to go naked."

"Well, I bet if you see me do it, you'll come in too," Janice said. "At least, come watch."

Brumley was almost beside himself. His desire had increased every day, partly from natural causes – delayed gratification naturally heightened desire – and partly because Jeremy gave him a little push every day. He pushed aside the risks. In fact, he momentarily forgot the suspicion that Mista had some way to trace them, which was why they had been locked in the secure room.

"Okay. Walk in front of me, so that I can be sure that you do not try to run." And so he could watch them in anticipation.

Janice went first when they got outside, stepping carefully on the ground, since she was barefoot. This also heightened the lift of her hips as she walked. Robin copied her, walking behind. Brumley followed, giving directions from time to time when they needed to turn.

When they came out into the open area around the pool, no one was in sight. Janice stepped up to the edge of the pool and waited for Robin. Then she put her hands under the hem of her dress, as if to pull it up and looked back at Brumley. He was bug-eyed with excitement. Janice winked at him slowly, and then jumped into the pool. Robin followed.

Brumley roared. "Hey! You were supposed to undress. You'll ruin those dresses. Take them off. Now!"

Janice said, "You could come in and try to make us."

Brumley sputtered. He had never learned to swim. "Just get out. You broke your promise."

Janice swam to the edge of the pool, about 25 feet away from Brumley, and signaled Robin to go to the other side. Then she put her hands on the edge and pushed herself out, turning and sitting on the edge in one motion. Robin tried to copy her, but couldn't manage. She had to throw her legs up and crawl out.

Brumley stomped over to Janice. "I said, take the dress off!" He reached out to pull it down. Robin sent a small fire into the palm of his hand, careful not to burn Janice at the same time. "OW!" He jerked his hand back. "You can't be that hot." He stretched his other hand out to touch her, and Robin burned it, too, just a little hotter.

"You won't get away with this," he shouted. He turned and stomped over to Robin. "All right, you take yours off. I mean, now." As soon as he turned his back, Janice pushed the secret button on her watch, just in case Mista was not watching the screen, he would get a call.

Brumley reached out to pull Robin's dress down. She burned him between the legs this time. He jerked back, lost his balance and fell into the pool. "Help! I can't swim!" Both girls watched him struggle. They did not particularly care if he drowned. Two guards ran from the trees and pulled him out.

Janice said, "Just you, huh? So much for your word."

"You broke your promise," he said.

"I never made a promise. I only said that it might be worth it. I decided that it wasn't."

Brumley looked at Janice with fury. "I'll … I'll … get back in your room."

Robin pushed her call button on her watch while he was yelling at Janice. Now Mista would have two calls.

Janice!

MOM! You found us!

Yes. We haven't been able to contact you. Are you all right?

Yes! I tricked him into taking us outside for a swim. It was fun.

All right. We on the way, be there in a day or so. I'm going to contact Robin. Robin!

MOMMY! You found us.

Yes. We've been trying.

They had us locked in a room.

I figured. Are you all right?

Yes. He hasn't touched us. Trying to make friends. Hah!

Well, don't forget, you have more powers than just fire. Use them!

I — we're going back in now. He's mad. We tric …

The contract was lost.

Brumley herded them back to their room and told the guard to lock the door again. He walked away to cool his anger. He decided to return that evening and have the girls, whether they agreed or not.

Janice stopped just inside the door, but Robin ran in and danced around in a circle. "That was fun. I thought you meant to go naked."

Janice did not say anything. They had hopefully made their calls. They had no way of knowing if the calls had gotten through until Sharra had contacted them, but Mista had assured her that it would. However, it reminded her of something else. Mista had had sub-vocal radio links implanted in them when they first came. They were only useful for short distances, but they allowed the team to communicate without anyone else being able to listen. Janice was trying to remember how to activate it. They had never used them..

She had been afraid to talk with Robin about anything serious, fearing that their room was bugged. But if she could activate the radio link... There was a tiny switch between two teeth. She was supposed to be able to activate it with her tongue, but she could not find it. She would need a toothpick. She didn't have a toothpick. Maybe a nail. She put her middle finger in her mouth and felt the gaps between her teeth. Most were far too small to have a switch. Then she found it. *Robin!*

Robin jumped. Janice's voice seemed to be right in her ear. "What did you say?"

Janice held her mouth closed with her fingers, and said, *We have radios. Remember? A switch between your teeth.*

Robin found her switch and clicked it on. *Oh. I forgot all about these. Now we can talk.*

Right. You made your call, didn't you?

Yes. I hope it worked. I tried when we first got here, too.

You knew it had worked when Mom contacted us. I think they kept us locked in this one room because somehow radio waves and cell phones can't get in it.

That would be why Mommy hadn't contacted us.

Right. And remember, the GPS thing doesn't work inside a building, anyway. That's why I wanted to go outside. That way Daddy knows exactly where we are. The call was just to alert him to go look, to tell him that we were outside finally.

Yeah, and it felt good to go swimming again. She squeezed some water out of her dress onto the floor. *Come on, let's go play in the shower.*

Sure, why not.

I wish they would give us shoes.

Janice said, *I guess we don't need shoes as long as we stay in this room.*

CHAPTER 47

When Mista left, Jania told Em that she did not have to stay. Em said, "No, I'll stay with you. You might need my skills before this is over. Besides, we both would need to take a break from time to time, and that way somebody would always be here."

"I'm going to have them bring in a cot. Do you want one, too, or will you sleep at home?"

"I probably should go home. I still need to help with the children, especially little Sam."

"Okay. I've got books to study, and I want to learn more about the brain while I'm here. What about you?"

"I'll go down to the book store and get a book to read."

Em went down to find the bookstore while Jania arranged for a cot. Then Jania pulled a chair up beside the bed, laid her hands on Sharra's head, and *looked* inside. She moved first one of Sharra's hands and then the other, trying to find what part of the brain showed activity. She could not localize that. She tried moving her head, but nothing showed up. *Maybe the activity has to start in the brain. Maybe that is what Sharra would do herself if she were here. Maybe if I do something inside the brain … no. too dangerous. I might really mess something up.*

She tried pinching a finger, sending a pain signal to the brain. That got a response. She saw the signal come in, but nothing happened. She reasoned that the information came in but was not processed. She gave it up for a while and sat back in her chair.

Em came in a little later. "How do you do your healing thing? I've often wished that I could do something like that for the patients I treat. I'd love to be able to fix Samantha's cerebral Palsy damage."

"So would I. That's one reason I am going to med school. I want to learn what makes the brain work and then learn how to fix it."

"We already know a lot about how it works. And a good surgeon can often fix problems."

"Yes, by cutting on something. Medicines affect everything, and some parts of the body respond differently to some chemicals. I want to be able to make a direct fix."

"But how?"

"I don't know how it happens. I can kind of see the inside of someone with my mind. It's kind of like looking at a picture, except it is the person. Then I can see if something is broken or leaking. I can see inflammation and infections. I didn't use to know what to call what I saw, but I am leaning things like that at school. I can move some things. I forgot that when I asked Jeremy to help when Sharra was first shot. I found the little pieces of bone and metal and he moved them out. The actual healing, though is something that God does. I just figure out what is wrong and pray for healing."

"Does he always heal what you pray for?"

"No, not always. Like Sharra, now. Physically, she seems fine, but something else is wrong, and I have no idea what. We'll just have to wait and see."

"That's fascinating. Can you read minds, too, like Sharra does?"

"No. That's not one of my talents. Sometimes I can sense something, but I can't actually read thoughts."

"I wish I could do something like that. I do know how to nurture, though, and teach. So I guess I just do what I can."

They were silent for a while, and Jania took a short nap. When she woke up, Em suggested that she go down and get some supper. After supper they talked about themselves. They both knew who the other was, but had not had a chance to get to know each other.

Em asked, "Do you think I could learn to heal like you do?"

"It's not something I learned. I was raised in a temple, supposedly being taught to be a priestess. I came to Mista's school to learn magic when I was 17. I was not able to heal anything at all. They had actually been training me to be a prostitute, similar to the ring that Sheila got involved in here. In fact, when we found her she was being used as a slave by the prostitution ring's leaders. She is my mother, you know."

"No, I didn't realize that. I thought Sharra was your mother."

"Mista and Sharra adopted me, before we had found Sheila. When we did find her, we just left it in place. Jasmine taught me how to pray for healing. And we discovered that I had a very unusual talent. It is God who does the healing. Jasmine taught me to pray."

"Well, I know how to pray. I guess I could pray for healing as well as I can pray for anything else. I became a nurse because I wanted to help people."

"I'm sure you do that a lot. I've seen what you do with Samantha. How long have you been a nurse?"

"Ten years, now. Worked in a hospital a couple of years, and then the Mayo Clinic. I've been here almost a year."

They talked for a while, and then Em left. "I'll see you in the morning."

Jania tried to probe Sharra again, but again had no success. She studied until she got sleepy, and then went to bed.

Nothing happened the next day except the bit of excitement about Mista heading out to sea. Em asked, "Why would he do that? Just sail around in circles?"

Jania shrugged. "He loves his boat and he loves the sea. He wanted a quiet place to think, and so I suppose he thought that would be the best place.

The next day started out the same way. No change. Sharra woke up at 3:00 that afternoon. She woke up, sat up and asked Jania, "Where am I?"

"MOM! You're awake!"

"Yes, I know. Where am I?"

"In the hospital in Tampa. You got shot in the head and were in a coma."

"So did they get you here in time to fix me?"

Jania giggled. "Yes. I fixed you. You were a mess!"

"How long have I been here?"

"Four days."

"Time lost. Where's Mista? Why isn't he here?"

"He out on his boat."

"Well he ought to be here."

Sharra called. *Mista?*

Coming, Darling.

Where are you? Where am I?

I'm at sea. I'll be there in two hours. You're in the hospital.

Oh. Hurry. I love you.

I love you, too.

Jania said, "Did you call Daddy?"

"Yes. He's already on his way here. Guess he knew. I have to get dressed."

"Mom, you can't leave just like that!"

Em said, "Let me call the doctor and see if he will release you."

"Jania is my doctor. Anything wrong with me that I don't already know about?"

"Nope. The only thing wrong with you is that you weren't here."

Sharra wrinkled her brow. "What do you mean?"

"I looked inside you and made sure that I repaired all the damage. Everything looked fine, everything was working like it should. But I couldn't see you. Like you weren't here."

"Maybe I wasn't. I was somewhere else, I think. It's only a vague memory, but then suddenly I was back. Where are my clothes? I need to get out of here."

"But, Mom, you don't have any clothes here. They had to throw your clothes away, they were ruined."

"Who are you calling, Em?"

"Your doctor. He will have to release you before you can leave."

"Jania is my doctor. Release me."

Jania threw up her hands. "You're released. But you don't' have any clothes."

"Oh. Well, I'll make some."

CHAPTER 48

She looked down at herself, unhooked the IV and threw off her hospital gown. She sat on the edge of the bed for a minute. "I'm weak as a kitten. Can you make me some food?"

"No, that's the kind of magic that doesn't work here."

Sharra snapped her fingers. "Oh well. But, I'm hungry. Em would you go down to the cafeteria and get me a couple of cheeseburgers to go? I'll eat them on the way over there."

"Uh... sure. I'll be right back."

"No, meet me at the front door."

"But ..." She shrugged. "Whatever."

"Mom, where are you going, and how?"

"Call me a taxi. You have money with you don't you?"

"Yes. Daddy gave me some."

"I'll meet him at the piers."

"But ..."

"Call me a taxi, please."

"Okay, but wha ..."

Sharra had made an illusion of one of her favorite pink dresses. She knew her size, and made it to fit. However, she had lost weight during her stay, and it hung loose on her. "Oh, dear. That will never do." She adjusted the illusion so that it fit.

"Well. Are we ready?"

"Just a minute... Taxi will be here in five minutes."

Two doctors came into the room, flanked by two nurses and an orderly dragging a portable EKG machine just as Sharra started out. One was Dr.

Baskins. The other wore a nametag that said, Simmons. Dr. Baskins said, "You cannot leave until we check you out, Mrs. Mictackic. Please get back in bed and let me examine you."

"My doctor has already examined me and released me."

"I am your doctor, Mrs. Mictackic."

"Correction. Jania is my doctor. I don't remember coming in, but I bet she cleaned me up. Correct?"

"Yes, but …"

"Did she also clean and close the wound?"

"Yes, but …"

"Did you do anything at all?"

"Not really, but she is not a doctor."

"Far as I am concerned, she is a doctor, and better than most. Please stand aside."

"But, Mrs. Mictackic, you can't just leave." His eyes widened. "Where did you get that dress?"

"Made it."

She walked through the crowd, parting them by the sheer force of her will. "Ask Jania if you have any more questions. Come on, dear. We have to go rescue the girls."

Jania grabbed her books up and ran. "Scuse me, please. Please let me through."

Sharra winced when she stepped on a piece of pencil that had been dropped. She realized that she had not made shoes, so she cast an illusion of pink high heels, and walked on, producing the click of heels as she strode to the elevator. Jania caught up with her at the elevator.

"Whew. Don't leave me. Mom, you are still shaven."

"Oh." She felt the top of her head. "No scar, right? Not that it will matter under my hair."

"Nope. No scar."

"Good." She made an illusion of hair in her normal style.

Jania looked her up and down as they rode down. "The Emperor's New Clothes look pretty good on you, Mom."

"Thanks, dear."

Em came running up with her cheeseburgers just as they reached the front doors. The taxi pulled up outside at the same time. Sharra got in first and Jania and Em sat on either side. "Give me a cheeseburger, please. I'm starving. To the piers, driver."

"Which piers did you have in mind, ma'am?"

"I'm afraid I don't remember. Tell him, Jania. Or Em."

Sharra frowned as she ate. "I don't remember being at the piers. Last thing I remember – was … Oh. We were heading for port and were going to try to meet the scum there."

"Do you remember who we were meeting?" asked Em.

"Of course. David Brumley. I just don't like to say his name."

"Looks like you've lost about two days," Em said. "That's pretty common for a person coming out of a coma. You might get it back, but probably won't."

"Who shot me?" Sharra asked. "And why?"

"We don't know, Mom. They found you on the deck, unconscious. Nobody heard a shot, but you definitely had a bullet wound."

"I presume that you have been working on finding the girls while I was out?"

"Not me, Mom. I stayed with you. Daddy was probably searching, though."

"Well, it's time to go look for them. Do you have any idea where they are?"

"Daddy said that he believes that they are in the Cayman Islands, probably Grand Cayman."

"Okay. Then we should go there and look for them." She thought a minute, and then called Mischal *Misch!*

Good to hear you, Sharra. We're on the way.

I'll meet you at the pier, but I just had a thought. Can you go by a gun shop or something and get a tranquilizer gun?

I suppose so. What do you have in mind?

I assume that you will be armed to the teeth, and if we are attacked, you will probably need them. However, we might be able to get inside the house by putting the guards to sleep.

I'll try. Should be able to find one. We'll talk about it later. I would rather have this closed permanently. That means all the key players dead, not just sleeping. If we don't, they will try again.

That is true. But they might not be on the scene. We don't need to kill otherwise innocent guards. Yes, I know that they aren't really innocent. If they are part of the operation, we could send police to arrest them. But they would not have a personal vendetta against us.

Right. No need to kill unnecessarily. I understand.

I knew that you would. See you soon.

When Sharra got to the piers, Mista was not in yet. She asked the driver to wait.

"But, I ..."

"We'll make it worth your while. You can keep the meter running, or name a flat fee." She did not need to tell him that he would pocket the entire flat fee, while he would only get a percentage of meter fare.

"How long?"

"Till my husband gets in. Shouldn't be long – less than half an hour."

He did not really want to stay, but ... "Fifty dollars?"

Jania said, "That okay, Mom?"

"Yes. High, but you will stay until he comes, right?"

"Yes. But if it is more than the half-hour, I will need more. I could be doing business."

"Up to an hour. Or keep the meter running."

"An hour."

They saw the masts of the Wolfhunter a few minutes later. Jania handed the driver two twenties and a ten and said, "Thanks for waiting."

They got out and stood on the pier until she was docked. Charly threw a line out from the bow and called Jania to loop it around a bollard and throw it back. When Charly had it secured, Mista put his rudder hard over and eased forward against the line, walking the stern in toward the pier. As soon as she touched, he killed the engines, ran aft and grabbed the stern line and jumped to the pier. He whipped it around the bollard there and tossed it back to Charly, who had come back and was waiting. "You can secure her."

He turned away and ran to Sharra, grabbing her in a bear hug. "I'm glad you're back."

"Was there any doubt?"

"You know there was. We do not presume on God." They shared a long, sweet kiss. Then Mista said, rubbing his hand up and down her back, "Hey. You don't have anything on!"

"I already knew that. They said that they threw away my clothes. I had to improvise."

"You mean, like an illusion?"

"Yeppers. I knew you wouldn't be fooled."

"Well, let's get aboard and get you something real to wear, before somebody else notices."

When they came back up a few minutes later, Sharra was wearing white jeans and a blue blouse. Mista stayed in the pilothouse, started the engines. "Jania, will you cast off the stern line? Charly, stand by the bow line, please."

Jania moved aft, but Charly just stood there. "We can't leave yet. Misch and Njondac aren't here yet."

"We don't need them. They deserted."

Charly's mouth dropped open. Sharra said, "WHAT?"

"Mista!" Charly said. "They did NOT desert!"

Mista shrugged. "They left. Said they were tired of riding around on a boat. Like it was all a waste of time."

Charly said, "Yes, they were frustrated with all the waiting. But they're *not* deserters. Misch said to be sure to call him when you had found them and were ready to make a frontal attack."

"Well, we don't need them, and I don't want to wait while someone calls them." He looked around. Jania had thrown off the stern line and was standing, waiting. "Jania, go stand by the bow line. Be ready to cast it off when I tell you."

Jania started forward, but Charly put her hand out. "Not."

"Let her go. We have to get underway."

"Not until Misch gets here."

"He's on the way," Sharra said. "What about Molly?"

"She deserted, too."

Charly doubled her fists in anger. "They did NOT desert. You want to see deserters? You don't wait for them, and I WILL desert. I'll take mother and Jeremy, too. Jania if she will come."

"Why are all of you resisting?"

"Because you need us, old man. Get your head straight. We are not leaving without them."

Mista said, "Every minute we wait is lost."

Sharra said, "Let's be patient, dear. We'll get there in good time. I asked Mischal to bring a tranquilizer gun. We might need that."

Mista looked over at her. She had walked out of the hospital clothed in nothing but an illusion, ready to hunt for their girls. Now, she was willing to wait. He sighed. He knew she was right. Mischal had really only asked for time off to visit his family. Taking it as a personal betrayal was a sign of Mista's own sense of frustration. He would never have taken out his own frustration in this manner in ordinary circumstances. Even unordinary.

"All right." He secured the engines, went to the rail and jumped to the pier. The gangway was still in place – he had been about to leave and have it fall in. He shook his head, angry at himself, and walked back toward the stern of the boat. "Pitch me the line, Jania. I guess I was hasty"

Mischal finally showed, half an hour later, carrying a suit bag over his shoulder and a long box in his other hand. Chandri followed, carrying Samantha and leading Tilly by the hand. Next came Njondac and Cato, carrying an extra-long golf bag with its open end covered by a burlap bag. Josie, Njondac's wife, came next with their son, Brut.

Mischal carried the bag and box down to the salon and laid it on one of the seats. It clanked, unlike most suits, when he laid it down. "Hope nothing is banged up," he said.

Mista followed him down, and asked, "You moving in?"

Mischal grinned. "No. I just thought that people might get curious about us carrying four long rifles on board."

Njondac came in and dropped the golf bag. "Not to say two shotguns and a long bow. And three swords."

"Well, I guess we might need them," Mista said.

"Jeremy said we were going on a hunt. Here is something new – tranquilizer pellet gun." He handed the box to Mista. "Don't leave just yet. We've got to go back and get two big coolers full of frozen food."

CHAPTER 49

"Daaadeee," Sam said and held out her arms.

Mista took her and said, "Hi sweetness. What you been doing?"

"Paaa." *I play.*

"Say it. Play."

"Paaa."

While Mischal, Cato, Njondac and Brut went back for the food, Jania took Sam and set her on the deck. "Let me see you walk, Honey."

Can't.

"Try. Here. Let me stand you up. Put your feet on the floor."

"Deck," Mista said.

"Hold her up, Daddy, with her feet just off the *floor.*"

Mista grinned, but knelt down and held Sam up. Jania placed one hand on each knee and looked inside. *Ah. Ligaments aren't quite long enough, and the long muscles are real tight.* "Honey, I'm going to stretch your legs, okay? It might hurt a little."

Hurt? I'm big. I not cry.

"Okay. Just a little."

Jania reached inside and pulled at the ligaments. They did not want to stretch. She worked with them for a few minutes, while Sam squirmed and winced. Finally, Jania just prayed for healing. She did not know why they would be drawn up like they were, but she knew that Sam would not be able to walk like that. Sam's eyes got big as she felt heat flow through her legs and then felt the legs relax.

"All right. Now you see how straight they are, Honey?"

Sam nodded.

Jania stood up. "I want you to stand on one leg, while Daddy holds you, and raise the other one like this." She stood on her left leg and bent the right leg back at the knee, raising her foot up behind her as far as it would go. "Can you do that?"

Sam scrunched up her face and told her leg to bend. The leg bent back and she relaxed. "I do!"

"Good. You need to do that every day so your legs get strong. Now put it back down."

The leg went half way down and stopped. "All the way down."

She got it there, and said, *Hurts.*

"I know it does, Honey, but if you keep doing this it will get strong and then it won't hurt any more. Then you can walk."

Em came up and picked Sam up. "I know what you are doing, Jania. I'll work with her and we'll get those legs strong, won't we sugar?'

"Eeeesss."

They brought four large coolers full of food and one large cardboard box. Mischal said, "I have body armor, too."

Then he opened another large box. "Hammocks. With safety harnesses. For the kids. I know most of the bunks are already being used, so I thought the little ones could sleep in the cabins with their parents. They shouldn't mind hammocks."

Chandri pulled one rifle out of the bag, and Mischal put the rest in a chest under one of the salon seats. She showed it to Mista, her eyes shining. "Remington M24. Mischal bought it in Atlanta this spring, but I haven't had a chance to really test it out yet."

Mista nodded. "Sniper rifle. You should be good with it. What scope?"

"The original 10X scope. There are better ones available, but this is good for a start. Maybe as good as I need anyway. Maximum range is 800 yards, and I doubt if I will want to shoot further than that."

"Never can tell. You going to try to shoot from the deck while we're underway?"

"If I find a target. I won't be able to get long range accuracy, but if I can time the rise just right I should be good for a few hundred yards."

"Hah. You probably will. I would never be good at that range from a moving deck."

Mischal waited until Chandri turned to put her rifle up and then walked up and placed a hand on each of Mista's shoulders. "We're going for him, now, right? That's what Jeremy said."

"Yes. I don't know exactly where he is, but we got one satellite report on Grand Cayman. We're going there and look till we find them. With any luck, we'll find one or both of his boats there and can get a clue from the people aboard them."

"Right! That's all I wanted to hear. Listen, Bro. I hope you didn't take offense when we took off. I was just tired of spending weeks at sea and getting nothing done. I want to get this man and all his team. You're not going to just argue with their version of the FBI, are you? Just go in and get them."

Mista looked him in the eye, a spark of blue in his own. "I'm getting my girls, whatever it takes. And I intend to take Brumley and crew down. They will die, one way or the other."

Mischal clapped him on the shoulders. "Finally. Let's go."

Mischal climbed up on deck. "Charly! Get the stern line. Chandri, get the bow line. Njondac! Lite off the engines." He jumped ashore, took the loop on the stern line off its bollard, passed the line around the bollard and tossed the end back to Charly. He did the same at the bow. Now all they had to do to cast off was let the end go. He came back aboard and pulled in the gangplank, then went up and took the bow line from Chandri and snubbed it around a cleat.

"Ready, Mista?"

"Ready."

"Cast off, Charly."

Mista put his rudder over and eased ahead against the bow line. Since the boat could not go forward, this move caused the stern to swing away from the pier, called 'springing out on the bow line'. When he was far enough out, he reversed the engines, gave four short blasts on his whistle, and backed out into the channel. Mischal released the bow line and let it snake around the bollard and drop into the water.

When they had cleared the last buoy, Mista set a course of 200 degrees. Then he asked Chandri to plot a course for a point 20 miles west of the western tip of Cuba, taking into account the offset of the wind. She came up a few minutes later and said, "This looks good. Good guess. I'll give you an update after we've run a few hours, and see how the wind affects us."

"Good. Don't forget, the Caribbean current comes up around the end of Cuba and becomes the Gulf Stream. We'll need to monitor the track closely when we get close to Cuba. I don't want to be pushed into Cuban waters."

Then he called Njondac. "I want to keep the engines running so that we can make the best speed possible."

"No problem. If you keep the boost moderate, we'll have enough fuel for about 10 days. Five days, if you push it."

"Let's keep it moderate. I'd like to gain about 10 hours on the trip."

CHAPTER 50

Just before dark after the first full day out, they crossed the edge of the continental shelf. Chandri noticed the change in depth and called Mista. "We're only making a little over 10 knots. Just dropped off the continental shelf – depth went from 50 fathoms to 1500 in a little over an hour."

"Well, we'll lose speed during the night, when we hit the Gulf Stream."

"Right. I'll watch our track. We should pass Cuba about eight in the morning."

They rounded the point of Cuba on schedule, and set a new course, direct to Georgetown. Jeremy sensed the change by the way the boat rode, and asked. Chandri told him that they had changed course. "Should be in Georgetown by tomorrow evening."

"Good." He called Molly.

Molly! We'll be in Georgetown tomorrow evening.

Good. I'll be there about noon. Will one car be enough?

Probably. Everybody came, children and all. You might as well bring Susan with you.

Mista kept his computer on with the girls' GPS program active. He had set his map to show about 300 miles square, with the Cayman Islands near the right edge of the screen. The screen showed a white dot for their location and would show a red dot for Janice and a blue dot for Robin. Only the white dot was showing as they neared Grand Cayman. Mista was half watching the screen, drinking coffee and half asleep. He hoped something would happen, but did not really expect it. When they were about 50 miles away from Grand Cayman, the computer suddenly beeped. A red dot and a blue dot popped up on the screen.

Mista sat up, instantly alert. He moved over to the computer and zoomed in so that Grand Cayman filled the screen. They were at the eastern edge of the island. He continued to zoom in until the map reached maximum resolution. They were on the beach near a town called Gun Bay. He wrote down the coordinates. There was also a sheltered bay there, and he supposed that it was Gun Bay.

His cell phone beeped. A computerized voice said, "ALERT! ALERT! ALERT! THIS IS AN EMERGENCY CALL. ALERT!"

He had just disconnected when it beeped again. Again, a computerized voice said, "ALERT! ALERT! ALERT! THIS IS AN EMERGENCY CALL. ALERT!"

He smiled. *Good. They both remembered to call.*

Suddenly, it dawned on him, that if the girls were outside – and they must be for the GPS finder to work – then Sharra would be able to contact them. She was on watch. He climbed up to the pilothouse. "I've got it. The girls are outside – I have a GPS location. You should be able to contact them."

"Oh. Of course."

Janice!

MOM! You found us!

Yes. We haven't been able to contact you. Are you all right?

Yes! I tricked him into taking us outside for a swim. It was fun.

All right. We on the way, be there in a day or so. I'm going to contact Robin. Robin!

MOMMY! You found us.

Yes. We've been trying.

They had us locked in a room.

I figured. Are you all right?

Yes. He hasn't touched us. Trying to make friends. Hah!

Well, don't forget, you have more powers than just fire. Use them!

I – we're going back in now. He's mad. We tric ...

The contract was lost.

"Lost them. They said that they tricked him into taking them outside to swim. Where? In the ocean? Or a pool. Anyway, they're fine, so far. They should feel much better now that they know that we are almost there, and know where they are."

"My map didn't give me much information. Just the location. I'm going to try to spot the place with Google Earth. You might want to watch. First, though, I need to change course." He called Chandri's room. She was not there. Then he spotted her, up in the bow, taking in the sun. "CHANDRI!" he called.

She sat up. "Yes!"

"We need a new course."

"Right now?"

"Yes. We found the girls."

"Oh! Be right there."

Mista brought the Wolfhound around to 090, due east. That was about as close to the wind as he could sail and still maintain acceptable speed, even with the engines running. He called Charly and asked her to take in the sheets on the mainsail until it was in trim. Then he sent her to adjust the mizzen sail.

"Okay. Now, take the wheel, please while we plot a new course. We found the girls."

"Oh. Great!"

Chandri laid out a course line at 090. "That clears the island to the north, but only by a few miles. The wind will be setting us down onto the island. We would need to come really close hauled – almost right into the wind to maintain our track. Might be best to go on south of the island and then turn north at the other end. We'd still have the wind setting us onto the island when we turn north, but that is only for a short distance. Or, we could go on past the island, turn north and then come down on the island from the north. And we could adjust course to compensate for the wind without having to turn directly into the wind."

"Yes. I see what you mean. Okay. Let's go back to 160 then and re-adjust the sails. You get the mizzen sheet and I'll send Charly to get the main sheet."

When they had reset the course, Mista turned the watch back over to Charly and went down to see if he could see what was at the girls' coordinates. Sharra sat on one side and Chandri on the other. Mista turned to Chandri, "Why don't you get Mischal and Njondac in here, too?"

"Okay."

Mista had Google Earth running and had zoomed down to the island level when they came back in. He brought the resolution up until he could see the coastal highway on the south side of the island, and followed the highway across the island. At the eastern end of the island, he zoomed in closer and then put the cursor on the coordinates given by the girls' GPS locaters. "There it is. Big house, private dock, swimming pool and two outhouses."

Mischal looked and studied the picture. "Think we could go right into that bay? They have a dock there."

"Looks pretty shallow. I don't think I want to try it with this big boat. The dinghy could get in."

"Yeah. When do we get there?"

Mista said, "Let's not just guess. Check the chart."

Chandri pulled up the chart for Gun Bay, on the east end of the island. "That house and dock are here. There are two entrances through the reef, but this one is pretty narrow. We have ten or eleven feet of water near the reef, but the rest of the bay is pretty shallow. I wouldn't recommend it."

"Well, we're about three hours away from the island, now. Two hours to sail by it, or maybe three. We'll be going into the wind, so not nearly so fast. It's four, now, so seven or eight."

"Barely dark."

"What are you thinking?"

"I'm thinking we put a team ashore in the dinghy to go in and get the girls. Take the sleep darts. Tranquilizers. Stubbs and I can do that."

"What do you use for cover?"

"Hmmm. No cover."

Chandri said, "Molly could make you invisible."

"Where is Molly?" Mischal asked.

"Oh. She went home," Mista said. "Someone should have called her."

"Maybe they did," Chandri said. "I'll go ask Charly." She ran up the ladder.

Charly said, "I think Jeremy did. Call him. I think he's in the room."

Jeremy said, "Yes. She's meeting us in Georgetown. Flying down. I gave her our ETA last night. Are we still on schedule?"

"Well, not exactly. We're changing. We found the girls."

"Oh. Better tell her."

Chandri went back down. "She's meeting us in Georgetown. She'll have a car for us to use."

"That'll be good," Mischal said. "We can attack from two fronts. Should we drop a team off in Georgetown?"

"No," Mista said. "We'd be splitting ourselves too thin. We'll drop you off here and then go on. We'll have to pass customs in Georgetown. Might not be able to get weapons off the boat."

"Yeah, that could be a problem. We can take extra weapons in when we hit the beach. Problem. Molly won't be with us."

"I'll go in with you, "Sharra said. "I can make you invisible."

"Are you sure?" Mischal asked. "You just got out of the hospital."

"They're my daughters," Sharra said quietly. "I'm going."

Chandri was studying the picture. "Drop me off on that breakwater on the bay. I'll sight in with my new toy and cover you. I'm glad you got the night scope, too, when you bought it."

"It's going to be rough, there. See how the waves break?"

"That's okay. Drop me in the water. I'll wear jeans and a black shirt. I'll be all right."

"Better let me paint your hair black," Mista said.

"You're not painting me black!"

"There are worse things," Jasmine said.

"I have camouflage paint,' Mischal said. "I'll rub it in your hair. Don't worry, it'll wash out."

"Will it wash off in the water?"

"Would in time, but you won't be in that long."

"Okay," Mischal looked around. "We don't want to be too early. Why don't we sail north past the island and then come back?"

"Good," Mista said. "Safer sailing that way, too."

"Can you anchor out somewhere?" Mischal asked.

"No. This island is just a mountain top sticking out of the water. Time we got close enough to anchor, we'd be ashore."

"Well, then put us out and then head for Georgetown port. Whoever comes in the car, blink your lights."

"We have radios," Mista said.

"Oh. We keep forgetting that, don't we."

Mista said, "I'm going to cut the engines. That will add a couple of hours, and we won't have to sail up the east coast and back again."

"Makes sense to me," Njondac said, and went down to secure them.

CHAPTER 51

It was a quiet afternoon on the boat as it sailed on toward Grand Cayman. Even the children sensed that something was up, and were subdued. Patches was Mista's shadow. Every time he went through the hatch down to the salon or back up, he had to hold the door open and wait for Patches. This was the first time that they had planned an assault in a long time. There had been attacks and battles, but nothing that they had planned.

They passed close enough to see the harbor and then Mista set a course due east. It was six o'clock, and they were right on schedule. Sheila served sandwiches to everyone, wherever they happened to be. She sensed that no one was in a mood for a sit-down dinner, but she also knew that they had to eat.

Mista had just finished his sandwich when his phone beeped. His first thought was that the girls had gotten out again, and answered immediately, even though he did not recognize the number. When he heard Brumley's voice, he started his recorder.

"Mr. Mictackic? I have sent you a picture in e-mail. Please look at it, now. It was taken just now with my camera phone. This phone, which I will discard after this conversation. So, don't bather to try to trace it."

Mista said, "Just a moment, please." He opened his e-mail and then opened the last message received. The sender's name was obviously false – not even a real name. The attached picture showed his two girls. Janice stared straight ahead, unsmiling. Robin had a sheepish grin.

"I have it."

"Your two girls, yes? Just so that you know that I have them. The next picture you see, they will be naked."

He signed off.

Mista called Sharra over. "Look at this. He called me to tell me that he had sent it, just to taunt me. However, if their door is open, you should be able to contact them.

"Right." She tried. "Nothing. Too late. Next time call me while he's talking – if he calls again. Of course, we don't know when that picture was taken. He might have taken it inside, and then walked out to call."

"Yeah. But it was worth a try."

Mischal called Chandri to their room. "Let's get you dressed for tonight. I need a denim skirt. Might ruin it, so make it an old one."

"Here. I've only got one. What are you going to do?"

"Make you a fanny pack what am."

He sewed the hem together all around, and then tied the waist to a leather belt with pieced of twine. "All right. Fasten the belt around your waist, and let's see how it works." The belt fit and stayed on, but the skirt made into a bag gaped too much at the top. He looked at it. "It has loops for a belt."

"Yes. I could have told you that."

Mischal looped a piece of line through the belt-loops. Then he tied each end of the line into a loop, fed one loop through the other, and tied it off, like a drawstring. "All right. That should hold. I'll put your night scope in a zip-lock bag and ammunition in another zip-lock bag, and then put the bags in your fanny pack. That should keep them dry while you are swimming."

"Okay. That will work. I better practice putting the scope on the rifle, just in case."

"Right. Now, what shoes will you wear?"

"I think my flats. They are hard leather, have a crepe sole, and fit pretty tight, so they should stay on, and give me good purchase on the rocks."

"Let me see them wet."

"What?"

"Put them on and stick your feet in the shower. I want to see if they come off easily."

"Oh. Okay." She did.

Mischal pulled at them and they stayed in place. "They seem tight enough. But I'd rather see you wear sneakers. I know they won't come off."

"Okay. Whatever you think."

"Put these in your fanny pack, in case you need to go somewhere later. I'll put you in, inside the breakwater, and then hand your piece to you." Mischal unconsciously still called a rifle a piece, a holdover from his Marine days.

"I can climb in."

"Might rock the boat. I'll just lift you and put you in."

"Okay. Just be careful what you squeeze."

"I wouldn't hurt you for the world." He did not crack a smile.

"You're sweet."

"Try to keep your piece dry. Hold it up out of the water if you can."

"And if it gets wet?"

"Should be okay. But take a cloth and some swabs in another zip-lock bag. I think you're ready. Keep your head down."

"You betcha."

The wind was out of the northeast, and they were on a close reach after they turned east. Since a close reach is defined as 45 to 90 degrees from the wind, they were at the near limits of a close reach. Their speed dropped to 4 knots. They passed the lights of a village at the end of the island at 10:00, and turned directly into the wind. Mista started the engines again to hold the boat in place while they put the dinghy in. The moon had not risen, but the sky was clear. There was enough light from the stars to see the breakers and the gap in the breakwater.

Mista said, "Be careful. We'll call you when we get there."

When the small boat was clear, Mista kicked the engines up to speed and brought the bow around. With the wind behind them and the engines at cruising speed, their speed came up to eleven knots. Mista said, "Making eleven knots. Maybe more, since the current is with us, too. He dropped his sails and came into the harbor under power an hour and a half later. Mista called Molly on their radio link when they were just entering the harbor, and she waited for them on the dock. However, the harbormaster radioed them and gave them a spot to anchor. "We do not have dock space for that boat. Send a small boat for the customs officer."

Mista sent back, "Our dinghy went over the side. We do not have a tender."

"Sorry to hear. We will send a boat out. Anyone needing to leave your boat tonight can ride back in with the customs officer. You should be able to replace your boat here."

Mista thought, *That won't work. I can see us unloading guns on the customs officer's boat.* He called Molly. "See if you can find us a small boat. Mischal has our tender. Get someone to bring you out, or buy a boat if anything is open."

"Buying a boat at midnight might be a problem," she sent back. "There are some guys on the beach, here. I bet one of them would take me out there." Molly was wearing a short skirt and high heels -- she had no trouble getting a ride out to the Wolfhunter, arriving a few minutes after the customs officer.

"Wait for me, please. I want to get something to pay you for your trouble, and a couple of my friends want to come ashore. We need to buy a boat tomorrow. Know where we can get a good deal?"

"Sure," the boat owner said, with a leer.

After the customs officer had left, Mista and Charly put their body armor on. Molly said she didn't need it, but she did change to jeans and a dark shirt. And sneakers. Mista put his Kimber .45 in his boot and taped it to his leg and snapped his staff to his belt. Charly said, "I want my swords, but I don't know how I'll get them by those guys in the boat."

Molly said, "I can make them look like pieces of a boom. You ought to take a rifle, too. You don't know what we'll find there."

"All right. What are you taking?"

Molly grinned and pointed to her head. "I've disguised mine as hair." She meant her mind. She did not use any other weapon.

Mista said, "You have the home guard, Jeremy. Is that okay with you?"

"Sure. With all these children aboard, and the ladies, somebody better stay."

Jasmine said, "Don't count me. I'm going. There's bound to be trouble."

"Me, too, Jania said."

The men in the boat were disappointed when Molly did not reappear in a skirt, but recovered quickly when Jania climbed down the ladder into the boat.

When they got to the docks, Molly asked how late the men would stay up.

"We got nothing better to do," one of them said.

"Well, we've got some business to take care of," she said, pointing to the disguised rifle and swords. "We will probably be back in a couple of hours. Think we could borrow a boat?"

"I'll sleep in my boat, lady. Be glad to take you back out. But I don't think you'll find a repair shop open this late."

"Oh, we called ahead. We have friends waiting for us."

They all climbed into the Suburban she had rented. "Biggest thing I could get," she said. I got another car, too, but it's smaller. Think we'll need both?"

"Yes," Mista said. "We will have the girls, and some of the others might want to come back with us instead of waiting for us to come around in the boat."

"Okay. Whoever drives, be careful. They drive on the wrong side of the road here."

There was very little traffic at midnight, and they were approaching the house twenty minutes later.

CHAPTER 52

Brumley had walked into the girls' room and snapped a picture, and then gone back to his office to send it and to call Mista. He had no idea that his boast that they could not trace his call had no meaning, and that Mista was only hours away.

He went back to the room half an hour later. The girls were not in sight when he opened the door. "Where are you?" he asked.

"In the bathroom, Janice called back. "Be out in a minute."

He did not wait for them to come out, but opened the door and walked into the bathroom. They had been playing in the shower, still dressed. Janice said, "You want to play too?" She turned the shower full on him, turning on hot water only.

He jumped back and yelled. "Hey! What are you doing?."

"Oh, well," Janice said.

"Come out here. You've ruined those dresses, too."

"Well, they weren't ours, and we didn't like them, anyway," she said.

"Take them off, then," he said.

Janice said, "We can't. We don't have anything else to wear."

He grinned an evil grin. "Exactly. Take them off."

"No," Janice said.

"I've had it with you two."

Robin reached out and loosened his belt, dropping his pants.

"Hey! How did that happen? Oh, well, just a little early. He stepped out of them and stood in his boxer shorts. "You two are here for one thing only. You know what that is."

"Yes. You want to raise us to be proper young ladies, something that our mother is incapable of doing."

"No. I will raise you, but you know what you're here for. I had hoped to make friends with you so that we could both enjoy it. But you refuse to cooperate." He stopped. His feet were getting uncomfortably hot. "I am not waiting any longer."

His socks began to smolder. He looked down, saw smoke rising from his shoes, and ran for the bathroom, jumping into the water that was still in the tub. He stepped out, untied his shoes and kicked them off. Then he walked back into the room. "All right. Who's first?"

They did not move.

"Then I'll pick one. I'll take you first," he said, pointing to Janice. "You watch. Take off the dress. I'm tired of messing around."

Janice tilted her head and said, "You'll have to make me."

"I'll make you, all right," he said between his teeth. He reached out to her, but could not bring himself to touch her. *What is this?* He thought. He reached for her dress, to pull it down. Just as he touched it, Robin put a little flame under his hand, burning the dress slightly and burning his hand.

He jerked back. "How did you do that? All right. I'll take you, then," He stepped toward Robin. She set his boxer shorts on fire.

He yelled and pulled them off. He stepped back over to Robin and reached down for the hem of her dress, started to pull it up. She set his shirt on fire.

He slapped at it to put it out, and then ran for the door. "This is not worth it. You girls must be witches," he said as he opened the door.

The guard outside was a native. When he heard 'witches', his eyes rolled up into his head. Janice said, "Shall I put a hex on him, too?"

He said, "No, no, miss. I have never hurt you. I'm out of here."

Brumley went out and closed the door. He called Smirnoff. "Get up here with a couple of guards."

When Smirnoff came up, followed by two guards, Brumley asked him if he had a trank gun with him. "Not with me. You need it?"

"Yes. I don't know what's going on, but I can't touch either one of them."

"Hold on. I'll be right back."

When he came back, they went back into the room, Smirnoff holding the gun at his side. The two guards followed. Brumley said, "You two hold that one," pointing at Janice.

Janice sent, *Let them. Let's see what happens. Be ready for anything.*

The guards walked over slowly and one took each arm. Janice said, "You act like I'm some kind of monster. Think you two big guys can hold little old me?"

Brumley said, "All right now, take off that dress."

"Why, granddaddy, I can't with my arms being held."

"I'll take it off of you." He walked behind her and reached for the zipper in the back of the dress. When he reached for it, Robin caused a spark to leap from the zipper and burn his fingers. He jerked back. "Shoot her!"

Smirnoff reacted instantly, raising the pistol and firing a dart. It hit her in the center of her chest. Janice looked down at the dart and then slumped, unconscious.

Robin screamed. "You killed her!"

"No, child, she's just asleep," Smirnoff said. He took another dart and started to re-load the pistol. Robin reached out with her mind, *moved* the dart and pushed the tip into Smirnoff's hand. He stared at it a moment in surprise and then collapsed.

Brumley shouted, "Seize that one! She's the witch!"

The two guards looked at each other, eyes wide and frightened. "You didn't say anything about a witch. We don't mess with witches." They dropped Janice and ran out.

Brumley fumed. This girl was making him look like a fool and he was anything but a fool. He stared at Robin. "Don't move." He grabbed Smirnoff by the shoulders and pulled him out of the room.

Robin called after him, "My daddy is coming. He'll take care of you."

Brumley called back, "He doesn't even know where you are." He slammed the door and locked it. Then he called Karackish and said, "Let's get him down to the office. He must have stuck a dart in his hand while trying to reload the tranquilizer gun. Then we need to figure out what we are going to do."

"What's happening?"

"I don't know. Those girls act like witches, and all the guards have run off."

"Well, voodoo is real to most of them. I'll get a few men from the boat. They're not afraid of anything. Be back in an hour."

"Well, check the guard house. Maybe they didn't all leave."

"I will, but if they are thinking witches, they're all gone. You think Mictackic is on his way here?"

"No. He can't know where we are. Probably still mourning his wife. Those silly girls think he is coming, though."

"Well, be safe. Take an MP5 and check the grounds while I'm gone."

The grounds was a two-acre strip of land between the coastal highway and the water. Brumley walked around behind the outhouses and then walked down to his dock. The dock was a string of wide planks leading out to a pontoon platform. Nothing looked suspicious.

CHAPTER 53

Meanwhile, Robin sat down on the floor and cradled Janice's head in her lap. Janice was breathing normally, long, slow breaths, like she was in a deep sleep. Satisfied that they were telling the truth – that she was asleep – Robin got up and put a pillow under Janice's head. She did not know what else to do. She changed her mind and tried to carry Janice to a bed, but she was too heavy for her. She pulled her over near the bed and sat down again, putting Janice's head in her lap, and leaning back against the bed.

Robin sat and thought. She did not know what more to do. She could not move Janice, and would not leave her. She hoped that she was really all right, and remembered that the security man had stuck her and Janice with darts the first time they had been captured. She could move things. Maybe she could unlock the door and get out. But she would have to wait until Janice woke up.

She tried the lock. It only took a minute to unlock it. Then she put the pillow back under Janice and tried the door. No guard. They really had run off. She was in a long hall with six doors on each side. She could see a staircase at each end. Her room was in the center of the hall, and there was a large staircase in front of it. It looked almost like a motel. She thought, *maybe it was a motel*.

No one was around. She walked to the next door down the hall and tried the door handle. It was locked. *Might be somebody's room.* She went back to her room and stood in the door, thinking. Then she closed the door, pulled her own skirt and top out of the drawer where she had stuffed them and put them on. She threw her wet dress in a corner. Next, she took Janice's clothes over to her. She managed to pull her shorts on, but

281

left the dress. No way was she able to manage the top while Janice was a dead weight. She laid the top on the bed and pulled Janice's dress down over her shorts.

She was still not happy. She opened the hem of her skirt and took the little Exacto knife out. She looked over at Janice. She wished that she had worn shorts instead of a skirt. She liked skirts better, but ... She looked at the dress in the corner. *If I could sew the bottom together ... Mischal gave us some string.* She cut the dress above the waist and ripped the skirt off. It had been a snug fit on her, so the skirt should stay up without a belt. Then she took the little knife and made two small holes in the skirt just above the hem. Two in the front and two in the back. She looped a few turns of string through the holes so that the front and back hem overlapped, and tied it off. It would do. She pulled the modified skirt on under her own skirt. *Phew. At least something down there.* She stretched out on her bed. She wasn't sleepy, but there was nothing else to do but wait. She did doze some, and woke a little later with a start. Her DVD clock said it was 9:00.

She shook Janice and called her name, but Janice did not stir. They had given them something on the boat to make them sleep all night. She hoped that Janice was not going to sleep all night.

She thought, *I could go get wet again. No much fun just getting in the tub and getting wet. Not like outside, wading in streams or in the ocean.* But, it was something to do. She sat on the edge of the tub and put her feet inside and turned the water on to get warm. Her mother used to fuss at her when she waded through puddles, but Mista said he didn't care. It actually would be more fun if he did care a little bit. Not enough to yell at her. She wondered why it was more fun to do something that was a little bit naughty.

The water was warm, and she turned the shower on. Just a little bit. The shower was a shower head on a long hose instead of a regular shower. She pulled her skirt up and sprayed her knees and then her legs, getting the skirt she had cut up wet again. She didn't want to do anything really bad. Some of the girls had talked her into taking a drink of whiskey once in school. That was bad. She hadn't liked it. All it did was make her head feel funny. She had tried drugs, once, too. She didn't like that either. That was really bad. She kept spraying herself a little here and there, eventually getting wet all over. It was more fun to do it slow. It was more fun to *get* wet than to actually *be* wet. She wondered about that, too.

She'd have to ask Daddy. Daddy knew everything. Maybe he would know when she would start developing. Janice was already way ahead of her. But she was older. There was so much she didn't know.

She went back and sat on the bed, forgetting that she was wet. Janice still would not wake up. She decided to go explore some. Nobody was out in the hall anymore, and Janice was never going to wake up.

She went to the first door to her left. She already knew that it was locked, but it only took her a few seconds to unlock it. It was empty.

She went to the next door and unlocked it. There was a girl inside, watching TV. She looked a lot older. The girl looked up, startled, when Robin came in. "How did you get in? They keep the door locked. And where did you come from?"

"Down the hall. I just fiddled with it until it opened. I'm Robin."

"What do you want?"

"I was just exploring, to see if anyone was up here besides us."

"Well, now you know. You can leave, now."

"You don't want company? You aren't lonely all by yourself?"

"No. I wish they would send me a man, but I don't want little girl company."

"You like it?" she asked incredulously.

"Of course. You will too, once you get used to it. Now please leave. I'm watching this movie."

Robin left, thinking the girl sure was crabby. She hoped that she didn't become like that when she started having sex.

She checked the room on the other side of her room. Empty. Checked the next one. She found two girls in that room, watching TV. "Hi," she said. "My name's Robin."

"Hi," one of the girls said. "How did you get in?"

"Fiddled with the door till it opened." Both girls appeared to be her own age.

"I'm Ruth and this is Sally. We're supposed to be models, but nobody has said anything to us since the first week we were here."

"How long have you been here?"

"About two months. The must have forgotten about us."

"Well, count yourselves lucky. Don't believe them. You were not going to be models."

"How do you know? He made us take our clothes off and walk up and down, like models, and then said that we would do."

"Yeah. You mean Mr. B? He told me to take my clothes off, too, but I wouldn't do it. He got mad."

"Well, we did like we were told, and he didn't get mad at us."

Karackish also returned from Georgetown with six of his men about 10:00. He sent two out to patrol the beach, posted two in the upstairs hallway, and he climbed up to the roof for a look around. These girls had been quiet for days, and suddenly they were stirring things up. He thought that maybe they knew something that was about to happen. Smirnoff roused when Karackish came into the office.

He went up with the two guards posted in the hallway. He opened the door to the girls' room and looked in, momentarily surprised that it was unlocked. One was sleeping on the floor, but the other was not there. The girl on the floor had begun to stir. He did not notice that she had changed clothes. He himself paid little attention to what any of the girls happened to be wearing.

He stepped back out. The door, two doors down, was open. He walked quickly down and looked in. Robin was talking to the two girls in there. "Nobody is supposed to be out of their rooms."

"Well, I was bored."

"Back to your room. No one is allowed out." He followed Robin out, locked the door behind him, and followed her to her room. "I don't know how you got out, but this door is supposed to stay locked." He walked out, closed the door and locked it and then turned to the guards. "These doors are to remain locked and no one is allowed out of their rooms."

"Gotcha."

Smirnoff went back down to the office. Brumley was waiting, dressed in dry clothing. "What happened to you in that room?"

"I don't know. Must have stuck myself when I was reloading the gun. What happened to you?"

"I don't know." Brumley shook his head. "My step-daughter used to pull tricks like that. Not with fire. I just couldn't touch her, and my head hurt so bad I had to leave her alone. Now her daughters are doing the same thing. You think there is something to this witch stuff?"

"Voodoo? The natives all swear it's true. I never believed it."

"Well, you saw what happened in there. Maybe we should just get rid of them."

"You mean, send them home? Or dump them? We have a lot invested in them. Try them on a client. Charge extra since they are virgin. They are virgin, aren't they?"

"So the doctor said. Virgin and no diseases. I like that. Then if they hurt the client we can say that since they are new, the client is taking all risks. New girls are an unknown."

"I'll put one of them with the next man to ask for a special girl."

"No. Not yet. They aren't really flesh and blood, but still, they are my step-daughter's. That's almost my flesh. I raised her from the time she was six. I will have them first. And I *will* have them. This is payback."

"Whatever. You are a glutton for punishment."

"Maybe. No. I'll figure out something, if I have to put them to sleep again and take them in their sleep. Not much fun, that way, but at least I'll have the satisfaction of saying that I raped my daughter's daughters. I'll take a picture, too, and send it to that Mictackic. That'll make him happy."

Smirnoff snorted. "Yeah, right."

They sat in silence for a few minutes. Smirnoff took a pipe out of his pocket and tamped tobacco into it, then lit it. He spent a few minutes getting a consistent smoke, and then blew a series of smoke rings.

Brumley said, "I like that smell, although I've never smoked. What kind of tobacco is it?"

"Cavendish. I love the smell, too. Only, after a few minutes, I can no longer smell it. It has a good taste, too. Some tobaccos smell good, but I can't stand to smoke them because they taste so bad."

After a few minutes, Brumley said, "Where's Arnat?"

"He went up on the roof. He's expecting invaders from the sea. You know, they have those old pirate ships at Georgetown. Maybe one of them is real pirates."

"Yeah. I'm going up to see him." He frowned. "I was going to send a picture of those girls naked to their father. But I can't get them naked. Give it some thought, will you? Maybe they'll let you touch them."

"After seeing what they did to you, I'm not sure that I want to try. I'll think about it."

Brumley climbed to the roof and looked around. He saw nothing out of the ordinary. "What do you expect? An invasion from the sea?"

"Could be. He has a big sailboat."

"He wouldn't risk coming into the lagoon with that."

"I don't know. He doesn't lack guts. I don't really expect him to show up. One he can't know where we are. Two, he wouldn't leave his wife. She's either in the hospital or dead."

"How can you know that? We didn't stay to see what was happening."

"I don't miss. Anyway, he could have been here by now if he were coming."

"Well, he hasn't showed. Meanwhile, we have a couple of uncontrollable girls. What do you suggest that we do with them?"

"Get rid of them. Sell them to another house."

"I could do that. I want to get my revenge on them first, though. Let's call it a night."

"What about all your servants and guards?"

"They'll be back in the morning."

They went back down to the office and talked for a while, drinking coffee and rum. Then about 11:30, Karackish went back to the roof for one last look around before turning in. He saw movement on the floating dock and fired a burst. Whatever or whoever it was fell back into the water. *I don't miss.*

CHAPTER 54

When they got to the breakwater they discovered that it was not a breakwater – it was a reef. Not only that, they had not measured the distance from the reef to the shore, but had assumed that it was about 300 meters. When they got there, Mischal said, "We can't leave you here. It would be dangerous to try to find safe footing on a reef in the dark. Besides, it is at least almost a mile to shore. The range on your night scope is only 300 meters."

"I could see …"

"Not well enough in the dark to see your target at that distance. We'll have to find a closer place."

They moved across the lagoon slowly, both to reduce any noise of their passage and to not make a wake or bow wave that would light up with the phosphoresce of the water. It took nearly an hour. As they got close to the beach they saw a pontoon float about 30 meters out from the beach, with a narrow walkway leading to the shore.

"Looks like about 50 meters to the house from here, Chandri. Let me lower you into the water and then hand you your piece. Ready?"

"Ready."

"I'll lower you slowly to avoid stirring the water. Try to swim without splashing."

It was hard to swim while holding one arm up out of the water with a heavy rifle. Its eleven pounds had not seemed heavy when carrying it on land and firing it, but holding it up out of the water was a different matter. She swam on her back, kicking slowly and using one arm to swim. Wet clothes and shoes did not help.

She finally got there and pulled herself up high enough to see the house. A man was standing on the flat roof looking around. He suddenly raised his weapon and fired a burst at her. She dropped back with a splash. Mischal called, *Chandri, you all right?*

Yeah. Not hit. I'm going to try a different location, where there is some shadow.

She had not had time to mount the night scope, so she pushed her rifle up on top of the dock. Braced her feet on parts of the frame and rose up carefully, showing just the top of her head. As soon as the top of her head came above the surface of the dock, the man fired again, but again, it was burst fire, not accurate. Chandri said, *Must be using a night scope. He can see me in the dark with any least part exposed. Have to think of something*

Want us to come back?

No. That'd just expose you. You all better be hiding behind the sides of the boat. Invisibility won't work if he is using a night scope.

Right, Mischal said. *That sees body heat.*

Chandri took her shoes off and stuffed them into the bag Mischal had made for her. Then she hooked her toes into the dock frame, hooked an arm through part of the frame that was out of water, and pulled out the night scope and mounted it. It was hard to control both rifle and sight while bobbing in the water, but she finally managed it. She knew that the dock floating on oil drums was no protection from billets, but she was depending on it shielding her from the watchman's night sight, or night goggles, whichever he was using. Next, she took one of the cleaning swabs that Mischal had given her and stuffed into the end of the barrel of her rifle.

I'm going to swim over to the rocks and see if I can draw his fire. I don't think it is legal to shoot just because I'm on his property.

Sharra said, Let's ask Jeremy.

She called Jeremy with mind speech. *Jeremy! How's it going there?*

All quiet. How about you?

Somebody's shooting at Chandri. Talk to her.

Right. Chandri!

Hi, Jeremy. Got a question. Is it legal to shoot someone just because they are trespassing?

What are you doing?

Going to try to get into the house.

No, what are you doing right now?

Nothing. Swimming to some rocks.

And he's shooting at you?

Not yet. I was at a dock that I don't believe is on their property. Could be.

And he was shooting at you? Why?

I don't know. Sharra can see him. Ask her.

Okay. Sharra! Can you see the man who is shooting?

Yes.

Take a look in his mind, see if you can tell why.

Right. It's the guy who was in the car when Robin set it on fire this spring. Arnat Karackish. He expects us to come and is mad because Brumley doesn't believe it. And he saw Chandri in the water and assumed that she was an intruder. In other words, one of us.

Well, he got that right. That's reason to shoot, but not legal.

Chandri! Jeremy called. *He is expecting us and thinks that you are about to invade. That's why he is shooting.*

That's not legal, is it? Can I shoot back?

If you are sure that he is shooting at you, and not just trying to scare you. But if you shoot first, he has a right to shoot back. Better alert Mista.

Right.

She reached the rocky spur she had seen and found that there was a little beach behind it. The beach was mostly rock and only a few feet from the water's edge to dry, rocky ground. The rocky spur was about two feet higher than the beach at the waterline, so she crawled up behind the rock and raised up. A bullet hit the rock about an inch from her head before she got high enough to see. It knocked a large chunk of coral off. That gave her an idea.

She pulled one shoe out and stuffed in inside her shirt to warm it up. Then she carefully pushed the coral chunk up on top of the rocky spur. At the movement, another bullet came, and another chunk fell off. She pushed that up on top, next to the first one. Her shoe felt warm, so she stuck it up next to the second chunk of coral. A bullet hit the rock next to her shoe and broke off a piece. She jerked the shoe down, waited a moment, and put it up a little further away. This time a bullet hit the rock in front of her shoe, breaking off a large chunk and knocking the shoe out of her hand. It landed on the beach a few feet away – far enough that she dared not try to retrieve it. But, she thought, maybe the man would think she was hit and not moving, if he could see it. It would cool quickly, just as a body would. He would be watching it. She reached out with her rifle and pushed it a little, waited a beat and pushed it again. Then she left it to lie.

Now she piled up two more rocks on top, leaving just enough space to push her rifle through. Since it was cold and dark, she did not think he would see it. He did not fire, so she assumed that she was correct. *I could ask Sharra!*

Sharra! Does the shooter see me?

No. He saw something and shot it. He thinks that it was you, and that you must be dead, since you aren't moving.

Good. That's what I was hoping. He shot my shoe.

She could not stretch out behind the rifle – that would expose her legs and feet. So she curled up, propped up on an elbow to make herself stable and sighted through the scope. It was an awkward position, and would not be the most accurate. But it was only 50 yards. She brought the rifle around carefully and then up until she saw the figure standing on the rooftop. *So that's Karackish. The one that killed Sharra's father. Shot at us in Louisville. Brought a gang to fire the B&B we were in. Now he's shooting at me and doesn't even know who I am or what I am doing here. Well, Mr. Karackish, say goodbye to this world.*

She could not hold the rifle totally steady in this crouched position. But the waver was small enough that the cross hairs stayed on his chest. She raised it a little until she had the sight on the base of his neck, in case he was wearing body armor. She already had one round in the chamber. She squeezed the trigger as the sight rose. The bullet took him in the base of his neck and he pitched off the roof and lay still. The crack of the rifle sounded like thunder to Chandri in the quiet of the night. Chandri realized that she had not heard the shots that had been fired at her.

Misch! He must have had a silenced weapon. He fired at me, but missed. I did not hear anything, though.

Neither did I. He hasn't seen us. Up! Just saw him fall. We're almost at the beach.

CHAPTER 55

Two men came walking along the water's edge. Both were carrying Heckler and Koch MP5 sub-machine guns. They had stopped when they heard the shot, but when nothing else happened, they continued on. They stopped again when they saw the boat.

One said, "Look. Somebody's boat drifting."

"Anybody in it?"

"Nope. Just a boat. I'm going to sink it."

"No, dummy. We can use another boat. If nobody claims it tomorrow, we'll take it up to the house." Mischal raised the tranquilizer gun and pointed it at the man who wanted to shoot the boat.

"Where did it come from? That's an expensive boat. People aren't careless with them."

"Maybe we have intruders?"

"Yeah. I'm going to sink it." Mischal fired a dart. The man heard only a thunk as the gun fired, but felt the dart hit him and looked down. The drug acted fast, and the man folded up.

The other man first looked toward the sound of the gun firing. It seemed to come from the empty boat. As he looked, he realized that it looked like there were people in the boat. Then his companion fell to the ground. He jerked back. "Hey, Al! What's up?"

By this time, Mischal had the gun reloaded, and put a dart in the second man.

There was no real beach here, just rocky shore that dropped off quickly. Mischal used his paddle to push the boat up against the shore, and Njondac stepped out. Mischal handed Sharra up and then followed, taking the painter with him. "Nothing to tie it to," he said.

"Tie it ta one uv them. They ain't goin' anywheres before we're through here."

"Good idea."

He slid the painter under the nearest body and had stepped back to tie it, when a voice called, "Who goes there."

Mischal froze. Sharra sent, *Just stand still. I don't think he can see you, but if you move it might break the illusion.*

"I see you down there. Stand up and raise your hands."

He sees the bodies on the sand, Sharra sent.

Mischal pulled the line and the body flopped. "Your last warning. Stand and identify yourselves or I'll shoot."

Mischal pulled the line again, and the man standing near the house fired a burst into the body on the beach. "All right. Who else is there? Stand up with your hands raised."

No one moved, and he fired a burst into the second body.

He turned to his companion and said, "That takes care of that. I guess that was their boat. We better tell Arnat." The two men went back into the house.

Mischal keyed his radio. *Mista should be getting here. It's almost midnight.*

I'll check, Sharra said. Then she sent by her mindspeech, *Mista? Where are you?*

On the road. We should be there in a few.

Better hurry or it'll be all over before you get here.

What's happening? I thought you were going to wait.

We were. However, one of them saw Chandri and shot at her. So, she shot him. Then two men saw the boat, so we put them to sleep. Their companions thought that they were intruders and shot them. Since they would not stand up.

Great. Anything else?

Not yet.

She keyed her radio. On the radio link, they could all hear, including Mista when he got close enough. *He'll be here in a few minutes. Let's go up to the house to wait. Chandri, you all right out there?*

I'm fine. I'm up on the beach, now. Wish there was something out here to hide behind. They can see me if they are using night goggles or night sights.

You have a night scope.

Yes. I have it attached, now. I see two men walking up to the house, but I don't see any movement around the house.

Mischal said, *Maybe you should work your way up near the shore and stand behind one of those barrels.*

Too deep, probably. That's why they use the barrels instead of pilings.

Oh. Should have known.

I'm okay. I'm lying behind a rock spur.

The two men found Karackish, but could not report to him. He was lying dead on the sand.

They went inside to report to Brumley.

He said, "What? Arnat's dead? What happened?"

"Don't know. Looks like he was shot."

Brumley started out to see for himself.

"I wouldn't go out there," his man said. "Somebody is out there somewhere. I don't know where, couldn't see anybody. Found a boat and two men down by the beach and shot them."

"I thought you had a patrol out there on the beach."

"We do. Haven't seen any sign of Al and Bobby."

CHAPTER 56

Mista drove up to the house. He saw a side road across from the house, so he pulled onto it and stopped, killing the lights. Molly pulled up behind him. She sent, *This the house?*

Mista keyed his radio. *Use the Radio link. That way everyone can hear. Yes, this is it.*

Mischal said, *We're behind the house. You won't be able to see us.*

Mista said, *We'll go to the front door and knock. Force the back door if you are sure that we are in the right place.*

They are shooting people. Has to be right. We'll wait for you at the back door.

Mista crossed the road and mounted the front steps, followed by Molly and Charly. Molly stayed far enough back that she was able to make Charly and herself invisible, leaving Mista apparently alone. Jasmine and Jania stayed by the cars. The door was answered by a short, rotund man, walking with a mincing step.

"Yes?"

Mista said, "I heard you have some girls here."

"You heard wrong, mister."

"I'm sure that my information was reliable. This is the residence of David Brumley is it not?"

"It is that, but we do not have girls here for hire."

"Well, now. I did not say for hire."

"We do not keep girls here." He started to close the door.

"I'd like to see Mr. Brumley, please."

"I would like you to leave."

Brumley stepped into the room. "Who's there, Ivan?"

"Some stranger. I think he has the wrong house. He was just leaving."

Mista said, "Well, hello, David. Nice seeing you again."

Brumley turned white. "How – how did you get here?"

"Let me tell you, it wasn't easy. But I made it. I came to collect my girls."

"I told him that we have no girls here, David."

"Ah, but you must be mistaken," Mista said. "David sent me an e-mail just a little while ago with a picture of them. He definitely said that they were here."

"I said nothing about where they were in that e-mail. You can't make a claim like that without some evidence."

"I have some evidence. Three people listened to your phone conversation, and I preserved a recording." Mista pushed the door all the way open and walked in, pulling his staff out of its pouch at the same time. Molly and Charly followed him in before the door closed again.

Smirnoff opened the door again and pulled a pistol. "I asked you to leave. Leave now, or I will be forced to take further action." He leveled the pistol at Mista.

Mista said, "I wouldn't do that if I were you." He snapped the staff out and locked it in its extended form in one motion, and then slapped it upward, knocking the gun out of Smirnoff's hand. "Not nice to point weapons at strangers."

Meanwhile, Robin unlocked her door again and stepped out into the hall. One of the guards said, "You aren't supposed to be outside of your room, little girl."

As she had stepped out, Robin had heard the end of the last radio exchange. She heard Mista say that he was coming in the front and Mischal say that they would be waiting at the back. She said, "I need some fresh air. Besides, I think my daddy is coming."

"Ha. Nobody here but us. Go back inside."

"No, I don't want to. Come on, Janice. Let's go downstairs."

The guard pulled his weapon. Robin said, "You going to shoot me? Mr. B. wouldn't like that. You'd get blood everywhere. And besides, I wouldn't be much good for sex any more."

He knew that she was right, but he had to make her stay in the room. He started to holster the weapon, and Robin reached out with her mind and squeezed the trigger. The bullet hit the floor and continued into the room below, hitting Brumley in his left arm.

Robin pulled the gun out of the guard's hand and tossed it down the stairs. "You shouldn't have a gun if you're going to be so careless." Then she dodged around him and ran down the stairs.

Mista saw her coming down, and yelled, "Stay up there, Robin. Stay up there!"

Robin was not about to stay up there. She ran to Mista, throwing her arms out. "Daddy! I knew you'd come."

When Brumley was hit, he assumed that Mista had somehow shot him, since Mista was the only other person that he saw. He pulled his own gun, an MP5, and fired a three round burst. However, he was not skilled in the use of a submachine gun. Two would have missed Mista by a fraction of an inch, and the other hit Smirnoff. He fell, dead. The two that would almost have hit Mista hit Robin instead, as she ran between Brumley and Mista.

She arched her back and flopped into Mista's arms, unconscious or dead, he could not tell. The back door opened and Mischal yelled, "Drop your weapons."

Brumley whirled around, but did not see anyone. He fired another three round burst in the direction of the voice. Two went wild, but the third hit Mischal's armor. He grunted at the impact, and fired one round, hitting Brumley in the heart.

Mischal said, "Let them see us, Sharra." She dropped her illusion just as the two guards came down from upstairs. Mischal said, "Drop your weapons and raise your hands." They did, stopping half way down the stairs.

The other two came running in from the kitchen. Njondac swung his shotgun toward them. "Stop right there, boys. Drop yer guns."

Mista forgot everyone else in his concern for Robin. He kneeled down and laid her on the floor, and then checked her vitals. Her pulse was weak and she was breathing. Her top was stained, front and back, blood pulsing out. He stopped both wounds as best he could with his hands. The other wound was a gut wound. There was nothing he could do about that one. He called on the radio link, *Jania! Get over here fast.*

Coming, Daddy. She ran across the road and into the front door, which was still standing open.

She saw Robin at once, and knelt down beside her. Robin was pale white, with a hint of blue. Jania put her hands over Robin's chest and *looked* inside. "Oh, this is bad. She's all torn up inside." The bullet had hit her lung right where the pulmonary artery entered. She was spilling much of the blood that was going to her lungs, and her left lung had already filled.

Jania prayed for healing and then began repairing damage. She sealed the ruptured arteries first, to avoid losing any more blood. She knew that Robin had lost a lot of blood already, but there was at least still some. Then the checked her gut. The bullet had done a lot of damage there, but had not hit any major organs. She prayed for healing again, and repaired the broken blood vessels and intestines.

Robin was still struggling to live. *All that blood in her lung. She can't breathe properly, but more important, she does not have enough blood left in her system.* She thought about it only for a second, and then began to move the blood back into the pulmonary vein, to return it to her heart and system. She chose the vein, since the heart would be pulling blood from the lungs, and pressure would be low at that point. She moved most of the blood back into Robin's system, but she was still dangerously low. Jania looked up at Mista. "She's lost too much blood. I don't know if she'll make it."

"Put some of mine in her. You can move things, can't you? Move my blood from me to her."

"But …"

"The type is right. She gave blood to me this spring."

"Oh, that's right. Okay. It'll leave you weak."

"Take as much as you need. I can't lose her here."

Jania had no way to measure, but she figured that she took over a quart before she was finished. Robin had her color back, but still was not breathing properly. Jania checked her lungs again. Still too much liquid in her left lung. Mostly blood, but maybe not all. She did not want to risk trying to reuse that blood. It had been out too long. She focused and moved the loose liquid at the bottom of the lung to the puddle on the floor. She had most of it out in less than a minute, but she was still not breathing right. Jania covered Robin's mouth and pinched her nose. When Robin breathed in, Jania blew as much air into her lungs as she could. She took a deep breath and repeated that every other breath that Robin took. Finally, she sat back, totally oblivious of the fact that she was sitting in a puddle of blood.

"I think she will make it. I can't find anything else wrong. It's going to take some time, though."

"Why is she unconscious? What made her lose consciousness, and why had she not regained it, if she is going to be all right?"

"She wasn't getting enough oxygen to her brain, and it shut down. She is getting oxygen now, I think. Let me check." She looked inside Robin's head. Blood was flowing and everything seemed normal. She did not see any signs of damage, like dead cells. "She looks okay. I don't see any damage – she was not deprived long enough. She should be waking up."

Robin opened her eyes and looked up as Jania was speaking. "What happened? I heard daddy downstairs, and that's all I remember."

Jania nodded. "Lost the last few minutes. That's pretty normal. You got shot in the back, honey. You'll be all right, now, though. I think your daddy wants to hold you. Our daddy."

Janice had been hovering, afraid to say anything or do anything. When Robin sat up, Mista took her in his arms and held her tight. Then Janice ran over and but her arms around both of them. "I knew you'd come, Daddy. Robin lost faith, but I never did."

"I did not. I was just scared that he might not be able to find us."

Mista said, "Sorry it took so long, Little Bird. We had some trouble."

Janice said, "You feel all right, Robin? You look pale. I'll give you some of my blood if you need it."

Robin looked at Jania. "I feel awful! Do I need some blood? Is all that blood on the floor mine?"

"It's all yours, honey. Your daddy already gave you some of his blood, and I think you have enough, now. But, we'll watch. Thanks for offering, Janice."

"Take as much as you need. I don't want her to die."

Mista said, "You girls sure are messy. You've got blood on everything."

"I didn't mean to, Daddy," Robin said.

"Oh, honey, I'm just teasing you. However, why don't you go to your room and get cleaned up?"

Sharra said, "I'll take them. Where is your room, girls?"

Jania said, "I'll come with you. I need to get cleaned up, too."

When they had gone, Mista said, "I guess I need cleaning, too. But it'll wait. We've got quite a mess here."

Chandri called in, *I'm coming in. Looks like it's all over.*

Mischal said, *Don't come inside. Police will be here soon. We can account for everything except the one you killed. We both know that it was justified, but it still could get us tangled up. Get the boat and take it down to that dock or somewhere. I don't want the police to know you were here.*

Okay.

Molly said, *I'll come out and go with you. I can hide us.*

CHAPTER 57

Mista called the police in the nearby village and told them that there had been a killing in the Brumley mansion. A car arrived a few minutes later with a detective and a uniformed officer. The detective said, "A killing?" He saw two bodies and the guards sitting under Njondac's watchful eye.

"Maybe I should have said a killing spree. There are more outside."

When the inspector came back in, he looked like he was angry at the world. "This is unconscionable. Is this some kind of gang war? Let me see all weapons, please." He had his own sidearm drawn.

Three of Brumley's guards produced their sidearms. The fourth had not recovered his yet. He said, "That girl took mine and threw it down the stairs. It's over there."

Mischal handed him his Kimber Desert Warrior, butt first. Mista offered him his club, and Charly held up her swords. Njondac held his shotgun steady on his prisoners.

"Keep the arcane weapons. I only see one gun, unless these men are your men. Has that shotgun been fired?"

"No, sir," Njondac said. "They been behavin'."

"Do you already know who is who, here?" asked Mista.

"No. Absolutely not. I presume that there are two sides?"

"That is correct. The four men under guard used to work for the man lying there. I don't know who the other people are. These two women, pointing to Jasmine and Charly, and those two men are with me. My wife is upstairs with my daughters and our doctor."

Mischal said, "You will notice that my piece has been fired only once. I believe that the rest of them killed each other."

The inspector turned to Mista. "Is this your home, sir? You are Mr. Brumley, correct? Did this gang attack you?"

"This house used to belong to that man lying there," Mista said. "That is or was David Brumley. Do you know who he is?"

"I know the name." He shook his head back and forth. "This is over my head. I must call the chief of detectives. You will not be allowed to leave until he releases you."

While they waited, Mischal called Molly. He was thinking about Chandri sitting outside waiting for something to happen. It would be a long wait. *Molly, you have keys to the car?*

Yes, the Suburban. Why?

I was just thinking, you and Chandri should drive back to Georgetown and go aboard the boat.

Good idea. But I don't want to take the big car. Mista, put your keys in your hand, unless you left them in the car.

No, they are in my pocket. Okay, I'm holding them.

Mista felt the keys change shape in his hand.

All right, Molly said, *you have the keys to the Suburban now. We'll take the small car back. See you back on the boat. Or, hey! There's enough of us, counting Chandri and me. Want us to sail the boat back here and pick up our boat?*

We'd still have a car here.

We could come get the boat and then go back.

Hmmm. No. By the time you get here it will be daylight. They will wonder about you.

They don't know that we are here, Chandri said. *I can swim in and bring the boat out.*

Okay, Mista said. *That will work.*

It took an hour for the Chief of Detectives and the medical examiner to get there. No one talked. They all just sat and waited. Mista called Sharra and told her to stay up stairs.

Neither girl wanted to stay upstairs. The wanted to go to their daddy. Sharra said, "We need to wait up here. Your room has a lot of stuff in it. He treated you well?"

"He was trying to bribe us," Janice said.

"Then he finally got tired of waiting for us to be friends – like we were ever going to be friends – and he demanded that we undress. He sent dresses in, and no underwear. I cut the skirt off mine and made my own. See?" She pulled up her skirt and showed Sharra her makeshift shorts.

"These are your own clothes, aren't they? How did you get them?"

"One of the servants let us have them. I got them out tonight after I ran Mr. B. off."

"Clever girl. Are you the only ones up here?"

"I don't know. We could go look, while we are waiting."

There were 12 rooms on the second floor, all of them locked. Robin ran to the nearest room and proudly showed her mother her new-found skill – manipulating locks. The room was empty. They opened every door on the hall, and found six more girls, all hungry and frightened. No one had brought them an evening meal. They had been locked in their rooms, but had heard the shots.

Two were eleven years old. They had been brought down early in the summer. They had thought that they were going to be models, but after Brumley had talked them into posing nude for him – and then could not touch them – no one had told them anything. Brumley had had a TV brought in for them and let them room together, but then forgot about them.

One girl was 15. She had been in service for four years, and had decided that this was her life and she might as well make the best of it. One girl was 13 and two were 14. They still had hope that they could escape some day.

All the girls were barefoot, and made no noise as they followed Sharra from room to room, collecting all the occupants.

The inspector downstairs could hear Sharra's heels clicking as she went from room to room. He asked, "What are they doing up there?"

"Sounds like they are exploring," Mista said.

After they had opened all doors and collected all the girls, Sharra said, "Anybody know where the kitchen is? We'll go fix something to eat."

The eleven-year-old named Sally said, "We've been locked in our room ever since they brought us here. We don't know where anything is."

"Well," Sharra said, "let's go find it. Those stairs in the center go to the front room, where everyone else is. We don't want to go there. Let's try the stairs at this end of the hall."

The stairs came down into a small room with windows lining one wall. A doorway on one side of the room led to a large room that looked like a formal dining room. The door in the other wall led to a kitchen.

"Aha!" said Sharra. "Anyone know how to cook?"

No one answered. "Well, let's see what we can find."

301

They found breakfast foods – bacon, sausage and eggs – and fresh vegetables. "Anybody for a midnight breakfast?" Sharra asked.

"Yes, yes. Anything."

When they had finished eating, Sharra asked questions about their backgrounds, how long they had been here, what had happened to them, and other things. She also wanted to know what they wanted to do, now that they were free.

Ruth said, "Go home. My parents are probably going crazy. I don't want to be a model if we have to live like this."

The oldest girl said, "I don't know what to do. I've been with Mr. B. for four years. My parents probably think I'm dead. When they find out – if they find out – they will probably wish I was dead."

"Do you wish you were dead?" Sharra asked.

"Sometimes. I thought I'd die, at first. But it's not so bad. You get used to it."

CHAPTER 58

The chief of detectives arrived and surveyed the scene with dismay. "Someone has tracked blood everywhere. This is a crime scene."

Mista said, "Sorry about your evidence. I considered my daughter's life of prime importance. It's her blood that's all tracked up."

"Is she dead somewhere?" he asked gently.

"No, but she nearly bled out before we could help her."

"You saved her life, and now she's up walking around, after a wound that bled that much?"

"Yes. Our doctor happens to travel with us, and she got her back on her feet."

"You are traveling, then. May I see some ID?"

Mista showed him his ID card and badge.

He raised an eyebrow. "A little out of your territory, aren't you?"

"I'm not here on official business. I came to get my daughters."

"Ah. They were visiting Mr. Brumley?"

"Not exactly. They were prisoners here."

"If they were prisoners, how did you know that they were here?"

"Because of the nature of our work, we all have sub-vocal radios embedded. Even my daughters. Not only that, but they wear a GPS locator bracelet, so I knew exactly where they were."

"I see. Then, you came in, demanded to see your daughters, and then shot Mr. Brumley."

"Not exactly. My weapon is a staff." He showed his collapsible staff. "When my daughters heard me down here, then came running to meet me. Brumley shot one of them, shot at me, and killed his man there by the front door."

"He killed his own man?"

"Find the bullets. Yes."

"So who shot Mr. Brumley?"

Mista pointed to Mischal. "He fired a burst from his sub-machine gun at my security chief. He had no choice but to defend himself."

Mischal said, "My weapon has been fired only once. Your man has it. It is a .45, and Mr. Brumley had an H&K MP5, which uses 9mm. Shouldn't be too hard to figure out who shot who. And it is self-evident that Mr. Brumley could not have fired at me after he was dead."

They dug out three 9mm bullets near the front door. They found three more near the back door. They found one .45 caliber bullet in the wall behind Brumley and a 9mm bullet in the floor near Brumley.

The chief inspector said, "Looks like we have an extra bullet. Any idea where it came from?"

One of the guards said, " Must have been me, sir. I accidentally fired my gun through the floor from upstairs. I guess it came down here."

"Which is your gun?"

"That girl threw it downstairs. I think it's still there."

They took statements from everyone there, and then called for Sharra to come in and took her statement. The inspector said, "I thought you said two daughters?"

"I have two. Looks like there were some other guests."

"Were you guests?" the chief inspector asked, "Or were you prisoners?"

The oldest girl said, "That man kept us here, locked in our rooms."

The chief of detectives fell silent. His face paled. "You were …"

Her lip curled down. "What do you think he kept us locked up here for?".

"He's been doing this for at least 25 years," Mista said quietly. "He deserves nothing but death, but we had not intended it to end this way. However, when he fired at Mischal, Mischal had no choice but to fire back."

"Yes. I believe that is the case. However, he must stand for a hearing before a judge. For professional courtesy, I will not arrest him, if I have your word that you will not leave the island until and unless he is acquitted."

"You have my word," Mista said.

"Thank you. Now, there is the matter of three dead bodies outside."

One of the guards said, "We shot two of them. We found them on the property near the beach. They had a boat drawn up."

"And why did you kill them? Did they threaten you?"

"No. As a matter of fact they did not respond to my challenge except to try to crawl away."

"All right. You two will also have to face a hearing. Now, there is still one more."

No one answered. Finally the guard who had shot the two men on the beach said, "Maybe they shot him. We heard a shot earlier, and that's why we were out looking."

"Where will you be staying, Mr. Yoeder?"

Mista said, "You want to stay here?"

Sharra said, "NO!" She shuddered. "You can if you want to, Misch. I'm not."

"We have a boat anchored in the harbor," Mischal said. "I'll be living there."

"We are pretty crowded," Mista said. "Some of you might want to take rooms on the beach. Now we also have an addition of six girls."

"The government will provide housing for them. We will contact their parents."

Melissa said, "I don't know if I want you to contact mine. How long can I stay?"

"Only until your parents claim you. If no one comes forward, then you must find other accommodations."

"Oh. Mr. Mista, would there be room on your boat for one more?"

"We can make room, if that is what you want. You might have to sleep in a hammock."

"I can do that. Anything is better than this place."

"I thought you had gotten used to it," Sharra said.

"I thought I had. But I do want to escape now."

"We'll make room for you and help you decide what you want to do. I'll even provide a home for you, if that is what you want."

"I don't know about that. I don't much like men at this time."

"Not trying to force you, my dear."

CHAPTER 59

There were no extra beds on the boat. Mista looked at the one remaining hammock and then looked at Melissa. She reminded him of what Candy would have looked like if she had stayed with them. She was a pretty girl with a well rounded figure. She had curly blond hair and a tipped up nose. Her light blue eyes were clouded with sadness.

Mista said, "We'll have to figure something out. All the bunks are taken, and the little kids sleep in hammocks. I guess we need to go ashore and get you a hammock. You could sleep on one of the sofas in the salon, but in any kind of weather you'd roll off."

"Hammock is fine. I used to lie in one in our back yard. Before I had to come here."

Janice said, "We could hang it in our room."

Molly said, "I have a solution. We're done here, right?"

"All over but the shouting. We just have to wait for Mischal's court date."

"Okay. I'd like to go home to my new husband. That will make some room."

That did not help all that much, since Molly had been sleeping in one of the girls' bunks.

Sheila said, "I'll be glad to help you, hon. We should get along fine. You know that I was taken when I was eleven, just like you. Only I didn't get rescued until 25 years later."

"He's been doing this for 25 years? And nobody caught him?"

"When I found my sister," Mista said, "we began to track him down."

"Yeah," Robin said. "We were bait."

Jania said, "I guess I better head back to school, too. I don't have a place to sleep anyway, now that the other girls are back."

"Okay, Kitten. Thanks for saving Robin. And Sharra. And me. We've kept you pretty busy, haven't we?"

"Yeppers. When I finish my school, I'll come back and then try to keep you out of trouble instead of fixing you after."

Mista and Sharra saw the two off from the airport, and then went to buy an easy chair for Mista. One that he could bolted to the deck. Next they went to the grocery to restock the freezers.

Janice was the first to test the new chair that evening at bedtime. Robin was five seconds late. She came running into the room still pulling her pajama top down just as Janice settled into Mista's lap. She stopped, put her hands on her hips, and said, "Daddy, you bought a chair too small. It won't hold both of us."

"Sorry, it's the biggest that I could buy that's designed for a boat. You'll either have to take turns, or go to bed without loving."

"Well, I'm not going to bed without my loving." She sat on the edge of the bed and waited, tapping her foot.

Janice was in no hurry. "I knew you'd come, but I was afraid you wouldn't be able to find us. The room had wires across the windows, and probably in all the walls. I used my watch to call you the first day, but since nobody contacted me I figured that everything was blocked somehow."

"You figured correctly. Jeremy tried to contact you while you were on the boat going south, but you were asleep the whole time."

"I know. They must have put something in the food. They'd feed us and then we'd go right back to sleep."

"I got an alert from the GPS locater when they took you from the boat to a car, so I knew that you were on Grand Cayman Island."

"I don't remember that. Going from the boat to the island. I guess they put us back to sleep."

"Mischal put some things in your hems and your shoes. Did you think about cutting the wires?"

"No, never thought about it. Not that it would have done any good. They didn't even take our shoes, and anyway, they made us go barefoot the whole time. They took our clothes right away. There was a nice lady who took care of us, and we talked her into bringing our clothes back, but we had to hide them."

"They didn't mistreat you, did they?"

"No. Even Mr. B. was nice to us at first. Bought all sorts of things for us. I think he was trying to bribe us. He gave us more things in a few days that you've given us in six months. Like he was trying to show how generous he was."

"It was working then?"

"No way. I knew what he was up to. All he wanted was to use our bodies to get back at Mom. And then he would throw us to the wolves. And, I didn't mean that you were stingy. You've given us everything that we need and lots of other stuff, too."

"I won't give you everything you see. If you have too much, and it's too easy to get, then nothing has any value."

"You've been good to me, and you love me. That's the most important gift. That's something I never had before."

"I haven't even spanked you yet, even though you gave me explicit permission."

"I know. I haven't tried very hard to earn one." She grinned. Then she sobered. She looked into his eyes. "I don't ever want to do anything to hurt you, Daddy. And if I ever start going off in the wrong direction, I want you to stop me, no matter what it takes. Lock me in my room on bread and water. Beat me. Take away everything I've got. Everything but the love. If I made you mad at me and lost the home and love you've given me – then I would deserve anything you chose to do."

"Hmmm. Pretty wise for a twelve-year-old. You have not begun to face the temptations and trials of a teenager. I just hope you keep that attitude as you grow up."

"I faced life on the streets of Atlanta for six years. I know what's out there. I love you, Daddy. Good night." She kissed him and hopped up. "Your turn."

Robin jumped up from the bed and curled up in Mista's lap. "I was getting real worried that you wouldn't get there in time."

"You thought I couldn't find you?"

"I knew you would. But it might have been too late. Then Janice tricked him."

"Oh, I never did find out what you did. Janice!"

She came to the door. "Yes, Daddy?"

"How did you trick Mr. Brumley?"

She blushed and looked down at the floor. "I ... I, uh, sort of lied to him."

"Sort of?"

"Yes. I dint actually lie. He told me to take off my dress and I refused. He said I would have to sooner or later, that he would make me. So I said, 'make me.' Then I thought, if I could get outside … so I said if he would let us go swimming it might be worth it. To undress. He said I would have to go naked because I didn't have a swimsuit. So I said, okay."

Robin said, "I told him I wasn't going naked, no matter what."

"So then?"

"He let us go out and down to the pool. But instead of taking my dress off, I just jumped in."

"And I did, too. And then he couldn't reach us out in the water."

"So, I didn't exactly lie, but I let him believe that I would. That's dissembling, right? Same as lying. Do I get a spanking, now?"

"Come here, Honey." She walked over slowly.

He put his arm around her and squeezed. "No spanking. That is what you call choosing the lesser of two evils. You had two choices, and only two. Be raped, or lie. If you had just asked to go swimming, would he have let you? He was giving you all sorts of things."

"No way. He had us locked in so we could not talk to you."

"But when he thought he was getting what he wanted, then he forgot about the danger of communicating. You took a chance and it worked. But when you do that, you must be sure that you truly *only* have two choices. There are usually more. I'm proud of you, Honey. You were able to think even in the face of danger."

Janice relaxed.

Mista said, "You were afraid to tell me?"

She looked up at him and then down at the deck. "Yes. A little."

"Don't be. Did you think I might find out anyway?"

Janice looked up at him and then at Robin. "Yes, I guess you would."

"Then you should tell me first. Robin did not say anything, by the way. I just asked. If you do something, you should always be willing to tell me. I won't promise never to punish you if you tell me first. But I will promise to consider that you confessed. And if I am sure that you've learned your lesson, then there is no point in further punishment, and I would not give any."

"Okay. Thanks, Daddy. Good night."

Mista squeezed her again and kissed her. "Good not, Sweetheart."

"That's a lesson that's hard for you to learn, isn't it, Little Bird?"

Robin stiffened. "I haven't done anything."

Mista squeezed her. "I didn't say that you had. But it is hard for you, isn't it."

Robin screwed up her lips, snuggled closer and whispered, "Yes."

Mista held her tight for a moment, thinking, *She is so afraid of disapproval. She wants to do what she wants, but is always afraid that somebody won't like it and so won't like her. Her mother must have just beat her into the ground.*

"You acted guilty, but I think it was just fear. Am I right?"

Robin snuggled closer and didn't say anything. Mista felt tears through his shirt. "I haven't done anything. Honest, Daddy."

"I'm not scolding you, Sweetheart. I have no reason to think that you did something wrong. I'm just trying to assure you that you have nothing to fear. Do you think I would have burned a whole tank of fuel hurrying to get here, rented cars, planned an assault on that house if I didn't want you back?"

"No. Could have just been Janice."

"Oh, no. I wanted Janice, too, but I wanted *you* back, and I wanted you back before he had a chance to harm you. Do you think you could do anything to make me stop loving you?"

"Yes. I'm sure that if I did some bad things you wouldn't love me any more. Then you'd yell at me like my mother always did."

"What did you have in mind to do?"

"I wouldn't do them! But if I did ..."

"Like what?"

"If I let Mr. B. do me, and then stayed with him and worked for him?"

"No. I'd be very sad and would miss you, but I would still love you."

"If I killed somebody?"

"If you mean murder, I would be sad, and you'd have to go away to prison, but I would still love you. If you mean killed, like Mischal killed Mr. Brumley, and it was the right thing to do, then I wouldn't even be mad."

"What if I turn out to be ugly?"

"Ugly? You think you have to be beautiful to be loved? You mean ugly like Chandri?"

"Chandri's not ugly."

"Not beautiful, either. Ugly like Charly?"

"No! Charly's not ugly."

"Who then?"

"Josie?"

"Josie's not ugly. She is a very beautiful person. Beauty is inside you and comes out. Pushing beauty in from the outside doesn't work. That's why it won't do you any good to use makeup."

Robin sat up straight. "How did you know?"

Mista grinned. "I know everything."

"You do not. Nobody knows everything."

"I guess I know little girls well enough to know that the temptation to make yourself beautiful before God is finished with you is just too great to resist."

"It's wrong to use makeup, then? I would have told you if I thought you wouldn't like it."

"Would you really? Don't answer that. I think you didn't tell me because you were afraid that I wouldn't like it. Am I right?"

"Yes."

"Well, you don't need it, and I would rather that you didn't use it, but there is nothing wrong in it. If you really want to, though, you should talk to your mother. She can show you how to use it properly."

"She won't. She doesn't want me to use it."

"Oh. Well, then you have a problem, don't you?"

"Yes. But I want to. Daddy, why is it more fun to do things that are a little bit naughty? Like that."

"It's human nature. People like to do things that are really bad, too. Some people would rather do a bad thing than a good thing if they have a choice. Like Mr. Brumley. What else were you thinking about with that question?"

"How do you always know? Anyway, I like to get wet. My mother always used to yell at me for it, but I did anyway. But you said you didn't care, so it's not as much fun."

"Well, how about if I said you really should grow up a little and not get wet so much? That it was all right, but ..."

"That would be more fun, then. But why is that?"

"Just the way God made us, I guess."

Robin snuggled and sighed. "How do you know God is not finished with me? I'm not pretty like Janice."

"Sure you are. You are not like Janice, but no two people are alike. But you're just as pretty."

"Am not. She's got big boobs and," she blushed. 'In for a penny, in for a dollar', her mother used to say. "And I've just got buttons. Will I get big like her?"

"Well, you know, you're right. I don't know everything. I don't know the future. You will be whatever God's design for you calls for. Does it matter that much?"

"I don't know. Candy used to say that if a girl had big boobs she could get anything she wanted. That's what the boys all like."

"Hmmm. Wouldn't you rather be talking to your mother about this?"

"No. I mean, she's all right but ... if you don't want to talk about it, that's all right."

"I don't mind. I just don't want to embarrass you. There is some truth in what she said. But only half the truth. Yes, boys and men like big boobs. But if a boy likes you because you have big boobs, he doesn't really like *you*. He only likes what he sees. You want him to like you, not your body. If you could stick a pin in them and let all the air out, what do you think he would do."

"It's not air."

"I know. Just a picture. If you could somehow reduce them to size AA, would he still be interested?"

"No, I guess not."

"No, he wouldn't. You want him to be interested in you. If he likes what he sees, then that's all right, too, but that is secondary. You are a very sweet little girl, and should not have any trouble attracting a boyfriend when the time comes."

"I'm no –"

"A very sweet little girl who is growing up real fast," Mista amended.

After a while, Robin said, "I just wish I would hurry up and grow up. It takes forever."

Robin was quiet for a long while, eyes closed and breathing quietly. Mista thought she had gone to sleep. Suddenly she opened her eyes and asked, "Daddy. What does 'having sex' mean?"

Mista started. "Are you sure you don't want to ask your mother that one?"

"No. I asked you."

"Well, ..."

"I know what people do, and I know that's how you get babies. But it doesn't make sense to me. Some people call it 'making love', but that doesn't make sense either. It doesn't seem to have anything to do with love."

"You've been exposed to the wrong end of it, haven't you?"

"I guess. Those men that came to that house to have sex with the girls there were not loving them. And they didn't have any babies."

"No, that certainly was not love. However, love ought to have everything to do with having sex."

"Well, I love you, and you love me. But we don't talk about having sex. I don't even think about it."

"Yes, well, I don't think about it either. Love takes many forms. I have sex only with your mother, Sharra. That's all I want to have. But I do love you, and Janice. I love Mischal, also, and I certainly don't think about having sex with him."

Robin giggled.

"We should not be having this conversation for many years. But you have been exposed to some really bad stuff, and the questions are quite natural, given your exposure. I'll try to answer any and all of them to your satisfaction. Ideally, you should fall in love with one person, marry him and then have sex as part of your marriage. That is how I hope it happens for you. You will find many people along the road that you love, but not deep enough to marry."

"They do it on TV all the time without being married."

"Yes, they do. But that brand of love is unsatisfying. It lasts a season, and then they have to look for somebody new. Your mother and I have 14 years, and we look forward to many more together."

He waited a beat. "Now, the way those men go about it, has nothing to do with love. It is an abomination and is against the law. If Brumley hadn't been killed, he would have gone to prison for a long, long time."

But Robin was asleep.

Another conversation was taking place in another cabin. Em and Sheila were talking to Melissa. Melissa would talk to Sheila, since she had been through the same thing. Em she was not sure about.

Sheila said,. "What are we going to do with you?"

"I don't know. Just don't send me home. Are you going on another job somewhere?"

"Yes. I don't know what my brother has in mind for our future. He does work for a living, but it is contract work. Sometimes we go for months with no contract."

"How does he afford all this?"

"He found treasure somewhere several years ago. Not the fantastic sums you hear about, hundreds of millions. But enough to keep us all going for months at a time. If he takes another assignment, and I'm sure he will, sooner or later, we could end up anywhere for several months."

"That's where I come in," Em said. "I am a nurse and a teacher. I set up a home school for all the children so we don't have to worry about finding schools."

"I don't think I want to be involved in that; I mean the jobs that you do. It's police work, isn't it?"

"Yes. Why don't we put you in a private boarding school in Atlanta?"

"I haven't been to school in four years."

"There are some very good schools there. They can bring you up to speed, and help you put the last four years in the background."

"Okay. That will work for me. But who will pay for it?"

"I'll pay for it. Mista wants to set up a trust fund for you, also, to help make up for the four years that you lost. It will pay your living expenses now, and give you full control when you turn 25 or so."

"How much?"

"I don't know yet. We'll have to work out the details with our lawyers. It'll be substantial."

"Over $10,000?

"Much over. More like $100,000."

"That sounds too good to be true. What do I have to do?"

"You don't have to do anything. We just want you to have it."

"That's an awful lot of money."

"I know. He was talking about suing Mr. Brumley in your behalf. Not just you, any girl who had been used by Brumley that he could find. Then Brumley would pay for the trust and school. Everything. However, now that he is dead ..."

"You could sue the estate."

"We could. Do you want to do that?"

"Why not? He has basically ruined my life."

CHAPTER 60

The first week went by quickly. They rented cars and visited the sights on the island, the Governor's Palace, the Botanical Gardens, the rock formations known as Hell. The girls went down to the beaches every afternoon. It was good not to have any pressing business, no threats, and no place that they had to go.

But after a week, everyone started getting restless. Jeremy and Charly took a room in a smaller hotel. Jeremy needed quiet to study, and Charly went with him. Karl and Molly came down for two nights, and that helped. While Karl was there, he and Mista visited the Chief of Police. Mista introduced Karl and then said, "I'd like to ask a favor. Time is beginning to drag. If we lived here, it would be different, but just to stay with nothing to do … I'd like to visit some other ports in the Caribbean. The hearing is set for July first, and we would be back before then."

"You agreed to stay."

"Yes, and I will honor my word. However, I would appreciate a little slack. It would be nice to be able to visit Jamaica, for example."

"You are not constrained, Mr. Mictackic. Only Mr. Yoeder."

"I cannot leave without him. It would be unfair to him, since he and I are part of a team."

Karl said, "He has worked for me for years. He has never failed to keep his word."

"I appreciate that, but we are already bending the rules, leaving him free without bail being set."

Mista said, "We have GPS trackers on board. You would always know exactly where we are. You could even send one of your men along to make

315

sure that we come back. I would be glad to pay his expenses, including salary."

"Where exactly do you want to go, Mr. Mictackic?"

"I'd like to go to Jamaica. Maybe Puerto Rico, if time permits. Mostly, I just want to stretch our sea legs."

"I'm going to assign a man to your boat. You will pay one month salary and provide him a berth and food. Then you can go wherever you want, so long as you are back here by July first."

"Thank you. It's crowded on the boat, but we'll make room. That's part of the reason I want to go to sea. Crowded is not so bad if you have something to do. I'll give you notice when we plan to leave."

"If you push him overboard, you will all be in trouble." He said it with a smile, but the threat was serious.

"I promise not to push him overboard. And if he should happen to fall off, I'll drag him up and make him testify that nobody pushed him."

"If he drowns, he might have trouble testifying. He won't fall off. These island people are used to boats."

The next morning a boat came out from the port with a passenger about 10:00. Mista looked. "I guess he has already come aboard. I didn't want him until we got underway. Oh well."

However, the passenger was not a local policeman, but a lawyer. He introduced himself and asked if there was a place to talk. Alone.

"There is no place on this boat that is alone, Mr. Smithson," Mista said. "However, we can talk in the salon and ask the children to stay out."

"That will do. Mrs. Mictackic needs to be there, too."

Mr. Smithson opened his briefcase and took out a thick manila folder and handed it to Sharra. "This is Mr. Brumley's will. It still needs to go through probate, but that should be a matter of form. Basically it is a simple will. He had no children of his own, and no previous marriage. He left his house in La Grange, Kentucky and a trust fund of $5,000,000 to his wife. All the rest was left to his step-daughter, Sharra Darkling."

Sharra's mouth dropped. "I thought ..."

"Thought that he hated you? No, quite the contrary, Mrs. Mictackic. I drew up this will for him some ten years ago. You were a senior in high school. He told me in confidence that you were a willful and stubborn child, but that he had loved you from the moment he first saw you. He had tried and tried to gain your confidence but could never get past your fear of him."

"All that time, I thought that he …" Sharra's eyes were moist and she could not finish.

The lawyer said, "When I reviewed the will last year, he wanted almost no changes. He told me that he did not know where you were, but that he still wanted it to go to you if you could be found. If not, he told me, as executor, to hold it in trust for you and give the proceeds to charity each year. If you could not be found within ten years, then it was all to go the Masonic Home in Louisville, Kentucky. You were hard to find, Mrs. Mictackic."

"Well, I didn't mean to be. I just didn't tell him where I was."

"Your mother knew your married name, but had no idea where you were. I sent a query to all state police agencies. Got a call from a Commander Spicewood of the Georgia State Police. He told me who you were and where I could find you."

"Karl always knows where we are," Mista said.

Mr. Smithson stood and handed Sharra a card. "I'll be staying overnight at the Hilton, Mrs. Mictackic, in case you have any questions. Our firm handled all legal matters for the Darkling enterprises. You may retain us, or choose someone else."

"I wouldn't know where to look. You have been his lawyer for ten years?"

"Twenty, actually."

"Then please stay on, for now. I can think of no reason to change at this time. I reserve the right to change that at a later date, of course."

"Of course. Good day."

CHAPTER 61

Epilogue

After the man had gone, they both sat in silence for a few minutes. Sharra stood up after a while and walked over to Mista. He stood and took her in his arms. "All this time I thought he ... and he loved me. He just wanted to love me, like you love your girls."

Mista said, "I will not speak ill of the dead. We know that he did some things, but maybe there was some good in him. Anyway, it's over now. He left your mother well fixed. Interest on 5 mil at 6% is $300,000 per year. Plus, she has the house."

"Yes, but he left everything else to me. All his businesses. I don't know how to run a business. Well, actually, I do, but I don't want to."

"You don't have to do anything right now. They are all incorporated, so there is someone in each business in charge of that business. Or, at least that's the way I would set up multiple businesses. Let the lawyers handle the transfer. It'll be awhile before the probate court gets done with it, anyway."

"Yes. It is just overwhelming, being so sudden. Something I never expected in my wildest dreams."

"Look, I have an idea. Let's not go to Jamaica right away. Let's go to Puerto Rico and talk to Don Miguel. That will give you time to sort it all out."

"Yes. I like that idea. Let's do it."

Mista called the police station and told them that he would be leaving at 8:00 in the morning. He called Charly and asked if they wanted to go. No, they did not.

Three days later, they rounded the northeast corner of Jamaica. Mista said, "I didn't think about it, but we have to sail close hauled, about as close to the wind as we can. We're only making 4 knots. It will take another week to get to Puerto Rico."

"We don't have that long, do we?"

"We do, but it's cutting it close, and no time to visit. Why don't we just spend a few days here, see the sights, do some shopping and then head back. We'll visit Don Miguel after we are done on Grand Cayman."

"Sounds good to me," Sharra said.

All the women and girls wanted to go shopping. Mista went to Port Royal. It had been famous as the richest city in the world – and the most wicked – in the seventeenth century. Most of the city had sunk in an earthquake. Mista wanted to see the archeological sites that were being worked. His girls were torn. They were not especially interested in history, and they wanted to go shopping. But they didn't want Mista out of their sight. They tagged along with Mista. He and Sharra took them shopping the next day.

Mischal was acquitted in just a few minutes. The chief inspector presented evidence that showed that Brumley shot Smirnoff, shot Robin in the back, twice, and fired three shots at Mischal. Mischal was justified in defending himself.

They sailed for Puerto Rico that afternoon. When they were close to Puerto Rico, Mista called Don Miguel. "I was in the neighborhood and thought I'd drop by."

"You just happened to be a thousand miles from home."

"Yes, as a matter of fact. We were engaged in other business, but now that that is finished. ..."

"By all means, do stop in for a visit. You know the way."

"Yes. We'll be in San Felipe sometime tomorrow, and we'll rent cars and come up."

"Be sure to tour Fort San Felipe while you are there."

After dinner the next evening, Mista and Sharra asked the don for his advice on their problem. He took them to his study and closed the door. "Maria, please bring coffee. You know how they like it."

Mista said, "You probably know that we have been on a quest for the last eight months. Something that I had to do. My sister was taken from us when she was eleven and put into prostitution. At eleven."

"Oh, my. So terrible for her."

"Yes. I found her a couple of years ago and rescued her. We spent some time restoring her health and letting her get used to living again. When she was ready, we went back in her memory to find out just what had happened. She still does not recall the worst years, and we will not attempt to force that. It is best left alone. When we found out how she had been taken and had a description of the man, we went looking for him."

"I assume that you found him. And removed him?"

"Yes. It turned out to be Sharra's stepfather. He had tried to rape her when she was a teenager –"

"Actua—" Sharra started to say, but Mista held up his hand.

"Let me finish, and then talk to him. That was her impression during her teenage years. When she graduated high school she left home and never returned. We took in several eleven-year-old girls and they helped us track him down. I ended up adopting two of them."

"Robin and Janice? Beautiful girls. It is obvious that they adore you."

"Thank you. It all ended when her stepfather was killed about a month ago. Only, it was not the end. Sharra can tell you the rest."

Sharra told Don Miguel about her problem. "I thought he was trying to rape me. Now I'm not so sure. I do know that he was at least involved in my own father's murder. I think he ordered it, but we'll never know. Both he and the murderer are now dead. The real shocker to me was that he left his entire business empire to me. We know that he was supplying drugs, and we know that he was taking young girls and putting them into prostitution. I want nothing to do with those activities."

"You think that some of his businesses were covers for the illegal operations?"

"Yes, I'm sure of it."

"Do you know which ones were fronts?"

"No. Not really. He had an airfreight business, and a shipping business. I know that he had container ships, banana boats, and charter sailboats and maybe charter cruisers. The prostitution might not have been a business. It would have been based in Grand Cayman."

"Maybe he had a Caribbean Air passenger and or freight business."

"I bet he did."

"Sell the ones you don't want, sell the properties you don't want, and hire someone to run the part that you keep."

"Thanks. That's about what I had decided to do."

"So, lovely Sharra, you did not need this old man's words at all."

"Not true. I needed to hear you say that, and it confirms that my decision was right."

"Your husband could have told you the same thing."

"Stop chiding me, my friend. I wanted to hear you say it. Besides, your coffee is the best I have ever tasted."

After breakfast the next morning, Don Miguel asked Chandri if she remembered her introduction to his plantation.

"How could I forget it? I thought that I had been sold into the same kind of thing that Mr. B. wanted to sell these girls into. And I'll never forget wading down your creek to get away."

The don smiled. "Yes, you covered your tracks well."

Robin said, "Creek? Where is a creek?"

"Just a little up the road in front of the house."

"Can I go see it? Can I?"

"Not by yourself," Mista said."

"Janice can go with me."

Don Miguel smiled at her. "It's safe on the plantation. Don't go up stream or you will get into wild country. Don't go down any further than the falls."

"Take your phone," Sharra said. "You can at least call us when you fall down the waterfall."

"Come on, Janice." She ran for the door and skidded to a stop just before opening it. "Melissa, you want to come too?"

"To see a creek? I don't think so."

"Not just to see it. To play in it."

"I'll come, but I don't see how playing is a creek can be much fun."

Karl Spicewood called a little later. "How long are you going to be lazing around down there?" he asked.

"I don't know. We still have to go to Antigua, Aruba, Martinique, a –"

"You've been down there for months. Why didn't you visit them already?"

"We've been kind of busy."

"Yeah, right. Busy getting a tan. Look, I've got a situation here. Can you be in Georgia in the next two weeks?"

"Sure can. Sooner, if you like."

"No, two weeks. I'll set up a meeting."

Mista disconnected and then said, "Karl. He has a job for us."

"You have to leave so soon?" Don Miguel asked.

"Not right away. But, I'm thinking of flying home and leaving the boat here. Is there someone who can secure it for us?"

"Yes, of course. I'll contact a friend in San Felipe. You want it stored long term?"

"Better think long term. I don't know when we will get back."

Mista said, "Sharra what about your new business? We need to wrap up loose ends."

Sharra said, "I'll go on to Louisville and have the lawyers sell off the shipping and air freight businesses. I think we should keep the house in Grand Cayman, but sell off any Caribbean business."

"Sounds good. Might want to keep that cruiser, too. We could travel the world between assignments."

"Yes, I thought so, too. Then I'll get Tom to run the Darkling Trucking Co."

"That should work. Then on to the next exciting adventure. We should spend a few days here, and then fly home. Give Robin time to find the creek down by the road and get thoroughly wet. I wonder what he has in mind."

THE END

AUTHOR'S NOTES

The activities of pedophiles are a controversial subject, compounded by the taking of underage girls. This book does not glorify these actions but rather is the story of taking action against them.

Every American is guaranteed the right to privacy and protection from forced self-incrimination. However, when they engage in criminal activities, they forfeit rights. Many means are available to identify them, including fingerprints, DNA and eye-witnesses.

But many clever men hide their actions well and use other people to procure victims for them, making it difficult to find them and prove their guilt.

Knowing a person is guilty of a crime, or thinking that one knows, is not enough. It must be proven, The investigators in this book struggle on a long voyage to prove their knowledge.

It is tempting to resort to entrapment. The difficulty is that the trap might entice a person to do something he would not otherwise do. Although these girls are bait, since he decided to come into their home —that is the boat – to take them, he has made his own choice, without any enticement.

LIST OF CHARACTERS

Chief Characters

1. Mista   Leader of investigator group
2. Sharra Darkling   Mista's wife and Psi user
3. Samantha   two year old daughter
4. Mischal Yoeder   Paladin for God. Formerly known as Cato mom
    Cato   Barbarian Fighter
5. Chandri di Freet   Ranger
                        Married to Mischal
6. Cato   Son of Mischal and Chandri
7. Chantilly   Daughter of Mischal and Chandri
8. Njondac   Dwarf Fighter
9. Josie Mithraldiver   Njondac's wife. Dwarf.
10. Brut Njondac   Njondac's son
11. Charly   orphan found when 10 years old
                Public name: Deisa, a paladin for God
                  Charlotte Talljohn -- full name
12. Jeremy Bates   Psi Instructor and lawyer
                        Married to Charly
13. Jasmine Taalong   Christian minister
14. Jania Mistletoe   Adopted by Mista
    Pre-med student,   Mista's niece
15. Sheila Demallis   Mista's long lost sister

16. Gary Demallis	Sheila's oldest son –24 years old
17. Molly Greene	Former Student
	Joined group as free agent
18. Susan Jones	Molly's daughter
19. Janice Stormes	12 year old girl
	Adopted by Mista
20. Robin Smith	11 year old girl
	Adopted by Mista
21. Em Evockovic	Nurse caring for Sam, teacher
	Emaroud Evockovic, full name
22. Shawnah Adams	11-year old girl

Children

Janice Stormes	12 year old girl
	Adopted daughter now, Mictackic
Robin Smith	11 year old girl
	Adopted daughter now, Mictackic
Shawnah Kingsberry	11-year old girl

Cato Yoeder	Son of Mischal and Chandri	7
Chantilly Yoeder	Daughter of Mischal and Chandri	4
Brut Njondac	Son of Sean and Josie	6
Susan Jones	Daughter of Molly Greene	4
Samantha Mictackic	Daughter of Mista and Sharra	2
Charles Jeremy	Unborn son of Charly and Jeremy	

Supporting Characters

| Karl Spicewood | Commander of Ga. State Police | Special investigation unit. |
| Paul Ross | FBI Agent | |

Joseph Aramson	Mista's Lawyer
Jeffrey Felder	Mista's banker
Catherine Golightly	Mista's broker
Don Miguel Ridrigos y Manteno	Coffee plantation owner in Puerto Rico

Agnon Moskeffet	Florida State Police Special Investigations
Tom Bronack	General manager Darkling Freight
Joe Brown	Police detective

Antagonists

Sam Smith	AKA David Brumley
Arnat Karackish	Security Chief, David Brumley
Jake Masters	Business agent for Brumley
David Brumley	Sharra's stepfather.
Kevin Smirnoff	Prostitution coordinator based on Grand Cayman

Boat accommodations.

Crew: Njondac and Josie

Crew 2: Brut and Cato

Guest Stateroom 1:
Mischal & Chandri, Tilly

Guest Stateroom 2:
Charly & Jeremy, Charles

Guest Stateroom 3:
Jasmine and Shawnah

Guest Stateroom 4:
Em and Sheila

Master's Stateroom
Mista & Sharra, Sam

Master's Stateroom 2
Jania and Molly (Robin and Janice)

"It's not for kids to read, no but it's for them to be aware of. This story is controversial and it is very well written. It is a great book and I can recommend it to a lot of people!"

– Kelly Brooks

"This story could really raise public awareness about the sex trade and trafficking, it should really be read by the people. I believe this story is essential for the world to know"

– Rachel Harris

"Every factor of the story drives me into the excitement and curiosity about what would happen next. It feeds your imagination in a sense of suspense and thriller."

– Mariah Correy

"It drives your imagination and creates images in your mind, that's a perfect example of creativity."

– Geoffrey Hampton